NO LUCK

KAYLEIGH SKY

ALSO BY KAYLEIGH SKY

Backbone

Pretty Human

Doll Baby

Trinkets

Angel Dork

Jesus Kid

This book is a work of fiction. Any references to historical events, real people, or real places are used fictitiously. Other names, characters, places, and events are products of the author's imagination, and any resemblance to actual events or places or persons, living or dead, is entirely coincidental.

Published 2018.

For information, address Kiss Drunk Books in writing at 712 Bancroft Road, Ste 277, Walnut Creek, CA 94598.

ISBN: 978-0-9904125-8-8 (ebook)

ISBN: 978-0-9904125-9-5 (paper)

Editor: Kiki Clark, http://betweenthelinesediting.com

Cover Art: Paul B. Moore/Shutterstock (background); Ollyy/Shutterstock (man)

NO LUCK

1

LA LA LAND

N*O, NO, NO!* The slide of Vane's foot under the edge of Fisher's fluffy white rug tossed him halfway across the living room.

What a lousy time to die. For one thing, Vane was only thirty-two. He was also close to naked, and while he loved his tiny black boxer briefs, they hardly hid anything. Not to mention, he was up for the lead in a brand new sitcom, so this was seriously not a good time to kill himself. Unless, of course, he flung Mongolian Beef all over Fisher's immaculate condo, and then it was.

Well, he'd blame it on the throw rug. Everybody knew those things were out to get people. And with his luck, he'd probably crack his chin open or poke an eye out on the corner of the coffee table to boot. He could picture the headlines now. *Blind, chinless actor attempts comeback. Stay tuned.*

Yep. That would be his luck, though he'd take it over spatter-painting Fisher's rug with Mongolian Beef.

How he got to the couch without spilling anything was beyond him, but he wasn't going to complain about it. He dropped to the cushions, snatched up his still ringing phone and gasped, "Hey, Ro."

"Sweetheart."

His stomach dropped at the sound of his sister's voice. Something was wrong. "What? What is it?"

"Dad's had a stroke. I hate telling you this over the phone."

"Is he okay? Is he still alive?"

"Yes. I'm with him. We're at the hospital. He can't talk, but hopefully, that will change."

The ache in Vane's body told him how hard he was holding onto himself. He exhaled. "So, he's going to be okay?"

"I hope so, but will you come home, sweetie? Just in case?"

Home. He'd never had a home there. But he said, "Okay. I will. I'm off work in a couple days."

"Today, Vane. Things can change any minute."

"But... Ro, I can't. I have an audition tomorrow. I have to go to that. I won't get another chance, and I wanna be able to tell Dad I got the part."

"Sweetie, Dad doesn't care. Come home."

"You said he was okay." He had to be. Vane wasn't ready. He needed this part. It was everything he'd worked for. "I want him to be proud of me."

"Oh, Vane."

"Just give me a couple days to get squared away."

"I would give you anything, Vane, you know that. But this isn't my call, and I don't want you to live with regrets if anything happens."

Too late.

He wasn't deliberately staying away from home, but he couldn't make himself return. What kind of success could he show?

The whole point to seeking fame and fortune was to go back home famous and rich. Other than acting in a couple commercials and half a season on a failed sitcom, he was a waiter. A good night for him was not spilling anybody's water or dropping their utensils on the floor.

Fisher said Vane didn't try hard enough, but that wasn't true. Having no luck was his problem. But now...

"This is for a real part," he murmured. "I can get this. I feel it, Ro."

She sighed. "Will this make you happy?"

"Real happy."

"Then I want it for you. You deserve that."

"I love you, Ro."

"I love you too, sweetie."

"I'll come home. I promise."

The word promise spilled out before he could grab it back. Sweat popped out under his arms at the thought of another promise to break. But no. Not this time. This time he'd get the part. This time he'd go home a working actor in the popular new sitcom, *Marvelous Marcel*.

"Call me," she said.

"I will."

After he disconnected, he took a bite of his Mongolian Beef, trying to get rid of the oily, sour taste in his mouth. The beef needed more garlic or spice. Something. *I could make this hecka better.* He'd convinced the chef at work to teach him how to cook, and he'd gotten pretty good at it, but... it wasn't acting.

He munched on another forkful of food, trying to ignore the ache in his chest over his dad. His stomach churned, too, because Vane's eating the leftover Chinese food was going to piss Fisher off. But he was hungry, and other than a chunk of cheese and a bell pepper, the fridge was empty.

He gazed uneasily at the room he sat in. White on white with a pale beech floor. The sole rug was white too—a fluffy shag that was undoubtedly a rescue from a '70s porno. Otherwise, the place was immaculate and too fragile for a klutz like Vane to walk around in.

An image of Fisher's frown floated into his brain. *"How do you trip on nothing?"*

Fisher's stares made him feel like a bug under a glass in a grade school science experiment. *This is the Vanepilegus Rileyoligus. A strange insect. Curiously unable to walk on any of its eight legs.*

He sank back on the couch and stared at the script on the coffee table. As much as he wanted to pick it up, another part of him didn't want to risk too much of his heart on a part he might not get. And anyway, the dark was gathering outside now, and he had to be at work soon.

He looked out at the dull sky, puffy with thin clouds that would never give rain. It was November, but Vane sat in his underwear in a room that was neither cold nor warm. If he didn't look out the windows, he'd never know what season it was.

The sounds of traffic grew louder.

He wished he could be as loose and free as Marcel.

If he got the part, would Marcel's crazy, adventurous spirit rub off on him? Would he figure out how to open up one of these dang windows and let the smoggy air blow in? Fisher would freak, but Marcel wouldn't care what Fisher thought.

Marcel was wild and reckless and full of life. He'd never sit around and wish he didn't have to go to work. Jobs were for chumps, not for guys who could live on a shoestring. Vane was the kind of guy who tripped on shoestrings. He was an embarrassment for gosh sake. How could he possibly go home?

Ignoring the script, he got up, took his empty carton back into the kitchen, and rinsed it out.

The part of Marcel—bizarre name—was perfect for him. Life changing.

Or life ending.

Supposedly, somebody had hung himself over not getting called back for another audition. That kind of desperation was something Vane understood, but he'd never fallen so low he'd wanted to kill himself. Getting the role of Marcel would be incredible even if it wasn't for a big network. It was still a lead and a... well, a great part.

Of course, it was also possible nobody had killed himself. Vane had never heard of the guy—Cory something-or-other—so maybe it was just a rumor. If he'd been a real guy, he'd been an obscure wannabe like Vane and even killing himself wasn't going to bring him any fame. In a couple of weeks—or days—the gossip would die down, and nobody would even remember him. Who in this town would care if Vane knocked himself off? Maybe Fisher.

He dumped his food carton in the recycle bin, grabbed the takeout bag, and looked inside it when it rattled. Fortune cookies. Cool. He could use a little positive news. He broke one open, popped half in his mouth, and unfolded the strip of paper from inside. The print was in faint pink letters. *Don't panic.*

He choked. *Don't panic?* What kind of lousy fortune was that? The hairs on his arm stood up as he coughed to get the cookie stuck in his throat to go down. *Okay. Be logical. It's not a real prophecy.*

Fortune cookie companies churned these things out by the millions. They were for fun. They never came true. Vane was going to get the part. His dad would be fine. He should forget it and take a shower, but he didn't do that. He snatched the bag off the counter and grabbed another cookie. A second later, his fingers shook on another strip of paper. *You will stumble and fall. A friend will catch you.* For Pete's sake. They'd had to print that in tiny letters to fit it all in.

Did Fisher do this?

The pink ink blurred.

Would he?

No. Fisher had no sense of humor. It made Vane sad to admit, but he doubted anybody would bother to catch him, including Fisher. No, he'd have better luck with his imaginary boyfriend in the building across the street. Nobody lived on the top floor as far as Vane could tell, despite the lit Christmas tree in the corner window. He'd never seen people over there, so he'd invented someone to watch him dance.

He never stumbled for a guy who didn't exist.

And he wasn't going to stumble tomorrow either. He was gonna nail that audition and make his dad proud.

Outside, a horn blared and a set of tires squealed. Vane tossed the takeout bag in the trash and grabbed a dirty coffee mug off the counter. It slipped out of his fingers and exploded on the floor. *No, no, no!* The tile cost a fortune. Fisher was going to kill him—or stick his tongue in his cheek before bestowing Vane with a withering smile. *Perhaps we should invest in Styrofoam.*

Vane dropped to a knee. The cup was in pieces, but the tile looked fine. "Thank gosh," he whispered. Maybe Fisher wouldn't even notice the missing cup. He buried it in the trash and hurried into the bathroom.

A few minutes later, he got out of the shower and stared at himself in the mirror. Once again, he wondered what would happen if he got the part of Marcel. Would Fisher be happy for him? His dad would be.

Vane ran a hand through his hair, jiggling water drops off the dark ends.

I'd be somebody.

An actor.

As he stared, he smiled at himself, trying to force the strain out of his gray eyes, but it didn't work.

"Vane!"

Shoot.

"In here."

He wrapped his towel around his waist and stepped into the bedroom.

Fisher appeared in the doorway, his coat over his arm, fingers at his collar, undoing the button. "I saw your car in the garage. Why are you still here? You're supposed to be at work."

"I'm just getting ready." *Tell him about Dad.*

But he didn't.

"You're going to be late."

"I have half an hour."

Fisher flung an arm toward the window. "Look outside. Why the hell does everybody get off work at the same time?"

Fisher's hair was tousled, which kicked up Vane's unease, because disheveled was not Fisher's style. He took a breath to calm himself.

"Most people work days, Fisher."

Fisher ran a hand over the top of his head and glared at him. "I know that. Thanks for the news flash." Vane swallowed, tightening his fist on his towel, but Fisher didn't come any closer. "Be careful out there."

He nodded, the air seeping out of his lungs. His fear was out of proportion to anything Fisher had ever done. Yeah, he had a temper. Yeah, he sometimes grabbed Vane's hair and shook him, but he'd never hit him. Okay, maybe a slap or two. Fisher joked. He teased. He ridiculed. But the ice water sloshing in Vane's belly was because Fisher was different from usual. On edge.

Maybe some of his investments had gone sour, or he'd made some other bad deals, but he'd never talk to Vane about it. He remained in the doorway, watching Vane dress.

"What did you do today?" Fisher asked.

"Rehearsed." Fisher's snort startled him. Vane buttoned his slacks. "What?"

"I didn't think you'd take it this far."

Stung, Vane bristled. "You were the one who encouraged me to audition."

A frown came onto Fisher's face. "Why wouldn't I? I've always supported you."

Vane's mouth opened, but Fisher turned away before Vane could do more than huff. Was Fisher joking?

He finished dressing, snagged his keys off the dresser, and headed to the other room.

Fisher stood at the refrigerator. When Vane entered, he shut the door and glanced over. "You ate my takeout."

"Come by work. You can have my dinner."

"I know what I can have. I own half the place."

He owned Vane when Vane thought about it. Fisher employed him and put a roof over his head. Even if the roof gave him panic attacks because of the glass everywhere. Too many white things to stain.

"I know, Fisher. I'm just trying to help."

Fisher's rough-planed face relaxed. He was all gold and bronze, fit and trim. All sunny LA. Vane's gaze darted to the window. *Usually sunny.*

"I'm not going back out in that. I'll order in."

"Okay." Vane grabbed the doorknob and pulled, but the door didn't open.

"Turn it, Vane."

Vane cackled, the sound like broken glass as he turned the knob and bolted downstairs to the garage.

Safe.

A shiver ran through him, and he tugged up the collar of his coat. His worry was stupid. Of course, he was safe. But the words from his fortune floated through his head as he set off across the garage to his car. *You will fall.*

2

THE FIGHT

T HE KID'S SMILE creeped Vane out. It didn't help that he wore shades on a cloudy day. His long jacket flapped like wings, showing off a lean body dressed all in black. He was heading to the same building Vane was. He looked like Vane, though younger, but that made sense. They were competing for the same part, so they were probably a type.

The kid got to the entrance of the building first, glancing back with his small smile before he stepped inside. By the time Vane entered too, the lobby was empty.

When he came out again, the only thing on his mind was the audition because it had been—*marvelous!*

Mary Grommet, the casting director, had even smiled and said, "Nice touch with the hair flick."

The most Vane had ever gotten from her before was a grudging nod. Now he practically danced to his car.

The lights on the streets reminded him of Christmas and small towns in the movies. He felt like he could fly he was in such a good mood. It didn't even bother him when he dropped his keys on the sidewalk. He just picked them up.

But then his gaze fell on the kid again, who was sauntering across the parking lot to the traffic light on the corner. He smiled at Vane as he passed, and not once did he step in a pothole or go sprawling to his knees off the curb.

Walking and snidely smiling at the same time was a feat of coordination Vane couldn't pull off in a million years.

With his hands in the pockets of his London Fog, the kid looked for all the world like a GQ model. Graceful little jerk. Vane frowned, trying to remember where else he'd seen him. It hadn't been at an audition, but the location eluded him now, and the memory tickled his brain like an itch.

Well, screw it.

This was too good a day to worry about it. He flashed the kid a grin, got into his car, and drove away.

His good mood tempted him to run home before work, throw his arms around Fisher and yell, *"I think I got it!"*

But he wanted hugs and champagne and hot sex in response to his good news, and was pretty sure that wasn't what he'd get. Not that Vane blamed Fisher over the hot sex part. It wouldn't be the first time Fisher got an eyeful of Vane's elbow in the middle of a passionate encounter. Though Vane's news seemed like a spectacular reason for someone to risk the danger.

Someone?

"Fisher," he muttered. *You're with Fisher.*

What an idiot. Who else was he thinking of? His fantasy guy in the building across the street? Well, maybe, because at least for a few minutes it would be fun to imagine someone eager to celebrate with him. Somebody brave enough to hug him in public, lay a passionate kiss on him, and not say, "*You screwed yourself. You aren't talented enough to call the shots, Vane, and now you're going to have to jump through hoops to prove yourself. Coming out was a dumb idea.*"

Vane hated it when Fisher berated him for that. He'd come out years before and only because he had no talent for keeping secrets. The kids in his acting class in high school had liked him and he'd been popular. Mr. Kam, his acting teacher, had liked him, and he'd had no boyfriend at the time, so it hadn't been a big deal to anybody at home.

Getting the part in *Ranging Wild* was like having a magic wand waved over him. Doors were supposed to open, but he guessed that's what Fisher was saying. Maybe Vane had shut those doors.

"*Trust me,*" Fisher had said. "*It's a mark against you.*"

So now Fisher tried to introduce him to people who could help his career, though Vane was a bit confused by that. He was pretty sure Fisher didn't know anybody who could help his career. Fisher was a start-up guru, part owner of a steak house, and real estate investor. If he knew anybody in the Hollywood crowd, it was only by accident.

While auditioning for *Marvelous Marcel*, Vane refused to go out at night. He drank ten glasses of water a day and ate only healthy food. Well... mostly healthy. He wanted this part. Ten years had passed since he'd played the sidekick of a rodeo clown in *Ranging Wild*. He'd loved that show, but it hadn't clicked with viewers.

He thought he had talent, but... *You're delusional.*

The fact that his inner critic sounded like Fisher was creepy, but he tried not to think about it. The reason he'd kept the screenplay he was writing a secret was another thing he tried not to think about. The thought of Fisher patting him on the head over it made him cringe. *"You keep trying."*

All the way to Ribbets, the intersections glowed like festooned Christmas trees. The spirit of the season hadn't worked its way into the drivers though. Cars cut Vane off and stole parking places he didn't even want. He was practically sweating by the time he grabbed his uniform and ran inside the restaurant.

He changed clothes in the bathroom, smoothed his hair into a headband, and faced himself in the mirror. *Take a deep breath. You might be looking at a real actor again as of tomorrow. I can't wait to tell you, Dad.*

He spent his shift rolling out dishes on a cart his boss, Duncan, had bought for him. The busy night helped push thoughts of his dad away.

At home, he drove into the garage and climbed the stairs of their building.

The lights on each landing were more decorative than useful, but the first floor was lit by the street lamps outside.

When he swung around the railing toward the second floor, Vane froze. So did the kid who'd been at the audition, now standing a few steps above him. They stared at each other while Vane's brain shot off in a dozen directions. Why was the kid here? Who let him in? Was he lost? The only people who lived here were... Vane and Fisher.

Vane's breath stalled, and all he could do was stare.

The kid stared back without any expression. Vane didn't know if he was trying to confront Vane on his own stairwell or just didn't care that he was. Another little smile like the one from earlier crept onto his face, but it didn't stay. It dropped with his eyes.

Vane just stood there as though he'd turned to stone. Or a block of ice. Of course, he'd run into this. Why did every good day disintegrate into misery? He knew he needed to be more positive, but shoot, the little jerk was screwing around with Fisher.

"Hey," the kid said.

His tone wasn't arrogant. He sounded shy and small, and maybe he was. Maybe Vane was wrong about him. Or maybe he wasn't, and the kid was paying in sex to meet one of Fisher's friends of a friend. But Vane didn't ask. His throat locked, and his feet stuck to the floor.

The kid darted past.

"See ya," Vane murmured into the empty stairwell.

The sound of his voice thawed his limbs. He climbed slowly up to his door, punched in the code and stepped inside.

Fisher wasn't in bed. He sat in a chair by the bedside lamp, clothed in pajama bottoms and golden in the light from the tan shade even in the middle of winter.

Vane stared at the medallion lying in the center of his hair-covered chest. It was a coin. Vane didn't know where it had come from or even if it had sentimental value. *"I've had it forever,"* was all Fisher would say. That solitary golden coin encapsulated him for Vane.

"I saw your friend."

Fisher raised his gaze from his tablet. "My friend."

The comment wasn't posed as a question, and Fisher chewed his lip with a frown, as though pondering his next move in a game of chess. Finally, a smile curved his lips. "Stan."

Stan? Vane clenched his fist around his car keys and took a breath. "Are you having an affair?"

Fisher choked out a laugh. "I wish."

"You *want* to cheat on me?"

"Cheating? Me?"

Vane gaped at the foggy wonder in Fisher's eyes. Was this Vane's fault too? Like every stain on the rug and every broken dish?

"Yeah," he said. "You. Having sex with another guy. Cheating."

"You're worried about sex?"

The floor seemed to collapse beneath him. Vane had gone from having a boyfriend to a roommate with benefits in the space of three flights of stairs.

Now his guts knotted, and he had to force his numb lips to move. "We live together."

A shadow of a smile crossed Fisher's face. He tossed his tablet onto the bed. "You live with me."

"Dang, Fisher."

Vane set his keys down and stared at their bed. Did they screw in Vane's bed? Was the kid good? He was thin and languid and graceful the way Vane wanted to be. He probably never poked Fisher in the eye with his elbow. Vane loved sex, but the damage he could do made him nervous, and losing himself was like a carrot held out of reach. He could never let go with Fisher.

He shook his head and imagined a fog clearing away. *A friend will catch you.* But not this friend. "I'm leaving."

Fisher sighed and stood. "What are you talking about?"

"I'm done."

"Over a peccadillo?"

Vane laughed. Only Fisher Fox would say peccadillo and suggest his infidelity was a minor lapse. "I was going to tell you I had a great day."

Fisher stopped a foot away, his smile widening. He stroked Vane's cheek. "Was?"

Vane stepped back. Electricity tickled his skin while his brain screamed—*Get out!* But his normal, everyday voice said, "I did well. Really impressed them."

"At the audition?" Fisher pulled his hand back and smoothed his hair. "That's good. I know it's important you make a good showing and keep your name out there. I hope this pans out for you, but you might luck into a good commercial if not. Now that people know you again."

"Mary doesn't cast for commercials."

"Okay."

"I'm going to get this part. I can feel it. I've earned it. I deserve better than this."

The smile pulling at Fisher's lips turned grim. "Really?"

Vane's words hadn't come out quite the way he'd

wanted them to. He didn't mean he deserved better than Fisher—though maybe he did. But what he really meant was he thought he deserved to imagine better. Being with Fisher was like being on a bumper car with no steering wheel and no way to avoid the poles and the walls. He bounced off Fisher's heart and went into a tailspin. A menace to Fisher's valuable things.

He took a breath and tucked his hair behind his ears. "That came out wrong, and I'm tired anyway."

"I am too. We'll sleep on it. Talk tomorrow."

"I can't, Fisher." He turned and headed into the hall.

"Vane."

"I don't want to talk anymore."

"We can fix—"

"No."

"Vane."

He patted his jacket pocket for his keys, but it was empty. Great. What a perfect exit. He turned back and ran the last few minutes through his memory. He'd had his keys going in there. Did he put them on the bed?

Fisher approached, bare feet silent on the perfect rug. "Will you stop for a minute?"

Vane edged by him and stormed back down the hall. His gaze went to the bed with its silver- and gold-striped comforter, but his keys weren't there. They weren't on the floor or on Fisher's chair.

"You put them on the dresser."

He turned back to the door where Fisher stood with Vane's keys dangling from his fingertips. "Give them to me."

"No." Fisher's face fell into a pensive frown, light lines streaking from the corners of his eyes. "You owe me, Vane. You aren't walking out on me."

Vane's heart beat in a shell of ice. "Or what?"

"Just give me a few minutes?"

"You can't talk me out of this."

"I think I can." His face was expressionless now.

The air froze, though Vane knew that wasn't possible. Fisher hurting him for real wasn't possible either, but his heart pounded anyway. He stuck his hands into the heat of his armpits, and Fisher backed out of the doorway. Vane followed him.

"Give me my keys."

Fisher tossed them to him. "Stay and talk?"

"For a minute."

He circled the room, keeping the coffee table between them until he reached the kitchen. Fisher sat, forehead flushing dark as Vane took a step closer to the door.

"You're being melodramatic."

"You cheated."

Fisher drew his arms in and leaned forward, elbows on his knees. "I needed somebody to talk to."

"You weren't talking."

"You aren't listening."

"You know what, Fisher? Screw you. This isn't my fault." He headed to the door and Fisher got to his feet.

"Vane!"

The sharpness in Fisher's voice triggered his inner klutz and sent him stumbling over the rug. He hit the wall but stayed on his feet, almost getting the door open before Fisher slammed it shut again.

Vane pushed him away. "Let me out!"

His pounding heart deafened him. *Don't panic. Don't panic.* He yanked the door back open and fled, but Fisher ran after him and punched him. The blow hit him between the shoulders and almost drove him off the top of the stairs. At the last second, Fisher grabbed Vane's shirt and slowed his momentum, but he flailed to get away and slammed face first into the wall.

Stars exploded in his eyes, and this time he fell.

The stairs rolled under him, and he crashed onto his hands and knees on the landing below.

"Dang," he muttered as a few dark red drops slowly spattered the carpet underneath him.

"Vane."

He scrambled back. "Get away."

Fisher crouched at his feet. "Are you okay?"

"You hit me."

"You fell."

"Go away."

"You aren't that hurt. You have a bloody nose."

"I bit my tongue."

"Come back inside."

"Not with you." His face hurt, and he'd swallowed blood, so now his stomach churned too.

"Get up and come inside. I won't touch you. I won't even stay."

Fisher backed up, and Vane struggled to his feet and climbed the stairs. He dropped his keys on the bathroom counter, wet a towel, and took it to the bedroom. Careful not to look in the mirror, he sat on the bed and lowered his face into the cool cloth.

His pulse pounded a beat in his cheek and forehead as he probed his mouth with his tongue. The blood must've come from his nose.

In the other room, a cupboard door opened and closed, and a moment later, ice clattered into a glass. Vane's body tensed with disbelief. Why not turn on the TV and order a pizza? How could Fisher go on as if he hadn't knocked Vane down the stairs? Was Vane supposed to play along? Well, screw that. He dropped his towel on the floor, struggled out of his jacket, and dropped that too.

Take that, you neat freak.

Clenching his jaw, he strode out to the living room where Fisher sat with his glass on his knee.

"You lied," said Vane. "You're still here."

"You lied too."

His head told him to shut up, but his mouth said, "I'm moving out."

Fisher lifted his gaze. A bleary-eyed squint creased his forehead with a frown. He set his glass down and stood. "I don't think that's a good idea."

Vane fled to the bathroom again.

"I want us to talk!"

How had his life tanked like this? But maybe it had always been a mess. Maybe he just hadn't seen the cracks that for some reason had picked tonight to rip wide open. He locked the door and slid to the floor. Would marvelous

Marcel let somebody trap him in a bathroom? *Well, you aren't Marcel, are you?*

He closed his eyes and let his head fall back.

Just one good day. That's all he wanted. A good day from start to finish.

No. You want love too.

Well, yeah, that.

And a real home.

He'd been an idiot to think anything good could happen to him. He couldn't go home like this, beat up and broken with no place to live. Now he'd never see Rose and her kids, or get to tell his dad about Marcel. *Great news, Dad. I'm starring in a new sitcom called Marvelous Marcel.*

Not now though. His last thought before he fell asleep was that he'd ruined everything.

3

ON THE LAM

THE RAIN HIT the roof like sticks rat-tat-tatting on a too-tight drum. But after a while, Vane realized it wasn't raining. That was his heartbeat in his ears. Tat-tat. Tat-tat.

He liked thinking it was rain though. The sound reminded him of the toasty puffing of the heater in the house he'd grown up in. It had smelled of a summer's worth of dust and heralded good things like Thanksgiving and Christmas.

At least it had until his mother's death.

Without her, the holidays had gone gray, and their father didn't seem to care about them anymore. It hadn't stopped Rose from cooking and decorating though. She'd taken on their mother's job, and maybe that was why their dad had thought she'd want to run the diner with him. But she hadn't. She'd wanted a husband and kids of her own to raise.

Why did everybody's dreams get blasted?

Why, Vane? Answer the question.

I can't. I'm stupid.

Half his body throbbed, and he had a growing suspicion somebody had hammered a nail into his hip. He must have hit the stairs at some point, but he didn't remember it.

His neck hurt, too, bent all night while he'd drifted away, listening to Fisher pace outside the bathroom door. The thinness of the doors here had only become noticeable when he'd heard the click of Fisher's ice in his glass on the other side. Vane wasn't sure what Fisher had been doing. He hadn't tried to get in, only shuffled back and forth and muttered things like, "You stupid ass."

The rain in Vane's head kept falling, drumming like a lullaby. He smiled, deciding he'd put that line in his screenplay. His story was important to him in a way he didn't want to analyze. Writing didn't carry any angst for him. It wasn't splashy, and he had nothing riding on it. But if he made it as an actor, people would recognize him and point him out in public, and he could tell his dad—*See. They like me.*

At least they'd like him until they got to know him.

He'd impressed Fisher, at first.

It was hard to be impressive hiding in the bathroom though. He needed to get up. Morning light, gray and white, flooded through the window now.

He sighed, knocking his keys off the counter as he pulled himself up.

No sound came from the other side of the door. He pressed his ear to it, turned the knob, and stepped out.

The bedroom was empty, so he stole to the living room where the light through the windows floated like a veil. Cars whooshed by, and he remembered the sounds of Fisher opening the closet and drawers. He looked around and locked his gaze on a yellow sticky note attached to the front door. He sidled over, not wanting to read it, but—

I have an appointment I have to keep. Wait for me. I promise to make it up to you. —Fisher.

Calm, clean, and to the point.

The rain song in his head faded away. Rain was never going to fall. The water spots on the window were a joke.

Go!

Yes.

He hurried back to the bedroom but found the bed made and his jacket gone. He'd taken it off here, hadn't he? Yes, he'd dropped it on the floor, so where was it? His breath burned his throat, and his blood crashed like a storm-thrashed ocean in his ears. Of course, Fisher would put his coat away. It was clutter to him and not the rebellious act Vane had meant it to be. No amount of tidiness could fix Vane's mess of a life, so why not throw his dang jacket on the floor?

Oh, so dramatic. He imagined Fisher rolling his eyes.

So what? He was dramatic and emotional.

High-strung.

Rays of dull sun glittered with a fine dust that always drove Fisher crazy when it showed up in the winter light.

Vane opened the closet door and let out a sigh of relief at the sight of his jacket hanging there. As he yanked it off and put it on, his gaze fell to the dresser with its lacquer finish as bright as a polished stone.

For a moment, he was taken back to his childhood home, sneaking into his parents' bedroom with a Mother's Day card. The dresser he'd set it on was old and beat up, nothing special, but he felt a pang of nostalgia for it now.

For some reason, the memory flooded him with grief, and his eyes stung with sudden tears. How weird. The emotion shook him and left him feeling strangely hollow.

He took a deep breath, grabbed some T-shirts and underwear out of a drawer, and opened his jewelry box. He stared, heart skipping into high gear when he didn't see his flash drive. It had his screenplay on it. He hurried to his nightstand and scrambled through the drawer. Not only did he not find his flash drive, but his phone was gone too. Panic swelled in his head. Losing Fisher was bad enough, but this...

You can rewrite it.

But it wouldn't be the same. He'd never get those words back.

Clenching his hands, he turned to the desk in the corner. Maybe he'd left it in the computer? *Please be there.*

But it wasn't, and it wasn't in any of the drawers either. Fisher would have taken the laptop to his meeting.

Vane felt sick, but he went back to the dresser to look again. This time he found his flash drive with Fisher's sweats and T-shirts. A giddy relief prickled him like goose bumps. Geez. Could he have done that himself? He'd been distracted, but... No. Fisher had done it, but why? Had he tried to look at it? Luckily, Vane had password protected it.

He pocketed the flash drive and a twenty-dollar bill and froze. *Was that a door opening?*

The sound came again.

He scurried through the living room and snuck a look into the hall as a voice floated up the stairwell. "Anytime."

He let out a shaky breath. It was just somebody heading down to the garage from the art gallery.

After stuffing toiletries and a few clothes into an overnight case, he rushed back to the door. Not a moment of regret tugged at his steps, though he was leaving most everything he owned here. For now, he just wanted to get out and worry about coming back for his clothes later.

Buy new. Use your head.

The voice shook him. It had sounded like his father's. He dashed downstairs with everything he really needed.

Except my phone.

Was that what Fisher wanted? To make sure Vane missed the call about Marcel? Catty jerk. Well, Vane would get another phone. Screw him. He'd call Mary and Rose. He didn't need Fisher.

By the time he made it to the garage, he half expected to find slashed tires, but his car was fine. He got in, took a breath, and drove away.

VANE FOUND A PARKING GARAGE AND HUNG OUT until nightfall. Then he drove to his bank where he shuffled to an ATM hidden under the canopy of a tree. A second later, he stared at the display screen as though it had words in French scrawled across it. But, no, that was English.

Geez. Fisher had emptied the account. What a dick.

And why wasn't Vane getting his card back? If the only problem was a zero balance, wouldn't he get his card back? Was the account closed? Would Fisher do that? Could he? Didn't Vane have any say?

No, idiot. You live off him. You have nothing of your own. Admitting that flooded him with fear and left him sick and shaky. What was he going to do?

You'll be fine. You have your car and a job and a shot at a starring role on a sitcom on cable.

But the last thought weighed on his shoulders like a ten-story building. Who was he kidding? He wasn't getting the role. Not now. Fisher's little twink, whose face wasn't beat bloody, would get it. What was the kid's name? Stan? Nothing memorable like Riley Vane.

How much energy had he spent pondering a name that didn't make him sound like a twit—Hi, I'm Vane, a vain actor living in vain Hollywood—before it occurred to him to switch his first and last names? After all, everybody knew a name was the important thing. A name was make or break. Not talent. Not looks. Not who he slept with. It all came down to your name. That's what wannabe actors needed to worry about.

Stan.

Stan the man.

Marvelous Marcel.

Dang.

He stood at the side of his car with no memory of the

walk back across the parking lot. He got in behind the wheel, and his stomach rumbled.

Great.

Penniless and hungry.

And he was supposed to work tonight too. But at least he'd get some food. Plus, if he was lucky, he could hit up his boss for an advance. Duncan seldom left before seven. The guy was Fisher's friend though, which was how Vane had gotten his job, but maybe Vane could guilt him. *Look at what your pal did.*

When he got to the restaurant, he rushed through the kitchen and ducked into the bathroom across the hall. Luckily, it was vacant. When he turned to face the mirrors, he flinched, and his eyes stung again. Knocking somebody down the stairs was such a rotten thing to do.

You fell.

Bull.

Fisher had hit him flat in the back and only grabbed onto his shirt after the fact. Vane hated violence. It scared him, and so what if he wasn't brave?

He was a decent person.

He covered his face with his hands for a moment, struggling to get ahold of himself. Then he looked again.

Well, it could have been worse. His cheek and the side of his mouth were purple and puffy. Blood crusted the skin under his nose, but when he ran his tongue around his mouth he still didn't find any wounds.

After the water had warmed, he cleaned his face and dried off. His hair was mussed but presentable. He tucked it behind his ears, zipped his jacket to hide his blood-spotted T-shirt, and headed out.

He saw Duncan behind the bar and made a beeline toward him, but it was Sandy the bartender who saw him first. "Jesus, Vane. Are you okay?"

Duncan frowned and patted the counter. "Sit."

He poured a glass of Jack Daniel's while Vane sat and set it in front of him.

The whiskey burned Vane's mouth but warmed him all the way down. He shuddered and sighed.

"What happened?" Duncan asked. "Car accident?"

"Something like that," he muttered. Duncan's eyebrows rose, but he didn't comment. "I wanted to ask a favor."

"Go on."

He wasn't sure Duncan liked him, but he'd always been fair. Maybe not as friendly as he often was with the other staff but not unfriendly.

"I was hoping to get an advance."

"Are you quitting?"

"No. I... I don't think so."

He downed the rest of his drink while Duncan studied him.

"Let's go sit."

He nodded, slid off his stool, and turned into Mary's gaze. For the life of him, Vane wasn't sure why he never had any luck, but there she was, sitting at a table across the room. He could tell she didn't expect to see him. She did a double take, and her face went white.

He bolted.

Seconds later, all he could think was *idiot!* Why had he run? He was sick at himself, but it was too late to go back. He swallowed and made his way to the booth where Duncan was already waiting for him. Why did things like this always happen to him? Of all the places for her to go for dinner, why here?

He dropped onto the seat and bit back a groan at the ache that ricocheted through his body. *Yesterday was such a good day.*

Duncan leaned forward, his voice coming close. "You're sure you're okay? I can drive you to the ER."

He lifted his head from his hands. "No. I just need a couple days. And that advance."

Duncan settled back against the tall tufted booth again. "And you're not quitting?"

Well... No? Could he stay? Take a chance of running into Fisher? His throat strangled him. He swallowed to clear it.

"Hopefully, you're not firing me."

"Should I? I don't want to. You're dependable. Personable."

"Fisher's boyfriend."

"Is that a problem?" Duncan asked.

"His ex-boyfriend?"

Duncan said nothing for a long time, and Vane didn't lift his gaze from the table. Confronting the look he imagined in Duncan's eyes had no appeal. He'd much rather stare at the tiny nicks in the varnished tabletop than deal with the fact he was a loser who'd gone from the pinnacle of success (for him) to the dumps (for anybody) in a day. And he'd screwed up again the minute he'd run from Mary.

Why hadn't he just gone over and told her he'd gotten into a car accident? People got in accidents all the time. Did he want to fail?

Well, you are a screw up.

Duncan cleared his throat. "Fisher did that?"

Yes.

"I fell."

He barely made a sound. Duncan leaned forward. "Was Fisher there?"

He nodded, not trusting his voice anymore.

"I see," Duncan murmured.

Vane coughed. His mouth was dry, and he swallowed again. "I think he's seeing somebody. We fought about it."

"Well, I..." Duncan waved his hand. "I don't think you're telling me everything, but that's okay. It's not my business. You can have your advance. What you've earned. I'll round up."

Round up? "Like in severance?"

Duncan gazed at the ceiling and stretched his neck, tipping his head from side to side. "It's not personal. But you being here... It could be awkward."

"Sure."

And now he had no job and no money to go along with no place to live and no phone. *Great.* He straightened, holding onto the edge of the table in a rush of wooziness. "Okay. Thanks. Can I get something to eat first?"

"Of course." Duncan rose and gave him a pat on the shoulder. "Stay here. I'll be back."

Stay here as in stay out of sight, but Vane didn't have the energy to resist and didn't want to deal with Mary now anyway. He was queasy with shame but ate all the steak dinner Duncan brought him. After a while, his hands stopped shaking, and he gave himself a pep talk. *It's gonna be okay. You'll figure it out.* He just needed a good night's sleep.

After he finished his meal, he pushed the plate away and drank a glass of water. That helped too. A few minutes later, Duncan returned with an envelope, and Vane stood and accepted it.

"It's all cash," Duncan said. "It should keep you for a couple days. Give yourself some time, and then call Fisher. Maybe you two can work it out."

Vane forced a smile that hurt his face. "Sure. Thanks."

This time he used the front door, avoiding eye contact with anyone, and hurried around the corner to his car. The shame still lit into him, as though he'd ruined everything in his life by his own hand.

He choked on a laugh remembering his fortune. *You will stumble and fall.*

Well, duh. When hadn't he?

VANE BOUGHT A phone at Target and found a dump of a motel that took cash. After locking himself in his room, he set up his phone, took a deep breath, and called Rose. He thought she might not answer, and his belly did a little flip of panic before a voice popped into his ear. "Hello?"

Well, that wasn't Rose.

There were other voices too. Was Rose having a party? On a Wednesday night the week before Thanksgiving?

And whose voice was that? It rose above the others, and Vane fixated on it. It was more of a sound than a voice, actually. Warm and husky, it coiled inside his belly in a way that made him feel safe. He lost himself in it for a moment until the woman on the other end of the line repeated herself. "Hello?"

"Um... I-I'm calling for Rose."

"Hold on, honey."

A couple of breaths passed before—"Vane?"

"Yeah."

His nerves stretched thin and quivering.

"Where have you been?" Rose asked. "I've been calling all day."

"I lost my phone."

"Vane. Couldn't you call some other way to get your messages?"

"I'm sorry."

"Sweetie. Dad—" He knew. She didn't need to say it, but she said it anyway. "Dad's gone."

You will stumble and fall...

4

DOUG VISITS ROSE

DOUG GRABBED THE pizzas and six-pack of Coke and hit the door of his pickup with the heel of his boot to close it. The FOR SALE sign that had been stuck in the lawn for months was gone now. Nothing about the house had changed, but to Doug, it looked bare and forlorn.

He took a deep breath, shifted the pizza boxes to his other arm, and knocked.

As he waited, he ran a hand through his unruly blond hair, remembering the feel of his wife's fingers in it.

With the holidays near, his memories of Meg rose close to the surface and the death of Rose's father didn't help. The guy had only been in his mid-sixties, buzzing around Eileen's as usual just the weekend before. And now he was gone.

It could happen at any time.

A shout came from inside, and he pushed away the

thought that he was almost forty himself and had no family to go home to.

The door swung open, and a little girl with a head of fire-red curls gazed up at him. She inhaled, chest swelling. "Hm. That smells good."

"Let me in and we can eat it."

She stepped back and hollered, "Doug's here!"

"In the kitchen!"

Moving boxes stuffed the hallway like an obstacle course. So far though, the combo kitchen and family room had escaped the upheaval. Rose stood on a step stool, head tipped back, scrubbing at the ceiling with a blue sponge.

Doug set the pizzas and Cokes on the counter. "What are you doing?"

She lowered her head and gazed over her shoulder. "Cleaning the ceiling."

Well... "Why?"

"I want it to look nice."

"It already looks nice," he said.

A smile softened her face, and she stepped off the stool. "I guess so."

This was where she'd planned to raise her kids and grow old with Marc, her husband. Doug wondered what it would be like to move out of his and Meg's house. Eventually, he'd finish the one he was building and move in there, he guessed.

On the day Meg died, the only thing on his radar had been coffee. Their machine had broken, so he'd left early to grab a cup on the go. He'd had no idea his life was going to change forever.

A year later, he met Rose, who'd lost her husband, Marc. He'd travelled for work, she said, but called her every morning. On the day he died, she cut his call short when two-year-old Ricky threw up on the kitchen floor. She never spoke to Marc again. An hour after his call, an ordinary suburban mom T-boned his car and killed him.

Doug knew he could confide the grief he was feeling to his best friend, Dorcas, but he didn't want to. She wouldn't understand. With Rose, he didn't have to explain or pretend he was over losing his wife. He and Rose had dated briefly. Now they were friends, and he was going to miss having her nearby.

"Let's eat," he said.

She turned off the faucet after rinsing her hands, approached the pizzas, and lifted the lid on the top box. Her eyebrows rose. "Hm. Pepperoni."

"Everybody's favorite."

She raised her chin and leveled a stare on him. "Well, not everybody's."

"Take a look at the other one."

She slid the box to the side, lifted the lid on a pizza covered in veggies, and cackled. "Now that's everybody's favorite."

He snorted. "The kids and I will eat pizza the way it's supposed to be eaten."

She rolled her eyes and looked over her shoulder toward the door to the living room. "C'mon, kids. Dinner." She smiled again at Doug. "Thanks for bringing this over."

He nodded. He didn't know what to say. Not only was she leaving a house that contained almost all her memories of Marc, but she was about to bury her father. Her smile was pure Rose though, and it was good she was cheerful because she didn't have the help of her loser brother, Vane the has-been actor.

Was he a redhead like Rose? A photo of him had hung in a collection in the hallway before Rose had packed it away. The guy's hair had been blond in the picture, dyed for some role he'd been playing in a silly sitcom about a rodeo clown.

As though reading his mind, she said, "Vane's coming home."

"I thought he couldn't."

At least that's what Rose had said earlier. Some mumbo-jumbo about Vane not being able to do anything to help and being in the middle of something he couldn't get out of. The kids barreled in before Rose had time to answer him though.

Lucy was the oldest, an eight-year-old replica of Rose. Confident, careful of others, and cute as a button. Ricky was the serious one. Four, and already suspicious of the world. He blinked at Doug, screwing his face up into a frown a second later. "Where's Hoyt?"

"Home. I had to see somebody about a job before I came over. No dogs allowed."

Ricky's face fell. "Oh."

"I promise," said Doug. "I'll bring him by before you move."

"I don't wanna move."

Rose met Doug's gaze and pressed her lips into a thin smile.

"Don't be silly," said Lucy. "We'll have adventures."

"I don't want adventures. I want Hoyt."

"Hoyt can come play with you in Pleasant Hill," said Doug. "It's not that far away. Nothing's going to change but your house."

Rose treated him to an *Oh really* look. He shrugged, set a Coke on the counter, and hefted Ricky onto a stool in front of it. Rose pushed over a piece of pizza on a paper plate, and Lucy climbed onto the stool beside Ricky. "I want the veggie," she said.

Rose crowed. "Yay! That's my girl."

Doug shook his head, got his own pizza, and took it to the couch. A moment later, Rose joined him, took a bite of her veggie monstrosity, and mumbled, "Thanks for this."

"You're welcome."

After eating his first slice in two bites, he started in on his second one. "So where's he staying?"

Rose frowned, turning her gaze on him. "Who? Oh. Here, I guess. On the couch. After we move, I don't know. Dad's house or mine, whatever he decides."

"You said he was up for a part?"

She nodded. "I didn't ask about it though. It's a touchy subject."

I bet.

Somehow the first few years of failure hadn't been enough of a clue for the guy to move onto something else.

Well, what about you?

Doug bit into his pizza, glowering around his mouthful of grease and pepperoni. It was easy to think the burn in his gut was spice and garlic, but it wasn't. He was an

KAYLEIGH SKY

overachiever himself. A high-drive kind of guy—at least he
had been. Now he was an asshole, passing judgment on
somebody he didn't even know. But he'd do anything to
have his family back, and Rose's brother had walked away
from his. Doug's parents were gone and Meg—Well, how
this guy could blow off two cute kids like his niece and
nephew was beyond Doug.

"You done?" Rose asked.

Doug nodded and gave her his plate. "What do you
need help on?"

"The bookshelves? The boxes are in the hall."

He stood, swiping his hands on his pants, and headed
to the living room.

The shelving wasn't expensive but not cheap either.
Doug liked dark woods, but Rose was a light-hearted
person and the rosy-colored oak fit her.

A stack of boxes marked Christmas decorations sat
next to the bookshelf on the edge of the hallway. Doug
hadn't bothered with a tree for the last two years. Curious,
he peeked into the top box and found a snowman grinning
up at him. He smiled, though he didn't want to. Christmas
had been Meg's favorite time of year. His too, though
Halloween came in a close second.

He scooped some books between both hands and
deposited them into one of the empty boxes. Three
transfers cleared the top shelf, and he moved to the one
below it. A few minutes later, Rose joined him.

"Are you coming to Dad's service?" she asked.

He puckered his brow at her.

"Of course." Bizarre thing to ask, as though he'd blow

off her dad's funeral. "What about Vane? Is he going straight there?"

"Maybe. He was supposed to be here by now."

"Did you call him?"

She opened a new box and took the books he held out to her. "Voicemail. It's a new phone. I hope it works."

"Maybe he got lost. It's been a while."

A slow smile slid onto her face. "You're being snippy."

"No, I'm not."

"I think he remembers the way home, Doug."

"Well, not your home."

"He can find it."

He ignored the shake of her head. "Dorcas is coming with me. I have to hit a couple job sites that morning, so we'll go straight to the cemetery."

"You're coming back after, aren't you?"

"I cleared the rest of my day."

"Good. I might take Vane to Eileen's and the house the day after if he wants to go. I have enough savings to keep the place running for about two months while he decides what he wants to do."

"Rose, do you really—"

"Think it's a good idea? Yes. I think that's what Dad would want, and I'm essentially using his money anyway. Vane can pay me back if he decides to keep the diner open, or pay it out of the proceeds if he sells. We have the house too."

"Which you said is not in great shape."

"It's up to Vane what we do."

"Can I say something?"

Rose pulled the snowman out of the box of Christmas decorations he'd opened earlier. "Why didn't Dad split it between us?"

He nodded. "It doesn't seem fair. You were the one who stayed."

She hugged the snowman. "I wanted to. And I think Dad felt guilty as he got older and realized all the things he'd done wrong and didn't know how to make up for. This is how he made up for it."

"What about you?"

She kissed the snowman's head and smiled. "I'm much lower maintenance than Vane."

Doug deposited another armful of books into a new box. "I'm serious."

"I have a house, a family, and a career. Vane has none of that."

Doug leaned in and kissed her cheek. "Any help from me you need with your dad's house is yours."

"We'll have to put money into it whether he sells or not."

"I'll take a look. Just give me the word."

She returned the snowman to its box and closed the lid. "Thanks for the help, Doug."

"It's nothing, Ro. Whatever I can do."

"I know."

They packed the last of the books.

Afterwards, Rose returned to the kitchen, and Doug sealed the boxes and carried them to his pickup. He planned to drop them off at her new place in a couple days and leave the big stuff for the movers.

On his way back into the house, he paused and took a picture. The impulse surprised him because he wasn't really thinking about giving it to the kids. True, they wouldn't remember much about this place, but they'd have other pictures. He wouldn't remember much about it either, eventually, and why would he? It wasn't special to him. But it was special to Rose. She'd lived here with Marc, and maybe that's what Doug was doing—trying to capture the essence of memory.

He imagined Meg in every shadow of his own house, so maybe Marc lingered here too. He'd send the picture to Rose someday, and maybe she'd see something in it.

Inside, he pulled his coat on and said goodbye to the kids. Rose met him at the door with a sweater over her shoulders. At his truck, she took his arm and brushed his cheek with her warm lips, and a stir of loneliness washed through him.

"I know this is strange," she said. "But I'm glad we're friends."

She turned and headed back to the porch before he could respond.

It wasn't strange. Maybe to others it would seem so, but not to him. It was something he didn't like to think about. He'd met Rose in front of Dorcas's shop after Rose had come out from her tarot reading. He'd liked her red hair and steady gaze. Doug had liked her and still did. And he wanted her friendship, but he only had it because Meg wasn't here. Her loss had left a hole in him that was filling despite his best efforts to stop it.

TWO DATES HAD MADE IT CLEAR TO DOUG IT WAS too soon to move on. But Rose had understood. So had Dorcas, though she'd been Rose's cheerleader from the minute she'd noticed Doug's attraction to her. So it had surprised him when Dorcas said, "Take your time, honey. You'll know when you're ready."

"It's been a year," he'd said. He wasn't sure when the pain would ever go away. Wasn't it three months or six months? Could it stay forever?

Dorcas had offered him a reading, but Doug had declined, trying his best not to blurt out, "Oh, hell no." Out loud, he'd only said, "Later, maybe."

Now, in his pickup, heading home, his chest swelled like a stretched balloon. Some days he thought he'd explode with the ball of energy growing inside him. It burned with a power he couldn't possibly contain forever. It was like an orgasm teasing the edges of his sanity. He needed somebody to take him out of himself for a while.

When he reached the sign for Poppy Brush, he turned away from the village. Oddly, the sign gave no indication which direction to take. It just stood there, taunting tourists with the nearness of town but not telling them how to get there.

About a mile later, the road broke free from the trees and dropped on one side into an open meadow. He swung onto the shoulder, his headlights barely pushing the dark back, but he didn't need to see now. This was where he was building his house for Meg.

He parked and got out, sniffing in the cold. Above him, garish stars winked in the sky, too far off to light the ground, too far off for anything but a cold promise. He took a breath but the pressure inside him didn't ease. The energy in his chest swelled until he let it out in a groan and whispered, "Meg, dammit."

He wanted her voice to come out of the dark and remind him that she had been alive and still was in her way, but it didn't. It remained silent, and he finally sighed and stared in the direction of the house. Its walls were up, doors and roof on, but inside was only subfloor, bare wires, and exposed plumbing. It wouldn't take long to finish, except he wasn't doing it.

He strode to the porch, his jaw stiff, but when he reached the steps, the thought struck him that it was a lousy idea to be here. He was wallowing, scooting closer to that rabbit hole of despair he'd tumbled into after Meg died. His guilt had crushed him under a weight he still struggled to carry because he hadn't been there for her. He'd been busy building houses. Owning his own company had been his dream, and he'd gotten lost in the effort. He hadn't even noticed how lonely she had gotten until—

"I wish..."

His voice trailed off because his wish wasn't going to come true.

For the first year, as illogical as the thought had been, he'd latched onto the belief that she'd come back to him. Losing her was just a test he had to go through. On the other side, he'd be better and stronger for the experience of having lost her and gotten her back. All he needed was the universe to heed him and let him prove it. He'd do it right.

Love her for all she was worth. But, despite all his promises and threats, here he was... Alone.

He turned back to the pickup, fetched his Maglite, and flipped it on inside the house. He knew every nook and cranny and didn't need the light, but he swung its beam around the room anyway. He'd planned for dark hickory floors and mission-style furniture. No carpets and no rugs because that was his preference. Just wood, gleaming and warm, like Meg's smile.

Idiot. Don't brood.

He should sell the place. Even though he'd probably get used to the house without her, he didn't want to wait for that to happen. He'd always been the kind of guy who took charge of his life and got things done.

A pair of French doors in the bedroom opened out on the back half of the meadow. The dark hid only matted weeds, but in the spring it burst into pinks and purples and oranges.

"You'd like her, Meg. Rose, I mean. She reminds me of you."

Not that he was going to be with Rose. The timing hadn't been right. But, damn, he was tired of being alone. Tired of mourning. Tired of himself. For fuck's sake, there had to be more than this. There had to be the family he'd almost had.

"Jesus, Meg. Why'd you go?" His throat strangled his voice. His words emerged raw and hot, and he took a breath to calm himself. "I was hoping we'd have a little girl like..."

You.

No. Don't go there.

He took another breath and turned away, itching to hit something. He'd probably break a knuckle though, so he kept walking until he got into his truck and drove away. Another half mile down the road sat a dive bar and a drink with his name on it.

Maybe a body to hold tight.

He sped up, glimpsing headlights in his rearview mirror before the curve of the road took him away.

5

VANE FALLS ASLEEP

D*ANG.*

Other than being on a street with other streets branching off it, Vane had no idea where he was. He didn't recognize any names on the sign poles. None of them flashed—*this is it!*—the place where he sent Christmas cards every year. Was he even in Poppy Brush? He'd grown up twenty minutes outside of the village, but these homes were all in a new development.

His eyelids drooped, and a weight as cozy and warm as a blanket pulled him under until the sway of the car jerked him back. Geez. He swung to the curb and got out his phone, but when he pushed the button to bring the screen to life nothing happened.

He pressed the button again.

Still nothing.

For Pete's sake. He'd charged it that morning, the piece of junk. *Well, you only paid thirty bucks for it, you know.*

"Screw you," he muttered to the voice in his head.

Why did his life always do this to him? Was it him? Sometimes he thought he had superpowers when it came to screwing himself up. He had to be operating at a much higher level than ordinary humans.

Well, now what?

Think.

Vane drove to the corner and headed in a new direction.

Occasionally, Marc would come to LA on business and meet Vane for lunch. He'd usually have pictures of the kids on his phone. One time, he showed Vane a two-toned blue house with an A-shaped roof, so Vane knew what he was looking for. The house was on Persimmon Way, but he couldn't find the street either. Any of a half dozen houses he'd seen could be Rose's if any had been on the right street.

He turned back onto the main avenue and drove toward Poppy Brush. When the sign appeared, he went in the opposite direction. He doubted the village stores would still be open, so he needed to find Target or Wal-Mart and buy a new phone.

A few minutes later, he sped by the turn off to his old home. A pang struck him at the thought of the house sitting empty and dark. Maybe he should go back.

He let up on the gas as he thought about it. His tiredness tugged at him, and he struggled to keep his eyes open. There'd be a phone at the house unless Rose had turned it off, but then he remembered he didn't have his key. He'd left it with his extra ones in his jewelry box at

Fisher's. He'd been too distracted looking for his flash drive to think to take it.

Shoot.

The hard plastic of the steering wheel pressed into his forehead. A few seconds—*minutes?*—later, the discomfort roused him, and he realized he was idling on the dark road, half-asleep. He debated breaking into the house, but how creepy would that be? Reduced to breaking into his own house?

Don't panic.

I'm not.

He yawned and pulled away, rolling down his window as he picked up speed. The gusts of cold air reached him with metallic fingers, and he hunched his shoulders against it.

If he drove a few more miles, he'd come upon a bar he'd never been old enough to go into when he'd lived here. And about two miles after that was Eileen's. The bar had fascinated him as a kid. He used to walk by it in the summertime. The place had always been busy, even in the middle of the day, and the blackened windows hiding the mysteries inside had entranced him. At night, a red *OPEN* sign glowed against the painted front window.

For a few strange minutes, he floated back in time. The hot gravel of the parking lot burned his feet. The sound of music floated through the bar's walls. Then a crash rent the memory out of his head, and something hit him as his eyes flew open.

His car smacked rocky ground, and a strange shape

loomed at him as he slammed on his brakes and jolted to a stop. *Holy—*

Relax... relax...

He was okay despite his death grip on the steering wheel and the racket his heart was making.

His headlights lit a house still under construction in the field in front of him. The windows still had stickers on them, and the driveway was a wide swath of gravel. He was pretty sure nobody lived there. There were no cars anyway, and no lights, even though it wasn't that late.

Vane released his grip on the steering wheel and rubbed his face with shaky hands. He'd fallen asleep for gosh sakes. He could have killed himself.

His heart slowed, and he didn't think he'd drop off again, but he needed air. Of course, that was a mistake because just about everything he did was a mistake. He had no idea what he stepped on, but the minute he shut the door and took a step, his leg gave out, and his keys went flying. He staggered across the clumpy ground and crashed to his knees on top of something piled under a tarp. Lumber.

The boards shifted as he struggled up. He slid his palms along slick plastic, but his keys were gone. Giggling like a maniac, he got to his feet. Well, he was wide awake now.

He brushed his hands off on his pants and turned back to the car, but his door was locked. Of course it was. After years of living in LA, he'd locked it without thinking. Depressed the button with his thumb and swung the door shut almost in one motion. That's what he got for buying a vintage car.

He turned away again and stuffed his hands under his arms.

Now what?

Would it be breaking and entering if he slept in the house but left in the morning?

Probably.

He could go home, but that was miles away now. Or he could continue on to the bar and call Rose when he got there. Two miles maybe. That made more sense, and the walk would do him good anyway. The cash he had on him wasn't much but probably enough for a beer. Plus, he'd get a look inside the place and maybe come away with a little color for his next screenplay.

Redneck Heaven.

Geez, where had that come from? He doubted it was that kind of bar.

This was Poppy Brush. Average annual income a million plus and a favorite pastime that probably wasn't beating up the gay guy.

Still... It was a good thing he had his leather jacket on. Maybe they'd think he was tough.

As he set off up the road, Vane ruminated on the fact he'd thought about another screenplay a moment ago. Not Marcel. Not acting, at all.

He shivered in the cold and picked up his pace.

6

A HOT GUY

DOUG TIPPED HIS beer mug and gazed at the amount that remained. Two swallows of a second beer. But it did nothing for him. He was too wired, and if he kept drinking, he'd be drunk.

Dammit.

He tipped his chair back until it hit the wall and tried to relax, letting his gaze wander the quiet room.

The bar's owner stood with his arms crossed over his chest, watching the TV mounted in the corner opposite Doug. About a dozen customers sat at the tables and a couple took up stools at the bar.

The interior was dark, lit mostly by the glow of the TV.

Doug was pretty sure the guy at the table beside him was sound asleep. The dreariness of the place hit him out of the blue, and he had a feeling he was just punishing himself by staying. There were other places he could be, even sitting in a movie theater with Dorcas if he'd thought about it. But that ball of energy in his chest had brought him here.

He let his chair tip down just as the entrance door swung open and somebody in jeans and a jacket with a hoodie underneath stepped in—and promptly tripped. After he righted himself, the guy fixed what had to be a glare at the raised section of weather stripping across the threshold.

Doug lifted his mug, laughing into it before he took a drink.

The newcomer headed to the bar and stood at the corner until the owner finished with another customer and turned to him. Doug couldn't see the guy's face in the shadows, but he heard the owner say, "Yeah?" in a surprised tone and a few words in return. "Real quick... couple miles."

Doug doubted the owner responded to whatever the guy was talking about. A useful reply would need more than the "You gonna buy somethin'?" he came up with.

Doug finished his beer and kept his eye on them. Maybe the owner made the guy nervous because the money he dug out of his pocket flew everywhere but on the counter.

"Shoot."

The almost curse rang loud and clear. Doug grinned as the guy chased the rolling coins, picked up a couple, turned around, and bent over again.

Nice. Cute little bottom in those worn-out jeans.

Doug watched him step back to the corner of the bar and count his coins. The owner shook his head. Doug sighed, guessing the guy didn't have enough money and the owner wouldn't cut him any slack. *What an asshole.* Doug wasn't coming to this place anymore. It had always been sketchy, but now it was a dreary, low-class dump.

He stood and strode to the bar. "Another one. For him too."

The guy raised his head from his pile of money, and Doug got his first good look at his face. He startled. "Jesus, are you okay?"

The guy frowned, looking cute as hell as he tried to figure out Doug's question.

Doug pointed at his own cheek. The poor light hid a lot, but he thought the guy blushed. And then he... giggled. A real-live giggle. Doug couldn't help but laugh. Of all the weird things. Though from the twitches running through the guy, his giggle was clearly a result of his nerves. Doug liked that. Meg had been shy too.

"Kick-boxing."

The words took a moment to register. Doug lifted the beer the bartender set down and motioned with his chin at the other one. The guy picked it up, nodded, and took a swallow. His sigh sounded happy.

"I didn't think kicking people in the face was allowed," Doug said. He didn't for a minute believe the guy had gotten his bruises in a kickboxing match.

"Well, it was an accident. I'm kind of clumsy."

No kidding. "Glad I have no interest in contact sports."

No, Doug was a baseball kind of guy and lazy about working out. His job was physical, and he put muscle on without even trying.

"I quit," the guy said.

"Better part of valor," Doug murmured.

A slow smile lit the guy's face. "Caution is preferable to rash bravery," he added to the quote. "You're a Shakespeare fan."

Doug hid his surprise with a nod. The guy was beautiful and charming and familiar, but Doug drew a blank trying to figure out where he'd seen him before. "Are you from around here?"

That changed things. The smile flattened, and the guy pulled back.

"Just visiting. My car broke down. Well, not actually broke down. I got out and dropped my keys." He gave a blustery-sounding laugh. "Now I'm locked out."

"I can jimmy it."

The guy stared at him with his mouth half open. The pink of his tongue showed. *Damn.* Heat built between Doug's legs. He shifted on his stool as his lust bloomed, a sensation he'd almost forgotten about. He hooked up with willing partners to expend some energy, but to be honest, attraction wasn't usually a big part of it.

"Are you a car thief?" the guy asked, shrugging his jacket off.

"Right."

The smile came back. "Just checking."

The guy shifted to the stool between them and his hair

swung, the dark ends brushing the tops of his shoulders. He tucked it behind his ears, then pushed up the sleeves of his hoodie. He had holes in his lobes but no earrings, and a tattoo of a sun done in black ink decorated the inside of a wrist.

Doug rocked forward, feeling the pressure on his balls, and set his elbow on the counter. "Drink up. I'll take you to your car."

The guy nodded. "That'd be great. I was going to call someone, but my phone's broken."

Of course it was. This guy screamed total disaster. "What's your name?"

A whisper of a hesitation preceded his smile. "Ethan."

Ethan. A nice name, but it wasn't his. Or maybe it was his middle name. *Interesting.* Doug wasn't afraid of him and didn't think he was a psycho serial killer or anything. When it came down to it though, he probably couldn't pick a serial killer out of a crowd to save his life. But this guy looked friendly, a little nervous, and a lot needy.

The perfect storm for Doug. He stuck out his hand. "I'm Doug."

Warm fingers gripped his, and a jolt like a zap from a live wire shot up his arm and down his spine. Ethan's mouth opened again, a slight part, the pink of his tongue a glimmer inside. "Nice to meet you, Doug."

"You too."

He wanted to do more than meet him though. He wanted to plant himself inside him. Ethan's eyes widened as Doug stared at him, his pupils stretching to the edges of his irises. He flicked his lip with his tongue, picked up his beer, and chugged it.

"Want another?" Doug asked.

Ethan set his mug down. "Sure."

Doug raised two fingers. "So whadda you do?"

"Write. I'm a writer."

"Oh yeah?"

"Well, wannabe. I don't have anything out, yet."

"You will if you keep at it. That's impressive. I have a tough time writing a two-page proposal."

"What kind of proposal?"

"Job proposals. I own a construction company. We do mostly renos and additions."

"Oh, that's cool. Like the *Property Brothers*."

Without the brother. Or the money. Or the fame. Doug nodded and pressed his lips into a smile. "Exactly."

Ethan grinned. "I love those shows. I can barely use a hammer."

"Somehow I think your thumbs thank you for not trying."

Ethan gaped. Then he inhaled as though to speak but laughed first instead. "Okay. Okay. That's probably true."

His hand rested on the counter, and Doug wanted to touch it. The fingers lay flat, long, and slender. The thumb twitched, and Ethan curled it under his palm.

He was elegant and clumsy. And interested in Doug. Heat glowed in his eyes.

Doug pointed a finger at the beer. "Finish up. Let's get out of here."

Ethan swallowed. "Yeah. Okay."

After he drank the rest of his beer and tugged his coat on, Doug gestured to the back door. "This way."

They went down a short hall to a door painted the same black as the walls. Doug opened it and looked back. A hesitant smile greeted him and a flutter of panic stirred in Doug's belly. *Too sweet.*

He knew with perfect certainty he should bail and also that he wasn't going to.

❧

VANE STEPPED INTO THE DARK. A DOZEN CARS clustered around the bar, and a few other shapes loomed in back, but that was all. Only the creep of woods surrounded them. Vane blinked, letting his vision adjust. Doug faced him, but his expression was hidden, only a hint of illumination across his eyes.

Vane shivered, the movement seeming to break Doug's paralysis as he stepped closer. He loomed over Vane. Taller, bigger. Gosh, everything Vane loved in a guy. A sure smile. Cynical humor. Calm and confident. Everything Fisher wasn't, except for the confidence. Every tick box ticked off. Even the gay one. But Vane didn't know him, and he'd already lied to him.

Great way to start a new life.

Well, I'm not starting a new life. I'm going back home in a couple days. I'm going to be Marvelous Marcel.

He had to check his messages. There'd be a call from Mary or his agent. He hadn't blown it. Nobody could hold bruises against him.

You ran away.

Oh, shut up.

The hoppy scent of beer and Doug's warm breath caressed his face. He bit back a groan as Doug came even closer, hazel eyes hidden in the shadows. Vane swallowed.

"Is this okay?" Doug murmured.

He didn't have to ask what Doug meant.

"Yeah," he whispered, and Doug flattened him against the side of the building and covered Vane's mouth with his.

Vane groaned out loud this time and leaned in, wrapping his arms around Doug's neck.

Was this cheating?

No, idiot. Fisher beat you up. You left.

Doug's arms tightened and lifted, and Vane hopped up and wrapped his legs around Doug's waist. *Heck, yeah.* This was his dream, to have a guy pick him up and hold him.

His back hit the cinder block wall of the bar, and Doug pushed his tongue into Vane's mouth.

A humming sound filled Vane's head, his or Doug's, he didn't know. He swallowed the sound and the rich taste of beer. Doug's face against his forced his mouth open wider. He let his head fall back and let Doug take over.

The air in his lungs burned, swelling his chest with a desperate ache. He wanted to let go. Needed to.

The waves of worry and grief drowning him swept away. He didn't want to think right now. He'd think later. Now... Now Doug's kiss stole his breath and his core burned with a devouring fire. He thrust, rubbing his crotch against Doug's belly.

After a moment, Doug pulled back and gasped. "Fuck, you're hot."

"You too," said Vane. *Oh, yeah, that was original.*

"Thanks," said Doug.

Well okay, that wasn't much better.

He leaned in for another kiss, sinking into the softness of Doug's lips. He wanted to do this forever, but a thought rose to the surface of his consciousness.

"Is this okay?"

"Hm?"

Doug had his face buried in Vane's neck now, and Vane shivered at the soft touch. *Oh gosh... oh gosh.* He moaned, feeling as though his body had become one giant goose bump. But then a car crackled over gravel, and his eyes snapped open. People could see them. He shivered and dropped to his feet.

Doug took his hand. "C'mon."

They headed to a pickup wedged between a garbage bin and a trailer. "Weird place to park," said Vane.

Doug chuckled. "I have a friend's stuff in back. I didn't want it visible from the road."

No chance of that. The truck was a monster with four doors, giant tires, and a back that was almost eye level. Whatever Doug was carrying hid in the bed under a tarp.

Hoping this wasn't going to play like the plot of a murder mystery, Vane hopped into Doug's vehicle. *A perfect stranger's vehicle. You with your great instincts.* His pounding heart told him he was crazy, but he ignored it. Who cared when every beat of his pulse drove sparks into his balls? And anyway, he wasn't really afraid. He liked the guy.

You liked Fisher too though.

Shut up.

Doug froze halfway into the driver's side. "What?"

Shoot, did he say that out loud?

"Hurry up."

Doug grinned and jumped in.

The light stayed on for a moment, and Vane drank in the sight of Doug's face. Solid with a hint of light brown stubble. Were his eyes brown or hazel? Hard to tell. His blond hair was wavy and thick. Vane felt a surge of worry at the fading grin until Doug brushed his cheek with a finger. *My bruises.*

Vane gave a wry smile.

When the light winked out, Doug slid over, and Vane sank into his arms. Their lips met, the tip of Doug's tongue teasing its way into Vane's mouth. Heat built in his crotch, his cock swelling against his too-tight jeans.

He pulled away. "Are we having sex? I mean anal? I don't have any supplies. Will this work?"

Doug laughed, his breath puffing against Vane's lips. "What a kook you are."

Vane giggled.

Shoot. Don't do that. He really needed to outgrow the giggling, but he liked this guy. It was crazy. "A little," he admitted.

Then he shivered as Doug slid his fingers under his shirt and stroked the skin over his hip. "I have supplies,"

Doug murmured. "We'll do whatever you want. God, your skin is so soft."

Gentle strokes brushed over the trail of hair down Vane's belly, and his shivers built into a shudder. At the press of Doug's palm between his legs, he threw his head back and cracked it against his window.

"Ow."

"Jesus. Are you all right?"

"Yeah." He rubbed his head and snorted. "Gosh, I'm a klutz."

Why would this guy like you? Maybe something was wrong with him. Maybe Doug really was a serial killer. The kind who disarmed his victims with gentle strokes to the back of their head, because that's what Doug was doing. Caressing the tender spot, fingers ruffling through Vane's hair. "Poor baby."

Doug pulled him closer until their foreheads touched.

"I'll probably put my foot through your windshield."

Doug laughed. "Can't have that. You'll have to sit in my lap."

Vane moaned. "I'll be too high. Somebody'll see in."

"No, they won't."

"Maybe."

Doug slid his hand under Vane's shirt again and ghosted it up his back. "The owner lives in this trailer, and the bar won't shut for a couple more hours."

Doug squeezed Vane's neck and rubbed down his goose-bumped spine. When he reached Vane's waist, he slipped his fingers into the back of his jeans.

"You're so warm."

"I'm hot," said Vane. "I'm burning up."

"Yes," Doug whispered, kissing him.

Vane tried to swallow that hot tongue and got a moan. His insides reverberated, and he wasn't sure he wouldn't shake apart in Doug's arms. He tugged at Doug's belt. *Oh yesss.* Liquid fire slid down the back of his jeans as Doug's scorching-hot fingers worked between his crack. His hole twitched, hungry for something inside it.

When Doug's belt fell open, he cupped the bulge underneath it and sighed at the heat radiating through the denim.

Golly, how did he get so lucky? Something had to go wrong. He pulled away. "You really want to do this with me?"

Silence met his question. He peered into the blur of Doug's face, but when Doug spoke, humor bubbled in his voice. "Is there something wrong with you?"

Like they had a million years.

"I try to be normal."

Doug laughed. "You're failing."

"Oh."

Doug pulled Vane's shirt up, tongue ghosting his skin until it brushed on a nipple. He kissed it with a warm, humid murmur. "Now, shut up."

"Yeah," Vane whispered. "I can do that." The kiss became a tug and pull as Doug sucked. *Oh heck, yeah.*

Vane returned his attention to Doug's pants and popped the buttons. He curled his fingers inside and touched hot silky skin. Doug pulled his head up. "Oh, fuck, that feels good."

"I want it," Vane whispered. *Wow. Articulate as always.*

But Doug didn't seem to mind. He lifted off his seat and pushed his pants and underwear down.

Vane wrapped his fingers around the dick that drew him like a magnet. Hot flesh baked his palm. He squeezed and scooted backward, belly on the seat, legs curled up against the door. When he ran out of room, he bent down and brushed the length of Doug's cock with his cheek.

Doug hissed and knotted his fingers in Vane's hair as Vane breathed in and brushed Doug's skin with his lips.

"You smell so good," Vane whispered.

"You talk a lot."

He stilled. "Sorry."

"No." Doug groaned and hitched his hips. "It's just an observation. You're... unusual."

Vane didn't know what to say to that, but his gums flapped anyway. "Unusual in a good way? I can shut up. I can—"

"Stop."

"Okay."

He nuzzled Doug's dick, grinding his own against the surface of the seat before he licked the tip.

The tang of Doug's precum sent sparks across his skin and soothed his flyaway nerves. Peace spread through him with the warmth and ache of pleasure.

He took the cock in his mouth and melted at the weight of it. It held him steady, but he was light as air. He circled his tongue under Doug's cockhead and flicked the tip against the sensitive nerves. The rhythm of fingers stroking his hair sizzled over his scalp. An overload of sensation bloomed in a powerful ache between his legs. He moaned and ground his dick into the seat.

"So pretty," Doug whispered.

Vane looked up from beneath his brows and dragged his lips to Doug's tip, sucking hard before sinking down again.

The flavor of Doug's skin was strange and intoxicating. Could a person get drunk on skin? Vane was jobless and homeless and didn't care, so maybe he was drunk. He buried his lips in crisp hair, worked his throat and choked.

Oddly, Doug was laughing. That was weird. "You're still talking. Or trying to."

Oh.

He fisted Doug's cock beneath his lips until a tug on the back of his shirt pulled him off with a pop.

"Whoa, whoa," Doug panted. "Slow down."

Vane crawled on his knees and whacked his head on the ceiling. "Ow."

"Jesus."

"I'm okay."

Doug rubbed his head. "Take your pants off."

"Yeah, okay. Good. Are we gonna do it now?"

A laugh filled Doug's voice. "I was hoping to."

"Me too."

But Doug held onto him for a moment, swiping his cheek with a thumb before letting him go. Vane stilled at the gesture. He hadn't expected affection. The kind he got from Fisher was akin to a pat on the head. Silly, clumsy Vane. But this... He melted.

When Doug nudged him sideways and reached for the glove box, Vane would have moved away, but he didn't have to. Doug wrapped an arm around his waist and tugged him close, reaching past him with his free hand.

The latch on the glove box clicked open, and Vane leaned into the weight pressing against him. Who had ever held him this close and kept him from falling? *No one.*

Doug kissed Vane's throat, just above his clavicle, and said, "Let me help."

Vane didn't resist. His excitement rose as Doug gripped the waistband of his jeans and underwear and pushed them down. The cold air hit his cock with a shock. He leaned over Doug's shoulder as Doug bent down and breathed a hot gust onto Vane's tip, yanking a shudder out of him. Vane groaned and dug his fingers into Doug's back at the touch of his warm tongue.

"Sweet," Doug murmured.

It was. Sweet and hot. Vane's head bopped the ceiling again but not hard. He closed his eyes, drowning in pleasure. Doug lapped and sucked until Vane thought his shaking would break the truck apart. He couldn't take much more, but it didn't matter because Doug stopped and pushed Vane's jeans down his thighs.

But he froze when his fingers brushed the waistband of Vane's underwear.

"Are those lace?"

Vane wriggled away and scoffed. "No. Just bunched up."

Sitting again, he kicked his shoes off and lifted his knees, working his pants to his ankles. The edge of his shirt brushed his pubic hair, and the tickle of it racked him with another shudder.

"C'mere," Doug murmured, scooting back against the door.

"You come over here."

"Why?"

"So I don't honk the horn."

After a moment of silence, Doug said, "I guess you mean the truck's?"

Vane giggled-snorted, and Doug laughed.

After a few more scoots and shifts, Vane straddled Doug's lap. Keeping his head low, he sank against the finger that circled his rim, feeling hot and snug inside the foggy windows. He thrust back and bit his lip at the slight burn.

"You're so hot," Doug whispered.

"Hm," he hummed. "Do it... do it to me."

"Like this?"

Doug pushed his finger in deeper, and Vane dropped his face into Doug's neck with a groan. His dick ached, his balls hot and heavy.

"Open this." Doug pulled his finger away, and Vane lifted his head, squinting in the dark until Doug tapped his arm. "This."

Vane fumbled for the condom packet and took it while Doug cupped his ass again. He pushed back into the warm hands. His breath came in ragged gasps.

Thinking was hard. *Don't think.*

He dropped the condom between his legs. Doug laughed and fetched it.

"Sorry," Vane murmured.

"For what?"

But he couldn't answer because a hand at the back of his neck pulled him down. Lips met his, brushing back and forth. "I haven't had sex in a car in... ever. You make me feel young," Doug whispered.

What would that be like, Vane wondered. To be back at a place where the wreck of his life didn't pile around his ankles like a dump heap. Where being a washout of an actor was something that happened to all the other wannabes, not him. Why did this guy want him?

But the question flew from his brain when the knob of Doug's cock pressed against his hole. He groaned and spread his knees on the seat, hitting the door on one side. No matter. Doug's cock inched in, and a wrench of pain and heat spiraled through Vane's belly. He clasped Doug's neck in his hands and pressed down.

"Oh, my gosh."

"Damn, you are tight, babe."

Babe.

The sound of the endearment penetrated his absorption with the stretch of his ass. The scream of muscle, and the heat of the friction. So fucking full. He bore down.

"You're big," he moaned.

Doug took a breath. His hands vibrated on Vane's waist. "Average."

Vane snuffled a laugh. "I don't think so."

But maybe he was. Maybe Vane was just used to Fisher. Their bodies fit out of habit. And habit for Fisher probably meant staying out of the way of Vane's elbows. But, in any case, it wasn't new like this. Doug stuffed him, and Vane wasn't sure he had enough room in him.

A frisson of panic joined the shivers of pleasure racing through him.

"Breathe," Doug whispered.

He grunted out a breath and sank the last distance. Doug's lap met his ass, and he moaned. His whole body was an itch only Doug's dick could scratch, and the scrape of Vane's cock against Doug's shirt set him on fire.

"Sweet baby," Doug whispered. "My sweet baby."

Vane's heart swelled. Of course, he wasn't Doug's baby. He'd never even been Fisher's, but he fell into the fantasy and groaned as he pumped his dick.

A tingle in Vane's spine gathered power like an electrical storm. "Gosh... I'm gonna... gonna come."

"All over me."

Yes! Mark him.

The tension built, burst, exploded in wrenching spasms. He clenched and threw his head back. Doug thrust up, and Vane spurted. His orgasm wracked him, and his thoughts disappeared until the ache in his dick pulled him back. He squeezed himself, milking out a last few drops of cum while Doug's hands slid along his thighs.

"Jesus," Doug murmured. "That was nice."

Nice?

Vane's hot skin crawled in a sudden chill. He lifted off Doug's lap and scooted sideways. *What the heck happened to babe?* Where were his jeans? He bent down and whacked his forehead on the dashboard.

"Ow."

"Are you okay?"

"Yeah."

Maybe he was reading too much into that comment. Maybe it wasn't a dismissal. He found his pants.

"I better get you to your car. It's getting late. You probably have someplace to go?"

"Yeah."

But it was too late. He'd have to sleep in his car until morning. Assuming he could find Ro's house. He hitched his pants up his hips while Doug got out, zipped up, and circled back around to the driver's side. Vane scooted closer to his door and buckled up.

"I didn't expect that," said Doug.

Please don't say thanks.

"Thanks."

Vane sighed. He never knew what to say to that. *You're welcome?* "I had fun."

"Yeah. Me too."

Doug started the vehicle and reversed. At the exit to the road, he stopped again. "Which direction?"

Vane pointed toward the right. "That way."

He wasn't good with north, south, east, west. Or acting. Or boyfriends. Or pretty much anything. *Cooking. You can cook.*

But you're a waiter.

He squirmed on his sore ass. He should be grateful he'd gotten off, at least, and forget about the ice in his belly and the Jell-O in his legs. As Doug drove away from the bar, Vane gazed into the dark.

Maybe in the light tomorrow he'd recognize his old hometown again.

Or maybe he wouldn't.

Maybe it had changed into something with no relation to anything he remembered.

Don't panic.

Yeah, right.

7

HIS WIFE'S PLACE

DOUG CRANKED HIS window open, desperate for some cold air to clear his head. His heart still throbbed.

What the fuck had just gone on? Jesus Christ, he'd been lost in the guy. A weirdly clean mouth and a hot, horny body. But a hookup. A have-fun-with-and-walk-away-from kind of guy.

His head swam from the day. It had to be a reaction to Ethan having the same name as Rose's father, and Doug still reeling from the sudden death. He hadn't thought about that connection at first, but it made sense. Any death cut into a place in his heart that was only Meg's and brought all the pain of her loss raging back to life. He was so careful to guard that place so he wouldn't be hurt, but this Ethan guy had somehow slipped past his defenses. He was stupid to think he could move on. *I'm sorry, babe.*

But his apology dropped into an empty space. He got

nothing back from her, not even the whisper of a kiss he swore he could sometimes feel.

But tonight, he was burned by the guy sitting beside him, and he fought against his longing to hold him close again. Doug ached for Ethan's weight in his arms, the scrape of Ethan's stubble against his cheek. But, no. Forget it. They'd had their fun, and this was all that was going to happen. Doug had his work and a house to finish. It was his and Meg's, and he was keeping it. *I won't let you go, Meg.*

He hated that he had new things in his life and jobs she'd never know about now. Rose would never have become his friend if he hadn't lost Meg.

As he drove, getting closer to the house, he frowned and rolled his window down a few more inches. Ethan was quiet now, and he'd been such a chatterbox before.

"How much farther?" Doug asked.

"Right up here, I think."

Ethan's voice was subdued and guilt swept over Doug. Then his headlights illuminated his house and... a car. A car smack in the middle of his and Meg's meadow. His head and neck grew hot, and his ears rang.

Squeezing his steering wheel in his fists, he drew himself up on his seat. "What the fuck?"

Ethan scooted closer to his door. "What's wrong?"

Doug swung off the road, bouncing over ruts. "This is my property."

"That's your house?"

"Yes."

He snapped it, and Ethan flinched.

"Sorry. I didn't drive off the road on purpose."

Ethan fumbled at his seatbelt, and Doug shook his head, grimacing at himself. He'd scared the guy.

"I'm not accusing you," Doug said. Though he was. He was ashamed of himself, too, and had no idea how a night could go up in flames so spectacularly in a matter of minutes. "It's weird, that's all."

"I fell asleep," said Ethan.

"Do you have far to go?"

"No. I'm wide awake now anyway. I just need to get into my car. I'll find my keys in the morning."

Doug popped open his door. "We'll find your keys now."

He was a jerk for scaring the guy like that. Ethan wasn't to blame for distracting Doug from the things that mattered. And God, did Ethan distract him. Doug wanted to hold him and run his fingers through that soft hair and soothe his fears. Instead, he got out of his truck with his Maglite and closed his door.

Now that he was calmer, he could appreciate the vehicle in the beam of his flashlight. The vintage Mustang coupe had a hard top and was probably black, though it was hard to tell in the dark.

"What year is that?"

"'65."

"Very nice."

"It pretty much sat in an old couple's garage before I bought it. They'd gotten it new and just used it as their regular car until they bought an SUV. I like it, but it's not in great shape. That's why I could afford it though."

"Well, it'll be easy to get into. Just give me a couple minutes."

"I'll look for my keys," said Ethan.

Doug nodded and found his door opener and wedge in his toolbox.

After a quick glance at Ethan, who was wandering in the dark with his head down, Doug said, "You won't find them that way. Take this." He handed Ethan his flashlight. "I'll work my magic while you look."

"Okay. Thanks."

Bastard, Doug thought. *Touch him. Be nice.* But he didn't. He returned to his truck and turned on the headlights. Ethan hadn't driven far into the meadow. He wasn't stuck, and the ground was hard and frosty. Rain was coming soon though. Maybe the next day.

His breath fogged the air as he worked the plastic wedge between the top of the car window and the rim. Once he'd wiggled a little open space, slipping the tool inside and popping the button was easy. He'd purchased the tools with Meg in mind and smiled now at his many memories of breaking into her car for her.

Only you, Meg.

And this guy.

He opened the door, closed it again, returned his tools to his truck, and turned off his headlights.

"Find 'em?" he asked.

"No. I'm okay though. I can sleep in my car."

"It's too cold. Give me that."

"Look," said Ethan. "I'm sorry I drove on your

property. You've been nice. You don't need to hang out with me. I'm not really your babe. I can survive."

"I'm trying to help."

"I don't need your help."

"You fell asleep at the wheel and plowed your vehicle into my field," said Doug. "You need help."

"I said I was sorry. It's not like I hit your house."

"I know that. Let me help."

"Fine. Here. I just want to go."

The frantic tone in Ethan's voice hit Doug hard. "You'll go. No worries." He took the Maglite and returned to Ethan's car. "It happened here, right? You got out. Lost your keys."

"Yeah."

Doug pointed the beam at his feet and swept a half circle at his toes, returned in another arc, and spread out inch by inch. Less than a minute later, metal caught the light, and Ethan said, "There!" and snatched his keys out of a shallow furrow.

"Check your car," Doug said. *Get him in it. Make sure he's safe. Get away. You'll forget tonight. Forget him.*

But he knew he wouldn't forget. His throat burned from the acid rushing into his mouth when Ethan opened the car door and light flooded out. Shadows washed across his face and settled in the hollows. The bruises that had blurred in the bar's dull light were livid now.

Ethan slid in behind the wheel and started the engine. "It's fine," he said. "I just lost my keys."

A picture of Meg gesturing in exasperation at her car

flooded Doug's head again. A kind of wounded look was in the eyes gazing at him now.

"Good. So, um... It was nice meeting you." *Did I just say that?*

After a silent minute, Ethan broke Doug's stare and ran his palm over the top of his steering wheel. "Yeah, you too. Thanks for the beers."

"Anytime," said Doug.

But there wasn't going to be an any other time. This was it, though the tie of this connection only seemed to grow stronger as he backed away. But he was lonely and raw with the prospect of a funeral in two days, not far from where he'd buried Meg. That's all this was. A phantom pain. Nothing connected to the quiet guy in the car.

The clumsy guy with a warm mouth and a round ass that had filled his palms.

"See you, Ethan."

He didn't wait for a response but turned and walked away.

8

AT ROSE'S HOUSE

VANE STARED AT the TV, wondering why the kids weren't watching cartoons the way he had when he'd been a kid. Power Rangers. Teenage Mutant Ninja Turtles. Not talk shows.

He stared at the screen.

Not that it mattered what was on because they weren't really watching. They were staring at him. He shifted his gaze sideways without turning his head. They were in the family room attached to the kitchen. Lucy sat in a chair with her hands flattened on the arms, as though about to propel herself out of it. Frowny-faced Ricky sat beside him.

Vane dug his fingers into the blanket folded on his lap. He'd slept under it last night, and now he vibrated underneath it, pinned by their patient stares. He looked over Ricky's head into the kitchen.

"Need any help?"

Rose smiled at him. "Nope."

His stomach growled, and a voice piped up beside him. "Are you hungry?"

"A little."

"Mom made oatmeal pie."

"Oatmeal pie?" Shoot, that had to suck.

"Well, I didn't make it," Rose said. "Luis did. I'm trying to use up everything in the house right now. We're going to have enough leftovers after the service."

"Who's Luis?"

"Our cook," said Lucy.

Her words broke the silence she'd been treating him to since her murmured, "Hello," that morning.

"You have a cook?"

"At Eileen's," said Rose. "I can take you there today, or we can come back after the move. We'll close up Thanksgiving week, so that might be a good time. You can see what you're up against."

"I don't get it. Why would you close? Won't we lose money?"

"We already are, sweetheart." She opened the oven, pulled a dish off the rack, and set it on the stove. "I'm trying to find a buyer, which is something I need to talk to you and Luis about."

He frowned and opened his mouth, but before he could get his question out, Ricky said, "Do you have a puppy?"

"A— No. No puppy."

"Why not?"

"I just don't. Do you have a puppy?"

"No."

"Why not?" Two could play this game.

"I'm a little boy, but Mom says we can have a puppy in our new house. I don't want to go to the new house though. I like this house. I wanna stay, but I can't get a puppy here. You don't need to ask your mom."

"No," said Vane. "That's true."

"Where is your mom?"

Rose spoke. "Ricky, honey, Vane and I have the same mom. Our mom is in heaven."

Ricky frowned without looking away from Vane. "I think there are puppies in heaven."

"Good golly, miss Molly, you are talking up a storm today," said Rose. "Time to eat. I hope paper plates are okay." Her gaze was on Vane now. "I packed up our dishes."

He smiled. "Miss Molly."

Rose winked. "Learned it from Mom."

He stood and sat at the counter. "I remember." No swearing for her. "Congratulations on the new job, by the way."

She grinned. "Thanks. I'm excited."

She'd gotten her paralegal certification and a new job, but the new job was fifty miles away. He guessed she hadn't expected their dad to die, and now they had a family diner to run. A soon-to-close, running-out-of-money diner.

He leaned on the counter, inspecting an egg casserole and a pie. A strange-looking pie that somewhat resembled a pecan pie without the nuts.

"I know," she said. "Weird breakfast."

"I'll eat anything. I like sweets."

"I remember."

He gazed at her while she set squares of casserole and slices of pear on the paper plates she gave the kids. Her skin was pale like his, her flame-colored hair as curly as he remembered. She'd been twenty-four when he'd gone away, and over the last fourteen years they'd only gotten together three times.

He bit his lip. "Looks good."

"Last of the eggs."

She cut him a slice of the peculiar pie to go with his portion of the casserole. "You're right that it's weird though."

Her eyes widened and she made an O shape with her mouth. "It's oatmeal. Besides, I know you hate milk, so no cereal."

Lucy leaned forward and peered at him from around her brother. "You don't like milk?"

Why did that sound accusatory? He shifted on his stool. "I like cheese."

"That's weird," said Lucy.

Rose leaned back against the counter across from them and tucked into her eggs, eyes twinkling. Vane scowled at her and cut into his pie, releasing a warm and nutty, pecan-like aroma, though the cracked brown crust that sank into the soft filling was clearly made of oats.

"Hm."

He wagged his head as he swallowed his mouthful. *Yep. Pecan.* Or rather a twist on pecan topped with a chewy oatmeal cookie. *Weird pie, Luis.* "Not bad."

It needed something though. A little pizazz. Not that Vane had any plans to send it back. But he could make it better. Pretty sure he could anyway.

"It needs something," he said.

"Like what?"

"I don't know. I have to think on it."

"I don't like oatmeal," said Ricky.

"I don't like milk," said Vane.

"That's weird."

"You know who likes milk besides you?"

Ricky scrunched his forehead. The kid was suspicious as heck. "Who?"

"Cats."

For a moment nothing moved on Ricky's face. Then a grin split his mouth and crinkled his eyes. "I love cats!"

"Better than puppies?"

"No. I love puppies too. After the puppy grows up, we can get a cat, and they can get married."

Okay.

He looked at Rose, who was smiling, watching him from under her brows while she ate. "That sounds like a plan."

"I have to go," said Ricky.

Rose shifted her attention. "Where do you have to go?"

"I have to color."

She nodded. "Oh. Okay."

He slid off his stool while Lucy took his empty plate and set it on top of hers. "Thank you, Mom."

"You're welcome, honey."

She disappeared too.

Vane sighed and leaned his elbows on the counter. Dang, kids were work.

Rose was staring at him again, but she wasn't smiling anymore. "I can't keep ignoring your face, Vane."

He groaned and shook his head. "I don't want to talk about that."

"Tell me you won't go back."

"I won't. Not to him."

She took a breath and held it, and he steeled himself because he doubted she believed him. He didn't want to think too much about the statement he'd just made.

What if Fisher wants you back? Will you go?

Was he that weak? Wondering about it hit him in the gut and turned the pecan pie he'd just eaten into a ball of concrete in his gut. He didn't want to think about it.

Luckily, Rose breathed out again with a half smile and said, "How are you doing otherwise?"

They hadn't talked much the night before. By the time Vane had found her house, all he'd wanted to do was pass out.

"I'm okay. I told you I got a call back for a really good part."

"That's not what I meant."

"I don't know what to say. You know Dad didn't like me."

She pushed off the counter and looked down at the pie. "That's not true. He regretted the way things turned out between you. I think he missed you a lot."

Probably not. People always said those feel-good kinds of things after other people died and nobody could prove them wrong. Vane had no memories of his dad that told him Rose was right.

He straightened on his seat and squared his shoulders. "This neighborhood is new."

She nodded. "We bought when it was still under construction. I like the layout here, but the new house is nice too. It was built in the fifties but remodeled. Whereas dad's house..." She paused. "Well, our old place needs a lot of work. I have a friend who can help, but you'll need to decide if it's worth it to do any improvements."

"You mean fix it up first?"

"You'll get a better price."

"Why are you saying I will? What about you?"

"This is what I wanted to talk to you about. Dad left both of us an insurance policy and the house to you. The diner is yours too. If, or when, you sell it, Luis and I will each get twenty percent of the proceeds. If there are any."

Her words floated around in his head like bobbing balloons. They didn't make any sense. They were just bright and colorful and bounced off the inside of his skull.

"Trust me," she added. "I get the better part of the deal."

"Mom?"

Ricky stood in the doorway.

"Yes, honey?"

"Can I color the sun pink?"

"Yes."

"Okay."

He disappeared again.

"So, I..." Vane frowned. "Luis the cook?"

Rose sighed and looked back at him. "I think Luis was a bit of a replacement for you. You know how stubborn Dad could be. I told him to call you more times than I can count."

"I was the one who was supposed to call. Only what was I going to say? I never knew what I'd done wrong."

"Nothing, sweetie."

The power that old hurt still had surprised him. It snagged on the breath he pulled in with a dull ache. He rubbed his face and sighed. "So, after tomorrow, we'll go see?"

"Unless you want to go alone."

"No."

"You have some decisions to make."

None that he wanted to. "I think I'll take a walk and look around."

"Sure."

"Can I wash some clothes when I get back?"

"Yep. The washer and dryer are staying, so they're still hooked up."

He didn't have many clothes, but the shirt he'd stuffed in his trunk was covered in cum.

After shrugging into his coat, he stepped outside where the air was gray and still with a mist that stung his nose. A wave of memories rushed over him with the scents of the place. No particular smell that was definitely home stood out, but something old and familiar was rushing through his bloodstream now.

At the end of the walkway, he looked in both directions before heading away from the highway.

The houses that must have been cookie cutter when built had taken on their own personalities now. Few had the same colors, and none the same garden designs.

No birds sang in the cold, dark trees, and no people appeared on the first block or second.

With his hands stuffed in his pockets, Vane sauntered, trying to wrap his mind around events.

He was a homeowner and a business owner now, and he didn't want to be either. He didn't believe his father had wanted him. There had to be some kind of catch. His dad had probably only wanted to get him away from acting, which wasn't a serious pursuit, according to him. It wasn't solid. Not something somebody could be proud of.

No, far better to own a diner that wasn't making any money. Why he'd bought it at all was inexplicable to Vane. His dad had retired from a successful accounting career to take on a struggling diner. He'd renamed it Eileen's after Vane's mom. Had it been her dream? Vane had been so young when she'd died he couldn't remember.

Rose had told him that a new housing development planned for the area had fallen through. As a result, no nearby residents had materialized to keep Eileen's afloat.

Now the place was Vane's.

His thoughts drifted to Doug and the night before. How something so wickedly wonderful had blown up in his face like that was beyond him. One minute, the guy had seemed completely into him and the next he couldn't kick Vane out of his truck fast enough. Though, he had stayed until Vane had found his keys. At least he hadn't abandoned him, but still... Vane racked his brain for what he'd done, but he'd thought they'd hit it off. *Well, you're no judge.*

Seriously, he wasn't. He couldn't be trusted to figure anything out.

So why'd his dad leave him a business he had a snowball's chance in heck of saving? *To make you fail? Stumble and fall?*

He hardly needed any help doing that.

He slowed in the middle of the sidewalk. Thinking about his disastrous track record in life reminded him that he hadn't called Mary or checked his messages. Maybe she'd called him. Maybe Fisher had.

He started walking again.

Maybe he didn't want to call and confirm everything he'd lost. The longer he put it off, the longer he could live with his illusions that he wasn't a failure.

The kind of guy who got dumped after letting it all hang out in a stranger's pickup.

Geez, he'd never been like that before—so far gone that he didn't care what people could see or think. In the back of his mind, Vane had been aware of how exposed they'd been. In fact, it had excited him, and even now his belly fluttered at the thought of it.

He walked on, slowing once to let a car back out of the driveway before continuing around the block. A few windows burned with warm lamplight, and one house had blue icicle lights dangling from its eaves. When he neared Rose's again, he saw strings of lights under her eaves too.

Had she put those up herself? Or never taken them down? Marc had been gone for two years now. She'd probably want her lights for the new house, and Vane decided to take them down for her. It was the least he could do.

Inside, he found her in the family room packing DVDs and some of the kids' games and books into a box.

"I hate the idea of everybody coming back to an empty house," she said as he entered.

"Nobody's gonna care, Ro."

She smoothed her palm over the cover of the book in her hand. He wondered if she was thinking about where she'd been when she'd bought it, or if Marc had bought it.

With all the turmoil going on in his life, Vane hadn't thought much about his dad's death and honestly didn't want to. He wouldn't be able to escape it at the funeral though, and the thought of what lay ahead the next day was heavy and suffocating.

What was it like for Rose?

Everywhere she looked she'd find memories of Marc, but after she moved... Would that be any better? Vane had loved Fisher once, and he still cared for him like the idiot he was, but he wasn't lost in his memories of him.

"Will you miss this place?"

She looked up, her gaze startled. Then it softened. "Sure. But it'll be fine. We loved this place though."

"I'm sorry, Rose."

She set the book in the box, crossed the room, and kissed his cheek. "Just don't be a stranger anymore."

"Promise," he murmured. "By the way, do you have a ladder?"

She drew back and frowned. "Probably. If I do, it's in the garage. Why?"

"I'm going to take your lights down."

"My lights?"

"The Christmas lights."

"Oh, my God. I forgot about those."

"I'll get them."

He headed to the garage through the laundry room and remembered the clothes he needed to put in the washer. He thought of his cum-stained shirt and Doug's flesh in his mouth, but his belly didn't flutter this time. Instead, his heart did. He shook his head at himself, lifted the ladder off the wall, and carried it through the side door.

The cord to the lights was attached to hooks on the underside of the eaves and lifted off. Vane wound the strands as he went along the back of the house. In front, he set the ladder on the edge of the lawn and repeated the process. Near the front porch, a glossy-leafed bush stuck out from the house a good two feet. He pushed the ladder against it and climbed back up.

"Hey! Are you—"

He panicked at the excited tone. *Oh gosh.* Was it somebody who recognized him? Would he have to explain why he hadn't acted in anything worth remembering in a million years?

Heart hammering, he twisted and—*Oh no!*

The ladder sank in the wet grass, and the rung he was standing on dropped out from under his feet. He scrabbled for something to grab onto as a blur of window flashed before his eyes, and Rose's shout rang in the air.

"Vane!"

He crashed onto the soggy lawn. The thud knocked the air out of his lungs, but he wasn't hurt. He blinked at the gray-blue sky and the face of a grizzle-haired guy peering down at him.

Rose dropped to the grass on the other side of him. "Vane?"

"Is that Riley Vane?"

Of course, it was. Who else would stumble and fall on his sister's front lawn on the dawn of a new day?

Me.

He giggled.

9

THE FUNERAL

I T RAINED AT dawn. By noon, the air was cottony gray, and the trees dripped. The service was at one, and Doug was dressed, tie knotted and jacket on, but he was forgetting something.

His brain had stalled today, unwilling to think about funerals, but he thought he'd be okay once he picked up Dorcas.

Now he squeezed his keys in his fist until the metal bit his palm, but he had no clue what he was forgetting.

Nothing new stood out. The books and vases and knickknacks faded against the familiar walls.

A whine from Hoyt drew his gaze. The dog stood in the hall, tail wagging slowly, his eyes fixed on Doug with a warm shine.

"Sorry, boy."

Hoyt approached, butted Doug's hand with his nose, and continued to the open front door where he chuffed.

"Nunh uh," Doug said.

When he returned to the kitchen, his gaze fell on a bouquet of daisies and carnations on the counter. How did he forget about those? He glanced back at Hoyt and said, "C'mon, boy, you're staying home."

The golden clacked behind him, whine rising to a plaintive pitch. When Doug pulled the cookie jar away from the backsplash and brought out a biscuit, Hoyt perched in a half-sitting position, tail sweeping the wood floor. "Sit all the way."

Hoyt whined again but sat, and Doug tossed him the biscuit. It disappeared in a single crunch. Hoyt cracked his mouth open, tongue lolling.

The scent of the flowers was strong up close.

In theory, Doug loved the cemetery where Rose was holding Ethan's service. Paths curved through low, grassy hills dotted with plentiful trees. But the trees were leafless now, and the birds were silent.

The pain of knowing about that bareness, imagining it —his Meg all alone—was as sharp and searing as a solar flare. It stole his breath, and for a moment, he blanked out.

As though worried for him, Hoyt clicked from paw to paw and nudged Doug's hand with his wet nose. With a stir of gratitude, Doug dropped to a knee and wrapped his arms around Hoyt's warm, wooly body.

The dog rested his head on Doug's shoulder and waited patiently.

"Such a good boy. Sorry you can't come with me today. Tomorrow we'll go on a walk, just you and me."

He buried his fingers and cheek in Hoyt's soft fur, and Hoyt thumped the floor with his tail.

After another moment, Doug gave him a pat, collected the flowers, and headed out the front door.

Dorcas lived in a townhouse about ten minutes outside of Poppy Brush.

She stepped onto her porch and threw the strap of her bag onto her shoulder before Doug could shut off the pickup's engine. Her pale curls absorbed the light under the clouds, and her eyes twinkled. She was more positive than happy, and her expression was perpetually bright. Other than Meg, Dorcas was the most spiritual person Doug had ever known. He tried to reimagine her from their school days, wondering if she'd always been like this, but couldn't.

She pulled open the truck door and slid in. "Okay," she said. "Let's do this."

"You make it sound like a top secret mission."

She rolled her eyes and took the flowers off the dashboard. "Meg's?"

"Yeah."

"I'm glad you're letting me be there for you."

"For Rose," he said.

"For Rose too, but I know it's hard on you."

"We'll get through it."

Dorcas had been Meg's best friend, so it couldn't be easy for her either. The good thing for Doug was that he could concentrate on Rose. The minute her life had started coming back together after losing Marc, bam. This. Her dad hadn't been that old either. He'd been active and worked every day. His dying was something she shouldn't have had to worry about for years. Now she was alone with her kids and a worthless brother.

But at least that gave her something to escape into instead of...

Well, Doug didn't want to think about being alone. Dorcas was the best friend anybody could have, but Doug wasn't going to lose himself in her. And he wanted to lose himself in somebody. *In you, Meg.*

He pulled into the parking lot and swung into one of the first spots. A few other cars had parked on the opposite side of the lot.

"You waiting here?" he asked.

Dorcas reached across and gave him a quick squeeze on the forearm. "I won't intrude."

"I wasn't—"

"I know. You need your space. I'll be nearby though."

That was the thing about Dorcas. There and not there. A part of all aspects of his life, so he couldn't imagine her not being in it. She was vivacious and cheery. Her grin made him happy. And even in her version of dressed-down business casual, she glowed.

Usually, she wore the oddest bits and pieces of things that made her look like she'd raided a taxidermy shop. But today she had on a dark gray sweater, pinstriped gray slacks, and black pumps. A curvy, brown-eyed, corporate-sleek, new age goddess. The only concession to her usual attire was her earrings, long strings of tiny black shells. Doug repressed a shudder. Like snail shells, similar to the tiny snails he found on the watercress in his backyard.

She stretched out a hand, and he took it, but she let him go when they got near Meg's grave and wandered off.

He finished the last few yards alone.

At least it wasn't raining. Meg had loved the rain, but he wanted her to have sun every single day. He gazed at the simple stone he'd bought her with a dove, her name, and *Beloved Wife* carved on it. He and Meg had grown up together, went their separate ways, and reunited. They'd been meant for each other, he was sure of it.

"Miss you," he whispered, but those were the only words he could strangle out.

God, he wasn't anywhere near ready to let her go. Was he supposed to be? Dorcas said it was okay to stay in the house and keep Meg's old things around him. But he wasn't sure of that anymore, which was why he'd gotten Hoyt, he guessed. The silly dog brought love and friendship without any of the pain of remembrance. The truth was, Doug couldn't hold onto his loss, even though he never wanted to let it go.

The pain was blunter already.

His tongue tingled with the memory of kissing that crazy, clumsy Ethan guy. He'd be watching the burial of another Ethan today, so maybe he could bury his desire for the other one at the same time.

"I liked him," he murmured. "He lost his keys. Remember when we had to drive all the way back to Tahoe because you forgot your keys in the motel room?"

They'd stopped to get dinner on the way back and ate on a patio surrounded by vineyards. As the sun sank, frogs had begun to hop across the twilit patio. "We made some good memories."

He'd turned thirty-nine two weeks ago. Was that it? A stab of grief that was unnervingly close to self-pity dug into his heart. *You don't want to be alone.*

No, he didn't want to be alone. For a moment, his arms ached to hold onto that lean, warm body from the night before again. The guy was the opposite of Meg, except for the parts where he was clumsy and kind of funny. But, no.

No.

"I have to go," he said, "but I got you these."

He set the flowers down and traced the letters for *Wife* on the stone with his fingertip. "Beloved."

A moment later, he crossed the grass, heading for the pathway where Dorcas waited for him.

When he reached her, she hooked her arm in his and gave him a small shake. "This is such a pretty place. You know how much she loved her garden. This is a perfect place for her."

Was that supposed to cheer him up? He had to struggle not to pull away. His jaw ached, and he was surprised he hadn't cracked through all his teeth.

Dorcas tugged on him. "They're over here."

A crowd had gathered down the hillside beside a tent that stood over the gravesite. Raindrops glistened on the tent's roof.

"Poor Rose," Dorcas said. "At least, she can get rid of Eileen's now."

"Maybe she doesn't want to. It was her father's, after all. He named it for her mother."

"It's for the best."

He wanted to shrug, but Dorcas was dragging on his arm. She didn't let go until they reached the edges of the crowd.

Almost everybody wore raincoats, except for a guy in a leather jacket talking to Rose. She was gazing up at him, her long lips pressed into a small smile.

Doug stepped away from Dorcas and skirted the crowd as he approached, aware of the casket off to the side. Rose's gaze shifted to him, and her smile widened. Then the guy with her turned and—

Holy—

Doug's stomach lurched and threatened to unload all over the gathering. No, this couldn't be. Not—Ethan. The other Ethan. Ethan the—

Fuck.

Ethan the brother. Vane Riley or Riley Vane, whatever he was going by.

The guy's eyes widened, a silver-gray color Doug hadn't been able to see when they'd met. The pale light here lit them with a metallic sheen.

Gorgeous.

And panic stricken. The guy's face, already pale, had gone pure white. His lips parted, and his pulse fluttered visibly in his neck.

This couldn't be.

"You don't look anything like Rose," he blurted.

Rose's mouth opened, but nothing came out for a moment. She blinked. Then she laid her hand on Vane's arm and said, "Well, as you've guessed, this is Vane."

She looked back at her brother, who'd drawn his lips into a thin line.

Dorcas took Doug's arm again, and he fought against his impulse to fling her across the cemetery.

Rose continued. "And these are my friends, Doug Moore and Dorcas Lundgren."

"Please accept my sympathies," said Dorcas. "I've lost family too. My heart breaks for you."

Doug swallowed and cleared his throat. "Yes. Sorry, but I'm glad you could make it for the funeral."

Vane's eyes narrowed now, and he looked at Rose as though bewildered and unsure what to say. She smiled at him. "I'm glad he's here too."

A tug came on Doug's arm again. "Nice meeting you," he said to Vane. "We'll see you later."

"At the house," Rose said.

"We'll come right over," said Dorcas.

Now Doug didn't want to go. A sledgehammer pounded inside his head. He'd gone from grief over Meg to outrage at Vane. How dare the bastard be somebody? The whole point of a hookup was its impermanence. Nobody was supposed to reappear. Especially when Doug couldn't get Vane out of his mind in the first place.

His senses sparked back to life, and his fingers tingled, seeking the softness of Vane's skin. He scented him on the air—at least in his imagination. Warm and earthy, the fragrance teased through the aroma of trees and grass and Dorcas's perfume. The guy smelled like sweet fresh-cut wood.

Fuck.

Well, he wouldn't be staying. He'd go home. Rose would never need to know Doug had fucked her brother. Jesus, there had to be some kind of law. Thou shalt not screw the brother of the woman you dated.

Vane was staring at him. The heat in his eyes had gone though. In its place was a look Doug imagined he'd see in Hoyt's eyes if he decided to kick the poor dog for no good reason.

"Gorgeous, isn't he?"

He stirred and turned to Dorcas. "Hm?"

"Vane. Rose's brother."

Yes. Vane. Not fucking Ethan.

"He's okay."

She snorted, and Doug glowered in Vane's direction again. He supposed he'd hidden his sexuality behind Meg, but he'd never outright denied it either. Dorcas knew he was bisexual, though it had never been a topic they talked about. "Too pretty," he added.

Vane was pretty, but he wasn't too pretty. His chin was solid, his nose strong, and he had a grace that was peculiar considering Doug now knew what a klutz he was. "I thought he was blond," he added.

Dorcas shrugged. "I've never met him before. I've never met any actors before. It's kind of exciting. I wonder if I can get his autograph."

Doug pulled his arm away. "Here?"

"No. Of course not."

Vane had been blond in the sitcom, but that was nine or ten years ago, so it was no wonder Doug hadn't recognized him. The dark hair suited him with the way it offset his pale eyes and marble-like skin. The thin, silky treasure trail Doug had tugged on would be dark too. *Jesus, don't think about that now.*

The murmur of voices faded away as the minister appeared at the head of the gravesite.

Dorcas took Doug's arm again, and he patted her hand. He assumed she'd be thinking of her sister, the way he couldn't help thinking of his parents and Meg.

His gaze strayed to Vane again and locked on the silver eyes staring back at him. Vane's face was even paler under his faded bruises and drawn now, and there were shadows under his eyes.

After a moment, he dropped his gaze to the ground and Doug hurt for him without wanting to. But how could he not? Vane's father was about to be buried under tons of dirt. Was Vane picturing it? Gritting his teeth against the flood of grief and regret?

It was easy to get lost watching him, following the dark strands of hair that blew against his cheek, the way he shifted his weight on... sneakers, dark jeans, and a leather jacket? Hardly funeral wear. Didn't he have clothes? He didn't have much of a career anymore as far as Doug knew.

"A fine example of industriousness and commitment to hard work..." the minister said.

Industriousness. Doug knew all about industriousness and the way it masked what was truly important. On the other hand, there was self-indulgence and a self-centered chasing after fame. And Vane wasn't even famous or successful enough for Doug to recognize him. What had he sacrificed his family for anyway? A puffball of a dream?

Doug would love to have a family to come home to. What an idiot Vane was. Walking away from his responsibilities. Not even visiting his sister after she'd lost her husband. And for what? Those looks weren't going to last forever.

As though hearing Doug's thoughts, Vane shot him another stare. But this time his eyes were hot, and Doug pictured a bubbling pot of silver. In the next instant though, the heat cooled, and Vane's gaze fell again. He stuffed his hands in his pockets and drew his coat tighter around him.

"And the legacy one builds," intoned the minister, "is all one leaves behind. We are just dust and the invisible marks we make on the hearts of others..."

Vane pulled a hand out of his pocket and took Rose's, and she smiled at him.

"That's sweet," murmured Dorcas.

Doug thought it was sad. They only had each other now.

"The Lord is my shepherd. I shall not want..."

A moment later, they watched the casket being lowered into the grave. Dorcas's grip tightened on Doug's arm, and he cupped his hand over hers.

After Rose tossed a handful of dirt onto the casket, Vane took her place but seemed to freeze for a moment. He clenched the dirt in his fist, and Doug's heart spasmed, as though Vane's pain had reached into his chest. It rocked him like a blow. He wasn't surprised when Vane met his eyes again, and he didn't look away.

A few seconds later, Vane took a breath and let the dirt spill through his fingers.

And then it was over.

Doug turned with Dorcas, and they made their way back across the grass to the parking lot.

"That wasn't awful, I guess," Dorcas murmured.

"Yeah," said Doug.

But it had been. It had been awful for Rose and awful for Vane, even if Vane was an asshole. And he was.

Ethan.

His dad's name.

10

BACK AT THE HOUSE

G OSH, VANE WANTED to drink himself stupid
and wake up back home again. If he could go home,
and if he had a reason to.

When he'd checked his messages, he'd found none
from Mary, but his agent Tabitha had left him one. She'd
sounded worried at first. *Are you okay? Where are you?* But
the end of it was calm and cool. *We need to talk.*

So he'd called, but he hadn't told Rose about it yet. His
pride stung, and he wished he could blame Fisher or his
dad or his stupid fortune cookie. But the only one who'd
taken off running when he'd seen Mary had been Vane,
and that's what it had come down to. Tabitha hadn't said
he absolutely *would* have gotten the part, but Mary had
told her she would never take a chance on him now.

The feeling of failure in his gut was a solid thing, and
the memory of the derision in Doug's eyes burned into his
brain on top of it.

What an idiot loser he was. Banging a total stranger

practically the night before his father's funeral. But it wasn't as though that had been the plan.

The minute they got back from the funeral, Vane made for the bathroom, afraid he was going to throw up, but the door was shut. People he didn't know sat on the couch and the folding chairs they'd set out that morning.

In the kitchen, casseroles, dips, hot and cold pastas, cheese, and cold cuts covered the counters.

His stomach roiled until his gaze fell on a cooler filled with ice and bottles. He grabbed two beers and headed outside. It was cold enough everybody seemed to want to stay inside. The first beer he drank standing up, the second in a plastic chair facing away from the house.

Now, with the little pool of beer warm in his belly, he shivered as the damp air cut through the thin blue sweater he wore. He wished he'd brought his jacket with him, but now he was stuck here. If he went back inside, he'd probably run into—

Doug Moore.

That was a solid, dependable name. The name of a guy who wouldn't want anything to do with a flibbertigibbet like Vane. Although, truthfully, Vane always thought himself as over-serious and plodding. That night at the bar —dang, that felt good. But he didn't know where the crazy impulse to let loose in the middle of the parking lot had come from. What if somebody had seen them?

But that was just it—he'd gotten off on the risk in a way he'd never thought possible. Doing something like that had never even been on his radar before. For all that Mary might think he was unreliable, he really did his best to be dependable and not screw things up. Getting arrested for public indecency probably counted as a screw up. Where had his excitement at having sex in a parking lot come from?

But when he thought about it, could he be an actor if he didn't have a bit of an exhibitionist in him?

He drank his beer, remembering the warm taste of Doug's mouth and the cocoon of his arms in the humid air of the big pickup. Vane had been safe the whole time. Now, he felt as though his skin had been peeled away and he flushed with embarrassment.

Geez, what a tramp.

When the sliding glass door opened, he took another quick swallow of his beer before turning.

That pretty lady—*Dorcas*—stepped out, followed by a glowering Doug.

Dorcas smiled and flipped her hair back. "Well, there you are." She pulled another chair over and sank down on it. "Sit, Doug."

"This is fine."

Great. Doug stood by the door, which put him behind Vane. How comfortable. Well, screw that.

Vane shifted his chair closer to Dorcas, swinging it around to face Doug. A still-glowering Doug. Big, strong Doug, who'd picked Vane up and carried him as though he hadn't weighed a thing. Vane shouldn't like that. But he did like it. It rang a lot of his bells.

He swallowed, trying to get sex thoughts of Doug out of his head.

No luck.

He forced himself to smile at Dorcas.

"I love this yard," she said. "It reminds me of mine growing up."

It wasn't big, but it had a lawn and some bushes and a play set in the corner. Vane thought he liked things a bit more wild, but he didn't have any kind of yard back home and no houseplants. Fisher didn't even like Christmas trees or garlands.

"Have you known my sister for very long?" he asked Dorcas.

Doug straightened in a way that made him seem to tower.

"No. Only since Marc died. Rose came to me for a reading."

"A reading?"

"I give psychic readings. Tarot, mostly. I own a—" She drew air quotes, "'New Age' store in town. We sell books, candles, bath oils, that kind of thing. I also have a small consignment section for clothes and two part-time employees." She grinned. "It's a bit eclectic. A little of everything. You should make an appointment with me. A loss is always a turning point."

"We weren't close," Vane murmured.

Under the sound of his own cold breaths, he thought Doug might have snorted. He glanced at him with a scowl, but Doug looked away and stared at something on the other side of the yard. Vane took a swallow of his beer. Maybe that prompted Doug to say something because he spoke a moment later.

"Do you want some wine, Dorcas?"

She smiled. "That'd be nice."

After Doug disappeared, Dorcas patted Vane's knee. "You didn't have to be close. You were connected. This is about you anyway. Talk to Rose about it. She started coming to me not long after Marc died, and I like to think it's been helpful to her. She met Doug after one of her readings."

Vane's belly froze. *Met him? Met him like...*

"Now they're close friends," Dorcas went on. "It just wasn't the right time for them romantically. Grief is distracting, and it's so easy to get off track. If you can avoid that, well..." She tilted her head at him, a smile playing on her lips.

She was oddly perky, considering she'd just come from a funeral. The vivacious type, Vane guessed, but he didn't give it much more thought because now his head was stuck on Doug and Rose. "They went out?"

"A few times."

He took another drink, hoping to drown the rising bile. Holy moly, he'd messed around with his sister's boyfriend.

If looks really could kill, Doug would have dropped dead the minute he stepped out the door. As it turned out, Vane's only reward for his glare was a slight hitch in Doug's step. Unharmed, he continued across the patio, gave Dorcas her wine, and sat in the chair on the other side of her.

"Really, I'd love to give you a reading," Dorcas said. "It'll be fun."

"I don't know." Vane shrugged. "I'm not sure how long I'm staying."

He fought against a shiver. Why had he left his coat inside?

"No," said Dorcas. "I suppose you wouldn't like it here. Just like I think I'd hate living in Hollywood."

"Well, I don't live in Hollywood," he murmured and stared forlornly at his empty beer bottle.

Doug rose, drawing Vane's attention. He didn't speak, just crossed the space to the house and went inside again.

"I think it's exciting though. Being an actor."

"Sometimes."

The play set looked skeletal in the cold light. As he stared at it, Vane found himself thinking about the guy who'd supposedly killed himself over Marcel. He hoped it had only been a rumor because the finality of somebody actually dying over a part was just...

"Who've you met? I mean famous people." Dorcas was leaning forward on her chair, elbows on her knees now.

He'd met Clint Eastwood once, his dad's favorite actor, but he didn't want to talk about that. Everything he'd ever done was—

"Here."

He blinked and looked up through a blur, only now realizing how close to tears he was. He blinked again. Doug swung a beer bottle in his fingertips and Vane took it. "Thanks."

"You're welcome."

"I'm trying to get Vane to tell me some exciting stories about Hollywood."

Vane forced a laugh. "I don't really have any."

"Poppy Brush Village probably seems dull to you," said Dorcas.

"I grew up here."

It had never seemed dull. It was only that everybody here knew him as Vane Riley, Ethan Riley's son, Rose's little brother. They'd never believed he could be anybody special.

So, you gonna follow in your dad's footsteps?

Now that question made a laughable kind of sense. Giving up a successful business to run a failing diner was right up Vane's alley.

"I always liked it here," he said. "You can get lost in a city."

"With your looks? I doubt it," said Dorcas. "You must have admirers falling all over you."

He blushed. "No. I recently broke up with my boyfriend."

She placed a hand on his knee. "Oh, I'm sorry. This has been a tough few days for you, hasn't it? Are you sure you wouldn't like to try a reading? I can't get Doug to do it either."

"I don't believe in it," said Doug.

"Yet, when I told you you were going to meet somebody you walked out the door and ran into Rose."

Doug's brows lowered over his eyes. "Because she had an appointment, and you knew that."

Dorcas laughed. "I could be insulted by that, you know."

"We should go," said Doug.

"I suppose." She stood and patted Doug on the arm as she went by. "Just give me a minute."

Great. Alone with Doug. Vane didn't want to look at him. Instead, he gazed across the dreary yard and drank half his beer.

"Look," said Doug. "If I'd known about your dad, I wouldn't've—"

"Dumped me in the middle of nowhere?"

"I didn't dump you. We don't even know each other."

Vane rolled his eyes. "Well... kinda. You know that's not something I usually ever do, actually. I'm not like you. I have limits."

"Excuse me?"

Vane raised his beer and lost his grip on the slippery glass, sucking in a breath as it dropped and—

Doug caught it and handed it back with a glare.

Vane huffed. "What?"

"Limits? I have no limits?"

Vane glanced at the sliding glass doors and hissed, "Yesss. You dated my sister."

"So what?"

"So what was I? Hooking up with whoever's there doesn't make you very particular."

Vane leaned away from the cold look in Doug's eyes.

"I'm not even going to comment on that," Doug said. He stood as Dorcas stepped back out with her bag on her shoulder.

She glanced between them. "Everything okay?"

"Fine," Doug said. "Are you ready?"

"Uh-huh."

Vane stood too, and Dorcas hugged him and patted his back. "I hope we see you before you go back. Talk to Rose. Maybe we can all have dinner or something."

Doug rolled his eyes behind Dorcas's back. The clench of his jaw was so tight, Vane pictured an iceberg shattering into bright white slivers. Well, too bad. Vane's whole life was falling apart. He wasn't sure why he was the guilty one, especially when Doug muttered, "Sorry for your loss," and walked away.

Why did that hurt so much? Why did he want Doug's solid and steady hands on his face?

The slide and click of the glass door closing him off on the patio sounded ominously loud.

11

HOME SWEET HOME

THEY WENT OUT for Thanksgiving dinner. The streets of their new town were quiet and Christmas lights glowed in the drizzle.

At home, they put Christmas shows on TV, and that was Vane's first holiday with his family in over ten years. In LA, he'd usually worked on Thanksgiving and had been grateful for something to do.

If Fisher had family, Vane didn't know it. As in most things, Fisher was vague about his past. Vane suspected he came from some small-town family in the middle of the country he was eager to forget. Considering Vane's relationship with his family, he had nothing to say about it. After Thanksgiving, he and Fisher would put up a tree made of two wooden, pine-shaped silhouettes. Slotted together, the two pieces made a four-sided tree. They threaded blue and white lights through star-shaped cutouts.

This year after Thanksgiving, he and Rose and the kids

picked out a Christmas tree at a garden center. Back home, Vane helped the kids decorate it while waves of loneliness rolled over him. Ricky's somber inspection of every ornament and Lucy's glee over tinsel filled him with wonder. Why had he stayed away?

When the tree was lit and twinkling in the window, he stood there by himself for a while. But he imagined he wasn't alone. Somebody else stood behind him and wrapped him in warm arms.

What if he dared to lean back and found a hard chest to hold him steady? His heart whispered to him—*Go on. Chance it...*

But another voice scoffed. *Idiot. You'll crash land on the carpet.*

Stumble and fall.

The next day, he stapled the icicle lights to the eaves with Rose holding onto the ladder. "I can do this," he complained.

"I know. I'm just helping."

On the Sunday before Eileen's reopened, they loaded the kids in the car and drove back to Poppy Brush. Vane sat with his hands in the pockets of his hoodie and a glower on his face. Hot air blew on him, and the sky was gray and gloomy like his mood.

"I guess I don't get how a place can make any money if you close every Sunday and Monday."

They were close to Poppy Brush when Rose gave him the news about Eileen's. Not only were they closed the week after Thanksgiving, they'd been closing two days a week for the past six months.

"We weren't making any money, Vane. Not enough. But Dad didn't want to give up. We have employees."

Luis. The dark-haired guy at the funeral, who'd worn a brown suit the color of wet clay. He'd clearly not liked Vane. Maybe he thought Vane was going to walk away with the whole diner. *Geez, who includes the cook in their will?* What place did Vane ever have in his dad's life? *None.*

So what he ought to do is sell everything and walk away after giving the vulture cook his share. The guy hadn't even offered his sympathies. The funeral was for Vane's dad, not the cook's boss.

So what if his dad had liked the cook better? Vane had been the one with the chance to do something important.

Not that *Ranging Wild* had been high art, of course. And not that commercials didn't sell people things they probably didn't need. But even fluff took people out of their hard lives. The same was true for books. His screenplay wasn't serious. It was fun. He loved to cook, so he'd devised a crime mystery featuring a chef turned jewelry store robber. And apparently he loved to write too, maybe more than—

No. He crushed that thought. He couldn't love writing more than acting. Would his dad have been prouder of that, though? It wasn't feeding families and keeping a business running, but Vane could do the cooking part. He was good at it. Maybe he didn't need Luis. *Can I fire him?*

"What are you thinking?"

He looked at Rose, who tossed him a glance before

turning her attention back to the road. "I'm just letting it sink in. I guess I didn't expect this."

Rose was quiet until a small smile moved her lips. "Yes. That's the hard part."

The hard part was remembering in the here and now how quickly things could change. Rose had lost Marc with no warning at all. Vane had spent fourteen years thinking he'd have time to make his father proud of him before he returned home.

"Well, I guess it won't hurt to take a look and see what I'm up against."

"Exactly. You don't have to decide today."

Strange. Her voice sounded hopeful, as though she wanted him to stay. For what though? For a place that was going out of business?

Dad's place.

"What kind of food do we serve?" he asked.

"What you'd expect from a diner, I guess. Burgers. Patty melts. The mac 'n' cheese is popular. Salads. Chef and Cobb. Breakfast. Pies."

"I wonder if people would like something different?"

"Maybe." She turned off the main highway. "That sounds like you're thinking about it."

He pulled his hands out of his pockets and ran them through his hair. "Lots of work."

"Well... There's Luis."

"I don't like Luis."

"Vane, you don't even know him."

"Luis is nice," said Lucy.

Vane glanced back. Ricky was crashed in his car seat,

head lolling. "I just met him," said Vane. Lucy scrunched her forehead at him. "I'm glad he's nice to you though," he added.

"He made me a flower out of a napkin once."

"Oh yeah? That's talented. Do you still have it?"

"No. It got torn."

"Too bad."

She nodded and looked out the window, and Vane shifted forward again. "Anyway," he said. "I don't have to like him. You didn't tell me about Doug either."

She shot him a quick look with a scrunched forehead that made her look like Lucy. "Told you what?"

He glanced into the back seat again and lowered his voice. "You know."

She laughed. "That's not a secret. We had two dates a year ago, but it was too soon for both of us. Doug lost his wife about the same time Marc was killed."

"His wife?"

"Vane... Are you interested in him?"

"I kind of make it a rule not to throw myself at straight guys. Besides, I just left Fisher."

Got kicked to the curb by Fisher.

"Well, for whatever it's worth, I don't think Doug is straight."

"Whatever. I'm not interested."

And what did that mean—not straight?

It means bisexual, you dip.

Gosh, why had he made that crack about limits? Of course, he knew why, and his body flushed with shame that he'd been such a jerk. Even before Fisher's twink had come along, he'd worried Fisher would find somebody else. Somebody who didn't stain his rugs or break his coffee cups or list waiter at the top of his résumé. Why in the world would Vane want his competition to double? A guy like Doug... Well, the world was easy pickings. He could find better than Vane anywhere. Cheat across the spectrum. *Unlike Fisher, the gay guy, who was completely loyal.*

Dimwit.

He settled back in his seat, and the stir of warm air woke the memory of Doug's scent. Musky and spicy, clinging to that so soft skin under his ear. Everything else like iron, rigid and crushing and... tender.

Stop it.

Idiot.

He pulled his thoughts back.

The road they were on was dark under trees that hung a canopy overhead. When they broke free into open space, the light shone with a hazy glare. Low winter-brown hills surrounded them.

Vane had been out this way when he'd been a kid but had forgotten about the diner. A shorter road led from the house to Poppy Brush, and that was the one he was used to. But this was nice. Still and quiet and... unpopulated.

The diner appeared in the distance where the road made a slow curve back into the hills.

"Interesting location," he murmured.

Rose laughed. "Back in the day, it was the only road into town."

The building was a blue-gray square with a smaller

roof on top of a bigger roof. The roadside sign was a white trapezoid with Eileen's Cafe in blue letters. It looked like the name on the sign was the only thing to have changed around the place.

The parking lot in front was empty, but a pickup sat by itself in the back. Rose pulled in, turned off the engine, and glanced in the rearview mirror. "Stay with Ricky, Luce. We won't be long."

"Why can't I get out?"

"Because we aren't staying. You can get out at the house."

"What if we get cold?"

"The car's warm. I had the heater on. But you can honk if you need to."

The back door of the diner flew open before Vane could reach it, and the Luis guy peered out. Vane caught a nervous look on his face before he disappeared inside again.

Turning, Vane waited for Rose.

When she got closer, he said, "I thought it was closed."

"It is."

"Why is the cook here?"

"I don't know." She arched her eyebrows and strode past him to the door. "We could always ask him."

He shook his head and looked around before following her. The wind made a lonely sound as it blew out of the empty space around the diner.

"C'mon, Vane."

Rose pulled open the door, and he followed her inside and inhaled the aroma of coffee. A pot sat on one of the burners in the dining area where the cook hunkered at the counter with a mug in his hands.

Rose took off her coat. "You're a workaholic, Luis. Why aren't you enjoying your time off?"

"I like it here," the guy said, but he set a sour stare on Vane as he said it.

"Coffee, sweetie?"

Vane nodded. "Yes, please."

Rose handed him a cup, and he took a sip. "You remember Vane, Luis. I wanted him to look around, but I'm glad you're here. I want you to have some input too, even though Vane is the one who's deciding whether to stay or go, so that affects you."

"I want what your dad wanted," said Luis.

"And you know what that was?" asked Vane, hearing a snap in his voice.

"We talked."

Just that. *We talked.* Just those words and a blank stare. Vane strolled away.

The place was kind of homey and comfortable in a way. The blue gray from outside had found its way inside. Blue and gray carpet squares covered the floor, and the booths and stools were blue too. The tables were creamy Formica with blue flecks. A half-wall with a decorative screen separated the dining area from the lunch counter. Wide picture windows showed the barren countryside.

"Have you ever been busy?" But he asked Rose not the sullen cook.

"Well... busier. Saturdays are good."

"One day? Where are the menus?"

"By the register," said Luis.

Vane picked one up. It had a blue-gray simulated leather cover. "How'd you get in?" he asked.

"My key."

"Luis opens," said Rose. "If you stick this out, you'll need to hire someone else if you want to stay open all week."

"Maybe," Vane muttered.

He opened the menu, and his heart sank at the selections. People ought to save their money and just go to McDonald's for all this menu was any better. Nothing special jumped out at him except the weird oatmeal pie Vane was positive he could do better.

Right. And you could get a plum role too. Prove everybody wrong about you.

Though the prize of a golden star on Hollywood Boulevard had lost some of its shine over the past few days.

"Let's look in back," he said.

He'd had no relationship with his dad. None at all. And it wasn't as though his dad's spirit lingered here. The diner was only a diner, so he didn't understand why he felt so comfortable in it.

"It's old," he commented.

"We couldn't make any improvements," said Rose. "But it's held up."

They stood peering into the kitchen. It had the usual accouterments and a large freezer against one wall. The vinyl floor on the far side of the room was peeling along the edges. Other than that, it looked clean, despite the smell of grease.

A door in back led down a short hall with a pantry on one side and an industrial refrigerator on the other.

Vane pulled the door to the fridge open. The pop of the light showed metal racks against the walls and boxes on the floor. He took a step in, shivered, and stepped back.

"What's wrong?" Rose asked.

"Nothing. That's old too."

"It was replaced at some point. It's definitely not original. The diner's fifty years old."

"Really?"

Rose nodded. "There was some remodeling, but that was done probably thirty years ago."

"I wonder what Dad saw in the place."

He wondered what drew him to it.

They returned to the dining area after Rose took a peek at the kids. Vane examined the floral prints hanging on the walls.

The lunch counter was vacant now, the coffee cups gone, the pot turned off. Vane was wondering where the Luis guy was when the bells on the front door rang and he strolled in. He rolled his shoulders in a thin leather jacket and said, "You make up your mind?"

"I'll let you know," said Vane.

"You don't think I got things to do? A living to make?"

Rose stepped up. "I know this is difficult for you, Luis, but it's difficult for Vane too. Selling Eileen's is a big decision, and we need to look over the financials first. I have no idea how soon we'd be able to liquidate or how much we might get. I know we have to decide on something though, and we will."

Luis snorted. "Who's gonna buy this place?"

"My dad did," Vane said.

"Yeah. For his wife."

"I don't know what I'm going to do," Vane said. "In the meantime, I want my key."

Luis rolled his shoulders again. "Your key?"

"Sweetie, Luis is the first in."

"I don't care," Vane muttered.

He was spiraling into the role of a jerk that wasn't him, but something about Luis got under his skin. The sneer directed his way didn't help.

"No, you don't care," Luis said.

"It's my business. My dad."

"The dad you didn't know anything about."

Vane repressed a shudder as ice flooded his veins. "Give me the key. Give it to Ro."

Rose sighed and stepped past him, setting her hand on Luis's arm and steering him outside. Vane followed slowly.

Hot and cold shivers ran through him, making him wonder if he was getting sick. Too much had been going on, and it was running him down. Usually, his life was pretty slow. He dreamed about fame, but he was a waiter. He wasn't special or strong, and the breakup with Fisher and the loss of his home and his job and his dad was wearing him down.

His eyes kept blurring, but he refused to admit that he was close to the breaking point.

For a split second, he remembered the push of Doug's chest against his, and the weight of his palms stroking Vane's back. He longed to rest there.

No, you don't. Try somebody who likes you.

But there wasn't anybody.

Then Rose came back to lock the door. Vane returned to her car and buckled up. When he glanced out the window, he found Luis staring at him, his eyes dark and sullen.

THE KIDS TROMPED THROUGH THE RAIN-MATTED weeds out front.

The house was bigger than Vane remembered. He thought reality was supposed to be the opposite of a kid's memory, but it was a good-sized house. Still dingy white though, with red window trim. The two-tiered roof was a style he couldn't remember the name of. The ground sloped down from the road, and the smell of damp earth was strong in the air.

"C'mon," said Rose. She had more keys. The red door was dark under the porch roof. "You, too, kids. You can play out back."

The crunch of Vane's shoes on the gravel walkway rang like a half-forgotten song in his head. The wood planks on the porch creaked just so, and a familiar, musty smell followed them inside.

Green carpet covered the floor, but it was clean and striped with vacuum marks.

A tiffany-style lampshade hung from a hook in the ceiling. Underneath it was a burnt-orange armchair beside a brown and cream plaid couch.

Gosh, they'd probably had the same furniture since

before Rose was born. It was all he remembered growing up.

A solid wood coffee table with drawers under the top sat in front of the couch. A mirror in a bronze-colored frame hung over the fireplace. He caught a glimpse of a too-pale face with purple smudges under the eyes.

"Looks okay."

Rose grimaced. "It needs new wiring, new plumbing. Everything works, and it's safe for now, but it's all out of date. Dad took out a second mortgage to buy the diner."

"Great."

"You can sell as is. I get postcards from people looking to buy houses all the time, but I don't think you'll do more than break even. Dad's insurance won't go that far."

"Didn't he *advise* people on money?"

Her smile was a grimace. "On taxes. Eileen's was... a gamble."

"You think?"

"We can ask Doug for his advice on the house."

They passed the hall that led to the master and the stairs to his and Rose's rooms and his mother's craft room. Vane's steps dragged like weighted things. *Doug?* His voice followed his thoughts.

"Doug?"

"He's in construction."

"Oh."

He remembered that now. His cock and balls remembered Doug's smell, and he ached to readjust himself. His face heated again, and he still wasn't sure he wasn't sick.

The kitchen was a big space and as crowded as he remembered it. A table and hutch took up one part of the room, a cooking area another part, and a cabinet attached to the ceiling cut the space in half. A greenhouse window without plants hung over the sink, and a door with a small window in it opened onto a porch.

Vane brushed his fingers over a corner of the table and drifted back to an afternoon he'd sat there with his mother. He'd been making a birthday gift for his father. He'd painted three aluminum cans at school that day and brought them home to decorate. His mother had Oo'd and Ah'd.

"Will he like these?" he'd asked.

"Oh yes," she'd said. "I guarantee it."

"Can you manage okay?" Rose asked.

He pulled himself back from the memory. "Sure. It's better than sleeping in my car."

She grinned. "Or my couch?"

"Or your couch."

A peal of laughter—Lucy's—pulled Vane to the back door. Face stung red in the cold, Ricky was swiping at something Lucy held above his head. Vane stepped outside, heart jumping like a kid on a trampoline when a blurry shape streaked past him.

"Holy—"

Rose murmured behind him. "I forgot about Dad's cat. Are you okay?"

"Cat? Dad?"

The cat, which had just exploded off the porch,

plunked itself down in a patch of brown weeds and yawned.

"Well, it's a stray," said Rose. "People dump them here sometimes. Maybe it lives nearby though. There's a subdivision about a mile away." She pointed toward more hills in the distance.

But right here was only this house. Only the oaks and the eucalyptus and the liquid amber. Only their mom's rosebushes gone wild and heavy. Their bright orange hips glowed like jewels in the winter light. She'd love roses, which was how Rose had gotten her name.

Vane stared at the cat.

It stared back.

Then it bolted again as a kid on a bike burst into view. The kid tore across a flattened path of weeds along the side of the property.

"Hey," Vane yelled. "Stick to the road." The kid flipped him off and continued pedaling madly. "Nice."

Rose laughed. "You really are making friends today, aren't you?"

"You can't just ride across somebody's yard."

"That's Isaiah," said Lucy. She was making circles in the air with a long-stemmed weed, and Ricky was standing underneath her, trying to swat it.

"I think he lives in one of the houses over the hill," Rose said.

Vane shook his head. "This is going to take some getting used to."

My life is over.

But he didn't say that. Rose had lost everything when Marc died, and it wasn't like he'd done anything to help.

Doug had helped.

Oh... Gosh.

Bile filled his mouth, and he swallowed. "I wish you didn't have to move."

She put an arm around his waist, and they leaned side to side. "I know. Me too."

The cat appeared again, farther uphill this time, and Vane wondered if it was hungry. "I can do some of the repairs myself and save us some money."

Rose laughed. "Seriously?"

"What?"

"Vane, you almost killed yourself taking down icicle lights."

He blushed and heard the voice of Rose's neighbor in his ear again. *"Is that Riley Vane? Wow. I remember you."*

The guy had spoken in a musing tone of somebody recalling something half forgotten, but then why wouldn't he? *Ranging Wild* had been a million years ago.

"I'm going to keep the diner open. I want to figure some things out and then open for the rest of the week too."

Rose shifted to look at him. "What about your career?"

He snorted. "Surely you jest."

"I'm serious, Vane."

He could tell now that this was what she wanted, though she hadn't been willing to push him.

He sighed, his gaze on the cat as it approached a lump near the top of the hill, sat down again, and gazed back at him. He thought of the fortune cookies he'd opened a few weeks ago. *Don't panic.* Why would he? What did he have left to lose?

"I'm serious," he said, wondering what that lump poking out of the ground beside the cat was. "I want to do this."

He smiled when Rose hugged him. "I'm glad."

He was too, surprisingly. He hoped he stayed that way.

12

THE PART OF AN ENTREPRENEUR

V ANE MOVED IN the next day. A cold wind blew the clouds away, and a bright sun flooded the kitchen with light.

It wasn't a cheery sun though. It was white and glary and brought out the dinginess of the walls and the thinness of the paint on the cupboards.

Fisher would have a coronary.

Luckily, Fisher would never see the place.

Vane stood still for a moment and let his surroundings settle around him. No matter that he hadn't lived here in fourteen years, it was home now. A place with worn-out, gray walls and random creaks, but his. And the cat's. *Not my cat.*

But after he put away the groceries he'd bought, he popped the lid on a can of cat food.

"Tuna Vegetable Medley," he said out loud and set the food and a bowl of water on the bottom step.

As he straightened, cold air worked under his shirt, and

he shivered, scanning the yard for the cat. Unless its fur coat had morphed into a ski parka, it had to be frozen after staying out all night. It couldn't belong to anybody or it would've gone home by now, and Vane had seen it skulking through the weeds most of the day before.

He felt sorry for it, but it was nowhere in sight now. All he saw was the glistening of frost on everything and the harshness of the cold sky.

He went back inside, got himself a cup of coffee, and sat down to make a list.

Number 1 — buy clothes

Rose had taken him to the bank, and after signing a few papers, he had access to their dad's accounts. The balances were low, but they would keep him until he got the insurance money. He could do this.

Number 2 — go to the library & check out books on running a restaurant

He had no internet yet and only a simple phone. He'd use the computer at the library and check out some books he could study at his leisure.

He supposed the diner had a computer, but he hadn't looked. He didn't want to take a chance on Luis finding out he had no clue how to run a business. The last thing Vane needed was to give the guy another reason to look down his nose at him.

He knew Rose had given Luis his key back because she didn't really have a choice and for some inexplicable reason seemed to like Luis. But it still pissed Vane off. One of the servers had quit too, Rose said, so now he'd have to fill in for her until he found somebody else. Plus... Doug.

Moore's Construction. We do more. It's our promise.

Vane had seen the logo when Doug had driven his monster of a truck out of the cemetery parking lot. Of course, he'd have a big vehicle to go with his big dick and his big ego, along with his bigger-than-life bestie, Dorcas. Were they more than friends? Did Vane care? No, he groused to himself as he returned his attention to his list.

Number 3 — check out some other cafes etc, think of ideas to bring people in

His zip of excitement at the idea of filling the diner with happy customers sank with his heart a moment later. Who did he think he was kidding? He'd never done anything right in thirty-two years.

Really?

Was that a true statement? He must have done something right at some point, but for the life of him, he didn't know what it was.

With a sigh, he finished his coffee, put his cup in the sink, and headed out.

At a Target outside of Poppy Brush, he bought a few household items and some extra clothes. They didn't have the underwear he liked to wear, but he'd already ordered some from Amazon.

After he packed his purchases into the trunk of his car, he drove back into town. The library was a block from Carleton High where he'd gone to school. On the other side of the high school, the commercial district of Poppy Brush began.

He parked on Main Street, fed the meter, and darted up the stone steps of the old library.

The place had always looked like a miniature castle to Vane. It even had a crenelated ledge around the roof. The inside was cluttered with beat-up tables and a maze-like configuration of shelves. He half expected a card catalog in the middle of the room. The whole setting was weird. Poppy Brush had a pretty high standard of living and the library looked like it had stepped out of the fifties.

Still, the musty book smell was nice.

Vane followed the sound of muted voices to a square formed of four desks. A woman with thinning red hair smiled at him. "May I help you?"

"I was wondering if you had a computer I could use."

She twisted and pointed to an alcove behind her. "Right there. Do you have a card?"

He didn't, of course, and also had to explain why his address didn't match the one on his license. But after learning that he'd just moved home, she set him up.

Vane had no sense anymore that Fisher's condo had ever been his home. Now he found himself plunked down in the house he'd grown up in, and he didn't really feel as out of place as he thought he should.

A strange discombobulation swept over him like a wave of dizziness. He didn't really belong here, did he?

As soon as he was seated at a computer, he took a deep breath, logged on, and checked his email. He found nothing from Mary or Tabitha, though he didn't know what he expected. Fisher had sent multiple emails. *Contact me. Where are you? Are you okay?*

The swell of Vane's heart scared him. Only seconds ago, he'd admitted he'd never had a home with Fisher, and now he wanted to run back to him. Why did Fisher care? Did he love Vane after all?

Call. We can work this out. I love you.

Well, he'd just said so.

A flutter of nerves sprang to life in Vane's belly.

He clicked out of his email and buried his face in his hands for a moment.

What the heck was wrong with him that he'd even think of going back? He had things he needed to do here. His family was here. He had a house he had to fix up and a garden he wanted to see come to life. Fisher wouldn't even tolerate a potted fern or an orchid in the bathroom. Vane owned a diner now. He had to think of Lucy and Ricky and Eileen's and... *Doug.*

Another guy to screw himself up over.

Warmth spread inside him, but it was the blush-from-head-to-toe-in-painful-embarrassment kind, not the feel-good kind.

He'd really screwed up with Doug. Making that crack about limits was brain dead once he'd thought about it. Fisher had cheated on him without ever having to branch out to the opposite sex. And Vane had loved being with Doug. Never for a moment had he suspected Doug wasn't into it or thought Vane was easy pickings. And the goody-goody in Vane hadn't made a peep about getting his ass pounded in the parking lot of a skanky bar. He'd felt silly and giddy and... floatable. As light as air.

Even now, he imagined stripping naked in broad daylight and exposing all the things he'd used Riley Vane to hide. Maybe it had been Riley The Actor who'd lived with Fisher, and according to Fisher, Riley wasn't a very good actor. Well, Fisher never actually said that, to be honest.

But he thought it.

Vane clicked the mouse and found a few articles on running a restaurant. The inventory and budget requirements made him chew on his lip. He wasn't good at that kind of thing, and money and numbers made his eyes glaze. Maybe they had a book.

He checked the catalog and found a list of three possibilities. Logging off the computer, he got up and searched for them. Two of the books looked as old as the library. He took the newer one to the desk, but the redheaded lady led him to a machine that looked positively space-aged in this dusty old space.

"Press start and put your card right here." He laid his card down on a screen and a red light traced the bar code. The machine beeped. "Now the book." He set it down and got another beep. "Do you want a receipt?"

"No, thank you."

She tapped the No Receipt button on the clunky upper screen and said, "You're all set."

"Thank you."

With the book under his arm, he strode outside and descended the steps.

The sidewalk was splotched with patches of damp, but the sky was still clear. An icy breeze froze his face.

He looked down the street at the row of shops where people exited a door with coffees in their hands. *Oh, heck yeah*. But the prospect of running into Doug slowed his steps before he got anywhere.

Cars and pickups filled diagonal parking spots and rolled through town at a crawl. Pedestrians flooded the crosswalks at every corner.

He spotted several white cars and one white truck, but it wasn't the monster that was Doug's.

Vane darted through traffic and hurried to the coffee shop. Warm air scented with cinnamon and coffee met him at the door. He spied pastries and cookies in a glass case and a boy smiling at him from behind the counter.

"What can I get you?" the boy asked.

"Cappuccino."

"For here or to go?"

"To—"

"Vane?"

He turned toward the voice that had come from across the room. A guy sat at a table in the corner, a smile creasing his face as he stood. "Vane Riley?"

Vane stared, his brain plowing back through time until —"Mr. Kam."

A weird combination of emotions tumbled through him. A smile of delight tugged at his lips at the same time another part of him wanted to slink home with his tail between his legs. But Mr. Kam was—his acting teacher. His biggest fan and supporter. No matter Vane had only been a bundle of dreams and nothing else. Mr. Kam had dreamed with him and made him believe.

"Sir?"

He glanced back at the boy behind the counter. "I'll have my coffee here," he said.

"I'll bring it over."

"Thanks."

He crossed the room, weaving through a maze of tables. Mr. Kam stood behind a large one in the corner, his cup of coffee and a script in front of him. The sounds of conversation faded as Mr. Kam stuck out his hand, and Vane shook it.

"Isn't this a surprise. Home for a visit?"

Mr. Kam sat, and Vane took the chair across from him. "My dad passed away."

"Oh, I'm sorry, Vane. I didn't know. Very sorry to hear it."

"Thank you."

"Will you be staying long?"

"Maybe. There are things to settle."

"Of course. Are you still acting? I remember *Ranging Wild.* I thought you were quite good."

"Wow. That was a long time ago. I—"

He paused, eternally grateful the kid with his coffee had picked that moment to arrive. Vane took the cup from him and set it down. Those few seconds gave him time to settle himself. *You're not famous. You never will be.*

"I've done a few commercials. My family owns a diner outside of town. Eileen's?"

Mr. Kam nodded. "I know it."

"Well, it needs some work, so I'm going to stay around for that."

"Excellent. It'll be nice to have you here."

Vane listened for some sort of pacification in Mr. Kam's tone but heard none. Mr. Kam was still Mr. Kam. Kind and unflappable. He wasn't old though, which made Vane realize how young Mr. Kam must have been when he was teaching Vane's drama class. He had dark buzzed hair, a slight tilt to his brown eyes, and a mischievous twinkle that made him look even younger. He was mild in an almost bland way, but Vane could remember the deep emotions Mr. Kam had pulled out of him. He'd helped Vane in ways that Vane had failed to live up to.

"Are you still teaching?"

"Absolutely. I run an off campus acting school as well. In fact, I—Wait." He smacked the table with the flat of his palm. "What are you doing tomorrow?"

"I'm not sure. Nothing definite. Why?"

"Tomorrow is Career Day at the high school. I'm on the organizing committee, and I must say, I've been challenged by the scheduling of the presentations. Two of my guest speakers have had to cancel. You would be doing me an enormous favor if you'd agree to fill one of those spots."

Vane frowned. "You mean talk?"

Mr. Kam bopped his head. "Yes. Talk to us about your experiences as an actor. Things the kids can expect if they choose to pursue your career. Best practices. Training that would benefit them. That kind of thing."

Apparently, Mr. Kam had missed the part where Vane was a failure. Heat crept into his cheeks. "I don't know. I haven't had a job in a while."

No *Marvelous Marcel*.

"Please. You've been in the thick of it. I know it's short notice, but I have faith in you. You'll speak for about fifteen minutes. Orientation is at nine a.m. in the auditorium. Your spot will be at ten-fifteen. We're going from nine-thirty to lunch, and you're welcome to stay for the entire event. We'll have refreshments afterwards as well."

"I just... don't think I'd have a lot to say."

"Vane, I remember you. You'll rise to the occasion. I could use help with my off campus school too. Think about that as well, but please agree to tomorrow. You'll be fabulous."

Vane chuckled—at least he hadn't said, *marvelous!*—took a swallow of lukewarm coffee and nodded. "Okay. Nine-thirty."

"Wonderful."

Mr. Kam pulled his script off the table, and Vane hid a frown. A strange pang struck him, and he thought of Fisher's pleas. *Call me.* What if Vane went back? What if he tried again?

Mr. Kam stood and set a hand on Vane's shoulder. "Again, my sympathies on the loss of your father. I know it's difficult, but I'm sure he was very proud of you. You pursued your dreams," Mr. Kam added with a squeeze to his shoulder. "So we'll see you tomorrow."

Vane nodded, swallowing in his dry throat. "I'll be there."

After Mr. Kam left, he stared at his coffee for a moment. The words "very proud of you" echoed in his brain in a voice filled with laughter. His dad hadn't been proud of him. He'd been disappointed. Heck, Vane was disappointed. It had all come to nothing. Why? Wasn't it what he'd always wanted?

Why would he let his dream burn out like that?

Weighted down all of a sudden, he stood with a grunt, left his cold coffee on the table, and went home.

13

SCREWING UP CAREER DAY

THE NEXT DAY, Vane got up early—for him—took a shower and returned naked into the bedroom he'd grown up in. The door to the master downstairs was closed. He hadn't opened it, wasn't going to, and he didn't want to think about why that was. His old bedroom was good enough. After all, he had no real plans to stay here, did he?

Fisher wanted him back.

So call 'im.

But he wasn't ready to do that yet. He had to wait until he'd gotten things squared away and could think with a clearer head. When he knew what he was doing and didn't look like a total loser anymore. In the meantime, he'd have to fake success at Career Day.

The light in his bedroom was gray and fuzzy like a scratchy old film. It didn't feel quite real. He imagined himself playing the part of a naked guy in a foreign movie. Some artsy flick called *A View in Gray* or something like that. His scene would be silent, so heavily symbolic nobody would really know what was going on.

Just like my life.

Or maybe the point would be clear to the audience and the real focus of the movie would be watching him figure it out.

He stood at the cold window and half expected a crowd to stare up at him, but the yard was empty, of course. It wasn't like he was really putting on a show for anybody. Even so, the idea of the silent gazes woke butterflies of excitement in his belly. Would he want that? Standing naked in the window wasn't exactly art. More like—

Washed-out Actor Takes Porn World by Storm.

His belly fluttered as his nerves danced a little jig.

The idea of an audience—it did it for him. What was that word? Fluffer. Yeah. Doug could be his fluffer.

Vane bit his lip and slipped back to the night in Doug's truck with its fogged-up windows and his bare ass hanging out, flashing anybody who wanted to walk up and peer in.

How weird that had excited him so much.

He inched closer to the window and brushed his fingers along his cock, the skin on his belly tightening.

Nobody was watching, but he shivered anyway.

He was an actor. This was a film. Artsy or porn, it didn't matter. Performance was exposure.

But standing in front of the window like this different. He'd only acted in commercials and a family sitcom for half a season. Nudity not required. He'd never have guessed a part of him would delight in naughtiness, though his underwear should probably have given him a clue. He stroked his fattening cock, squeezed it and pulled, rising onto his toes with a groan.

Of all the weird things to be doing.

The air brushing his skin had gone cool, but his dick was hot, the slide of his dry palm electric. He stared out at the low hills and trees and weeds, and the strange clump on the low slope in the far corner of his property. *The well.* Shoot. How had he forgotten they had a well? A dry well. He pictured his mom's roses blooming all around it.

His breath hitched.

He rolled his thumb over the tip of his cock, rubbing a drop of precum into his skin, and shuddered. A faint gray outline wobbled on the glass. Now he was the voyeur, watching himself, creating a scene he'd play for Doug. With every stroke, he'd entice him, drawing him nearer and nearer. Soon Doug would be the one cupping his balls, sliding a finger over his taint, soft as a feather.

A gasp escaped his lips. *Yesss.*

He blinked, focusing past his image on the glass, drawing his pleasure into an ache that set fire to his skin.

He stared at the empty hills and the bitter blue sky. The grass stirred in the— No, not in the breeze. From the skulking cat. So Vane had an audience after all.

He tipped his head back and closed his eyes. His belly clenched and his balls tightened.

He pulled faster and faster, the column of flesh in his hand like hot silk. The vein underneath the tip of his finger throbbed. He rubbed his slit with his thumb and pleasure pulsed through him like lightning bolts.

Imaginary hands tightened on his ass, pulling him in. The breath of warm air on his face was Doug's. Sweet, strong arms holding him close.

He moaned.

His spine was electric, his body lighting with sparks. He let go of his sac and cupped the tip of his dick as he shot, the force of it doubling him into the window. With his forehead resting against the glass, he panted.

Bells rang in his ears.

Then the thump of the furnace broke in, and warm air stirred the dust again.

Shoot. You idiot. You're gonna be late.

Rushing now, he washed and dressed, grabbed his jacket, and trotted downstairs. After setting out another plate of food for the cat, he headed to his car.

There were two ways to get to Poppy Brush from his house. One road wound through the country and came out on the other side of the village. In the old days that one was quicker because hardly anybody used it, but now, with the new developments in the area, Vane wasn't sure it still was, so he took the straight route.

On the outskirts of town, a car in front of him turned into a wooded neighborhood of mansion-sized houses. Vane picked up speed, relieved that he was making good time. He hated being late and the reason he would be this time made him blush all over. But still... His mind drifted back to the window and the heat in his belly and the feel of Doug's hands and—

Oh no!

The squirrel came out of nowhere. One minute the road was empty and then—

The thing sat staring at him as Vane bore down on it. Why? Why? Why couldn't anything good happen?

He swerved, tires squealing. The shadows of trees whipped across his windshield. His heart slammed and his legs shook, but—*I didn't hit it... I didn't hit it.* He gasped and slowed, looking for a place to pull over. He was on a street with ditches on either side and giant houses on giant lots. A car approached behind him.

Shoot, shoot, shoot.

He sped up, but the street rolled onward. Soon the houses stopped, but ditches lined either side of the road. He drove for about a mile before another house behind a gated driveway appeared. Here he swung into the space in front of the gate and turned around after the car behind him passed by.

Great.

When he got to the school, there were cars everywhere. Holy moly. Whatever happened to walking to school?

He drove to the end of the parking lot and stopped by a building near the corner. An access road behind the building appeared with a Do Not Enter sign beside the exit to the lot. Vane edged to the side of the red-painted curb and let a car behind him squeeze by. After it passed, he reversed in a three-point turn and backed into the corner by the building.

He was blocking the exit to the access road but doubted anybody would be using it during Career Day.

Hurrying now, he crossed the empty quad to the other side of the campus. The doors of the auditorium stood open, the warm air inside mixing with the cold outside.

After he checked in, he got himself a cup of coffee from a canister on a table by the door and put on his happy Riley Vane face. The kids threw him questions about the parts he'd gotten, people he'd met, how he spent his time.

They were good kids.

They listened and smiled and nodded and didn't judge him, but they had no idea who he was, which was a kind of judgment in itself. These kids had been toddlers when he'd flashed and burned.

One season. Half a season.

If Mary had really wanted him, she'd have pursued him, and at least made sure he was okay. His bruises would have healed.

But the truth was, he was too old to play the twenty-something Marcel. He was pretty, and he could pull it off, but for how long? He was thirty-two. A failed thirty-two. If he were ever going to be anybody, it would have happened years ago. He could hang on the outskirts, but the accolades and the fame? He'd missed it.

And who cared anyway? His father was dead. Vane couldn't prove anything to him now. The world belonged to these kids. Kids who didn't even know who he was.

He bolted as soon as the session let out.

CLOUDS HAD GATHERED, AND RAINDROPS spattered the ground.

Vane hurried across the quad while his memory ran with the shouts and laughter of his old school days here. It had been fifteen years since he'd had a cheese zombie—though the aroma of greasy, cheese-stuffed buns flooded his nostrils again. Close to ten years since he'd lost most of every summer in Fisher's temperature-controlled condo. He swore he could feel the heat of the pavement here instead of the chill of the drizzle. At least until the wet slap of tires reminded him of where he was.

Halfway across the parking lot, he slowed in surprise at the sight of two figures standing in front of his car. His stomach dropped. *Doug.*

Doug and Dorcas.

He hurried to them.

Doug glared at him, hands on his hips. "Yeah, I thought so."

"Thought what?"

Doug waved a hand at Vane's Mustang. "This car. I doubted there were two of the same running around town. Were you never taught any manners? You blocked us in."

Doug pointed over the roof of Vane's car toward the access road. Dorcas grabbed his arm and pulled it down.

She smiled at Vane. "He's sorry, honey. He's just grumpy today."

"I'm late," Doug said, grinding the words out.

"You are not late," Dorcas said. "That's why you're your own boss." Her smile on Vane turned into a grin. "I didn't know you were participating. I would've come take a peek."

Vane kept his distance from Doug, who'd pulled his mouth into a tight line and turned a frown on Dorcas.

"It's the principle," Doug muttered.

"I didn't know I was doing it," Vane said, focusing on Dorcas. "I ran into Mr. Kam yesterday."

She waggled her eyebrows. "I'd like to run into him any day."

Doug's eyes widened, his frown gone. "Seriously?"

"I think he's cute. I would've definitely taken up acting if we'd had a teacher like Mr. Kam at our school."

Now Doug rolled his eyes. "I have a job site to get to."

He had on a tweed jacket in various tones of brown that brought out the darker strands in his blond hair. The woodsy color in his hazel eyes looked dark in the gray light. Smoldering. Vane imagined the warmth of Doug's palm cupping his balls.

Quit it. Jesus. That's why you were late.

Maybe he should tell Doug that. *Well, I was rubbing one off to my fantasies of you.*

Would Doug forgive him?

"Don't let us hold you up," Doug said.

"Stop." Dorcas waved her hand in the air, sending her bracelets into a bell-like melody. Her earrings—giant filigree butterflies—fluttered in the same breeze that blew her voluminous skirt against her legs.

"Were you a presenter too?" asked Vane.

Doug groaned and leaned back against Vane's car.

Dorcas ignored him. "Of course, I was." She grinned. "Everybody needs to hear from the new age witch."

"Witch?"

"Well, according to one of the kids. I'm not even Wiccan, but it does make me more interesting, don't you think?"

"I think you're interesting anyway," said Vane.

"That's sweet," Doug muttered.

"I have no control over squirrels."

Vane's comment clearly took Doug aback. He blinked, and the frown returned to his face. "Is that a witch thing?"

"It ran out at me."

"Oh, my God." Dorcas reached for his arm. "You didn't—"

"No. I swerved."

"Which you aren't supposed to do," Doug said. "And what does that have to do with blocking us in?"

"You can back up."

"The gate is closed at the other end."

"'Cuz you're not supposed to park there either," Vane said.

Doug glared. "That's beside the point."

"Not really."

"You wouldn't want him to run over a squirrel," said Dorcas. "Doug is an animal lover."

Vane snorted. "You wouldn't freakin' know it."

Doug stepped away from Vane's car and straightened to his full height. "You should have gotten here earlier."

"What about you?"

"I was at a job. Then I had to pick up Dorcas."

"I'm sorry," Dorcas said, wincing a smile at him.

Doug glowered. "You shouldn't be sorry."

"I should?" asked Vane.

"Yeah," said Doug. "You should."

He bit off the words in a way that the real meaning behind them slowly sank into Vane's consciousness. *Oh yeah.* The catty limits comment.

Doug's eyebrows had formed a ridge over his eyes and puckered into a deep crease at the top of his nose.

A part of Vane chided himself for being a romantic idiot about the guy. Doug was a jerk who made no bones about the fact that he didn't like Vane. And yeah, Vane had said something stupid, but people made mistakes. And for Pete's sake, he'd been upset. His dad had died. He hadn't asked Doug to come over.

"Well, get away from my car, and I'll move."

"My pleasure."

Vane dug his keys out of his pocket and felt his stomach drop the second they slipped from his fingers. Of all the times. He cringed inside, picked them up, and bobbled them again. This time they hit his fender and bounced a foot away.

Doug stared, and why not? Vane was a train wreck.

Geez, he wasn't always this way. Put a camera on him and he was Fred Astaire, but in front of Doug? Why couldn't he not embarrass himself for once in his life?

The next time his keys clattered to the ground, Dorcas raised a finger and came closer. "Honey, wait. Let me."

"Maybe you shouldn't be driving," Doug said.

"You're making him nervous," said Dorcas.

Vane blurted, "No, he's not," at the same time Doug said, "No, I'm not."

They glared at each other. Dorcas picked up Vane's

keys and held them out. Vane took them, closing his fingers into a fist.

Now Dorcas glanced between them. "Why don't we get a bite to eat?"

Their voices crashed together. "No!"

14

A GOOD IDEA

VANE HATED DOUG.
The thought settled in the front of his brain with the thump of a headache. He stood in the middle of Raley's, staring at the shelves of crackers. Round crackers. Square crackers. Wheat crackers. Rice crackers. Crackers with seeds. Crackers with herbs.

Screw the crackers.

He moved down the aisle until the display changed to cookies. Chocolate chip. Chocolate brownie. Iced Raisin. Oreos. Mini Oreos. Were those better? Who cared? What did it matter if he lived on cookies and Coke and got fat? Nobody wanted him anymore.

He stared at the nutritional information on a bag of chocolate chip hazelnut cookies. Geez, why had he done that? One cookie was an effing meal. Not that he gained weight. He made good choices, but he could eat whatever he wanted and could probably even live on cookies for all Doug cared.

And he was never going to be Marcel, so why did he care? *You have your screenplay.* But he hadn't looked at it in weeks.

No more Hollywood.

You could turn your screenplay into a book. You don't need Hollywood.

Maybe.

He set the bag of chocolate chip hazelnut death-by-cookies back on the shelf. Were there healthy cookies? Whole wheat? *Yuck.* Oatmeal.

Yeah. Oatmeal.

He frowned, and the packages in front of him blurred while an idea for the diner surfaced in his brain.

Could he possibly have a good idea?

He wasn't sure, but what did he have to lose?

Bottom was bottom, so he grabbed the handle of his cart and set off for the bakery section. Here he examined all the pies. When done, he parked his cart by the shelves of bread and tugged his phone out of his pocket.

Of course, he didn't fumble it—*why would you without Doug or Fisher waiting to roll their eyes at you*—and called Rose.

She picked up and said, "Please do not tell me you fired Luis."

"No, I didn't fire Luis."

"Good."

"I need his recipe for oatmeal pie. Do you have it?"

"Um... No. That would be Luis who has it."

"Well, I know Luis has it. Can you get it for me?"

"You are odd, Vane, but yes, I guess so."

"I mean like now. I'm at the store."

Rose sighed. "And you need to have oatmeal pie right now?"

"We need a gimmick, you know? Something to get people to come to the diner just for that."

"Vane, sweetie, we already sell it."

"I'm gonna make it better. And market it somehow. Give it away. Coupons. Something."

After a short silence, she sighed. Vane returned to biting his lip until she took another breath and said, "Okay. Give me a minute. I'll call you back."

"'Kay."

Piecrust. He'd definitely need that. He typed piecrust recipes into his browser and set off. By the time he'd wandered the aisles and collected the items he'd need, his phone pinged.

—*Here you go, sweetie.*

His gaze traveled down the ingredient list. But the new pie was going to need something else. Something extra. Lemon zest? Orange zest? He wasn't sure.

He dropped all the other items in his cart on the way to the produce section where he grabbed a head of lettuce, a couple of apples, and a bag of carrots since he was there.

He'd need oranges too, he guessed, for the orange zest.

But as he turned the cart around his gaze fell on something that looked like a pile of grubs. *Gross.* Maybe they were grubs. People ate lots of weird things nowadays. He eased his cart closer and inspected the lemon grass and tamarind and—

Oh, hey. Ginger.

Would that work?

It would be a different kind of pie that was for sure. Vane loved gingersnaps. Maybe he could put gingersnaps in the crust and dried ginger in the filling. He'd have to test it though. Maybe he could try candied ginger too. He grabbed what he needed, picking up a box of ginger snaps on his way to the register.

His idea excited him, and that made him nervous in a different kind of way in case his pie turned out to be a disaster. *But what if it doesn't? What if it's good and everybody loves it?*

Vane's inner voice wasn't usually positive, but he wasn't going to argue with it now.

He hurried home, put his groceries away, fed the cat and himself, and sat down with a beer to plot out his recipes.

Ginger Oatmeal Pie.

Way better than chocolate chip hazelnut cookies.

ON FRIDAYS, ROSE ONLY WORKED HALF DAYS, SO AFTER Vane made his pies, he packed them up and headed to Pleasant Hill.

An hour after setting off, he pulled up to the curb alongside a stockade fence. Rose lived in a cul-de-sac tucked away at the end of a private driveway.

Hugging the box he was carrying his pies in, Vane squeezed between the fence and a delivery truck and came out onto a common space shared by the cul-de-sac. An array of potted plants in front of Rose's greeted him.

The house was cute. Cuter than he remembered from a few days ago. He'd never lived anywhere he'd really cared about except for his parents' house. But he didn't wander around there or do anything to the place. He lived there, but he didn't explore. He kept to his bedroom, his bathroom, the kitchen, and sometimes the living room because that's where the TV was.

Not that he watched much TV anymore. The thought of *Marvelous Marcel* popping onto the screen made him sick.

The garage door was open, a hose dangling from a hole in the wall next to the water heater. *New washer and dryer?*

He entered the house and gazed through the sliding glass doors to the backyard where the kids were playing. While he watched, Rose brush off Ricky's butt and give him a push toward the play set she'd brought from the old house. When she turned around and headed inside, he slid his hands into his back pockets and waited.

Rose's eyes widened. "Hey, you."

"I have a surprise."

"Oh?"

He nodded at the box. "I need your opinion."

"You came all this way for my opinion? Must be important." She peeked into the box. "Pies. Oatmeal?"

"Sort of. You get to taste."

"Why am I scared?"

"Give me a break. I cook better than that idiot Luis."

"Why two?"

"They're different."

She lifted the top one from the box and set it on the counter. "What do you have against Luis?"

He rolled his eyes. "I don't have anything against Luis. I don't trust him."

"So you have something against him?"

"No." She removed the other pie, and he pulled his hands from his pockets and approached the counter. "I think he wants to get in the office."

She blinked at him, frowning a moment later as she rummaged in a drawer. "Luis?"

"Yeah. I went in to use the computer, and he kept hovering. Skulking—"

"Skulking?"

"Skulking. Can I tell this story?"

She straightened with a cake knife in her hand. "Well, what did he say during these skulks?"

He glowered at her. "Nothing. Something dumb like he was looking for register tape."

"Well, sweetie, that sounds pretty reasonable. Why didn't you let him in?"

"I didn't keep him out. I had to lock it up when I left though. There are boxes of papers just sitting out. Applications and stuff. They should be locked up in the cabinet."

Rose looked toward the ceiling and winced. "Oh, God. I forgot about that. Dad was going to store it, make room for other things. The office is so small. Most of those papers are old. You can shred a lot of it, probably."

"Yeah, okay. I'll get to it. I don't mind locking up for now."

"Of course not," she said, drawing the knife through the first pie. "It annoys Luis."

"Luis annoys me."

Metal scraped on the garage floor, followed by a clang. A moment later, a head popped in the door. "Gonna turn off the water for a sec. Won't take us long."

"Take your time," said Rose.

"You got a new washer and dryer?" asked Vane.

Her eyes brightened. "Front loading. They are *gorgeous.*"

He snorted. "Okay."

"Tell me about your pies, sweetie."

Maybe it was the endearment that flashed him back to their old house—his house now. For a moment, he was seven years old again with thirteen-year-old Rose sitting on the porch beside him. Her arm had been heavy on his shoulders, the cheer in her voice almost brittle. *We'll be okay, sweetie. Mom's in Heaven. It's a good place.*

From then on, she'd been mom to him. She must have been broken inside too, but she'd never shown it.

"You know I love you, right?"

She smiled. "I know, sweetie. I love you too."

The sound of a foot on the step drew their attention to the garage door.

A skinny blond guy wearing a backwards baseball cap, jeans, and a gray shirt leaned in. "I wanted to give you your packet here. Instructions and stuff." He held out a plastic pouch Vane took and set on the counter. "Wow." The guy remained in the door and took a whiff of the air. "Something sure smells good."

"My brother made pies," said Rose.

"You're welcome to share," said Vane. "I'm doing a taste test."

"Oh yeah? Never made these kind before?"

"Nope. I'm experimenting."

Rose laughed. "So you'll be our guinea pigs."

Another guy appeared behind the blond and peered in. The blond glanced back at him. "Offerin' us pie."

"I wouldn't mind a piece. How about we finish up here. Ten minutes?"

"Sure," said Vane.

"Incentivized," said the blond with a wink.

The other guy guffawed as they ducked back out. "Look at you with the big words."

Vane turned to find Rose studying him with a smile. "I haven't asked you how you're adjusting," she said.

"To what? You're the one who moved."

"So did you. For which I am eternally grateful. I never thought you were happy."

"I had to try. I just... I didn't mean to be gone forever."

He really hadn't. He thought he could make it. Even after *Ranging Wild* was cancelled, he thought he'd get another part if he stuck with it. But he hadn't. And at some point, not giving up had become hiding.

He hadn't been here in the real world for a long time. Not for his niece and nephew, and not for Rose after Marc had died. He'd never even sent a housewarming gift when they'd bought their house. If it hadn't been for Rose or Marc keeping in touch, he would have disappeared completely.

All his dreams had deflated like old balloons.

Rose sighed. "I know life with Dad was tough on you. I—"

Something thudded against the back door. Vane turned to find Ricky standing there with both palms and his lips smashed to the glass. The kid was laughing, bubbles of spit forming on the clear surface of the door.

Vane laughed too. This might be only the second time Ricky had laughed in his presence.

Rose groaned. "Oh, for God's sake." She crossed to the door and eased it open. "Look at that mess."

Ricky cackled.

"What are you doing?" she asked him.

"Saying hi to Uncle Vane."

"That's how you say hi?"

"The door was in my way."

"Oh, is that right? Go get your sister. It's time for pie."

Ricky threw his arms into the air. "PIE!"

He raced away, and Rose returned to the kitchen.

Vane chuckled. "That was..."

"Ricky's good mood." She grinned. "He's a cheerful kid once he gets to know you."

"Everybody else watch out."

She laughed. "Pretty much."

"Okay." The appliance guys stepped in. "You're all set."

"Perfect," said Rose. "Just in time for pie."

"You can tell us which one you like best," said Vane.

The blond craned his neck to peer over the counter. "They look the same."

"Try and see," said Vane.

The blond shrugged. "I'm game."

"Me too," said the other one.

Vane took a stack of plates out of the cupboard just as Ricky rushed in. He grinned as Ricky rocked to a sudden stop and stared at the appliance guys. A frown slowly formed on his face. Lucy slid the door shut behind him.

After he set the plates on the counter, Vane picked Ricky up with his hands under the kid's arms and set him on a stool. "Counting on you to help me with this, Ricky."

Ricky turned his glower on Vane. "Okay."

Vane grinned at him and passed him a plate. "You eat this and tell me what you think."

"Okay."

After serving Lucy too, Rose said, "This does smell good, Vane."

The bigger appliance guy nodded in agreement. "Like Christmas."

Rose transferred thin slices of each pie to the plates. "Which one is which?" she asked Vane.

"I can tell," he said. "Try them and tell me what you think first."

She handed out the plates and forks.

"It's really good," said Lucy. "Like cookies."

The blond guy cut into his pie and raised his fork, studying Vane for a moment. "That's an unusual name you have."

Vane's pulse sped. *Please don't know me.* "I guess so."

"Are you?"

"What?"

"Vain."

The other guy snort-laughed, and Vane grimaced at him. "Good one." *Like I haven't heard that fifty thousand times.*

"Hmm," said the blond, nodding his head. "I'm likin' this."

Vane took a bite of the pie with the fresh ginger. It was milder than he thought it would be.

"I like both," said the big guy. "But this—" He pointed his fork at one of the slices. "I really love. I don't like real sweet stuff. This isn't as sweet."

"I like the sweet one," said the blond. "The sweeter the better. I really like the chewy pieces."

"That's candied ginger," said Vane.

"Candied, huh? My wife makes a killer cupcake with cinnamon hearts." He patted his chest. "Gets me right here."

"Aw," said Rose. "That's sweet."

"I'm a lucky man."

The guys finished their pie, and Rose walked them outside. Lucy slid off her stool and flashed Vane a smile. "I like both. Ricky likes both too."

Ricky glowered at her until Vane grabbed him again and swung him down. "Okay. Go play."

Tilting his head back, Ricky grinned. "That was like candy-cake."

Candy-cake.

"I like the sound of that."

"Me too," said Ricky.

A minute later they were both outside, and Vane

took another slice of the pie with the fresh ginger. It tingled on his tongue. He liked it, but the universal appeal question was still up in the air. Would Doug like it? He wanted to watch Doug eat it, even though he hated Doug. *The jerk.*

He swallowed his mouthful of pie and took a bite of the other piece.

"The one with the candy," Rose said. She laid her hands on his shoulders as she went around him. "Much better than Luis's, and Luis's is good."

His cheeks burned, but he smiled. "Think so?"

"Yes." She pulled a container out of the cupboard under the stove. "You have to give this back."

"Keep 'em. The pies, I mean."

"You sure?"

"Yeah, I don't need anymore. I haven't worked out in weeks."

She rolled her eyes and took a tube of aluminum foil from a drawer instead. "You know it's going to take more than pie to put butts in those seats."

"That's a charming way of putting it. And not true. People go to McDonald's for the fries."

"And the burgers and the shakes and the prices."

"We'll market it."

She pulled open the refrigerator and turned back for the pies. "That takes money, sweetie. I want this to work. I just don't want you to get your hopes up too high."

"Do you want me to sell?"

"No." She slid the pies into the refrigerator and shut the door. "I don't. I want you to stick it out and give it all you've got. Just be realistic. You have a lot of inertia to overcome."

"I'll think of something."

"And if it doesn't work, you did your best."

"It has our mom's name attached to it."

"I know."

He flipped on the water in the sink and rinsed off the dishes. Through the window he watched the kids play.

Lucy was swinging, and Ricky was bouncing a ball off the bottoms of her shoes as she swung toward him. As though sensing him, Ricky turned his gaze to the kitchen window. The sun poured over the roof of the house, and Ricky scowled into its glare.

Vane was pretty sure he was hidden behind the window until—the kid stuck his tongue out at him.

Weirdo.

At home that night, he fell asleep on the couch and dreamed stacks of pies filled every room from floor to ceiling. He had to walk through mazes in every room. In his dream, somebody knocked on the front door, and when he opened it, Fisher stood there. Vane let him in and watched him work his way to the middle of the room where he stopped and gazed at the walls of pies. Frowning, he looked back at Vane, said, "I won't live in a mess like this," lit a match, and tossed it on the carpet.

Flames erupted, and Vane turned for the door in a panic, threw it open, and... woke up.

Holy—

Geez.

He sat up.

The lights were on and everything looked normal. The dream didn't linger, but the echo of the knock floated through his brain and drew him off the couch. He opened the front door and stared into the dark.

The wind blew and something cracked. Then it was silent, as though somebody had gone still in the night, waiting for him to go back inside. A sweet scent tickled his senses. Cookies? Or a flower. But what bloomed in winter?

With a shiver, he shut the door and locked it. Then he went to the back and locked that door too.

Probably just the cat.

He turned off the TV on his way upstairs but left the light over the couch on.

15

STRANGE NOISES

CREAKS AND GROANS and the whistle of the wind made its way inside the kitchen. The house was old with cracks and gaps and drafts.

But this time the sounds were different.

Vane set the coffee pot back on the burner, turned in the direction of the living room, and held his breath. The wind died. It wasn't late yet and was barely dark. He took his cup with him and approached the front window.

Now it was quiet. No whistle. No rustle. No snap of breaking branches.

Nothing.

But the silence bothered him. He set his cup on the window ledge and eased open the front door but didn't bother with the porch light.

The sky was clear and filled with bright, hard stars.

He slipped outside, and his breath puffed in ghostly wisps. The crunch of grit under his shoes accompanied him on the walkway, and a faint clomp like a car door floated on the air. If anybody was out there, not wanting to be seen, they were doing a good job of skulking around.

Vane stilled, holding his breath again.

A whisper reached him. Or was he imagining it?

He cast a glance around him, but all that met his gaze was darkness. The smudge-shape of trees in the distance loomed closer. Their branches winked out the stars while the smell of blossoms floated on the air. The fragrance was strange for winter. Something like jasmine or vanilla.

He crept deeper into the yard, aware of the door behind him and the safety of the house. The farther away from the light he got, the faster his heart beat.

He waited, took a step back, and something flew at him. Okay, it probably didn't fly *at* him, but it got close enough for him to feel the wind of it zooming by. He stumbled backwards, breath stuck in his throat. The thing —demon—whatever it was, hit the tree beside him and scrambled up into the branches.

Vane bent, gripping his knees in his hands as he pulled in a shuddery breath.

"You maniac," he muttered at the thing with glowing eyes that hunkered in the crook of a branch above him. "See if I ever feed you again."

The cat said nothing. Vane was facing away from the sudden, thunderous crashing of the bushes behind him. He whirled, and a dog ran out of the dark and dashed around him. Vane spun in a circle. Tail thrashing, tongue lolling, the dog stopped in front of him and wagged his whole body.

What the heck?

The dog confused him. He kind of understood the cat, but the—

"Hoyt! Hoy— Oh, Jesus."

No. No, it couldn't be. The dog ignored the shadow shape pursuing it. Doug. This was Doug's dog.

Screw my life.

"What the heck?"

"Sorry." Doug trotted up and reached for Hoyt's collar. "He got away from me."

Vane stared into the shape of Doug's face, trying to catch details while Doug patted the side of the dog.

"Are you spying on me?" Vane asked.

Doug snorted. "With a dog?"

"Well, what are you doing here?"

"Rose hired me to do the remodel on the house."

Oh heck, no. "In the middle of the night?"

"Right. And it isn't exactly the middle of the night."

"You were sneaking around."

Doug guffawed. "I wasn't sneaking. I just—didn't want to disturb you."

That wasn't what he'd been about to say.

Heat surged into Vane's face, making his skin sting in the cold. His thoughts had been spiraling around Doug for days. He couldn't get him out of his mind, but clearly Doug didn't feel the same way. If he could've snuck off without Vane knowing he'd been here, he would have.

"You didn't want to see me."

"Disturb. You. I was on my way home. I thought I'd stop and get a quick look."

"In the dark?"

Something moved, rising, and a light flashed in Vane's eyes. "Shoot." He swatted at it, and the dog nudged him.

"Back," said Doug. "Go wait."

"I am waiting," Vane murmured, rubbing at his eyes. "I'm waiting for you to tell me what you're doing here."

"I told you, and I meant the dog."

"Oh." Hoyt whined and snuffled and pranced in a circle. "What kind of dog is it?"

"A golden."

He said it as though it were bright sunshine outside and Vane was an idiot for not knowing a golden retriever when he saw one.

"I can't see it."

"Hoyt. Go wait."

The dog yipped and ran off. Doug turned back and stood with his hands on his hips.

"Where'd he go?" Vane's voice had fallen, rumbling somewhere in his throat.

Doug didn't answer. He took a step closer, approaching so slowly Vane felt everything around him slow and stop. He couldn't move. But he didn't want to move. His heart raced. He was pretty sure he nodded right before Doug cupped his face and stepped him back against the tree.

Warm breath fanned Vane's skin, but Doug didn't come any closer. He waited. Waited until—

Vane lunged against him, and their mouths crashed together, and Vane groaned. His back rolled against the tree, and his chest swelled against Doug's. This was stupid, of course. They didn't like each other, and Doug wasn't even gay.

No, no, no, don't go there. Vane had bungled that enough already.

Don't say anything. Just shut up.

Luckily, his mouth was busy.

He grabbed the back of Doug's neck, and his lips mashed against teeth. Doug's breath was as warm and rich as Vane's morning coffee. The delicious aroma and taste pulled a moan out of his belly. Doug dug his fingers into Vane's head and the side of his neck, and his dick thrust hard against Vane's belly.

This was nuts.

Now Vane pushed back and slid his arms over Doug's shoulders, holding him close. The air heated up around him and the tree pressed into his spine as Doug's chest and belly pushed in hard against him, pinning him out in the open.

Were they visible? Could passing headlights slice across them?

Vane's heart beat faster as Doug's kisses stole his breath. He flung his head back and knocked it against the tree trunk.

"Ow."

"Jesus," Doug said and cupped the back of his head, massaging through his hair. "Are you okay?"

"Yeah." Just a couple sparks and a feeling of *déjà vu.* "People can see us."

"Naw."

"That's okay. I don't mind."

Doug's teeth gleamed, catching the seep of light from the house. He leaned in again, his hand protecting Vane's skull from the back of the tree. "You want an audience?"

Vane giggled—*Oh shoot, stop that*—but Doug laughed with him. "It's an occupational hazard," he whispered. "Acting."

"Hm. I bet."

The space between them had disappeared. Now Vane moaned at the caress of Doug's lips across his face like little flames in the cold. He shivered as warm fingers brushed his belly under his shirt and rocked against the touch.

"I like that," he whispered.

Doug dipped his face to Vane's neck, nuzzling and breathing warm air on him. The starless dark under the tree filled Vane's eyes, and his shivers came faster and faster. It was cold and he was warm. "I want you to do it."

"I don't have any supplies," Doug said. He hooked his fingers inside Vane's waistband, slid them down and... "Is that lace?"

"No."

The only sound for a moment was the drumming of blood in Vane's ears. Doug didn't speak. He pushed his fingers under the material, brushing against Vane's pubic hair. "Feels like lace."

"It's just... Just rough," he said. "They're old."

"I—"

"Gosh." Vane shucked his jeans and briefs, scraping his ass against the tree. He kicked free of his pants and toed off his shoes. Clammy leaves clung to his feet. "Oh shoot, that's cold."

"Goofball. Jump up."

Vane frowned, about to mutter, "Jump where?" when Doug grabbed his ass and hefted him off the ground.

"Let's go in," said Doug. "Use your stuff."

"I don't have anything. Just... just lube. I didn't—Oh."

A finger slid into his crack, and Doug chuckled. "Fuckin' exhibitionist, aren't you?"

"Yeah." The tree against Vane's back and his legs clamped to Doug's waist supported him, allowing Doug to let him go and reach between their bodies. He squeezed Vane's cock, and Vane shuddered. "Yeaaah."

"Hm. That's right," Doug agreed. "Show me whachya got."

Vane rocked his hips and rolled his pelvis against Doug's torso.

The brush of Doug's fingertips from taint to tailbone vibrated into Vane's belly. A moment later, he stroked back again, tailbone to taint. "Tight little hole," he whispered.

"I want your dick in it."

"Not tonight."

Another night? "Why not?" he moaned.

"No supplies," Doug said against his mouth. He pinned Vane's dick between them and rocked him against the tree. "And I like you out in the open anyway."

Vane's shirt snagged on the rough bark, pulling it against his ribs. The cold numbed his skin, but he was shivering anyway, pushing against Doug, seeking his warmth.

"I'm sorry."

The words spilled out of Vane's mouth, and Doug

swallowed them. He stroked Vane's cock again, and fireworks exploded in the dark sky. But a moment later, Doug pulled his mouth away and gasped, "Sorry?"

"I say things."

Crazy things. Stupid things.

"You're nuts," said Doug.

He squeezed Vane's cock, loosening his fingers a moment later to drag up its length. The feeling was both mind blowing and nerve wracking, and Vane clamped his thighs even tighter around Doug's waist. The raspy burn lit him up, and a thrill of fear raced through him.

Nobody'd ever had his cock pulled out by its root, right?

Would Doug do that?

No. He stroked back down, only a flutter of a touch, which wasn't enough anymore, and Vane pushed down on the finger at his hole.

"You're teasing me."

"I should leave you like this," Doug whispered.

"No."

"Stand on my feet."

Vane frowned. "What?"

"The ground's too cold. You're cold. You're shaking."

"Dude, I'm about to have sex."

Doug laughed. "Stand up against me, an' I'll get you off."

Vane nodded. *Yes, yes.* Getting off. That was good.

He released Doug's waist and dropped his feet, hip hopping until he stood on the top of Doug's boots.

"Just like this," Doug whispered, stroking Vane's ass.

"More than this?" Vane asked hopefully.

He wanted it. He didn't want to think why or about what was happening. Not tonight.

Shivers ran through him, wracking him in time to his heart hammers. Doug's cock was as hard as a metal pipe. He rocked his hips into Vane's.

"Take me out," Doug whispered.

Oh, pretty please. Yes, yes. He fumbled at Doug's buttons and giggled again. *Stop that.*

But Doug laughed. "That's the cutest damn giggle."

Then he groaned as Vane wrapped his fingers around him. *Good. Shut up.* Vane wasn't cute. He didn't want to be cute. He wanted to be irresistible. He wanted another night doing this with Doug.

The cock in his hand was thick and hot. He slid partway to his knees before Doug cupped his elbows and pulled him back up.

"It's too cold. C'mere."

Doug pulled him closer and pushed his cock against Vane's. Another explosion of fireworks burst in Vane's eyes.

Well, probably not fireworks, but they seemed like fireworks. His whole body shuddered, and he thrust into the heat of the flesh sliding against his.

Doug's fingers closed on both of them. He slung an arm around Vane's waist, helping him balance.

Vane had wanted a good fucking, but now he didn't. He wanted it quick and hot and furtive. He wanted cars flying by, his shirt off, his naked skin gleaming in the starlight.

"Fucking gorgeous," Doug whispered.

Me?

Vane opened his eyes and wrapped his arms around Doug's neck, thrusting into the fist that held him. "Feels so good."

"You like it?"

"Yeah..." His balls ached, drawing close to his body.

He rested his chin on Doug's shoulder, and his chest echoed with the drumming of Doug's heart. Faster and faster with his fist. They were both panting, Vane moaning, the sound kind of desperate and frantic. Doug's free hand slipped lower, and he grabbed Vane's ass and pulled him in. The feel of Doug's thumb rolling over the head of his cock made Vane thrust hard.

"You're wet," Doug said.

"I wanna come."

He was going to. A tingle grew at the base of his spine, and heat pushed the cold into distant places. He dug into Doug's shoulders and rose onto his toes.

"Oh, my Gosh."

Doug grunted, his voice a rasp. "Do it."

Hot cum splashed Vane's belly under the hem of his shirt. The smell pushed him into a spiral. Light spread inside him. Light and heat. He jerked, spurting again into Doug's fist, stiffening in the curve of his arm.

"Yeah," Doug whispered. "Yeah."

His knees wobbled, and he dug in with his toes for a purchase on Doug's boots. Doug slung his other arm around him now and held him close, brushing Vane's cheek with his lips. "That deserved an audience." Vane giggled and Doug laughed. "But you need to go inside. You're cold."

"Come with me."

Doug squeezed him, kissed his face, and let go. "I've got to get Hoyt home. Go inside. Make some hot chocolate or something."

Or something.

"Hot chocolate seems kind of wholesome."

Doug smacked his ass. "Like you, Joey Johansen."

Vane startled. *Oh, my gosh.* That was his part from *Ranging Wild.* He slipped off Doug's boot, and his ankle gave in the cold mud.

Doug caught him. "Okay?"

"Yeah. You watched the show?"

Doug released him, and dropped his gaze, buttoning his pants. "I looked you up."

"Oh. I was probably pretty bad. It was my first part."

"You were cute as a button. Too cute for LA."

"It's not that bad," he murmured. LA was exciting, and he wanted to go back, but Doug didn't say anything to that.

"Go on. Get inside. I'll have to come back for another look at the house and take some measurements. Sweet dreams, beautiful boy."

Vane scooped up his pants and shoes. "G'night."

"Go."

"I'm going."

He backed up, watching as Doug headed to the roadside. The dark soon swallowed him. Vane turned toward the house. When he opened the door, he whirled at a sound behind him, and something dark shot into the living room.

"Hey," he said. "You don't live here."

The cat—a giant cinnamon, chocolate, and cream furball—ignored him and sauntered into the kitchen without a glance.

"Well, la-de-da," he muttered, closing the door behind him.

16

DOUG CHECKS OUT THE HOUSE

DOUG FOLLOWED DORCAS into Vane's house and jolted to a stop when she froze a foot inside. Gazing past her, he met the glower of the thing she was staring at.

"Look, Doug. A cat."

"Can't hardly miss it," he murmured.

It sat on the coffee table, its fur looking like an ice cream sundae that had exploded vanilla and various shades of chocolate. But at least it didn't have glowing cherry-red eyes. The golden, baleful glare was bad enough. Leave it to Vane to be the owner of a demon cat.

When Dorcas reached out to it, Doug murmured, "I wouldn't do that," and she snatched her hand back with a breathy laugh.

Vane cleared his throat and stuck his fingers in his pockets. He stood in the middle of a living room that looked as if it had been catapulted out of the eighties. It even had a brass and glass curio cabinet in the corner by the couch.

"You have a cat," said Dorcas.

Doug gazed at Vane, holding down a smile.

Vane's cheeks brightened with a pink glow. He waved his arm at the furball on his coffee table. "Yeah. I... Trout. That's Trout."

"I didn't know you had a cat," said Doug.

Vane gave him a glare as though it were Doug's fault he had a cat. The flush of his cheeks brought a brightness into his pale eyes. When Doug's smile widened, Vane's blush deepened. Good to know. Doug intimidated him. He—

No, you don't. You aren't interested. You aren't dating. This is business.

Doug smoothed his face and returned his attention to Dorcas. She was edging nearer the cat again, whose gaze had turned even more baleful than before. Thinking better of it, Doug guessed, she stopped and folded her arms across her chest.

"He doesn't seem to like me."

"Maybe he's gay," Doug said, surprising himself. Vane snorted, and Dorcas gave him a sour face. "Anyway," he added. "I need to look around. Any objections?"

A smile tickled Doug's mouth again as he watched Vane's brows form a furrow above his eyes. He was pretty sure Vane was scrambling to figure him out. Good. Fair was fair. Doug couldn't figure Vane out either. Or his own emotions. How far was he willing to go with this guy?

Well, nowhere.

He wasn't willing to go anywhere with Vane, which was why he'd brought Dorcas with him. Dorcas was a force of life that could pretty much distract anybody from anything. Vane had looked dizzy after two seconds in her presence.

The night under the tree had been two weeks ago. It was past Christmas now, but the memory of Vane's heat still warmed Doug in the cold. The salt of Vane's skin still clung to his tongue.

"Show me around?" Doug asked.

Vane nodded and waved his arm. "Living room."

"Your house is homey," said Dorcas, stepping away from the cat. "I can picture the Walton's living here."

Doug laughed, knowing that wasn't any kind of compliment. Doug's house was more Dorcas's style, and he had no doubt she'd pull it out from under him if she could.

But Doug liked Vane's place, too, and wanted to keep most of its character.

It was a white house with a red trim and a red saltbox roof in the center of a green hollow. Inside, the look was tired, but solid and workable. The living room was dusky from the shade of the trees outside and the winter gloom.

Vane crossed to the staircase. Alongside it, a short hall led to the back of the house.

The hall had the same white walls and narrow baseboards the living room had. White was Doug's preference, but he pictured fat baseboards in a dark walnut for this house.

"Bedroom?"

"Yes. The master... Don't open it!"

Doug froze mid step and gazed back into Vane's stricken expression. *What the hell?* You would have thought he'd threatened to put a bullet in Vane's damn cat to get a reaction like that.

He glimpsed Dorcas's eyes darting between them and raised his palms. "I just need a look. I won't mess your stuff up. Is there a bath attached?"

"Yeah, but I don't use it."

"What's wrong with it?"

"Nothing."

At first, Doug was about to argue. Fixing the rest of the place and leaving one bedroom in a fifty-year time warp made no sense, but whatever Vane was hiding had its claws in him because he was wringing his hands over it. If he'd had a set of keys, he would've thrown them through a window by now.

Which was nothing like Meg and her keys, Doug reminded himself. *They are not alike.*

"Okay. How about upstairs?"

Vane nodded. "Yeah, okay."

Doug backed up, and Dorcas shot him a wide-eyed stare before she followed Vane up the stairs.

Here the light came in, clear and gray. One bedroom led off the landing and overlooked the backyard. Two others opened off a hall around the corner and looked out on the front yard.

Vane pushed open the door to the first room, which was clearly the one Vane was living in. So *what the hell is wrong with the one downstairs?*

His own master had a nook he'd converted into a space

for Meg. There'd been just enough space for a cushy chair and ottoman, built-in bookshelves and a writing desk. She'd disappear in there to read or pay bills. Now he sometimes sat in her chair and buried his nose in her old blanket as though her scent still clung to it.

His heart ached at the memory of her, but he ignored it and crossed to a door near the corner of the room. The closet inside was small, barely the size of a coat closet, but the floor was cedar lined. *Nice touch.*

The floor throughout the rest of the room was oak, but dull and scratched and too light for Doug's taste. Walnut in narrow boards, he decided. And yeah, this was definitely the kind of place for white walls. Ideas floated through his head.

"Well, aren't you in contractor heaven."

He came back to himself and stared at Dorcas. She stood with a hand on her hip and her head tilted. Turning to Vane, she took his arm and leaned up to whisper *sotto voce* in his ear. "Careful. You don't know what you're getting into with him."

"It's called a remodel, Dorcas."

His gaze met Vane's, and Vane murmured, "I don't think I can afford it."

"I worked it out with Rose," Doug said.

Dorcas tugged Vane toward the door. "You really need to think about letting me read for you. This is a new adventure."

Vane gave her a startled look but didn't say anything.

"You guys do whatever," said Doug, "I'm going to get some measurements and make some sketches."

He strode into the hall ahead of them, eyeing the cat sitting at the top of the stairs as he went by. At a sound coming up behind him a moment later, he stopped and turned. Trout sat at his feet.

"I have a dog," he said.

Trout stared.

Weird cat. Doug shrugged and proceeded into the first room across the hall where he tapped at the thin windows. He'd have to replace them, along with the hardwood and drywall.

Nails scattered behind him, and he turned, but he was alone now.

He shook his head and got back to work, listening to the voices downstairs float up to him. The soft buzz reminded him of what living with somebody else had been like and hit him with another stab of pain. He stilled for a moment, eyes closed, holding his measuring tape across a closet door.

His feelings had nothing to do with Vane and the way his laugh made Doug want to pull his giggle out of him, of course. Anybody could stir him this way and make him think of Meg.

His grief came out of nowhere and had no remedy, so he pushed the thoughts away, took a few more measurements, and finished his inspection.

A few minutes later, he found Dorcas and Vane in the kitchen, Dorcas sitting at a big wooden table. They were drinking tea Doug was pretty sure Dorcas had made. Luckily, she didn't have any of her own concoction here.

There were times Doug thought she was trying to poison him.

He looked at Vane, who fixed him with a panicky stare as though Doug was about to tell him his house was beyond repair and they might as well burn it to the ground. "You have a nice house here."

"Very homey," said Dorcas. "You'll get a good price for it. Especially after Doug gets done with his magic."

Vane frowned. "How long is that going to take?"

"Months."

"Well, that's firm," Vane muttered.

His scowl dug a divot between his brows. Doug found it comical on such a pretty face. He drew in a breath—well, that was a dismissive thing to think. Meg would have ripped him a new one for that. The guy's life was like a spinning top and this house might be the only solid thing he had. Being pretty probably didn't make anything any easier on him.

"I'll draw you up a schedule," said Doug. "I'll be doing most of the work myself."

"Don't you have people working for you?"

"I do." He opened a cupboard door. It wasn't aligned. The construction was solid, but the cabinets were old and didn't utilize the space in the best way. He closed the door. "I have other jobs I need to keep them on."

"Paying jobs," muttered Vane.

Doug looked over his shoulder at him. "Oh, you'll be paying."

A slow flush crept up Vane's neck and settled in his cheeks.

"What's that?" Doug asked, heading across the kitchen. "Laundry room?"

"Yeah. The water heater's in there too."

The room was narrow but stretched to the other end of the house. A door led outside and windows that covered the full length of the space let in streams of light. Trout crossed his line of sight, wading through the weeds. Overgrown bushes and wooly trees nestled in the hollow and crept up the hillside.

"Where's the property line?"

"I'm not sure," Vane answered. "Top of the far hillside, I think."

Outside the laundry room a small desk stood next to the back door. Vane's phone lay on it with a pile of mail in his dad's name and a book called *Join the Club: Everybody's Dream is to Own a Restaurant*.

A second after Doug glanced at the cover, Vane approached and flipped the book upside down. Of course, that brought it to Dorcas's attention, as did the pink in Vane's cheeks as it deepened to red. He buried his face in his mug of tea while Dorcas approached from behind him and snagged the book.

She looked at the cover and rolled her eyes. "Oh, honey. You definitely need a reading. Do you really fit into the Everybody's Dream is to Own a Restaurant category?"

Vane lowered his mug and stared into its depths. Maybe Dorcas was rubbing off on him and he was reading his tea leaves. Whatever he saw didn't seem good or bad. He looked up and shrugged. "Well, it's not permanent."

"Maybe not," said Dorcas. "Best to listen to your heart."

She took her mug to the sink and returned to tug on Vane's arm. "Seriously. A reading. On the house. I'm confident you'll come back for more, and you need to see my shop anyway. We'll do lunch."

Chuckling, Doug stepped outside. Dorcas was a pest sometimes, but she'd wiped the desolation off Vane's face and replaced it with amusement for now. Dorcas believed in her ability to guide people through life, though her own was as muddled as anybody's.

Doug hopped down the back steps to the ground. The cold cut like knife blades, and he shivered as he said, "We'll need to get this cleaned up too."

"I like it."

Vane's voice was a rumble near his ear. Doug turned. "It's overrun."

Vane shrugged while Dorcas huddled beside him with her arms across her chest. "Freezing, guys."

"Maybe it'll snow," said Doug.

"It hasn't snowed in decades," she replied.

He cast another glance across the yard. His gaze fell on something that rose above the surface of the ground on top of a low hill. Weeds about buried it, but not quite. "What's that?"

"A well... Or it was supposed to be."

Doug started across the yard toward it.

Behind him, Vane said, "Hey, you!" and for a moment Doug thought Vane was talking to him, but then a kid on a bike flew by, and Vane bellowed after him.

"Get off my property!"

The kid flipped him off and sped down a path toward the hills in the distance.

"Oh, I bet you're popular in the neighborhood," said Doug.

"Well, geez. I don't need the liability."

"The kid's just riding a bike for God's sake."

Doug continued with Vane in tow to the protuberance on the weedy slope. When he reached the well, he walked a circle around it. It hadn't been mechanically drilled. This was a dug well and wide enough to fit an adult.

"There's no pump. Has this always been here?"

"As long as I can remember. I think it's rock at the bottom, but my dad had wanted to hire somebody to finish it. I guess he never got to it."

A brick enclosure encircled it, but the vinyl cap on top was bleached from the elements and cracking.

"Do you want it?" Doug circled it again while he spoke and found the lock.

"There's no water in it. Might be nice, but I don't think I can afford it."

"Oh, God," said Dorcas, appearing behind them. "Holes in the ground give me the creeps."

"I know a contractor I can talk to. If you want to abandon it, we'll need to fill it in. No worries," Doug said as Vane's eyes widened. "I can do it myself if you want to go that route. As long as it's not too deep."

"Twenty, thirty feet, I think."

"Above the water table then."

"A portal to hell," said Dorcas.

"Damn, you're superstitious," said Doug. He tugged on the lock, and the latch wiggled against the brick.

Dorcas shrugged. "I don't care."

Doug retreated a few steps. "I'll work up some options for you. You'll need to replace the lock if you want to keep it. It's loose."

"Okay."

They turned and headed back to the house. On the porch, Doug stomped his feet. "That's all, I think. I'll be in touch."

He held Vane's gaze and watched the color surface in his cheeks again. A shy boy. That made no sense given Vane's erstwhile career and exhibitionist tendencies.

But Doug didn't get far in his thoughts before Dorcas grabbed his arm and tugged him through the kitchen door. "C'mon, lover boy. Off we go."

He glanced back, but Vane didn't follow.

17

LUNCH WITH DORCAS, BUT FIRST...

S OMEBODY WAS KNOCKING on the diner's back
door. Vane opened it on a stranger, who frowned at
him but said, "Hello" in a friendly enough tone.

Vane squinted in the bright light that bounced off the
parking lot and hit him in the face. "Can I help you?"

The guy handed him a business card. "My name's Eli
Johnson. I'm with the Environmental Health Division,
here to inspect the premises."

Vane's stomach plummeted to the floor. "Is something
wrong? Did I do something wrong? I filled out the
transfer."

"Not at all. This is routine."

Yeah, right. Like this wasn't fated to go cock up. It was
his life after all. He was such an effing—

"I didn't think you'd be closed."

The guy was peering over Vane's shoulder. Vane
stepped aside to let him pass. "We've been closed Sundays

and Mondays for a couple months. Next Sunday we'll reopen for the full week again."

The guy looked around for a moment. He had an actual clipboard with forms attached resting on his forearm.

If Vane had been casting for a part, he'd never pick this guy. Maybe a long-haired hippie in tie-dye or a grandmother. Yeah, a grandmother was even better. But this guy was a stereotypical authority figure.

He had the same solid build Doug had—*no thinking about Doug*—and looked comfortable in his own skin. They didn't look alike though. This guy was black with a receding hairline on a high forehead and a short, compact build. *See, nothing like Doug.*

Stop thinking about Doug. Think about the fact you're screwed.

"I generally like to see an establishment at work, but I am here," the guy said.

"I'm... not really familiar with things."

"What is your position here?"

"I own it."

A small smile floated across the guy's face. "Oh yes. The transfer? So you've recently purchased it?"

"It was my dad's. He died."

A grimace appeared now. "My condolences. Very sorry to hear that."

"Thank you."

"May I look around?"

Vane half shrugged, half nodded. "Sure." The guy set

off, and Vane followed him. "I've never run a restaurant. I'm still trying to get up to speed."

"I'll leave you a packet. There's a lot of good information. Do you still have Mr. Flores?"

Unfortunately.

"Oh yeah."

The guy—Eli—peeked under the tables as he made a circle of the dining room. Vane peeked too. *Please no rats. Please no mice. Please no cockroaches. No dirt. No broken things besides... me.*

"It smells good in here," said Eli.

"Those are my pies. I'm trying to invent something special."

"Well, you've invented a wonderful smell."

"Thank you."

He wanted his pie ready for Sunday's reopening. He wasn't sure about the ginger. He'd found a recipe for a cake with coffee in the batter, so he was trying a pie with espresso and orange. It did smell good.

When the guy headed in back, Vane followed and tripped over a mat. He caught himself and giggled. *Shoot. Stop. He's going to think you're storing nuclear waste in here the way you're acting.*

But Eli didn't seem to notice. He ducked into the first bathroom. Popped back out. "No soap in the dispensers."

"I know. I was going to fill them."

Eli wrote something down and continued to the kitchen. *Oh gosh.*

"This isn't as clean as I'd like to see," Eli murmured.

"I was gonna get to that after my pies."

"Were you planning on offering those pies for sale?"

"No. Honestly, I wasn't. I'm just testing."

Eli stared at him. Then he smiled. "I tell you what. I have been called a neat freak before. This isn't bad, just not what I'd really *love* to see. I'd like to come back when you're open, and talk to the employees, so I'm going to give you a to-do list and return in a week."

"A week? Monday?"

Eli chuckled. "Monday. And let me tell you—" He paused while Vane's heart raced in his chest. "I just hope those pies are ready for sampling."

Vane giggled. *Stop.* "Me too."

"Good. I'll just finish here and write up my report. Trust me on this. You don't want people getting sick or seeing something that spurs a complaint. There's nothing here that warrants closing you down, but make sure you do what you can today. If you're trying to reinvigorate your business, and it seems that you are, you want to control everything you can. The department wants you to succeed. I'm readily available, and if you ever have questions or concerns, I'm happy to help." He lifted his clipboard. "Let me write this up, and I'll be out of your way."

Vane nodded. "Okay. I'll take care of everything."

"Why is that open?" asked Eli, looking over Vane's shoulder.

Vane turned and faced the refrigerator. "Oh..." *I'm afraid of it.* "I was going in and out."

"Keep it closed when you aren't in it."

Vane nodded and watched Eli step over the milk crate

holding the door open. He didn't follow. He remained in the hall and swallowed the dread squirming in his gut.

Baby. It's a refrigerator.

But it wasn't. It was a portal to Hades like the well in his backyard. *Beware all ye who enter here.*

He didn't know why he thought he was going to get locked in and die, but he did. After a moment, Eli pushed the crate into the hall with his foot and let the door close.

"Boxes of foodstuffs need to be up off the floor. Also, your temperature is just on the line. You'll need to watch that. It's a pretty serious violation, so you might want to have somebody check the gaskets on the door."

Vane chewed on a nail and followed Eli back into the dining area.

"Mind if I sit at a table while I write this up?" Eli asked.

"Go ahead. Would you like some coffee?"

"I'd love it."

Vane poured him a cup and set it down right when the timer for his pies went off. He put the pot back on the burner and hurried into the kitchen.

The aroma of sugar and orange wafted from the oven in a wave of heat when he opened the door. The first pie was a deep russet color, the second as dark as the coffee inside it. He set them on a rack to cool and returned to the front.

Eli swallowed the last of his coffee and stood. He handed Vane a copy of his report. "I'll get your packet for you while you look that over. I know Mr. Flores has an inspection binder, so make sure you get that from him."

Vane stared at the report, but the words blurred. He was buried under a million other things he had to do now. And heck if he was calling Luis. This was his place.

AFTER WAVING ELI OUT OF THE PARKING LOT, Vane covered the pies with a clean towel and headed to his car. It was eleven-forty, and he was supposed to meet Dorcas for lunch at noon. He was really too busy, but she was Doug's best friend, and apparently Vane was turning into a sap for the guy.

His Mustang was the only vehicle in the parking lot now. The white sun shone on it, but the inside was still cold. He turned on the heater and drove away, keeping his eyes peeled for squirrels.

Dang things.

They lived in the tree outside his bedroom window. Or maybe only one did—a deranged one that woke him with its enraged chattering every morning. Today, he'd awoken to find Trout sitting on the windowsill. He could've sworn the cat was smiling.

As he drove, he mulled over his lunch date with Dorcas. On the one hand, interaction was good while becoming a hermit was not so good. But on the other hand, Dorcas was connected to Doug, and he ought to resist Doug. Did he need the complication?

Besides, for all Vane knew, Doug was Fisher in disguise, waiting to show his true colors. Vane was a sucker for that kind of guy.

At least Dorcas was friendly and cheerful. She'd have nice friends, wouldn't she? Doug would have to be nice.

When he hit Poppy Brush, Vane slowed again, looking for a place to park on Main Street. The bright winter light blazed down on the colorful awnings over store entryways. People strolled along the sidewalks and sat under the heating lamps in front of delis and cafés. Why anybody would want to go to a diner in the middle of nowhere...

Oh well. Stop thinking about it.

Vane pulled into an empty spot against the curb, got out of his car, and yanked his coat tight.

Holy moly. It was false advertising to be this sunny.

Holding his collar to his neck, he headed down the sidewalk. Ahead of him was the green and white awning Dorcas had told him to look for. It lay a chilly swath of shadow that looked like a black puddle across the pavement.

Vane shivered but let go of his collar and waved as Dorcas approached from the other side of the café. She waved back and then...

He slipped.

Colors pinwheeled. Red brick. Blue sky.

But it took only seconds before he hit something solid and staggered backwards with it. Luckily, the solid thing held him up. He moved away into Dorcas's path as she skittered up to him—*in freaking heels*—and latched onto his arms.

"Oh, my God," she gasped. "Thank you for catching him."

Her eyes were wide on something over his shoulder. The solid thing. Vane twisted and looked back.

A guy stood there, swiping the front of his overcoat.

"Careful," the guy said. "Looks like we're having some icy weather."

"Sorry. I didn't mean to land on you. I'm a klutz."

"No problem."

The guy strode off, leaving Vane with Dorcas, who released his arms and rolled her eyes. "Oh, my God. You are so accident prone."

He laughed. "I like how you pull your punches."

She grinned back at him. "You're getting to know me already. Now c'mon. Let's get you inside where there are safe chairs and tables."

"Wonder what I stepped on."

"Ice?"

"It's sunny out."

"It's freezing. Into next week they say."

She was wearing a coat that looked as if it had been made out of a couple dozen of Trout's relatives.

He plucked at her sleeve. "Is this real fur?"

"God, no. That's gross, Vane."

"I didn't say I wanted it to be real fur."

They stepped inside a space that had been done in various shades of green. Sage-colored walls textured like grass, moss-green upholstery, drapes the color of asparagus. The floor looked like birch. Everything in the Elm Street Café was light and airy and nothing he could afford for Eileen's. A weight settled on his shoulders.

Dorcas led him to the hostess station. "They have the

best salads," she murmured. "That's why everybody comes here."

Well, okay. Food he could do.

"I'm making pies," he said.

"Pies?"

"For the diner."

"I like pie."

But she said it in a normal voice, not the reverent whisper she'd reserved for salads.

A woman appeared in the long hall that separated the dining space, smiling as she approached. She wore green. A snug forest-green skirt and a loose spring-green blouse.

One half of the café was snug and cozy with darker green curtains in a leaf pattern. The other half was light and bright with a wall of windows on a garden. The garden was bare now except for the pink-petaled magnolias.

The hostess tucked two menus under her arm and led them into the bright space.

Vane held Dorcas's chair, a hint of a tremor in his fingers. That almost-fall had scared the bejeezus out of him. He sat across from Dorcas and took his menu.

"We have two lovely seafood specials today," said the hostess. Vane was pretty sure the word *lovely* would never be used to describe the fare at Eileen's. *Plentiful. Hearty. Stick to your ribs.* He tuned back in. "... We also have sole in a delicate chive sauce with a half Caesar or spring green salad with herb vinaigrette."

Definitely wasn't Salisbury steak. Or chicken-fried steak. Or hot turkey sandwiches.

Vane chewed his lip and stared at the menu.

"Your server will be right with you," said the hostess.

Barely a second after she stepped away, Vane looked up and blurted, "The health inspector came by today."

Why he shared this with somebody he barely knew stumped him, but Dorcas didn't indicate she thought it odd. She frowned and said, "I didn't think you were open today."

"The inspector didn't know that. Of course, Luis wasn't there, and I don't know anything I'm supposed to know. And why—" He leaned against the table and spoke in a murmur—"would anyone come to Eileen's when they can come here? Or any other place on Main."

Dorcas set down her menu and smacked it with the flat of her palm. "Stop that. You can't think of it that way. It's your unique selling proposition that's going to bring people in."

"You mean my pies?"

"Maybe. Just remember. The diner isn't your life. Don't sink all of your energy into it. Figure out how to make it a comfortable place for a certain crowd of people. You cater to them. Their unique needs. Make it simple. Sinking yourself into Eileen's isn't a good idea unless that's the life you want. You need to be able to pick up and go home without a lot of trouble. You have a goal."

The words stuck into him like needles. Annoying pricks that shivered up his spine. Dorcas understood him. She wasn't consoling him over his lost life, because it wasn't lost. He could go back to it, and this time without Fisher weighing him down. Without all the doubts. Without...

Doug.

He swallowed and flipped through the menu. "Wagyu Beef Steak Salad. Tilapia Piccata with Lemon Tarragon Sauce. Do you know the demographics in Poppy Brush? A little over 5,600 people. Over fifty percent are in the twenty-five- to sixty-four-year-old age group. Those are the people who come to places like this."

"Well, honey, that figure doesn't include the several other towns in Poppy Brush's vicinity, so that ups your ratio. You just concentrate on the age group that might want the casual atmosphere of a diner. Especially one that has some sort of appealing feature."

"Like world famous pies?"

"Like world famous pies."

He snorted a laugh.

Their server arrived, and Dorcas ordered the Caesar salad. Vane went with the Wagyu beef and a bowl of pasta e fagioli.

He raised his glass of water and toasted Dorcas with hers. "Thanks for getting me out."

"My pleasure. I plan on pumping you."

"Pumping me for what?"

"Stories about Hollywood."

"I waited tables. And before that I answered customer questions for a credit union. I hated that job. And before that, I acted in a sitcom that was cancelled halfway through its first season."

Dorcas sighed and pursed her mouth. "Well, I understand disappointment."

"Yeah."

"You might not want the way your life turns out, but sometimes you might like it better." He waited. "I expected to be happily married," she continued. "I was married."

"But not anymore."

"Nope. But that's what I mean. I'm a forever and ever kind of girl. We tried. It just didn't work. So I took my half of the house when it sold and moved back home here."

"You grew up here?"

"Meg was my best friend. Doug was kind of our third. We lived in the same neighborhood and went to the same school, but things change and hardly ever turn out the way you think. We went away to college, and a few years later my sister died."

"Oh gosh, I'm sorry."

"It's okay, honey. My parents were devastated, of course, though that was the only possible outcome. She'd been sick for as long as I could remember, but I guess knowing it was going to happen didn't help at all. They sold the house, and when I got out of school, I moved to be near them, met my husband and got married. I'm grateful now there were no kids. It made our split easier. There was nothing negative. I just think we married too soon."

For Vane, splitting from Fisher was still hard. He dealt with it by pushing it to the back of his mind every time it surfaced. "You seem happy here."

"I am. That's what I was saying. Doug and Meg split up too. They went to different colleges. We all met again at our ten-year reunion. We held it at the Covey Mansion. Do you know where that is?"

He nodded and took a drink of water. "We took a field trip there once."

The house was at least a hundred years old, but people mostly came to see the poppies. Every spring they bloomed in bold strokes of orange like an impressionist painting. That meadow was how Poppy Brush Village got its name.

"We had a blast," said Dorcas. "I still can't believe how good we got along. I never saw myself coming back here, living with my best friends again, and starting a business. I saw myself married. That's all I'm saying."

"Your shop does well."

"I have to be flexible."

They were silent as the server set their plates down. Vane took a bite of the steak. It was meltingly good, garlicky and spicy, and served on a bed of crisp butter lettuce.

"You have to come see it. You still need a reading."

He was about to decline the reading, but instead he said, "I'm sorry about your sister."

Dorcas sighed, her fork poised above her salad before she put it down and gripped his wrist. "And I'm sorry about your dad. Even if you weren't close. Sometimes that makes it even worse."

That definitely wasn't anything he wanted to think about. He pulled his arm away and stuffed another piece of steak in his mouth.

"I want to keep Eileen's for him," was all he said.

"I think that's wonderful. Just don't forget your own life."

Her voice fell a little at the end, and a pained look crossed her face.

"Mr. Kam called," he said. "He'd asked me about helping with his after-school class before Career Day, but I forgot until he called again. I don't know. I might do it."

Dorcas's eyes brightened. "Oh, me too. Can you get me on? I always wanted to be a part of the acting world. Fortunately," she said with a laugh, "I knew not to bother. I can't act, but I can do makeup and costumes. Will you put in a word for me?"

"I said I wasn't sure."

"You have to. Consider it a way to keep your skills sharp."

"My skills are dull," he said and marveled at the lack of self-pity in his voice. He'd begun to wonder if maybe he'd gotten lucky snagging the part of Joey Johansen. Maybe he'd had the right look, and that was all. Maybe he had no talent, at least not for acting.

Dorcas shook her head. "You're going to do it. Me too." She gave his arm another squeeze. "You'll be my new best friend."

"What about Doug?"

She fixed her gaze on his. "Oh, I think Doug has his eye on another prospect."

He blushed, and Dorcas returned to her salad. When they finished, she paid, slapping his hand away from the bill. Then she hooked her arm in his elbow and walked him to his car.

"I don't usually trip over my feet," he said.

She laughed but didn't let go. "So when do you want us?"

Her mouth made words that made no sense to him. "What?"

"You said the inspector left you a list of items to address."

"You don't—"

"I'm calling Doug. You call Rose and see if she can make it. Maybe you should stay closed on Sunday. You haven't announced you're reopening or anything. That'll give us a whole day."

"Shoot, you're as bossy as Doug."

"That's why we get along, honey." She smiled and kissed his cheek.

They were at his car now. He stood on the sidewalk and watched her stroll away. The fuzzy coat that reminded him of Trout swung gracefully with every step.

She bowled over him the way Fisher always had. Only Doug didn't overwhelm him, which Vane couldn't explain. Doug blazed confidence too. Solid and strong like a Gary Cooper, but young and hot like—*nobody*.

Doug wasn't the actor. Vane was. *Remember that.*

"An actor," he whispered. An actor with a career and a life in LA.

Fortunately, the roar of the traffic drowned out the sound of his snort.

18

CLEANUP

DORCAS PULLED TO the side of Eileen's and shut off the engine. "C'mon," she said. "It'll be fun." Doug eyed her. "I'm using my day off to scrub bathroom floors. Not seeing the fun."

She made a sour face and reached behind Doug's seat for her shoulder bag. "Your reward for patience and good deeds is a dream come true."

"You've been inhaling too much incense, Dorcas."

Her laugh pealed in the frosty air. Doug blew into cupped hands as he followed her inside.

Liking Vane was as annoying as opening a can of sage-green paint and getting avocado. *That wasn't what I wanted.*

Doug wanted a family, the sound of voices in his home, and busy holidays. The flibbertigibbet bobbling the sponge Rose had tossed him didn't want any of that. He didn't even come home for his sister's wedding. Doug's parents had been old when they'd had him. Now they were gone, and he had no brothers or sisters nor any distant family.

Vane stooped to snatch up the sponge he'd dropped, fingering his hair back as he stood, his gaze lighting on Doug's. A smile flashed across his face, but then he turned to Dorcas, who flung her arms around him and kissed his cheek.

Doug turned away and found Rose. "I didn't think you'd be able to make it," he said.

She looked up from a binder she had opened on the counter and flicked a loose strand of hair out of her face. The rest of it was tied into a ponytail on top of her head. He relaxed in her presence. The timing hadn't been right for them, but he was always aware of her appeal. If only things had been different. But then there was Vane...

Though Doug resented it, Vane cast a shadow over Rose. He invaded Doug's thoughts and intruded into his workday. His to-do list went ignored while he researched wells and sketched house plans with Vane in mind. Would he like homey or old-fashioned? Sleek or modern? Then he reminded himself it didn't matter because Vane wouldn't stay long in a place like Poppy Brush. He was—*vain.*

All that glitters. Fame and fortune.

Doug watched him where he stood in the alcove at the back of the main eating area, staring outside with Dorcas. He pointed at something.

Then Rose spoke and drew Doug's attention back. "I got somebody from work to watch the kids." She laughed. "Mel has four of her own. She probably won't even notice mine."

Other voices carried over from the kitchen. "Who else is here?"

"Luis, much to Vane's annoyance. I guess I wasn't supposed to invite him."

"Dorcas will keep Vane occupied. Don't worry."

She smiled and pushed a piece of paper to him. "We need to take care of these items, but I thought since we were here..."

"Top to bottom," Doug finished for her.

She nodded. "I'd love to hire somebody, but it's really expensive."

"No worries."

"We'll pay you in pie."

"Pie?"

"Vane has decided to attract customers with his Famous Oatmeal Pies. They're actually pretty good."

Gonna take more than pie.

He gazed at the paper Rose had given him, lifted his head, and said, "Okay, people. Come on over. Let's make a plan and divvy this up."

Dorcas saluted him.

A few minutes later, they got to work scouring and scrubbing every surface. They vacuumed and mopped and washed windows and ceiling fans. Later, as Doug rinsed out the bucket he'd been using to clean the walls, Vane's voice drifted back to him. "What are you doing sneaking around in here?... I saw you... Like heck I don't..."

Doug left the bucket in the sink, wiped his hands off on his pants, and took the few steps down the hall to the office.

The room was small and crowded. The furniture—desk, chairs, and worktable—was too big for it. Opposite the desk was a shelving unit for office supplies and a file cabinet.

Vane and Luis stood beside a stack of banker boxes next to the desk, glaring at each other. Luis's glare was a lot more impressive than Vane's.

"What's up?" Doug asked.

"Caught him snooping."

"Snooping?" Luis practically spat. "I'm here helping you. I don't know why when you're just gonna run this place into the ground. You wanna take over with the cooking? Well, whatever. Go ahead. I guess you don't need me no more."

"I didn't say that. I said I wanted to help with the cooking. I was talking to Rose anyway, and don't get me off the topic. What were you looking for?"

"I was cleaning!"

"Inside the boxes?"

"I don't need to do anything to help you out here." Luis stuck a finger in the direction of Vane's chest. "You fix this mess."

"Can you just finish up the walls for me?" Doug asked, focusing on Luis. "I left a bucket in the bathroom sink. I'd appreciate it."

Luis stared at him, eyes narrow, emotions battling on his face, and Doug wasn't sure which one was going to stick. It wasn't just anger. Luis bristled with an energy that was more like frustration. But the emotion that stuck out for Doug the most was one that hit close to home too. *Grief.*

The boss Luis had liked and who'd liked him back was gone, and now Vane was in his place. But Luis was the employee, and his temper wasn't going to get him anywhere. After a few tense seconds, he threw a glare at Vane and stalked out.

Doug shook his head. "Seriously?"

Vane's face was shiny red. "He's up to something."

"Like what?"

"I don't know." He licked his lips. "Somebody's been calling me."

"Calling you about what?"

"I don't know. They disconnect."

"Have you called back?"

"It's blocked."

"And it just started happening?"

Vane shuffled and peered down into a box on top of the stack by the desk. Folders piled inside. "It's new."

"The phone is new? So maybe it's not for you."

Vane raised his head. "It is."

Doug's exasperation came out in a sigh. "Why would Luis prank call you?"

Vane's eyebrows met in a glower. "I don't know."

Doug stepped closer. A hint of a tremor ran through Vane's body. "Luis has no reason. Would somebody want to bother you?"

The frown disappeared, and Vane's eyes widened. "No."

Nothing in that sounded truthful, and it was Doug who frowned now. "Are you hiding out?"

Vane snorted. "No. I had a life, you know."

"I don't know anything," Doug said. "I just know you're here. I also know Luis isn't out to get you. You have a vivid imagination."

Vane scowled, looked toward the door, and drew closer. "I'm not making this up. He was looking through the boxes."

"For what?"

"How would I know? That's what I'm saying."

Doug rolled his eyes. "You're paranoid. Come help me in the fridge."

He stepped into the hall and looked back. Vane's stare was locked on him, his eyes blazing silver. "Help you?"

"Clean."

"Oh."

He still didn't move. Doug ignored him and proceeded down the hall. He found another bucket, filled it with water and cleaning solution, and took it into the cooler. The door didn't close behind him. He glanced back. Vane slid in with his white-knuckled fingers gripping the door's edge.

With a grin, Doug returned a few steps, and leaned past him into the hall. "Hey, Rose!"

"What?"

"We're in the cooler. Don't forget us."

"I'll make a note."

"Ha, ha."

He backed up, and Vane let the door close, crossing his arms over his chest after he stepped all the way in. "I guess they can hear us if we can't get out."

Doug laughed. "Well, now you have another reason to

be pissed off at Luis. You're gonna need him to fetch you the cold stuff if you're too scared to come in here."

Vane didn't move, but their gazes connected until Vane's rose as he tipped his head back and stretched his neck.

The movement was strange, slow and languorous, and so lovely Doug caught his breath. He tingled, electrified at the sinuous, sexy dance that was taking place in front of him.

Vane lifted his arms like wings and twisted his body in a lissome circle. The fridge wasn't large and longer than wide, but it allowed a few feet of space for him. His hips swayed and his hair clung to his face.

Doug's mouth opened, his heart quickening.

Then, just like that, Vane stopped. He let his arms fall and tipped his head slightly toward the floor. "See? I'm in here. Big. Effing. Deal."

Against his flushed skin, and in the dim light, his eyes glowed. His lips looked as rosy as a flower's petals, his hair like silk. Though Doug would swear it was against his will, he was bizarrely smitten with him.

"Those boxes," Doug said. "They can't be on the floor."

Vane blinked. "What?"

"The food."

"Oh. That just came in."

"Needs to be off the floor though."

Vane swiveled his head and stared at the box of cheddar cheese. "Okay."

Doug breathed out. *Here to clean. Just to clean.*

He wasn't here to get involved with an irresponsible actor who couldn't be bothered to be there for his family. Doug closed his thoughts on Meg and the time he hadn't given her. Time he'd spent on work sites and in other people's homes.

Then Vane bent over and pretty much wiped out every thought in Doug's head except ripping the guy's pants off. A tiny strip of underwear appeared. Were those boxers? Briefs? He glimpsed orange, red, and green. The colors reminded him of sherbet.

Vane squatted at a box. Above the multicolored waistband, a dusting of dark hair crept up his tailbone.

Damn.

"Where do you get your underwear?"

Vane jerked upright and spun around. "Are you looking down my pants?"

"Can I?"

"Perv."

Doug stared at Vane's parted lips and slightly flared nostrils. Color was seeping into his cheeks, but he frowned, and the frown flirted with becoming a glare.

"You think I'm a waste of space, don't you?"

Doug blinked. "What?" *Where the hell did that come from?*

"I'm gonna make this place work. I have my reasons for doing things."

"Okay."

"I'm serious, so don't tease me."

The tone plucked at Doug's heart and filled him with pity. He hated bullies, always had, and it shocked him to stare into the mirror of Vane's eyes and see somebody he didn't want to be.

But he'd been careless, he realized now. Everything he had churning in his head about Vane had shown on his face the way Luis's emotions had shown on his. The hurt in Vane's voice scraped his skin like broken glass.

"I didn't mean to tease you," he said, sticking out his hand as he stepped closer. "Friends?"

Vane giggled.

Damn, that was cute.

"Well, we don't have to be totally serious," Vane said.

"Good. So on that note..."

Contrary to everything he should be doing, Doug sank into Vane's heat and scent with a deep internal groan. He backed him into the shelves, gripped his blood-hot nape with one hand, the wire rack with the other, and leaned in.

Vane didn't move, his eyes tracking Doug's, his breath warm and dry. "Is there air in here?" he whispered.

Doug paused and smiled. "Why, yes, I believe there is."

"You're doing it again."

"You won't die in here. I promise," he murmured and brushed Vane's lips with his.

Vane's breath puffed faster, and Doug imagined that the drumming in his ears was the echo of Vane's heart. His nervous heart, beating a continuous stream of adrenalin through his high-strung body. His nervousness was physical, like a vibration from a tuning fork. But when Doug pressed in, his lips softened and opened, and he slung his arms around Doug's waist.

Doug squeezed his neck and pulled him closer. Vane's cock poked him. He pressed a thigh between Vane's legs and rocked a groan out of him. *So sweet.*

He dipped his head. The tip of his tongue met Vane's. Vane opened wider, and something in Doug's brain snapped and blew his thoughts away.

He absorbed the softness of Vane's lips, the damp heat of his nape, and the silkiness of the hair brushing his fingers. The sunny, metallic scent of sweat filled his head. The slide of Vane's tongue and the smack of their mouths were as melodic as a song.

He scraped whiskers with his thumb and shivered at the warmth of Vane's fingers under the back of his shirt.

Reaching down with his free hand, he grabbed Vane's ass and pulled him in.

"Um... Guys."

Shit.

Doug broke away and twisted around, steadying himself against the sway of Vane's chest against his back. His heat burned through Doug's shirt and melted his bones. Why wasn't there a cot in here? Or a blanket in a quiet corner where he could lay Vane down and bury his dick in his warm body?

He cleared his throat. "Hey, Dorcas."

She smirked, a hand perched on her thrust-out hip. "Hey, Doug. I wanted to let you guys know we're done out here. I guess you're not... Done, I mean."

"Funny."

She grinned. "I know."

"We'll be right out."

"Take your time."

"Damn pest," he muttered when she'd gone.

Vane stepped out from behind him. He bit his thumbnail and dropped his hand a second later. "I guess that wasn't very hygienic."

"My kiss?"

"No. Doing it in the refrigerator."

"Oh, that." Doug moved closer again, the flighty nerves in Vane's eyes enticing him. He pressed another kiss on him. "I liked your little dance," he murmured.

"That was nothing," Vane whispered.

"Are you holding out on me?"

"I might be."

Doug reached around him and snapped the waistband of his sherbet-colored briefs. "Guess I'll have to come round again and investigate."

"You know where I live."

Doug nodded and took a step back. The space between them yawned. "Yep. And we start work on your house bright and early tomorrow."

Vane groaned. "I don't do bright and early."

"Get an alarm clock."

He headed across the floor and hit the light switch. The dark fell, and Vane muttered, "That door needs an alarm."

"You're not gonna get stuck in here."

But when Vane stepped back into the hall, a frown pinched the skin between his eyes, and woke a warning inside of Doug.

19

STRANGE BEGINNINGS

THE AIR WAS like ice, but Doug opened a window to let out the dust Vane would probably delight in pitching a fit over. The guy was already a pain in the ass, and they were only four days into the job. Other than Sundays and Mondays when Vane covered for Luis's days off, he was always here in the house, pestering Doug and complaining about every little thing. Paint color. Doorknobs. Window frames. The floor.

Doug stared down at the stripped and sanded boards beneath him. They should be dark. It should be a whole new floor, actually. But not for Vane. No.

"I want my old floor," he'd said.

"Your old floor is junk. And light. It should be dark."

Doug was still stuck on his vision of dark floors, dark baseboards and white walls. That's what he'd first imagined, and Vane would like it too, he just needed to trust Doug. Though why Doug thought he knew what Vane wanted was a mystery. Or why Vane would trust him after knowing each other only two months. But Vane's quirks—his giggle and thumb chewing and klutziness—had gotten under Doug's skin. The guy was a disaster, and Doug really, really liked that.

But Vane's love of the beat-up red oak floor?

Just. No.

"We can spend the money on something else," Vane had said.

We. Doug had been careful not to let that word sink in too far. *We aren't a we.*

Contractor. Client.

Brother of a friend.

Eventually, Doug had gone along with it though. "I guess I can replace the worst boards. Patch and stain it." *Dark.*

"Okay."

In the room across the hall, Doug opened another window, trying for a cross flow.

Downstairs, his crew boss, Geff, was leaning against the counter, his phone to his ear. "That'll work... Couple weeks... No worries."

Doug poured himself a cup of coffee and stared down at the sketch on the kitchen table. It was more intricate than it needed to be, but he liked to sketch. Liked to build the things he sketched. He had five miniature homes he'd built into a miniature neighborhood in his garage. Then he'd started building the house for Meg. *You had time for those things but not for her.*

And time to create a dream kitchen for Vane on a piece of paper.

"Mario finished the Wagner job today."

Doug looked up. "That's perfect."

Geff tapped a corner of Doug's sketch. "Fancy smancy."

He didn't say *too* fancy smancy, but that's the impression Doug got. "What?"

"Nothin'."

He was probably wondering why Doug was doing most of the work himself after the teardown. Doug didn't tell him so, but no way could Vane afford his usual fees. Throwing in the labor for free kept the cost down, but Doug wasn't paying his crew for things he could do himself.

"Top a the line," said Geff.

"Yeah," Doug agreed. "I wouldn't mind these cabinets for myself."

"I want the cabinets I have."

Fuck.

He turned to meet Vane's frown. It wasn't a glare though, but maybe that was worse. He wasn't mad. He looked hurt and nervous—and stubborn—as though Doug and Rose were trying to push him out of the only thing he had right now. Well, the only thing besides a diner that had been on its last leg for years.

But it was Rose who was Doug's friend and had hired him, and Doug had to remember that. Vane wasn't staying. He'd sell this place eventually and dump the proceeds back into the diner. Or sell the diner too and use the cash as seed money for a revival of his career.

Wanting to keep things out of sentiment was a lousy

idea in the short term. Reimagining somebody else's house the way *he* wanted it was a lousy idea for Doug.

Dark wood and white walls. White on white in the kitchen.

"Your cabinets aren't salvageable."

"Why not?"

Okay, they probably were. They were solid wood. All Doug had to do was strip the old paint, refinish, replace the hardware, and reinstall them. Voilà.

"I can get you new. A modern design at cost."

"This isn't a modern house." *True.* "I want my cabinets."

Doug shrugged. "Okay. You're the client."

Vane flinched—barely—but it was there, and Doug grimaced. "We'll make them good as new," he added.

"Blue," said Vane.

"Blue," Doug echoed.

"Have you seen Trout? I can't find him."

"I thought you didn't like him."

"I don't."

Vane turned and left, and Doug looked at Geff with a raised eyebrow. "Blue," he murmured.

Blue. Something with a gray tone. He pictured it pretty easily when he thought of it.

In the other part of the house, a door opened and closed. A few seconds later, footsteps pounded on the stairs.

"Anyway," said Geff. "The windows'll be in in a couple weeks. You'll need help with that. And the plumbing for the new bath. Me an' Mario can start on that tomorrow. I'll pull up the floor today. I was expecting asbestos, but turns out we're good."

"I'll pick up the tile tomorrow."

Geff pushed off the counter, and Doug headed outside to his pickup. He took the back door and rounded the corner of the house, tracking the stir of weeds in the distance. The cold bit through his coat and stung his nose. He blinked to clear the sting in his eyes.

Was that Trout over there?

Doug wasn't sure. The breeze wasn't strong, but the weeds moved, rolling in the sunlight toward the shadows under the trees.

After he grabbed a vinyl binder out of his pickup, he returned to the house and climbed the stairs.

Vane was in his room, rubbing a thumb over a red line on the closet door frame. It was one of a couple and looked like the kind of thing people did to mark their kids' height as they grew up. The ink had faded over the years but was still visible.

Vane didn't look at him when he asked, "Are you going to paint over these?" As though Vane had no say in the matter.

Doug shook his head, sympathy rising inside him. "Not if you don't want me to."

Vane shrugged. "You think I'm an idiot."

"I think you're beautiful," Doug said without thinking.

Vane shot him a startled stare. Surprised too, Doug just stood there, staring back through a pale light as still as an old photograph. Nothing seemed to move, not even time or space. If someone later told him he'd spent a hundred years with Vane in his gaze, he'd believe it. But the moment broke when Vane looked back at the marks and a shiver ran through him.

Doug crossed to the window, but instead of closing it, he rested his hand on the frame and said, "There's Trout."

He motioned with his chin when Vane pressed against him, his body heating Doug's.

The cat had planted itself in the middle of the yard and sat staring at the house. "Looks like he's just waiting us out," Doug said.

"I don't want him to freeze."

Doug glanced at Vane's torso in his thin T-shirt, nipples straining against the thin fabric. "You're more likely to freeze."

A slow smile curved Vane's mouth. "Warm me up."

"We have company," Doug murmured.

Vane's eyes widened slightly as though only now noticing the sounds down below. His gaze shifted to the door, his expression heavy-lidded, color rising in his cheeks.

"I feel strange," he said.

Doug laughed. He didn't know what to make of that. "You do?"

"Yeah."

This guy was strange. Maybe Vane made sense to himself, but to Doug he was a land mine. One minute annoyed and anxious, the next pensive and sad, now lascivious and playful. He was nothing like steady Rose. And nothing like Meg, come to think of it. Doug wasn't sure they had anything in common, any real reason to get together. Even so, in the last week, they'd met for coffee one day and gone to a movie the next. Were they dating?

"I'm going for a drive with Hoyt on Saturday. Want to join us?"

Vane smiled. "Sure."

He slid graceful fingers up his shirt. His clumsiness had disappeared for the moment. The steps moving him backward on the floor were fluid and strong. His faded jeans clung to his lean legs and narrow hips.

"Do your guys know you're gay?" he asked.

"Bi," Doug said. "And I doubt it."

"Hm. Secrets."

"Some."

With mesmerizing slowness, Vane tucked his fingers under the hem of his T-shirt and lifted. As the cotton slid over his skin, Doug fixed his gaze on the growing strip of pale flesh, goose bumped in the cold. A tantalizing treasure trail formed a dark shadow into Vane's jeans. Doug's mouth went dry as he drank him in, naked in the daylight. All that fair skin. How hairy was he? What color were his—

Pink.

His nipples were small pink rounds on his chest. No six pack, but his belly was lean with ripples of muscle. His chest had a hint of definition and a patch of sparse hair in the center of it. When his arms rose over his head, he tugged his shirt off and spun in a slow pirouette.

Pure grace, though Doug expected him to take a header across the room at any second.

"Somebody might come up," Doug said.

Vane's eyes twinkled. He licked his lips and grinned.

Interesting. When Doug crossed to the empty doorway and stood in front of it, Vane giggled.

"Protecting my reputation?"

"Mine."

The T-shirt flew into a corner of the room, and Vane hooked his thumbs in his jeans. His hips swayed as he hummed a low tune that floated like a tantalizing whisper. His movements were seductive and bewitching. As lissome and flowing as a willow tree. Doug's heart quickened as he inched his jeans lower with every twitch of his hips. The vee below his lean belly dipped into shadow. Then, as another sinuous spin took him closer to the window, the deep crack between his pale ass cheeks appeared.

Doug swallowed. "They might see."

"My house," said Vane.

That should have sounded arrogant, but it didn't. Doug thought he detected a hint of surprise. Was this the first thing Vane could really call his own? A beat-up house? Well, he owned his Mustang, but maybe that didn't mean anything to him. It wasn't his history or his family's.

Doug straightened in the doorway, gaze pinned to a tiny strip of—*blue?, lavender?*—across Vane's ass. "Turn around."

Vane obeyed, the pale white light streaming around him. He kicked off his shoes. The strip of lavender was there in front too, hugging Vane's pubic line. Something about the filthy look of those dark curls against the delicate purple color heated Doug's blood.

He squinted. "Is that lace?"

Vane didn't answer. He pushed his jeans to the top of his lean thighs. The hair was a light dusting, and his briefs were—

Fuck.

Lace. A strip of thin cotton that barely covered him. The pouch for his junk was loose, the weight of him tugging at the flimsy material.

Holy fuck.

Doug's dick strained against his jeans. His heart pounded a mile a minute while Vane chewed on his lip, his eyes in sleepy-looking slits. The sinews in his pelvis were tight as wires.

Voice grating like sandpaper, Doug forced words out of his dry mouth. "Where'd you get those?"

"Amazon."

A laugh burst out of him. "Seriously?"

Vane nodded. "I like sexy underwear."

"Oh, hell yeah. So do I."

Vane grinned and tipped his head back, gazing at Doug along the line of his nose. The light glowed around him like a halo now. He dropped his jeans and kicked them out of his way.

"Put your socks back on. The floor," Doug added when Vane hesitated. "It's been sanded, but just in case. No splinters."

"Don't you want to do it on the floor?"

"No. You're gonna jerk off for me."

Vane groaned. Mesmerized, Doug watched him slip off the briefs. "Throw those my way."

Vane did. An underhanded toss. Doug snagged the

lacy fabric and pressed it to his lips, breathing in Vane's scent. Musky and floral. Christ, did he spray perfume down there?

Doug's heart pounded again. His eyes feasted on the body in front of him, on its glorious composition of muscle and bone. It was spare but with a hint of fat under his belly button that Doug just now noticed. His chest and shoulders flared, broad and flat. For as vain as Doug had imagined him, Vane's body didn't bear the signs of somebody who cared much about his appearance. But he had to be vain, didn't he? Or did he really see something else in the mirror?

As Doug watched, Vane sucked in a breath and shivered. His dick bobbed, pointing straight out, flushed red, tip wet. Doug's mouth watered, and his balls ached as heat pooled low in his belly.

"Go on," Doug murmured. "Stroke it."

Vane blew out a breath, and a smile flitted across his face. Now he seemed nervous. He brushed his fingers down his length, and his hips strained, following his touch.

Doug curled his toes. How hot was Vane's skin?

But Doug wasn't going to touch him. He was going to torture himself by watching him. For now, Vane was his wind-up toy.

He ought to feel guilty for treating Vane this way, but his body only grew hotter. Besides—he knew Vane wanted it. Deep in his eyes, a part of him was begging for it, imploring Doug not to hurt him. If anything could pull Doug into him, it was that. The need. The offer of a trust he hadn't earned. The gift of Vane's nakedness. His exposure. Goose bumps covered him as tiny shivers ran over his skin, and Doug could tell he liked Doug's eyes on him. Maybe anybody's eyes, and the desire to watch that surged through Doug's body was a shock.

He wanted this too.

"Faster," he said.

Vane's groan deepened. He backed toward the window, covering the pane of glass with his body. He blocked the light and took on a stronger shape in the shadows.

Doug tossed his underwear back. "Come on that. Not on the floor."

Vane snorted and twirled the strip of lace like a tassel. His body mirrored the motion, flowing in a half turn. His ass appeared. He wiggled it, and Doug grinned, feasting on the little ripple. "Yeah," he murmured.

Vane's slow spin continued until he faced Doug again. He thrust his hips out and pushed his dick through his fingers. His cock was as straight and slender as he was. He leaned his head back and licked his lips again, pointing his gaze at Doug as he reached down and cupped his balls. The panties, still hooked on a finger, dangled in front of his thighs. Then he stepped wider, easing the finger into the dark between his legs.

Doug bit back a groan, imagining Vane's heat, and fumbled behind him for the door. He batted the edge with his fingers and closed it quietly.

"Chicken," Vane whispered.

He shrugged. Geff had no reason to come up here, and he'd call out first anyway. Vane rested his ass on the windowsill. Geff had no reason to be out back either —hopefully.

"Close the window," Doug said.

"No."

"It's too cold."

Vane frowned. A shudder ran through him, but that was from his thumb rolling across his slit, probably. He straightened anyway and twisted sideways to close the window. As though sensing a trigger, the furnace kicked on and blew a gust between Vane's legs. His eyes widened, but he stayed there, though it was slightly to the side of the window.

Doug leaned back, relief flowing through him. Now he could enjoy this.

"No noise," he said.

"Bossy."

"Of the guy downstairs, yeah."

Vane leaned against the wall, head tipped back, stroking faster. But he kept his eyes on Doug's the whole time. The pleasure he was feeling played out on his face in his frown and bitten lip. Doug held onto Vane's gaze as though holding onto him, soothing and caressing him through this strange scene.

Vane panted. "I'm gonna—"

"Shhh."

Vane bit his lip again. Then his eyes flew wide with a vague look of surprise. He rocked against the wall, the smell of cum strong in the warm air, and still Doug didn't look away.

Vane's head fell. "Jesus," he whispered.

Now Doug moved. He crossed the room, throbbing in his jeans, aching in his chest, and pulled Vane into his arms. Vane hugged him in return, resting a cheek on Doug's shoulder while Doug stroked his sweaty back. "That was so damn sweet."

"Sweet? I was going for sexy."

"That too," Doug murmured.

When Vane lifted his head, he brought his lips to Doug's. The kiss didn't last long. It was soft and warm. A shared breath. He smiled into Doug's face, and Doug ran a thumb over Vane's cheekbone.

This was such a lousy idea.

20

SLIP AND SLIDE

A HAND STOLE under the blanket and brushed Vane's belly while lips tickled the back of his neck. He snuggled into the warmth of his dream until it exploded like wisps of mist.

Shoot.

Now cold stole under his blanket. He thrust his arm out and shivered. The warm breath on the back of his neck that he'd imagined was Doug's blew away, and goose bumps popped out in its wake.

Geez, why was it so cold? What was that noise?

His head pounded with a tinny jangle that stabbed him in the ears until the sounds formed into Rose's ringtone.

He slapped at the hair stuck to his cheek, pushing it away. The room was gray and strange looking. Well, of course, it was strange looking. It wasn't his bedroom. Doug had moved his furniture into his mom's old craft room while they finished his floor, but he'd fallen asleep on the couch under a blanket that did nothing to warm him.

The cold crept in through the leaky window casements and under the door.

He smacked at the coffee table, and something thumped in the kitchen. The music stopped.

"Oh... Dang."

With a groan, he sat forward on the edge of the couch and dropped his forehead onto his palms. His pulse pounded against his skull. With a headache like this he deserved to be hungover, but he wasn't. Instead, he felt as though he'd woken up in the center of an iceberg.

The cold reminded him he'd turned the heater off for some brain dead reason and Doug wasn't wrapped around him. Though he'd take the cold over the mild air in Fisher's condo any day. No summer or winter. No world with sun and rain and sweet flowers.

This was better.

But geez, it was cold.

After another moment, he struggled to his feet and staggered into the kitchen. The edges of counter and cupboards blurred in the dull light as he gazed around. Trout blinked at him from the top of the desk by the door. When Vane went over to him, he hit something with his toe and sent it thudding into the wall. Great. His phone.

"Did you knock that on the floor?"

Trout didn't answer.

Vane crouched down and grabbed the blurry device. "Feed you in a minute."

He stepped into the pale light seeping through the window in the back door and called Rose.

"Ugh," she said. "Call Luis, please. I texted you his number."

"What for?"

He turned his gaze outside where a silver shimmer lit the gray landscape. Frozen grass. Frosty trees. A blanket of low clouds in the sky.

"Alice and Ceejay quit."

He scowled at the motionless yard, furrowing his brow. "Who?"

"Our waitresses. *Your* waitresses."

Clarity snapped into his brain, pushing the blur away. But they were open every day of the week. Everybody had more hours, so why quit now? "What the heck, Ro. They can't just quit."

Of course, they could though. They could do what they wanted. They were probably working at the Elm Street Café and making a lot more money than they'd ever made at Eileen's.

"They stuck with us for a long time, sweetie. Now you're changing things to try and stay open. All they see is risk. Call Luis. I have to get ready for work, and you are going to have to deal with this."

"Me?"

"Vane, sweetie, I can't anymore."

Right. It was his turn. Karma. Payback. He gritted his teeth and stared at Trout, whose fluffy body was taking on shades of brown in the growing light. *Effing wonderful.*

"I guess I'll go in."

"Call Luis."

Heck, no. He didn't want to. He got a can of Halo from

the cupboard and opened it. Trout dropped to the floor. "I'd better go," he muttered.

"Call me later."

"'Kay."

Upstairs, he turned on the water in the shower in the bathroom across from Rose's old room and stripped. His head still ached from being wedged into the arm of the couch. He bent under the hot stream with a sigh but couldn't stay.

He should call Luis.

But he didn't want to.

He wanted to call Doug.

Who isn't your boyfriend, you dip. Geez.

But Vane wanted him to be. He wanted somebody he could gripe to. Somebody who had good ideas and could see a well outside and know it shouldn't stay there like that. Vane had had no idea. That was Doug's thing, and he had no trouble speaking up. He'd invaded Vane's life, but Vane had only known him a little over two months.

Think of Fisher.

It had been only three months before Vane had moved in with him and look at that. Had he ever been happy? In love?

Well, hello, you aren't in love with Doug either.

He turned off the water, got out of the shower, slipped, and grabbed onto the edge of the enclosure with a gasp.

Shoot, he needed a keeper.

A few minutes later he was dressed and hurrying downstairs. He let out Trout and hit the number in Rose's text.

Luis's voice rumbled. "Whadda you want? I'm busy. You aren't."

"What the heck does that mean?"

"I don't see you here."

"Well, duh. I don't read minds. I just found out."

"I don't get paid good enough for this."

"Are there customers?"

"You ask that? You can't just assume the best? Shows how much you care. Oh, that's right. You don't care. You probably don't want customers, so you don't have to sweat it. But, yeah. We have customers."

Vane yanked open the back door, skin shrinking in the cold. Trout padded on in.

"Why don't you just do your job? You don't know me."

"I am doing my job," said Luis. "I'm here. I know you. I got to know you with everything your dad never said."

"Screw you."

"You too."

"Are you quitting too?" Vane asked. "Are you just gonna run?"

A low chuckle rolled into Vane's ear. "You first."

"I'll be there in fifteen."

He disconnected the call, shrugged into his jacket, and fetched his keys from the pocket. Trout lay on the blanket on the couch, one paw stretched out across the cushion. "Use your litter box."

No response.

Vane opened the front door, stepped outside, and flew. His brain blanked out for a few seconds as the world spun. The weeds and trees and sky swooped away, and he was staring at the underside of the porch roof.

His mind grabbed at an explanation, but he was upside down and couldn't make any sense of it.

He flailed and hit the porch, something sharp smashing across his back and knocking a grunt out of him. A strange, numb grip held him tight, and he blinked at the porch roof again.

A split second passed.

From the grunt to the bolts of light bursting in the dark behind his now squeezed-shut eyes was no time at all. Pain dug into him and broke him on the icy porch steps. His lungs stalled, and he sank into a dark he wanted to stay in, but he had nothing to hold onto and floated up again. The ache in his chest made him gasp for air, and the pain flared like a sunburst.

"Oh gosh... gosh..."

He took another breath and—*Don't move!* No, no. He wasn't going to move. He was going to stay right here. The pain hit like a wave with a brief respite before the next wave and the next. The cold nipped at him, and a cat sat on his chest. No. Not *a* cat. His cat. Trout.

Trout stared at him.

"Hey," Vane wheezed.

Trout blurred as tears welled hot in Vane's eyes and ran cold on his skin. He swiped at them.

Now Trout lay down, stretched his paws across Vane's shoulder, and inched his nose under Vane's chin.

Comforting me?

Was he going to die? Did Trout sense that?

Vane swallowed and slipped the fingers of one hand into the warm fur. Trout's rumbling purr vibrated inside him. Weird. He never would have thought Trout gave a frig about him. He wondered where the cat had come from. Wondered if something was broken inside him.

He bent his knees, flattening his shoes on the porch, and the pain loosened its hold. The high-crested waves fell to a rhythmic lapping. He took a slow, deep breath as the throb rolled in and out.

It still effing hurt though.

He turned his head and stared at a sheen that spread across the porch like a shallow puddle. He stretched an arm to it, and ice crumbled under his fingers. Ice? On his porch?

He gripped a rail, muttered, "Sorry, Trout," and rolled onto his side.

"*Ow*," said Trout.

Yeah, me too.

A second after he pushed onto his elbow, a burst of fluid gushed out of his mouth, and his head pounded again. Oh, geez. Images flashed in his eyes with each thump. He saw Fisher's condo, the ranch where they'd shot some of *Ranging Wild*, and his mom, smiling at him from the couch in their living room. *"I'm okay, honey. Go out and play."*

No, no.

A wave of pain flowed from his back into his belly, but he gripped the railing again and dragged himself to his feet. "C'mon, Trout."

The slide of his foot scraped up ice as he inched his way to the door. Trout slipped past him, and Vane shut him inside and turned back. A lacy outline of frost showed where he'd lain. It was thin, but too thick to be on his porch under the roof with no rain.

Luis?

The thought was like a shot of adrenalin to his heart and for a moment the rush of his blood was a roar in his ears. Could Luis have wet the porch so it would freeze? Set him up? How much more of the diner would he get if Vane died? Vane wasn't sure. He hadn't asked Rose for any details but thought she and Luis would split forty percent. That wasn't much, but with Vane's portion added to the pot it was fifty percent each.

Was it enough to kill over?

He shivered. Those were crazy thoughts. He shouldn't think them, but the possibility was stuck in his head now.

Holding onto the railing, he clung to it as he descended to the walkway. From there, he stepped onto the crunchy weeds and made his way to his car. At least his head was okay. He probed it to be sure. The pain in his back tightened like a corset around his waist, but it was dull now. A couple vehicles passed him on the road. One came roaring from behind and left him in a wash of taillights.

Whatever. He'd get there, eventually.

It took him longer than usual, but soon the glow in the diner windows appeared in the gray dawn. Three cars dotted the parking lot. He parked and got out.

The aromas of bacon and coffee met him in the hallway. He headed to the kitchen where Luis turned at his entrance and glared at him. "Glad you could make it."

"Look—"

"Just take this out. Middle booth."

He accepted the two plates and swayed. *Oh shoot.* Still shuffling, he made his way into the dining area. A pair of older guys sat at the table and watched him approach. *Please don't let them talk. Please don't—*

"Are you Ethan's boy?"

He nodded and set the plates down. "Yeah, I am. Vane."

The heftier guy on the right stuck out his hand. "I'm Dave. And this is Ollie."

Vane shook hands with both of them.

"We're glad you reopened on Sundays," said Dave. "This is our place. Every Wednesday and Sunday morning you can find us right here. Very sorry about your dad though. Losing a parent is always a hard thing."

"Not a day goes by that I don't think of my folks," said Ollie. "My mom was eighty-eight an' my dad went three days before his ninety-sixth birthday. That's not bad."

"Soundin' younger every day," said Dave.

Ollie hooted. "That's true."

The words in Vane's mouth jumbled. He swallowed and said, "More coffee?"

"Yes, please," said Dave.

Vane took small steps, picked up the coffee pot, and circled back around the counter.

"Your dad was super proud of you," said Ollie over a mouthful of Denver omelet.

Vane bobbled the pot, sloshing coffee. He tightened his fingers on the handle. "Oh." They went on eating as though that hadn't been a dumb response. "Well... Enjoy," he added.

A couple at another table and one lone guy at the counter still worked on their meals. Vane filled their coffee cups, poured himself one, pulled his keys from his pocket, and unlocked the office. The boxes of files and invoices were still stacked by the desk. They probably didn't need the invoices, but he needed to sort and lock the personnel files in the cabinet again.

A buzzing filled his head, edging toward pain. He grimaced at the chair—a million miles away. Really only a few steps, but the sitting part... He set his cup on the desk and sank. His back screamed until his ass hit the cushion.

"Holy moly," he whispered.

But his head cleared again, the only sound the churn of the computer after he tapped the space bar.

He picked his cup back up and took a sip.

Up front, the bells on the entrance door jangled, and the place grew quiet again.

He logged onto Craigslist. It wasn't like Luis couldn't handle those customers himself. He wasn't rushed in the kitchen. No dishes had piled up in the bins.

Vane finished his coffee and focused on the screen in front of him. He needed at least one server. The rest of the time he'd fill in himself. That wasn't what he'd planned, but his plan clearly wasn't working anyway, as another wave of pain confirmed. He wanted to get back to his screenplay, but that was a joke. He hadn't even plugged in the flash drive.

Because you're a failure. A screw-up, and you'll see it the minute you read those words again.

But he'd liked his characters and the setup he'd given them. Robbing a jewelry store to save a restaurant might not be a probable storyline, but that was the fun of it. It was goofy and colorful.

Right. Delude yourself.

He posted his ad and peered into his empty coffee cup.

"Resting after your busy day?"

He spun in his seat. The room swirled for a moment, and he had to blink a few times to settle it. Luis stood in the doorway, arms braced on either side of him—*blocking me in?*—his face twisted into a glower.

"You couldn't handle that?" Vane asked. "Three effing customers?"

Of course, he couldn't. Not if his plan was to get Vane rushing outside onto a frozen porch. The dizziness hit him again as he imagined the sky spinning above him. The ice hadn't been natural. Not that much of it on a covered porch after a dry night. Vane's heart raced, and he squeezed the handle of his cup. He'd throw it if Luis came any closer.

"Leave it to you to come in after the rush," Luis said.

"Rush?"

Luis straightened and smacked the doorjamb. The sound hit like an electrical jolt through Vane's body, making his heart beat double-time.

"Selling this place is better for me," said Luis. "But I'm the one here trying to make it work."

"I'm here."

"Sitting on your ass."

Before Vane could make his mouth work, Luis had pushed away and headed back to the kitchen. Jerk-off. The shake in Vane's body woke the pain in his back. He rested his elbows on the desk and his head in his hands. His stomach growled, but acid flooded his mouth at the thought of food. He sat still for a while, drifting until the bells rang again.

A lady with two kids took a seat at one of the tables.

The customers seemed to roll in one at a time. Nothing that could support the place, but he was glad of it today. He got a couple hits on his ad and arranged for an interview in the afternoon. Afterward, he took a break and headed outside.

The cold shook him, but Luis not being out here was a giant selling point, so he burrowed in his coat and got into his car. With the doors locked, he let go of some of his nerves. Luis wasn't likely to attack him with a chainsaw in a parking lot during the lunch hour.

When he opened his eyes later, the side of his head felt frozen to the glass, but that was okay. The corset around his waist had loosened and let the pain seep out.

He drifted again until the clomp of a car door roused him and he looked out his window.

A girl stood by a purple Kia, yanking her black skirt down over red- and black-striped tights. The sweater under her bomber jacket was black too. Her hair was dark brown like his and tied in a long braid around her head like a crown. She was pale with delicate features. In fact, she looked like him. *Weird.*

But Vane had never known he was a type until he'd auditioned for *Marvelous Marcel* and an army of look-a-likes had appeared.

As he watched, the girl tucked a manila folder under her arm. He guessed she was there for the interview. Black ballet slippers covered her feet. Excellent winter gear.

Kids these days.

He stepped from his car and stood still, clamping his hand down on the top of the door. Wooziness left a prickly sweat on his skin, and an echo rumbled in his hollow belly. *You need to eat.* A donut. He might be able to keep a donut down. Or pie. How was his pie selling? He closed his door, arms stiff at his sides. In the office, he found an application.

The girl waited near the register, bouncing her manila envelope against her legs as she shifted side to side.

Well, at least she had energy.

"Hey."

She swung her head, and her gaze locked on his for a moment. Then she flashed him a mouthful of teeth. Bits of her braid had come loose and wispy curls clung to her face. She thrust out her hand. "Hi, I'm Penny."

Vane held his ground against the force of her. She pumped his hand.

"Nice to meet you. I'm Vane. Would you like some pie?"

Her smile didn't waver, but she tipped her head to the side. "Pie?"

"To eat."

"Um. Sure. Cherry?"

"Oatmeal."

Her mouth opened. She showed him the silver ball in her tongue. "Oatmeal? That's a pie?"

"Yeah. Like sour cream and raisin."

"You lie."

He laughed and said, "Dang, that hurt. Really. Do you want to try a piece?"

"Bring it on."

"Okay. Go sit down. Anywhere."

Geez, she was bold. What was that like? To shake it out in the parking lot and not care. To approach a stranger with a neon smile. Maybe she was acting. Maybe she was that good. Vane's smile was an act, a thing he put on and wore. In public...

A shiver ran through him as the memory of standing naked in his window came back to him. He felt the burn of Doug's eyes on him. Peeling him bare to his real self, as though no skin existed between him and who he really was.

He plated a piece of a pie nobody had eaten yet, got himself a donut, and brought both to the booth she'd picked by the window.

She wriggled at the sight of the pie. "I approve of your interview style."

He swallowed his laugh before it could get out too far and wake the ache in his back again. He relaxed against the booth. The smell of sugar and vanilla tickled his senses. Perfume? Probably his donut. He stared at it, and his stomach rolled.

"You okay?" she asked.

He nodded. "Thanks for coming in."

"Oh, my pleasure. Is it always this slow?"

His heart jittered inside his chest. Of course, she wouldn't want to work here. "No. We, uh... We were closed a couple days a week. Some... issues, but now we're open seven days, so business'll be picking up soon."

She nodded and took a bite of her pie, eyes widening as she chewed. She pointed at her plate with her fork, smacked her lips and said, "Wow. This is good. You'd never know. Oatmeal pie. I would never order this," she added, taking another bite.

"Really?"

Nodding, she munched through her mouthful of pie in a few chews. "I will now," she said after she swallowed. "I love it. It just doesn't sound like a pie, does it? It sounds like a cookie. Or breakfast."

Well, heck.

He touched the application with his finger. She'd already completed some of it. "You've been a server before?"

"Uh-huh. Wanna see my résumé?"

"Sure."

She tugged it from her folder and passed it to him. He studied it. "Cottonvale. Where is that?"

"About an hour from here. Up 49. Used to be called Anderson. I don't know why they changed the name, but I go to the community college near there. I'm hoping to transfer to UCLA next year. They have a film and television program I'd love to get into, so working here won't be my career or anything. I want to be upfront about that."

Her face was distracting as heck. She was made for drama. Violet shadows under her eyes gave her a tragic look, but her lips were thin and curled like a harlequin's mouth. She'd be an indie film darling. Quirky and dark.

He sank back against the booth and pulled off a piece of his donut but didn't eat it.

"You sure you're okay?" she asked again.

"I might be coming down with a cold."

"That sucks. Drink lots of mango tea with lemon."

"Mango?"

"Antioxidants and vitamin C from the lemon. Oh, my God." She leaned against the table. "A friend of mine was taking those chewable vitamin C tablets, and they ate the enamel off her teeth. For real. Now she's using Dead Sea salt to remineralize. Mango and lemons."

He nodded, entranced with the crimped and curled corners of her mouth. "When can you start?"

She bounced on her booth. "Are you giving me the job? Seriously? Anytime. I'm real flex except for a class I'm taking at an acting studio in town here. I really, really want to keep that if possible." She pushed back in the booth and bit her lip with a pensive frown on her forehead.

Vane sighed. "Are you acting now?"

"No." She laughed. "It's important."

"Mr. Kam's studio?"

Her eyes lit up. "Yeah, that's it."

"Mr. Kam was my first acting teacher."

"No way. Really? You're an actor?" She cocked her head, the smile on her lips flickering. "A real one?"

It was strange how she hit him in the heart like that as though she'd meant to. "Not anymore," he said.

She pouted. "Why not? Why would anyone Not. Want. To. Be. An. Actor?"

She laughed, and he snorted, forgetting about the pain waiting to spring out at him, but it didn't come this time. Instead, the stabby fingers in his back loosened their grip. "Oh, I don't know," he said. "All the glamour's in the food industry nowadays."

She winked. "Good for us."

"Lot a work though."

"I'm up for it."

Vane nodded. "Tomorrow at seven?"

"Cool." She bounced to her feet, shimmying her skirt down her legs. "See you in the morning. Love that pie, by the way. "

Well, that was somebody. Now he had to figure out how to get people to order it.

The bells on the door jangled behind her. He dropped the plates on the counter, his uneaten donut still on his.

"Cottonvale?"

He jumped and forced himself not to give Luis the satisfaction of seeing him clamp his hand over his heart. The guy had snuck into the dining room and stood there, staring at him. A creepy suspicion that Luis had some kind of voodoo doll of him hidden in the kitchen shivered over Vane's skin. Vane imagined him hiding in the dark, sticking needles into him. *Jerk.* He glared into Luis's frown. *Cottonvale? What of it?*

"So?"

"That's an hour away. Too big a commute for no tips."

"Why won't she get tips?"

"Look around."

"Well, you're gonna be out of a job too, you know?"

Maybe that's what Luis wanted. Maybe Vane had wrecked his plans by reopening.

But Luis just snorted and returned to the kitchen. It was almost time for the dinner crowd if there'd be one.

Vane smelled meatloaf and pork chops and pepper steak cooking. He ate his donut. The sugar helped. He took a bottle of water into the office and sat down. A wave of weariness crashed over him and weighed him down until he laid his head on his folded arms and closed his eyes.

Like a memory and not a real sound, the bells on the door clattered. Voices floated back, and the bells jangled again to the clack of plates and Luis's laugh. The sound of his laugh swelled in Vane's head like a physical thing. A gray cloud with a face in it. A slash of teeth.

His heart jumped, and he floundered to escape his dream, gasping as he flung himself back in his chair.

A shadow filled the door.

21

TAKING CARE OF VANE

THE MINUTE DOUG opened the door of his pickup, Hoyt knocked him flying into the diner's parking lot.

He staggered with a laugh he probably shouldn't be laughing. "Damn, Hoyt."

The golden spun.

"I don't have a ball. Go on. Do your business."

"*Ruff.*"

"No ruff. No ball. Go on."

But Hoyt didn't go. He stared with a befuddled look instead, as though Doug had spoken to him in Cantonese.

"What?"

"*Grrr... ruff!*"

The dog's face cracked into a grin.

What the hell do dogs think about? "Go on, you weirdo." For some reason that seemed to do the trick and Hoyt bounded off.

While he waited, Doug cupped his hands and

breathed into them. He nodded at a guy who emerged from inside the diner, got in his car, and drove away. Now only three vehicles remained—Vane's, a silver Camry, and a pickup Doug assumed was Luis's.

A jingle of tags carried on the air. Doug whistled, and Hoyt shot out of the shadows, racing across the lot. The goofy dog's ears flapped like wings. He panted through a happy smile, spun in a circle, and dropped his chest to the ground.

"No ball."

Hoyt whined.

Behind them, a couple with a little girl in tow emerged from inside and crossed to their car.

Doug opened the truck cab and patted the seat. "Up."

Hoyt dropped his ass.

"C'mon." He patted the seat again. "Be a good boy."

Hoyt didn't budge for a moment, exploding into a scrambling leap a second later when he launched himself into the cab. After turning in an awkward circle, he plopped down and huffed again.

Doug closed the door and strode into the diner to the clatter of bells. Luis peered out from the back, his shoulders drooping like deflated balloons a second later. "Oh. I thought you were somebody."

"Slow?" Doug asked.

"I give 'im a week."

Irritation stirred inside Doug. He wanted this to work for Vane because he knew what it was to have his business on the line and devote everything to it. Support helped, but Vane wasn't going to get it from Luis.

"Where is he?"

"In back sleepin' it off, probably."

"Sleeping it off?"

Luis shrugged. "See for yourself."

He veered around the counter and strode down the hall. A light was on, but the atmosphere was gloomy. Vane sat at the desk, head resting on top of his folded arms, eyes closed. Maybe he was hungover, but... a frown creased his forehead, and the fingers of the hand Doug could see twitched against the desk.

With a tingle running down his spine now, Doug entered the office. His step fell quietly, but Vane reared back with a gasp and fixed blown pupils on him as he took another step closer.

"Vane?"

He kept his voice low and approached slowly. Vane's frown turned into a grimace, and he bit down on a moan. *Drunk, my ass.*

"Vane, what is it?"

He took the last step. Vane raised his hands and gripped Doug's waist. He dug his fingertips in, transferring the vibrations inside him to Doug. A breath later, he released the lip between his teeth and said, "I was dreaming."

"You were more than dreaming. What's wrong?"

"I didn't have a server today." He pushed himself upright, palms flat on the desk now and said, "My other one quit on me too."

"I know. Rose called. Why didn't you call me?"

Though why should he? Were they friends? But then

Vane stepped into his arms and leaned against his chest, pressing his chin into Doug's shoulder. A faint odor of sweat wafted off him. His skin was warm, but a shiver ran through him. Doug stroked his back, trailing his palm downward.

"I got caught up in trying to fix it," Vane murmured. "I hired a girl though."

"Already?"

Vane nodded, and Doug tugged him in closer, only to freeze when the muscles under his hand went rigid.

A breath whistled over Vane's teeth. "Shoot."

Doug released him and leaned back, holding his arms now. "Are you hurt?"

"No... I fell."

"Where?"

"At home. This morning."

"This morning? Tell me what happened."

"I slipped, that's all. On my porch. I landed on a step."

"Jesus—"

"I'm okay."

"No, you're not. Let me see."

But he turned fussy as a little kid and pushed Doug away, sitting on the edge of the desk and forcing a smile. "Want something to eat? On the house."

"No. I'm taking you home. We'll order a pizza."

"We're not closed yet." An uncertain look came onto his face.

Doug took his hand. "You're going home."

"What about Luis?"

Gritting his teeth, Doug struggled to clamp down on

the heat building inside him. *Sleeping it off.* "Luis should have noticed you were hurt. There's nobody out there anyway. Sorry," he added, pulling Vane's jacket off the back of his chair.

"People don't like the sound of my pie."

"The sound of it?" Doug held the jacket out, and Vane slipped an arm into it.

"They think it sounds like breakfast."

He leaned in and kissed Vane's cheek, the sweet scent of his sweat filling his head. "It's oatmeal."

"Breakfast."

"Call it something else."

Doug led Vane into the hall and glanced at Luis, who opened his arms in a what-the-hell-is-this kind of gesture. "We're leaving," Doug said.

"I guess so."

"Vane hurt himself."

Luis frowned but dropped his arms. After waiting for Vane to lock the office door, Doug ushered him outside.

"It was him," Vane whispered.

Doug leaned in. "What?"

"I slipped on ice. I think he wet my porch down, and it froze."

"Jesus, Vane." Doug opened the side door of his truck and pointed at his boisterous, wriggling golden. "Get back... That's a serious accusation."

"Who else would do it?"

"Nobody." Hoyt squirmed closer to the door, chuffing at them. "It froze last night. Why would he anyway?"

"I—" Vane went white, one foot on the runner, a hand

clutching the top of the door. He swallowed and wheezed a laugh. "Sorry."

Doug's stomach flip-flopped. He stroked Vane's shoulder and the back of his neck. "I think we need to go to the hospital."

"No, we don't. I'm okay. It's your dang truck that's the problem."

"Need a lift up?"

"Gimme a sec."

Hoyt sprawled with his paws at the edge of the seat. "Get back," said Doug.

The dog retreated, and Vane hefted himself high enough to slide onto the seat. After he scooted in, he blew out a breath and smiled. "See?"

"You're in a lot of pain."

"I just need aspirin. I didn't eat, so I didn't take any."

"We'll order in. Whatever you want. Buckle up."

"Doug."

He paused, gripping the top of the door in cold fingers. Vane whispered, "It was Luis."

Though he thrummed with tension, no hysteria wove through Vane's voice.

Doug pulled his lips against his teeth, thinking for a moment. Vane was melodramatic as hell and could believe something that wasn't even remotely true. Yet... ice on his porch? And Luis?

According to Rose, Luis had worked at Eileen's almost from the day her dad bought the place. Did that give Luis incentive? Doug had never thought of him as anything but an average, hard-working cook. Now he was seeing shadows where he knew there were none, but Vane was so sure he didn't fall by accident.

"I'll check around outside," he said. "Maybe one of my guys left the hose on. I hope not."

He closed Vane's door, hurried around to the other side and climbed in. Condensation fogged the windshield. Muttering, "Look what you did, dog," Doug swiped the glass with his forearm.

Hoyt's tail thumped the seat.

"Nice puppy," Vane murmured.

Doug started the engine and backed up. "Do you like dogs?"

Stupid question. It wasn't like he'd never met Doug's dog before. Thank God, they weren't on a first date. *So whadda you think of those Seahawks?*

"I guess. Fisher didn't want any."

Fisher. Right. The ex. Doug didn't want to think about the ex. "I had a dog when I was a kid. Riley."

A smile hid in Vane's voice. "Really?"

"Yeah. He was a mix we got from the pound. But you definitely like cats."

"No."

Doug glanced over, and Hoyt turned to stare with him. When Doug spoke, he made his voice a low whisper. "Did you tell Trout?"

Vane giggled. "He wouldn't care."

"True."

Vane went quiet for a while.

When Doug glanced over, he saw Vane's shadow

against the door and his head against the window. "Will you let me take a look at your back?"

Vane straightened. "Perv."

"Well, a guy's gotta try. But seriously."

"Okay. After I eat."

"Deal."

"I was looking at the brochures and stuff the health inspector left. They inspect farmer's markets too."

"Um. Yeah?"

"I was thinking. I can sell the pie there. Give away samples and coupons. Half off a second entrée kind of thing. The market's year round."

"How much is the space?"

"A hundred and fifty."

"That's a lot of pie."

"Well, I'm hoping they come in and buy meals. It's just something to tide us over. I have to come up with something."

"I don't know if you know this, but when your dad bought the place a development was planned for Moon Valley."

"Rose said something about it."

"The valley's about half a mile down the road, but the deal fell through. Environmental stuff and other contingencies the developer didn't want to deal with. The guy was a jerk. But what I'm saying is, your dad staked his investment on the Moon Valley development."

"I know. Rose said."

"Without it... Well, it's a slow bleed for Eileen's. I

didn't know your dad or why he'd take this chance, but Eileen's has always been a couple heartbeats from closing."

He swung onto Vane's road.

"Must've pissed Luis off that I kept it open."

"That's not why I told you this. Luis isn't trying to kill you."

"Or get rid of me. I know somebody did that on purpose."

"How do you know that?"

"I just feel it."

Doug ignored the pouty tone in Vane's voice. Something else was in it too. Something heavy and immovable. Maybe Vane was the kind of guy who'd never budge once he set his mind on something. Was Doug wrong? Could Luis have done something like this? He almost snorted. No. Even if Doug didn't trust his own instincts, he trusted Rose's.

He turned into the driveway and rolled down the incline to the garage door.

The trouble was, Vane believed himself.

"I'll look around," said Doug. "Let's get you inside first. Is Hoyt okay to come in?"

"I'm okay with it," said Vane, opening his door. "I don't speak for Trout though."

Luckily, Trout wasn't anywhere around. Vane sat on the couch, and Hoyt bounded up beside him.

"S'okay," he said, waving Doug off when Doug reached for Hoyt's collar.

He sank back, closing his eyes, and Doug stuck out a finger at Hoyt, whose ears perked as he stared wide-eyed at Doug.

Be good, Doug mouthed.

Outside, he took his flashlight from the glove box and panned it over the porch.

The lamp by the door was gummy with cobwebs and dirt, and its thin yellow light barely pushed at the shadows. The porch looked wet, but it was damp and dark out. The air was cold, but not cold enough to freeze anymore.

A brush of his fingertips over the boards didn't tell him anything either. Was it damp enough to be melted ice from this morning? How long would it stay wetter than normal winter damp? It wasn't like Doug had ever timed it. Frosty grass became wet grass in the afternoon. The icy lacework on the windows steamed off in the daylight.

He stepped off the porch and walked to the side of the house where the hose was coiled in a heap. He supposed one of the guys might have left the tap open, but the nozzle wouldn't have done more than leak. The ground was hard-packed mud, tromped by what looked like boot prints. He gripped the handle of the spigot and turned it. It was off.

Now he straightened and swept the light in a circle. Wooly bushes loomed and disappeared. The place needed a pair of pruning shears taken to it, but Doug liked the yard. He liked the old-fashioned house, even though it needed white walls and dark wood.

A minute later, he strode back inside and froze midstep. Vane eyed him with a put upon smile. Trout sat on his chest, glaring at Hoyt, who rested his chin on Vane's shoulder and gazed forlornly at the cat.

Doug shut the door. "Get off."

Trout didn't budge, but Hoyt scuttled back. Vane gave Trout a nudge as Doug approached, and the cat jumped down and sauntered into the kitchen.

Doug sat on the coffee table. "The hose wasn't on."

"Well, there was an ice slick on my porch."

Doug shrugged. He wasn't going to argue. He couldn't wrap his mind around it being Luis for a good reason—it made no sense. But Vane had been hurt and was grasping at straws to explain why.

"Can you get out of your jacket?"

"I guess."

Doug helped him, tugging the sleeves off his fingertips. "You doin' okay?"

"Just stiff." He bent forward and let Doug pull his shirt up his back. "Am I gonna walk again?"

The bubble of laughter in Doug's chest felt good and blunted some of the ache inside him. He knew a part of him was connecting Vane's injury to Meg, but that was too raw a place to go, and he was grateful for Vane's humor.

"Very funny."

A wide, purple swath stretched across Vane's back. Luckily, though, the blow had hit above his kidneys. Doug ran a hand over his ribs. Nothing felt broken.

"I barely hit the step. My feet flipped up, and I landed mostly flat."

"And you didn't conk your head?"

"No."

Vane straightened, and Doug lowered his shirt.

"The one an' only time," Doug murmured, and Vane laughed. It wasn't loud, but the sound was wonderful to

Doug. "I'm gonna make you something to eat. Delivery will take too long."

"I have soup and sandwich stuff."

"Cheese?"

"Yeah."

Vane scooted to the edge of the couch, and Doug helped him stand. Hoyt tagged along. While Doug warmed the soup and made grilled cheese sandwiches, Vane sat on a stool, chin in his hand. "You don't like the farmer's market idea?"

The cupboard that hung over the counter cut Vane's head off from Doug's view. He ducked underneath it. *Yep. Definitely getting rid of that.*

"Not sure of your return in investment," he answered.

"I need people to know we exist."

"True. At least you'll be taking charge of your situation."

Vane's smile grew, and Doug's heart pitter-pattered.

A silly happiness brimmed in Vane's eyes as though he didn't get a lot of compliments. Doug didn't know how that could be, but Meg's confidence had been frail too. It hadn't mattered how many times he'd told her how smart she was. How pretty. But he'd liked that about her. It was a good look on Vane too, that shadow of vulnerability in his eyes. Doug was sorry, all of a sudden, that he might have ever hurt him.

"C'mon. I'll put the soup in mugs. We can eat in front of the TV."

Vane nodded and pushed off his stool, Doug taking up the rear, and Hoyt dashing out of the door ahead of them.

The minute Vane sat, the golden circled the coffee table and jumped onto the couch beside him.

"Hey," said Doug. "Off."

But Hoyt had no time to obey before Trout charged out of nowhere and leaped over Hoyt's head. The dog flattened on the cushions, a desperate plea for help filling his eyes.

Doug set down the mugs and plates on the coffee table and said, "Don't look at me."

Hoyt rolled his eyes up as Trout sprawled across the top of the couch and bopped Hoyt on the head with his paw.

"Is he in your way?" Doug asked.

"No," said Vane.

When Doug sat, Vane snuggled close, Hoyt on his other side, and ate more than Doug thought he would. When he was done, Doug put an arm around his shoulder, and Vane leaned into him. A few minutes later, he slumped like a bag of sand. Heavy, solid, and sound asleep. Doug kissed the top of his head and tried to let the TV distract him from his memories of Meg.

How many evenings like this had he spent with her?

Hardly any, because he'd been too busy with work. The things she'd wanted, the things they'd fought about, he was giving to Vane. He wanted to walk away and build Meg's house and live in it and forget about Vane. But he hugged him closer and closed his eyes, feeling Meg slip farther and farther away.

22

THE DATE

I T ISN'T A date, Doug reassured himself.

But it was a date and entirely different from the movies and coffees and hikes with Hoyt he'd shared with Vane so far.

For one thing, Doug had made reservations and dressed up. He wanted Vane to enjoy himself and have a good time after all his hard work. He'd gotten his booth at the farmer's market and had been giving away samples of pie and coupons every weekend for almost two months, trying to pull business in. Doug had brought him to Little Tokyo, the closest to Benihana's they had in the area, and a place where people came to celebrate birthdays and anniversaries and... first dates.

So it's a date?

Well, it wasn't pizza or a game of pool or a trip to the snow with Hoyt, so...

The woman across the table from them, Darelle, clinked her water glass against her date's. The place was busy—it always was—warm and cozy and buzzing with conversation and laughter.

"What are you celebrating?" Vane asked.

Doug followed his gaze to Darelle, who flashed a smile and leaned against her boyfriend. "Malcolm's promotion. He's the assistant manager at his store."

"Congratulations," said Vane. "What store?"

"PetsMart," said Malcolm.

"Oh yeah? The one in Poppy Brush? I shop there. I have a cat."

"What kind of cat?" asked the little girl sitting between her mother and father at the other end of the table. A toddler in a booster chair sat beside her.

Her mother smiled at Vane. "We have five. Somebody is obsessed."

"I approve," said Malcolm. "That's my kind of obsession."

The kid was one giant tattoo. Doug counted at least a dozen tribal patterns in a dark ink that blurred like shadows on his skin.

The little girl peered around her mother and grinned at him. "I named them."

"Oh yeah? So what'd you come up with?" Malcolm asked.

Vane and Trout were forgotten as the girl prattled on about her cats. Her parents had introduced themselves after they'd been seated, but Doug couldn't recall their names now. *Ann? Paul?*

He kept quiet, letting Vane carry on their part of the

communal conversation. Something had changed since the night of Vane's accident, but he wasn't sure what. Or why it had. Doug supposed he'd fallen for the guy. Vane wasn't as shallow as he'd imagined no matter that he still seemed as flighty as ever. He went back and forth with Doug on every detail of the remodel. Just last week he complained he needed double ovens for his kitchen after they'd decided on one.

"Now I have to change the layout," Doug had said testily, annoyed that he'd become the one to complain.

Maybe they spent too much time together. Doug had no idea why he'd brought Vane here of all places. This had been Meg's favorite restaurant. She'd liked sitting with other people. If she'd lived, they'd have had a kid not much younger than the one in the booster seat.

Vane leaned against him, and Doug had to resist not pulling away as he gazed into Vane's eyes. How was such a pale color not cold?

"We should bring the kids here," Vane said.

Doug nodded. "Maybe on Rose's birthday."

Vane's eyes widened. "That's coming up? I should know that."

Flighty.

The little girl was staring at Vane again.

"What's your cat like?" she asked.

"My cat," Vane murmured.

Doug smiled to himself and watched Vane try to explain Trout. The damn cat followed Doug around the house every day. Not getting too close though. He planted himself at a distance and stared. A fluff ball with long wispy hairs on the tips of his ears. Doug wondered where the cat had come from. It had never been skinny.

"Looks like a Siberian," Malcolm said, gazing at the picture on Vane's phone. "Great cats."

"I think Malcolm should be a vet," said Darelle.

"Soon as I win the lottery," said Malcolm.

After they put in their orders, Vane asked Darelle, "What do you do?"

Doug watched her cock her head and roll her eyes. "Well..."

By the time their soup arrived, Vane had gotten her to promise to come down to the diner for an interview. Doug had had a hard time keeping his mouth shut and had snuck his hand under the table, clamping Vane's thigh in his fingers. Vane had ignored him. Of all the dumb ideas. The diner couldn't support the employees it already had.

The talking stopped as they watched the chef toss and flip their food. Seared strips of steak mixed with vegetables. Chicken and shrimp sizzled. Bowls of fried rice appeared in front of them, and they dug in.

Doug leaned closer to Vane and murmured, "Can you afford to hire somebody?"

"I have to do something," Vane whispered.

"Like what?"

A strange look crossed Vane's face. A hesitancy. Then it disappeared, and Doug frowned, wondering what Vane was hiding.

"I want to bring in more money."

"Save it," Doug said. He lowered his voice again and

gave a quick look in Darelle's direction. "You can't expand right now. Concentrate on the farmer's market angle."

A stubborn look came onto Vane's face. "I'm not sure that's going to work. I want to do this."

Doug sighed and returned to his meal.

The kid in the booster seat gurgled, "Yum," after every bite of the teriyaki chicken his mother fed him.

Doug had to admit the food was good. When Vane leaned in and murmured, "I can make this hecka better," he bit back a laugh.

"Just get somebody else to name it for you."

"Crazy Crunchy Stir Fry?"

"Well, it's descriptive."

In the parking lot after dinner, Doug said, "Go for a drive?"

"Sure."

They dodged a few cars pulling out ahead of them, got into the truck, and drove away.

"That was fun," Vane said.

"Glad you had a good time." Christ. How formal.

"Have you been there before?"

"A couple times." *A lot.*

"You seem weird," said Vane.

That made him laugh. "I do?"

"Yeah."

"Preoccupied, maybe. The job?"

Which was true in a way. Or maybe it was exactly the job. "An old friend of mine is moving back to the area this summer, and I already know he has a few projects he'll want help on. I'm not sure I'm ready to take on more work, but I probably will. It'd be stupid to turn it down. I'll be done with yours though."

"I wasn't worried about that. I would've been happy with a paint job."

Doug snorted. "No kidding."

He swung off the highway onto an old, windy road that would take them back toward Vane's and the bar where they'd met. "I might be pretty busy," he added.

Vane was quiet for a moment. He cracked his window. "We haven't talked about us, really. I don't even know if we're together. I mean, I know we go out and stuff, but... you know. Just in case we are together. Are you breaking up with me?"

Doug wanted to blow off Vane's comment like a joke they could both just forget. And maybe Vane would even go along with that, but Doug had heard the hurt in his voice and felt it like a knife in the chest.

He huffed a chuckle. "No, I'm not."

"I don't know how long I can stay here anyway."
Flighty.

But something in Vane's tone didn't ring true.

"We're together," Doug added.

The only sound that came from Vane now was the creak of his leather jacket. The wind through his window blew over a woodsy scent Doug knew was Vane's. He wanted to bury his face in Vane's neck and drag it out of his skin with every breath. It wasn't strong enough to catch except in the cold wind sending it to him.

Meg had drenched herself in cucumber lotion, and the

scent had mingled with her own. It had lingered in sheets and towels and blankets for weeks after she'd gone.

Why had Doug brought up work? That was what he'd done with Meg. Put the job first. Work over love. Over her.

"I want—" Vane stopped and Doug glanced at him. "I want to help Luis cook."

That wasn't what he'd been about to say. He'd pulled back from the truth at the last moment. Not that what he'd said wasn't true too, but Doug sensed something else underneath it.

"You can do that without hiring Darelle. You aren't that busy."

Vane huffed. "Thanks for the vote of confidence."

"I'm not saying you're going to fail. I'm just saying take it in stride. You aren't there, yet. You have Penny for now. Spell Luis some time off and take over for him if you want, but don't sink yourself trying to take on more than you can."

"I do spell him, but I want to change the menu and try other things too. I want this to work."

"I know."

"The menu sucks. I cook hecka better than Luis."

Doug laughed. "Don't tell Luis."

Vane snorted, and Doug turned his attention back to the road as it curved into the trees. Moonlight drifted through the branches and lit the under-foliage in a glossy silver. The road lifted and broke out of the trees, and the moon was bright in the sky. It lit the edges of the landscape and the shape of Doug's half-built house.

"Wow," murmured Vane.

"This is a great spot," Doug agreed.

Vane shifted, twisting close, filling Doug's nostrils with the wisps of his cologne. *Did he wear that for me?*

He nuzzled the side of Doug's face. "I'm glad we're together."

Doug squeezed the steering wheel with a pain so deep he thought his heart would break. Why had he taken him on a date? Why not their usual casual and comfortable nights falling asleep on the couch and having sex that meant nothing, except...?

He pulled over, his headlights on the house. He'd bought the lot for their sixth wedding anniversary and had stopped construction after the seventh.

"C'mon," he said. "I'll show you around."

The night was cool, but the last few days had been warm. Doug took his coat off and grabbed his flashlight.

"It's big," said Vane.

"Four bedrooms, three baths. We were planning on kids."

He had the flashlight on, slightly lifted, its glow on Vane's face. Vane looked down at the ground, not at Doug. "That has to be hard still."

"I'm lucky though. Dorcas," he added when Vane raised his head again.

"You've been friends a long time. It's good to have somebody you've known your whole life."

Wistfulness softened Vane's voice, and lit a warm glow inside Doug's gut. He wanted to put his arm around Vane and give him some of that warmth. But at the same time, he knew Vane had always had the person he could count on in Rose and had walked away from her. Doug's family couldn't be there for him when Meg died. They'd been gone already. But Vane could have been with Rose.

"Up here." He led Vane to the porch steps. "I was going to put a swing here."

"You still can."

With you?

That was the thing. He was getting in too deep with somebody who seemed to have no staying power. But nobody had made him ask Vane out on a real date. The guy hadn't changed. His circumstances had, and those could change again at any time. Was Doug willing to risk that? And for what?

He swung the light across a house that looked more gutted to him than unfinished. "It's for a family," he said.

"Is Meg the only one you can have a family with?"

Doug didn't know where that question had come from, and the sound of Meg's name in Vane's voice hit him hard. "She was the one I'd planned to have a family with."

Vane dropped his head and scuffed the tip of his shoe on the bare wood. "I know about plans," he murmured.

The pain in Vane's voice spoke to him. Doug wanted to hold him and ease his own heart. He was standing here inside walls he'd built to share with somebody else. It struck him again that he'd only met Vane because Meg was gone. A deranged voice he couldn't banish kept asking him if he'd trade Vane to get her back. And underneath that voice was another—deeper, darker, and slippery as silk— asking if he'd trade Vane's life for hers.

"Me. Pick me."

Meg.

"Me..."

"C'mon." He might've growled it because Vane resisted Doug's grip on his hand for a moment until Doug squeezed his fingers. Then he relaxed, squeezed back, and followed him across the floor.

They passed through the frame for a door. "This is the master. I put French doors onto the deck here. It looks out on the meadow. Careful..."

Doug pushed aside a tarp, slid open the glass slider, and jumped the few feet down to the ground. A moment later, Vane jumped too. Then Doug shut the door and gave him a push. "Go over there." He waved his light at the field.

Vane hesitated. "How come?"

Vane's reluctance surprised him, but Doug had to admit he'd been acting as moody as Vane usually was. The on again, off again, cold and hot wasn't him. Doug wasn't *flighty*. He had roots and staying power. This was where he'd been building Meg her forever home. Now he was here with somebody he wanted to let into his heart and was too scared to. But that wasn't Vane's fault, and Doug needed to let up on him. "I won't hurt you."

Vane laughed. "I wasn't thinking that until you said it."

"I promise. You'll like it."

He wasn't lying. He thought of Vane stripping down in front of his bedroom window.

Vane backed up, stumbled but caught himself, and Doug waited until he was a few yards into the meadow.

"That's good."

He pointed the light waist high, throwing Vane's face and the thumb he was chewing on into orange relief. His nerves showed in his shifting foot to foot, but he was excited too. Doug sensed it. His chest rose and fell in shallow breaths.

"Strip for me."

Vane froze. No breaths. No bitten thumb. Slowly, he dropped his hand and squeezed his fists at his side. "Here?"

"Yeah."

Vane looked sideways where the road was in plain view. "What if somebody drives by?"

"You'll be naked."

Vane's breath wheezed in a quick intake. His excitement shot across the space between them and bloomed in the pit of Doug's stomach.

"Go on." He whispered it but knew Vane heard him.

Vane dropped his jacket first, letting it slide down his arms. The sleeves caught on his wrists, and he shimmied his shoulders.

"Shoes and pants next. Then put your shoes back on."

"You're a weirdo, you know that?"

Doug chuckled. "I'm in good company."

Vane toed his shoes off. "Socks?"

"Keep 'em on," Doug instructed, swallowing at a sudden roughness in his voice.

Vane just did it for him like this. All his clumsiness disappeared, and he was shy grace instead. The boy next door doing a strip tease by the roadside. Doug was hard enough he hurt, but he didn't move, didn't adjust himself.

He let the discomfort pulse through his body with every heartbeat.

Vane's pants slid down his legs, his hips swinging side to side as a strip of fabric appeared. It was light colored, white—

"What color are those?"

Vane didn't ask what he was talking about. He lifted his chin and gazed at Doug from under his brows as he gave another shimmy.

"Pink."

Fuck me. Doug swallowed again. Cutouts on the hips revealed Vane's pale skin. "Pink, huh?"

"I like pink."

"Looks good on you," Doug agreed. Truthfully, the color faded in the dark, but Doug had no doubt it was a spectacular shade on him.

The briefs hugged his hips, low on his belly. While Doug watched, Vane shucked his pants and straightened again. His shirt hung down, inching over the pink bulge in his panties. Doug lowered the beam of light to the ground, and Vane faded like a shadow in the dark. Then, slowly, the landscape lightened into a ghostly blue. Vane's body seemed to absorb the moonlight.

"Turn around."

He made a smooth swirl and planted his feet apart. His legs were long and strong with a slight swell on the inside.

Doug's mouth ached to fill itself with Vane's flesh. "Around again," he said. Vane complied. "Shirt off."

Vane moved his hands over his belly, pulling his shirt

higher with each stroke. His cock was a thick pole, its head poking out of the waistband of his panties.

"You like this," Doug said.

"Just as much as you."

Doug nodded. "I do." He watched Vane drop his hand and stroke himself through the cloth. "Are you wet?" he asked.

Vane stilled his hand, his thumb rolling over the top of the head now. He moaned and thrust. "Yes."

Next, he let himself go and skated his palm upward again, grazing a nipple, while he grabbed the hem of his shirt with his other hand and tugged it off, dropping it on his pants by his feet.

"Tell me what you feel."

Vane laughed. "Cold. Nervous. I'm shivering."

"Too cold?"

"No. I'm excited." A roughness turned his voice throaty.

Doug raised the flashlight again. He loved the curve of Vane's body when he rested his weight on one leg. Loved the pads of flesh over his hip bones and the dips and angles in his shoulders and arms. *Beautiful boy.*

"The rest," Doug murmured, not quite sure that the pounding of his heart didn't drown out his voice.

"Do you want to do it to me?"

"Not here."

"Why not?"

Meg. This was Meg's place. But that wasn't right anymore. He watched Vane hook his thumbs in his panties and slowly push down.

"I don't want to fuck you." Vane stopped. "I want to make love to you. I want you on your kitchen table." Vane's hips jerked. "Bent over your tub."

"Yes," Vane whispered.

"On your porch," Doug said. Vane's cock bobbed in the air. "I'll sit on the steps, and you'll sit on me and spread your legs, so I can play with your balls."

"Squeeze 'em."

"At noon. In the daylight. With the cars driving by."

Vane stepped out of his panties and dropped his head back. In the cone of Doug's light, he turned the color of marble. He was stone, but flesh and blood shivers ran through him. His hands slid down until he cupped his balls and fisted his dick.

"First time you knew you liked guys?" Doug asked.

Vane was quiet for a moment. He rolled his hips against his fist and lowered his head. "I don't know," he said on a gasp. "I think I always did. You?"

"Twelve. A neighbor kid—I don't even remember his name—snagged a *Hustler*." He laughed. "Raunchy things. I realized I liked the guys just as much as the girls. I didn't know what that meant exactly, but that was my first clue. Your first time?"

"Eighteen. I messed around with a kid in my dorm. He pretended he was straight afterwards. At least he didn't beat me up." His hand flew. "I don't want to come."

"I don't want you to either. Drop it."

He let himself go and laced his hands behind his head. His dick bobbed as he rocked his hips. "Your turn."

"Sixteen with a girl, and no, it wasn't Meg. Twenty with a guy."

"You know I'm sorry about that crack I made after my dad's service, right?"

"I know."

"I just... don't have a lot of experience."

"With what? Sexuality? Life?"

"All of the above." His hands slipped away from the back of his head. "I wasn't partying like a movie star every night, you know? People didn't recognize me. I was a customer service rep and a waiter. I took acting classes. Not that that ever helped. I didn't go clubbing or do the gay scene. I didn't fool around. Fisher cheated on me."

He sighed and took his deflating dick in his fingers again.

"I'm sorry."

"I'm not real exciting."

"You're fireworks," said Doug, heading over to him now.

Vane stood still, watching him approach. A shiver met the touch of Doug's hand to Vane's shoulder. He let his fingers slip along smooth warm skin until he reached Vane's wrist. He gripped the strong bone and pulled Vane's arm away from his body. "You don't have to make yourself sound like a homebody. You didn't want to come back here."

"Maybe I did," Vane whispered.

Doug stared into his eyes, stroking his waist with a fingertip. Vane shivered. Heat came off him, but his skin was cold.

Doug leaned in and brushed his lips against Vane's cheek. "Aren't you sure?"

Vane shivered again. "I don't know."

Is that true? Trying to figure Vane out was like trying to catch butterflies in a summer field. Looping bits of color that burst into flames in the sun.

Doug didn't know why he didn't believe him. But right now he couldn't reconcile his own place in the world. Being in the meadow where he'd been building Meg's house had clouded his mind. How could such contradictory desires ever live in harmony? Could they?

He put his arms around Vane's body and stroked his back.

"Let's go home."

23

LUIS MAKES A GOOD SUGGESTION

"DUDE." LUIS SPREAD his arms and turned in a circle. "This is a diner."

Vane sat at the counter with his arms folded across his chest. Luis glowered at him. At least he wasn't knocking him over the head with a frying pan or pushing him into traffic or something. Doug wasn't worried about Luis's murderous intentions, so maybe Vane was wrong. He took a breath and decided he'd give Luis a chance.

"This is the style our customers expect," Luis added. "Like home."

Vane rolled his eyes. "Nobody makes blue plate specials at home. And anyway, we don't have any customers, which is my point. If it wasn't for the little bit of insurance my dad had, this place would be closed."

"Which makes no sense you hiring another waitress. What for?"

Except for the two of them, the diner was empty right now. They closed at three on Sundays after the lunch crowd. Though calling it a crowd was probably generous. They'd been half full this morning though. Better than ever. Maybe the sun was getting everybody out of the house now. Through the windows the sky looked white, but outside it was blue, and the day was bright and breezy.

Luis half smirked at him. Vane had asked him to stay and talk about the menu and Vane's plans. "Darelle's taking over for me."

Luis's eyes brightened. He sat on the edge of a stool and crossed his arms over his chest too. "Yeah? You goin' home?"

"I am home."

Cold prickled his skin and crawled over his scalp at the sound of that statement coming out of his mouth. He fought the urge to jump up and run away. The words had erupted from his gut. *I am home.* How could that be? Was he giving up?

As though confirming his thoughts, Luis snorted. "You had enough a this? Workin' every day?"

Vane scratched his back, giving himself time not to blow his top. A ticking noise pricked at his nerves, too, but he wasn't sure where it was coming from. It sounded like a drip, maybe from the coffee machine, but it wasn't even on now.

"You're lucky I don't fire you."

Luis snorted. "You wanna do this yourself?"

"Yeah, actually. I also want new menus." He tapped one still lying on the counter. "These things are ancient. And new dishes, like I said. And I want to cook. With you. As my job."

Luis's frown darkened his face, and a muscle twitched in his jaw. "You?"

"Why not?"

"And me? You think I'm takin' orders?"

"My dad was the other cook. Now I want to be that."

Luis shook his head. "I don't train people."

"Look, I cook already to cover your days off. I don't need training, and I'm not asking you. Either things change around here, or we go under."

Luis lowered his chin, the dark frown on his face again. "You wanna do that, you better pay me off first, cuz I put my sweat into this place, an' nobody's pushin' me out."

Vane's belly went cold. He clenched his fist on top of the sticky menu and sat still, not wanting to give anything away. The racket his heart was making probably squashed that plan though.

He inhaled slowly.

Luis wanted him out and was willing to hurt him to get him out. That fall on his porch could have killed him.

He held onto Luis's gaze and let go of his breath. "You can help me or not. I'm trying different things, and I'm changing the menu with or without you."

Luis stared for a few long seconds. "You do what you want. I've got nothin' to say."

"You can help."

He shrugged. "I can cook whatever. Let me in the office. I'll make a new menu on the computer."

An alarm bell rang in Vane's head at the memory of Luis pacing outside the office. Worry had dug lines into his face.

Vane still didn't know what that had been about. The office had nothing of value in it. He'd gone through everything. It was only locked because he still hadn't put the contents of the boxes back in the cabinets, and he wasn't giving Luis a key. No reason to, so he said, "My friend's going to do that for me."

He wondered if Dorcas even knew how, but he figured she did because she'd done the coupons he gave out at the farmer's market for him. And he loved her fashion sense. She probably had great design skills too, and he needed a reason not to let Luis do it.

He got a look from under Luis's brows. "You mean your boyfriend?"

"Screw you. You can keep your effing comments to yourself."

Luis lifted his hands, glowering again. "Hey, I'm not sayin' anything out of line. I'm not prejudice."

"Do you have any ideas?"

"No. I like the menu."

"What about my pie?" Vane asked.

"That was my pie."

"I do it better."

Luis guffawed. "I'm going home."

"Come on. Just give me some effing ideas."

"Oh, now you get mad. Almost with the bad words even. Fine. You need a... a—" He rotated his finger in the air. "A point. Like you sell only fish or a bunch of different kinds of burgers."

"A theme."

Luis nodded. "Yeah. You know. Like diner food."

"Ha, ha."

"You can call your pie Sugar."

The suggestion got Vane another glower as though it had torn Luis's heart from his chest to offer it.

"Sugar? It's not sugar."

"So what? It's sweet. It looks like brown sugar. Sugar Pie."

"Eileen's Sugar Sweet Pie."

"Yeah. Like that." Luis stood. "Figure out the rest an' tell me later."

He strode by, and Vane unpeeled his fingers from the menu and wiped his hand off on his jeans. Then he got up and went behind the counter where he found a rag and swiped the plastic surface of the menu. When he turned, Luis was standing there, and his heart jumped again.

Luis half laughed, glee in his eyes. "Water heater broke."

Vane went past him, his stomach sinking as he confronted a sheen of water across the hallway. "What the heck did you do?"

Luis sneered. "You don't need no help from me. You're goin' up in flames all on your own."

Vane half sputtered, but Luis grabbed his jacket off a hook in the kitchen and stormed outside.

24

VANE'S DISCOVERY

A LINE OF light lit the trees, and a hint of blue colored the sky, but the sun wasn't up yet. When Vane pulled in the next morning, Doug was already waiting for him by the diner's back door.

Vane got out of his car and stood watching as Doug sauntered toward him. His hips swung loose and strong in his beat-up jeans, and a flutter started in Vane's belly.

When Doug reached him, Vane opened his arms and leaned against Doug's chest, nose to nose and chin to chin. He sensed Doug's smile and shivered at the breath of his words.

"What are you doing?" Doug asked.

"You look so good."

"I'm a slob."

"You smell good too."

Like soap, but not the bubblegum-scented solution Vane had used to clean up yesterday. He'd tried sweeping the water outside, but the more he stepped in it, the dirtier it got.

He pushed into Doug's kiss, opening to the touch of his tongue. Warmth swept through him. He sighed as Doug cupped his face before he pulled away.

"Come on," Doug said. "Let's open up. Vic'll be here in a couple minutes."

Vic, the plumber. Coming to fix the effin' water heater. "I don't know if this place is worth it. It's gonna be over a thousand bucks."

"It's a write-off. Cost of doing business. You don't have a choice anyway. That's what you tell yourself."

"It's not working."

"C'mon."

Inside, Vane started a pot of coffee. Watching the slow drip from the machine relaxed him until a door slammed outside. Doug's voice followed the sound a moment later. "Mornin'."

Vane swiped his palms off on his jeans and approached a redheaded woman Doug was leading inside. *Vic.* Wasn't that a guy's name?

"Vane, this is Vic." He turned to the woman, who sported a big smile, laugh lines, and a red ponytail on top of her head. "Vane'll bring you up to speed. I've gotta go."

He gave Vane's arm a squeeze and headed out the back door.

Vic shifted a leather bag stuffed full of tools from where it perched on her hip to her front and said, "Lead me to 'er."

He gestured to the kitchen. She stepped in and pursed her lips. "At least, I don't have to worry about draining it."

Vane forced a grimace of a smile. "That's good."

Wonder if I get a discount because of Doug.

Vane watched her work for a couple of minutes before wandering off into the dining area. At least, he had his coffee. He poured another cup and sat down at the counter, facing the windows.

The tree line had grown more prominent, the thin blue border widening in the sky. The stars faded, and the headlights of the occasional cars passing by cast a glow as blurry as his old life. It was fading day by day. There were times he struggled to picture Fisher's condo or Ribbets or even Fisher himself. It had only been four months since he'd left, but his old life had a dreamy quality to it now, as though it had never been his.

He let the thumps and clanks from in back lull him while he drank his coffee until Luis's voice reached him. "How you doin'?"

"Fabulous. Yourself?"

"Good."

Vane got up and wandered into the alcove on the other side of the diner. It wasn't a bad view from the window here. Wooded hills and a few wildflowers surrounded them, but the parking lot itself was a long stretch of gray. Nobody parked there. Eileen's sat on half an acre of pitted and crumbling pavement. He'd have to fix that too. The alcove he stood in was a secondary dining space they never had enough customers to fill. It was a waste of a view.

Clamping down on the anxiety rising in him—*you're going to fail*—he returned to the kitchen. Vic was reattaching the pipes now.

"Almost done," she said.

Luis ignored him, chopping peppers and onions with a blur of his knife.

Vane wasn't that fast. Well, so what? He'd learn.

Today though, he waited tables, taking orders and chatting with his few customers. Later, he drew a sign on a piece of paper and taped it to the pie case. Eileen's Sweet Sugar Pie. He'd covered the paper in red hearts. It looked like something a third grader would do. By midafternoon, Darelle had arrived, and he got ready to leave.

After staring at him for a moment while she tied her apron on, she cocked her head at him. "You okay?"

"Our water heater broke."

"Oh no."

He shrugged. "Could be worse. It's fixed now."

"Hm. I get that 'could be worse' thing from Malcolm all the time. Some days though, I can do without the inspirational quote. Just gimme a bubble bath and a glass of wine."

Vane laughed. "Yeah. Me too." He pulled on his coat and fumbled for the keys in his pocket. "Call me if anything comes up."

She patted his arm and pushed. "Go."

The day was bright and sparkly now but cold for April. Getting into his car, Vane drove away, keeping an eye peeled for squirrels.

He passed the turn off for home and continued into Poppy Brush. Mr. Kam's studio was in a narrow brick building at the end of a strip of businesses two blocks off Main Street.

A walkway separated the building Mr. Kam's was in from the rest of the strip. A business called Left Brain Enterprises occupied the bottom floor. Vane parked in back and took the stairs to Mr. Kam's.

A loud laugh that sounded like Dorcas's met him as he opened the door, but he didn't see her.

The space he stepped into was a long, empty rectangle that looked like a lobby nobody used anymore. Instead of a counter, a metal desk and plastic chair stood against the wall. A fake ficus, gray with dust, occupied a corner and other than thin, gray-blue carpets that was all that was there.

Vane headed toward the voices coming through a door in the corner. "Nothing sad... A love story!... an anti-love story, ha ha..."

He paused in the doorway and looked into a space that took up the rest of the second story.

Windows bordered the room on three sides. A stage was set under the window opposite Vane. Mr. Kam had told him the kids put on performances here, but no curtain hung over the stage now, and the chairs for the audience were stacked against the walls. A handful of other chairs made a circle in the middle of the room. Dorcas stood in front of a metal easel, writing things in a felt-tipped marker on a giant pad of paper.

He gaped in horror at the feather boa she wore. Were those baby owl feathers? Where did she get these things?

"Hi, Vane!"

He smiled at Penny, who stood beside a beanpole of a kid in wire-rimmed glasses. Mr. Kam smiled too and waved him over.

"Vane. Come on in. I've been telling the class all about you."

Now the rest of the kids turned and stared. Vane smiled. "Hey."

A girl with short purple braids patted a folding chair. "Welcome. We were just throwing out ideas for our next performance."

"When is that?"

"Founder's Day."

"June twenty-third," Mr. Kam added, as though Vane hadn't been born in Poppy Brush.

From the other side of the ring of chairs, Dorcas pointed her marker at him. "The kids have decided. You get to be stage manager."

"Oh no. That's Mr. Kam's job. I'm happy to help though."

"There's no shortage of things for you to do," said Mr. Kam. "I'm just pleased that we have a real actor joining us."

Vane sat down and slid half out the back of the chair. Why the heck didn't they make the seats level?

"You don't act anymore though," said the purple-haired girl.

"That's not true," said Penny. She shot the girl a look and dropped into the chair on the other side of Vane with a puff of that perfume she wore. Cotton candy? Honeysuckle? "Vane's taking a break. I get it. Hollywood kills."

"Well, not literally." Vane chuckled.

Then he remembered the rumor about the kid who'd supposedly killed himself when he didn't get the part of Marcel. Shoot, that could have been Vane for all anybody would have noticed. When he thought about it, did he really miss LA? "I came home for family reasons."

"Are you going to go back?"

"That's the plan. We'll see."

Mr. Kam stepped away from Dorcas's side and stood behind the purple-haired girl's chair. "Let's start with introductions. This is Carol. That's Justin. Matt. Samantha..."

There were nine kids in the class. They smiled at him. He got a finger waggle from a couple. Fresh-faced. Pimple-faced. Purple hair. Blue hair. Pierced eyebrows. He was a thousand years old. His bones hurt from just looking at these kids.

He glanced over his shoulder.

Dorcas's eyes twinkled. "Hey," she said. "Did you guys know Vane won an Emmy?"

Oh gosh.

"Really?"

"Wow."

He squirmed, trying to get comfortable in the idiot

chair that didn't have a lower half to its back. "The commercial won, not me."

"That's modesty," said Mr. Kam. He returned from his circle around the room to stand at Dorcas's side.

Vane glared at her. She batted her eyelashes.

"An important thing to remember," said Mr. Kam, "is that you are always going to be a part of a group effort. Now let's settle on a plan. We have twelve weeks until Founder's Day. We won't be meeting the Monday after Easter or the week of spring break, so that's only ten sessions."

Dorcas uncapped her marker and swept her arm at the easel. "Okay. So this is what we have. Romeo and Juliet."

"That's dumb," said Matt. "Everybody does that."

"I want Equus," said a kid who pushed his glasses up his nose and then clamped his hands between his knees. *Adam.*

"No dead horses," said Carol.

Adam peered at her from under his brows. "Blind horses."

The kid beside him wrinkled her nose. "With their eyes poked out."

Adam twisted a look at her. "Well, you don't see that part."

"Why don't we write our own play?" said Carol. "A mock presidential campaign. We can add our own twist."

Mr. Kam nodded. "That's a good idea. I like it. Just remember that our time is limited."

"Who's going to write it?"

Carol looked at Mr. Kam. "All of us?"

"Of course. You should all participate. But..." He lifted a finger. "This is a volatile topic. The trick here, besides meeting our deadline, will be showing each other respect."

Carol bounced to her feet. "Wait. I have an idea. It's Founder's Day, right? Why don't we do a mock-up of the signing of the Declaration of Independence? We can have a bunch of citizens get together and talk about their ideas. Then the Founders have to make a decision about what kind of government we end up with."

Adam shook his head. "What if I don't like what the Founders decide?"

Carol shrugged. "I don't know. Maybe we stop before we get to the actual decision. We can make it more about people getting together to decide than the decision itself."

"Okay," said Mr. Kam. "What's the consensus? Is this a doable idea?"

"I like it."

"We can try."

"We always have Romeo and Juliet if we can't figure it out."

Matt shook his head. "No way." But he laughed with the other kids, and Vane joined in.

Carol leaned closer. "Are you going to act with us?"

Vane gazed into her eyes. They were a light hazel, swimming with clarity. He had no doubt at all. This purple-haired kid was never going to waste her time on Hollywood or Broadway or any indie films. No commercials. No Oscars. She didn't look like she gave a fig about applause. Not like him.

"I think I'm okay behind the curtains for now."

A slow smile curved her lips. "The Great and Powerful Oz?"

Vane guffawed. "Not exactly."

"Smart girl," said Dorcas. She leaned over and hugged Vane from behind. "You don't need to hide, you know? It's time to go shopping for a pair of red shoes."

He craned a look over his shoulder, but by then, she'd released him and turned back to her pad of paper.

VANE RAN THROUGH THE NAMES IN HIS HEAD AS the kids started packing their bags.

Carol, Adam, Matt, Justin, Samantha, Naomi, Kris, Sean, and Emma.

Carol and Matt were the leaders, Adam, the grump naysayer. Justin and Naomi and Sean wanted to be actors. But, as he'd guessed, not Carol.

"An investigative reporter," she'd said. "My mom and dad are super political. I didn't get fairytales. I got *All the President's Men.* They *loved* that movie. They watch it all the time. I love it too, though. I got hooked on reporting after seeing it a dozen times. *Wag the Dog* was a good movie too."

The glow in her eyes had stirred him. He'd always wanted to make people laugh or cry with a character he'd brought to life. *Yeah, like the ones you made up for your screenplay.* Which he hadn't touched in months. He hadn't even looked at it.

He'd smiled. "A writer, huh?"

She'd grinned back. "I plan on it."

Not want or hope. No maybe. *Plan.* She was going to set her life in motion, and that's what Vane needed to do too.

He pulled his jacket on and waved at Dorcas and Mr. Kam. "See you guys."

Quick footsteps sounded behind him though, and he glanced back as Penny hurried after him. She hooked her arm in his and walked him into the lobby.

"Juicy, Vane. I'm counting on you to write me a juicy part."

He laughed. "I'm just doing lines."

She leaned in. "For a really yawntastic idea. For reals," she murmured. They stopped at the outer door. "You have the legit talent, Vane. You can't walk away from it."

He leaned down and whispered, "I wait tables, Penny. Like you."

With a sigh and a roll of her eyes, she slapped the back of her wrist to her forehead. "Alas, we bore ourselves."

"Goof. I gotta go."

"Okay." She skedaddled back into the other room, wagging her fingers over her shoulder as she went. "See ya!"

Outside, the day had fled. Vane emerged into a purple-gray twilight. Thin layers of clouds blurred the sky. He headed home. The repairs on the house were a few months from completion, mainly because Doug was doing most of it himself. That gave Vane time to focus on Eileen's, get his head clear, and make a plan to get his life back. *Go back to Hollywood?*

He stopped at a traffic light and chewed on his lip.

Was he going to leave Doug? His skin went cold at the thought of that. What would he do? Move away? Moving wasn't leaving though, because he could always come back when he wasn't on set. He wouldn't be working all the time.

The light turned green, and he stepped on the gas.

Outside of Poppy Brush, the dark deepened, and wisps of mist broke apart in front of him. He turned onto the road home and wound through thick trees.

Soon his house appeared like a pale white ghost. He pulled into the driveway, turned off the engine, and listened to it tick.

Strange to think of the house as his and not his dad's. He pictured a strange family moving in and painting the outside blue or taupe or some shade of gray. Maybe they'd buy the diner too and put up a sign that read Anders Grill or the Moon Valley Café and not Eileen's anymore. In his dad's opinion, if Vane left here, he'd be running, not moving away.

Dad's dead.

But Vane didn't want to dwell on that or admit he had nothing waiting for him in Hollywood now anyway. Unless the impossible happened and the casting for Marcel fell through. He could always hope. Would Mary or Tabitha call?

Where are you?... I have a script for you to read... It's perfect!!!... You are going to shine...

Like he had in the moonlight in the glow of Doug's eyes?

A shiver ran through him.

He entered the house through the back door and kicked off his shoes in the laundry room.

In the kitchen, he gazed at the paint samples on the table. Egg shell. Sand. Buttercream. Dandelion. A sticky note was stuck to the center of the table. *I like white.*

Warmth enveloped him, as though Doug were still in the house somewhere, a part of Vane's everyday life. He touched the yellow square of paper.

"*Mow.*"

"Hey, Trout."

The cat jumped onto the table, landed on the paint samples, and sprang straight into the air in alarm. The card-stock rectangles flew, and Trout hit the floor with a thump.

Great.

Vane retrieved the samples and dropped them on the table. The cat glowered at him. Vane bent down and rubbed under Trout's ear. "It's okay," he murmured.

"*Mow.*"

"Dinner time?"

He got a can of food out of a cabinet without doors, set the can down, and looked around but didn't see his doors anywhere. *Whatever.*

While Trout ate, he heated a microwave burrito and took it upstairs to his mom's old craft room. It was mostly empty again, so he'd bought a small writing table at a garage sale. He sat in his chair, opened a drawer, and found his flash drive. He set it down and stared at it while he ate his burrito.

It wasn't hard to figure out why the flash drive had sat

in his dresser drawer and now the desk drawer the entire time he'd been here. It was safe, and he was safe from looking at his screenplay and thinking it was a piece of crap, because who was he kidding? Elmore Leonard wrote crime capers, not Vane Riley.

But just thinking about his story made his skin tingle. He was on pins and needles as he inhaled his burrito and new ideas for the robbery scene flooded his brain.

He opened his new laptop, started it, and popped the last bite of burrito into his mouth. After a quick swipe of his fingers on his jeans, he plugged in the flash drive and clicked to open it. A list of files came up a moment later, but they weren't his scenes, and at the same time, he realized—*It didn't ask for my password.*

He stared, confused by what he was seeing for a moment. The file types were images and videos. Feeling uneasy now, he clicked on an image, took a breath and straight-armed himself away from his desk.

Holy—

He swiped his mouth and stared at the dark shape of the tree outside the window. He had no thoughts.

For a moment, his brain stalled.

Then he got up, pounded downstairs, snagged himself a beer, and returned to his chair. He drank half the bottle before he opened another image.

Well... "Shoot." *Shoot, shoot, shoot.*

The kid on the screen was a little younger and prettier than Vane but still his mirror image. Fisher's twink. The little creep Vane had met on the stairs his last night with Fisher. Was he on set playing Marcel right now? That was Vane's part. That was Vane's bed he was sprawled out on.

Vane couldn't tear his eyes away. The kid had Vane's pale skin and shocking splash of dark pubic hair. Fisher stood by the side of the bed, but Vane kept his attention on... *Stan*. Stan, with his pretty dick poking up from his crotch.

Jerk.

He inhaled the rest of his beer, stood and fetched another one. By the time he got back, a text had appeared on his phone. —How was everything?

—Good. Done.

—Acting Class?

—Fun.

—Movie tomorrow? Your pick.

—Okay. After work.

—See you.

He pushed the phone away and let his eyes roam the list of images and... the videos.

Spectacular.

This was a spectacular night. And typical. The minute a bit of happy snuck into his life—the minute he got a little energy and hope inside him—*bam*. Reality check. *You are a loser.* Replaceable by somebody who looked like him but was probably better at everything.

He opened another file and got a close-up of Stan's hole, which was pink and fresh looking and slightly agape. The hair between his cheeks was dark and sparse.

Like Vane's.

His dick twitched. *Seriously? You're seriously getting turned on by yourself?*

He closed the file, took a breath, and clicked on one of the videos.

Fisher was fucking him, Stan's calves over Fisher's shoulders. It wasn't particularly close up, but Stan's slack-eyed gaze and pink tongue was easy to see. The kid was so pretty and tender. But he was messing around with somebody else's boyfriend.

"My boyfriend, you rotten cheater."

Vane wanted to look away, but he kept his eyes on Stan's face and watched his features twist. Was he struggling to come? Pinned to a bed he didn't want to be in but lured by the promise of Fisher's friend of a friend to make his career? Or did he want to be with Fisher? As Vane wondered, Stan turned toward the camera and met Vane's gaze. His eyes rolled up and cum spattered his chest like fallen pearls. But Vane would swear he wasn't happy.

"You made a bad bet," he whispered and lowered the lid on his laptop. His head followed, too heavy now to hold up. He let it rest on the desk and bit his lip until a whomp of heat burst in his gut, and he sat back up and grabbed his phone. *Well, screw you, Fisher.*

Like heck he wanted this garbage on his laptop.

When Fisher answered, his voice was suspicious. Of course, it was. Fisher didn't recognize Vane's new number.

"You creep. You have my screenplay."

"Vane?"

"I want my screenplay. I didn't take anything of yours, Fisher. I don't want your effing pictures. I—"

"You took them."

"No, I didn't. I took my flash drive."

"I don't know anything about that," said Fisher. "All I know is you quit your job and walked out, so I gave your clothes to the Goodwill. You were the one who cut off contact."

He almost sputtered at that. Leave it to Fisher to blame him. "You cheated on me."

"I don't know what you're talking about."

Vane grabbed his empty beer bottle and squeezed it. "I have the pictures."

"I want them back."

"You can have them. After you give me my screenplay."

Fisher roared. "I don't have your screenplay!"

Vane jerked back and swallowed in a tight throat. *Don't panic. No, no, I'm not going to panic.* And he wasn't going to let Fisher scare him either. He still felt sick, but he swallowed again and pulled the phone back.

"I took the wrong thumb drive," he whispered. "You have mine."

"It's not here."

"In the drawer—"

"No. There's nothing. You don't write, Vane. You barely act for that matter. You blew your one chance for that part, and I can't say I'm surprised."

Vane gasped as though Fisher had punched him in the chest. How could he say that? Vane had stuck it out for years, scraping by with crummy, low-paying jobs, always hoping for his next break. It had been Fisher who'd taken that all away.

"You beat me up."

"You're imagining things."

Now his heart galloped, thudding hard against his breastbone. Why would Fisher say that? What did he think Vane was imagining?

"Imagining what? You hit me."

"Those pictures aren't what you think they are. I was helping Stan with a role."

Vane laughed. He couldn't help it. In the back of his mind, his laugh sounded thin and too high. "By putting your dick in him? Give me a break, Fisher."

"I won't repeat myself. I want those pictures back."

The bonfire in Vane's belly flared to life again. "No. Look for my flash drive. We'll trade."

"Vane—"

"I mean it, Fisher."

"You little—"

Shaking, Vane disconnected the call and dropped his phone on the desk, not sure if he was furious or about to throw up.

What had he ever seen in that guy? How had he given so much to somebody who'd steal his screenplay?

Cheating on him was bad enough. Though Vane could live with that, he guessed, because it wasn't what was bubbling in his gut.

The only thing Vane's screenplay would be to Fisher was something to use or sell. He'd never see Vane's heart in it any more than he'd paint Vane's cupboards blue just because Vane asked him to. Vane had put his emotions into his story. Emotions he'd probably never given to Fisher, so maybe he was to blame too. But he hadn't cheated and filmed it for the whole world to see either.

Gosh, what an idiot he was to get so worked up about it though. To Fisher, it was probably just a sex tape. Everybody had them nowadays.

Heart aching, he finally returned downstairs and drank the rest of his six-pack of beer.

25

VANE INTERRUPTS A BURGLAR

THEY WERE STANDING by the stage in a flood of light through the wall of windows in Mr. Kam's studio.

Carol tossed her hair—loose and pink today—out of her eyes and removed a sheet of paper from her bag. The other kids had flocked around the computer with Mr. Kam, researching costume ideas. Dorcas had an appointment, and Vane had gotten there late.

"Here," said Carol, handing him the piece of paper. "You take care of the founding fathers and mothers parts. I wrote down what each citizen is going to talk about. You just have to write the prompts we respond to. We're switching this up, so now the founding fathers and mothers are going to be stuck in their ways. The citizens, us kids, are socially progressive. I'll write those parts."

Vane stared at her, wondering when he'd gotten so old he'd become the perfect fit for the "stuck in your ways" crowd.

"Is that okay? You can do that, right?"

"Yeah, sure."

Vane blinked at the list of topics he was supposed to write prompts for. Shoot. Was he losing his eyesight already? Thirty-two years old. Blind. *Chinless.*

He sighed and folded the paper.

He had to start rewriting his screenplay anyway. This would get him back in the swing of things, except his story was going to be a book this time. When he thought about how he'd rewrite it, it didn't flow the same way. It wasn't the same story.

He might like it better, but he wasn't sure.

As he stood on the edge of the group, he mulled over Carol's list of topics and let a few ideas run through his mind. The sunlight slid along the wall and out the window. A few minutes later, somebody flipped the lights on, and Vane looked outside at a sky gone gray. He stuffed the folded piece of paper into his pocket and ran into Fisher's flash drive. *You idiot.*

He tapped Mr. Kam's arm.

"I have to go. I have something to drop off at the post office."

"It's closed."

"What about the lobby? Doesn't that stay open late?"

He gazed at the clock on the wall, but it had long since stopped and nobody had bothered to rewind it.

"I don't know. I've never gone at night," said Carol. "I have a stamp if you need one. Or you can get them at an ATM."

"That's okay. I need an envelope too. I'm gonna give it a try. I'll see you guys."

He grabbed his jacket and hustled downstairs. *Shoot, shoot, shoot.*

He wanted to get rid of Fisher's pictures. Not because he was afraid of Fisher.

You are.

He wasn't. But he didn't want to owe Fisher anything and didn't want any links to him. The desire to go back to his old life was still there like a needle under his skin, but he didn't want Fisher to be any part of it. He'd write his story because he was more than a guy struggling to get by, and he'd prove it. But he didn't need any loose strings dragging him back either.

He trotted to his car at the curb, got in, and took off.

The post office was only three blocks away on the opposite side of the street. He swung into the parking lot, got out of his car, and darted up the front steps. Though the lobby was dark, he tried the door anyway, but it was locked.

Dang it.

He banged his head on the glass before he turned away.

Well, what did he expect? This was Poppy Brush not LA. He could mail Fisher's flash drive off tomorrow and get his clean slate then.

As he stood there, thinking about his options, his gaze drifted across the street to a shopping center. It was a little run down but had a CVS with a brand new sign over its entrance in the middle of the row of stores. They'd have what he needed. Maybe even postage.

He headed over.

A half an hour later, he didn't have an envelope, but he did have notebooks, pencils, and pens, none of which he needed to write. His laptop was good enough, but the thought of the cold screen filled him with apathy. The notebooks were different from his old way of doing things.

So, with his arms full of office supplies, he bounded to the checkout line, a smile he couldn't suppress pulling at his lips. He probably looked like a dimwit. *You are a dimwit. So what?*

By the time he stepped outside again, the sky was smoky with wispy clouds and speckled with a few pale stars. The light from a deli next door spilled on the walkway and drew him over. He went inside and got a sandwich and chips to go. At home, he set his bags on the kitchen table, waiting for Trout at the back door, but he didn't appear.

Vane stepped onto the porch. "Hey, kitty."

Stupid calling for a cat he didn't like.

The weeds caught the light like molten silver. Hidden farther back in the dark, a pair of eyes glowed at him, but Trout didn't come near at first.

"C'mere, kitty."

The cat still didn't approach, and Vane frowned with unease. That was weird. Maybe an earthquake was coming, though Vane didn't think Trout was the kind of cat who could sense that.

"You want dinner, you better come in."

When nothing changed and those glowing eyes didn't move, Vane turned away. He barely got one step back inside before a streak of fur blasted past him and knocked him into the doorjamb.

What the—

Trout skidded across the floor, scrabbled like a mad thing, and shot out into the living room.

With a shake of his head, Vane shut the door and took his sandwich from the bag. After he got himself a beer, he carried his dinner into the other room and sat on the couch.

Trout hunkered by the front door.

"What's with you?"

Trout didn't say anything.

"Come sit with me."

He didn't budge either.

Vane took a bite of his sandwich, set it down, and turned on the TV. Then he turned it off and stared at Trout, a frown coming onto his face. He thought he'd heard something. It had sounded like a nail easing out of a board or a cupboard door opening. Now his heart quickened, but he told himself it was nothing. He'd heard noises before, even when Doug had been here.

Trying to be quiet, he padded to the window and peered outside.

A faint gleam revealed his car and the tree in front of his house, its branches swaying in the breeze. Nothing else was out there.

He glanced down.

Trout was nosing the door, sniffing at the air coming through the crack. The house was drafty, that was all it was. He stood still, listening again, but everything was quiet.

"You aren't going out."

He returned to his sandwich, but as he took another bite, something creaked again. This time his skin crawled and his hair prickled. Moving slowly, he retrieved the remote and turned on the TV. As the sound filled the room, he stood.

Trout jumped on the windowsill and disappeared into the shadows behind the drapes.

Vane's gaze shifted away from him and rose to the ceiling. The sound had come from above. It couldn't be the floors. Those had been repaired and refinished. But not replaced, he reminded himself, so maybe a few boards were still loose. He swallowed, throat tight.

Fisher.

Who else could it be? It was Fisher looking for his flash drive. But did he know where Vane lived? Would it be hard to find him?

"Fisher!"

His voice croaked.

He needed to run. This wasn't the movies. No way was he sneaking up on a psycho killer in the basement with only a chef's knife for defense. Not his chef's knife anyway. He'd paid almost six hundred bucks for that thing. He probably had a box cutter in the junk drawer, but it was quiet again upstairs, so he was probably worrying over nothing.

He hit the light switch on the wall and took a step. The TV droned behind him.

Criminal Minds?

Perfect.

He hesitated and let his foot slide off the step. *Get a grip, Vane.* Nobody was up there. He strode back to the couch and sat down.

Maybe he should call Doug.

Really?

Candy ass.

Trout's tail flicked the curtain after whacking the glass. That was it. Something was in the yard. A raccoon or opossum. The air seeped out of his lungs, and he sank against the back of the couch. It—or they—must have gone over the roof to the tree out front. He was losing it over nothing.

Geez. *Idiot.*

He grabbed his beer and drank it. Then he put his feet on the edge of the coffee table and called Rose.

"Hi, sweetie. How are you?"

He turned down the volume on the TV. "Okay."

"You don't sound okay."

"The water heater broke the other day."

"Yours?"

"No. At Eileen's."

"Oh, geez."

"Yeah. The plumber cut me a break, and it was still almost a thousand bucks."

"Well... Write it off."

"You sound like Doug." She chuckled, and thumping sounds followed. "What are you doing?" he asked.

"Emptying the dishwasher."

Vane tipped his head back, gaze on the ceiling. "Do you ever hear random sounds?"

"Like what?"

"Um... I don't know. Creaks?"

"Like the house settling? It's an old house, Vane."

"I'm going broke."

She sighed now. "You said you didn't want to sell."

He got up and headed into the kitchen. "I think I want to now. And the diner. The best idea I can come up with to turn things around is pie." He grabbed his bag of notebooks and pencils.

"And what will you do? You can't go back."

"I don't have to go back to Fisher." He could make it other ways. If he sold the house and the diner, he'd have enough money to keep him for a while.

He headed upstairs, the hairs on the back of his neck prickling again.

"You weren't happy."

"I almost was." His heart hurt again at the thought of how close he'd been to getting the part of Marcel. But in the next second, he flashed on Stan, beating his dick in a frenzy to come on Vane's bed, and some guy he'd never even met so distraught over losing a part that he'd killed himself. "I can make it work."

"Vane."

"Okay, okay," he muttered. "I was just talking. I'm kinda hung up on Doug anyway."

In his mother's old sewing room, he put the bag down on his desk and lifted the lid to his laptop.

"I think you should see things through here," Rose said.

"You didn't care either way before."

He brought up his email, scanning down the list, but found nothing worth looking at. He clapped the lid shut again.

"That was before," said Rose.

"Before what?"

"Before you put effort into it. Before you called me so I can talk you out of quitting."

"Is that why I called you?"

He closed the door behind him, fingers hovering over the light switch in the hall.

"You like your pies, Vane. You wanted to do this."

"I can't. Nobody can."

"Miracles happen."

He hooted. "You're putting saving Eileen's on the level of a miracle, and you think I should stay?"

Her voice was light and airy. A door clapped on her end of the line. "I think you need this, sweetie. I think you need home. I think you need Doug. And... I think you want this."

He stepped off the stairs and crossed to the couch. "I called you so you'd agree with me."

"No, you didn't."

He sank down and leaned back. "I don't want to mess it up."

"Just give it your best shot, sweetheart. We were failing anyway. We can lose everything, or we can gain everything."

He groaned. "You were supposed to give me an easy out."

"You called the wrong gal."

"I guess."

But he didn't argue anymore. He asked about Lucy and Ricky and Rose's job and talked about Mr. Kam's acting school and Doug's fixation on white walls. Then they said good night. After he hung up, Vane ate his sandwich and watched another episode of *Criminal Minds*. When the show was over, he took his plate, Trout following, into the kitchen.

He looked down at the cat. "I have an idea for a pie."

Trout strolled past him and sat down at his food bowl, which he'd apparently emptied when Vane wasn't looking. "I don't think so, chubby."

After he tossed the chips he didn't eat into a cupboard without a door, he turned off the lights and TV, and went upstairs. His heart thumped faster, but when he turned on the light in his room, the shadows blew away. There were no boogeymen or ghosts up here. He brushed his teeth, stripped to his underwear, and returned to the top of the stairs.

"Trout."

After he hit the light switch, the hall fell dark, but a faint gleam seeped out of his mother's sewing room. The bottom of the door was almost an inch off the floor to accommodate the carpet that had once been in there. Now a dim gray light filled the space. *His laptop?*

With a frown, he turned on the light again and opened the door to the room. A square glowed on the desk. He must have left the computer on, but a part of his brain screamed that the screen would've gone dark by now.

Somebody had turned it on. No, woken it. It had already been on, but somebody had been in here and had tapped it, and it could only have been a few minutes ago, or... or just now.

Head swelling as his ears rang with the surge of blood through his veins, Vane spun.

Pain exploded in his head, blinding him with a brilliant light.

He stumbled into the hall on his knees, and something hit him again. He toppled and rolled onto his back. If somebody was still there, they lurked within a dark that was slowly filming his eyes. He blinked, trying to focus on the attic door and the accordion ladder unfolding from inside. In the cottony dark descending on him, his mother appeared and stretched her hand to him with a smile. He reached up, but touched only air. She was gone, and he tumbled into the scents of snickerdoodles and hot chocolate.

26

DOUG'S NIGHTMARE

DOUG'S LIPS MOVED. He was singing *Fields of Gold*. No, that wasn't right. A ringtone was singing *Fields of Gold*. He opened his eyes in the dark, rolled sideways, and took a look at the illuminated screen beside him. *Fuck*.

His heart sped into a gallop. "Vane?" He fumbled for a light, and the bed moved as Hoyt jumped off.

"Doug?"

"Yeah. Yeah. You called me."

"Oh. I... Sorry."

He got the light on and sat up. Hoyt laid down, head on his paws, and huffed. Vane's voice was thick, blurred and soft, and Doug's belly clenched at the sound of it. "Hey, what's up? Are you okay? It's..." He looked at the clock. "After one."

"My head... hurts."

"Why?"

He stood, and Hoyt rose too, scrambling back. The

golden whined as Doug shucked his pajama bottoms one-handed and got his jeans off the chair. He sat back down and stepped into one of the legs. "Talk to me."

"Um... Somebody hit me."

Doug put the phone on speaker, set it on the nightstand, and dragged his pants on. "Where are you?"

"Home."

"Alone?"

"I... think so."

Doug yanked a T-shirt on and grabbed his boots. "Okay. I'm coming over, but I'm gonna hang up first and call 9-1-1. I'll call you right back."

"No, no, no, no. Don't. I can't afford it. Just come over."

"I'll pay for the ambulance. You don't have to worry about that."

"No, I'm... I'm okay. I don't need it. Just... Don't hang up."

Doug's heart lurched against the wall of his chest. The pain of it made him light-headed. "Vane—"

"Don't. Please. Talk to me."

Doug hesitated. *Hang up. Call 9-1-1.* But what if he did? What if Vane wasn't there when he called back? What if Doug left him in the dark to—

"I'm talking." He got his keys off the dresser and tapped his leg for Hoyt to follow. "You talk too."

"Okay."

But then he didn't.

"Vane?"

"Hm."

"Talk, honey."

"Okay."

Doug got in his truck, Hoyt beside him, and sped out of his driveway onto the empty street. He gunned it, a low squeal following him around the corner. The tip of the vehicle tumbled Hoyt against his shoulder.

Vane's breath rattled. "I heard noises."

"Inside?"

"Yeah." Now he laughed, a soft, choking sound. "I didn't want to be scared."

"Vane. Jesus. I'm—"

Beep.

Fuck. He looked at his phone. "I might lose you. Don't panic."

The console beside him was stuffed with things he dumped and forgot about. Why wasn't his charger on top? He dug to the bottom before his fingers latched on a cord, and he yanked his charger out. But now his phone was dead.

"Fuck!"

Hoyt emitted a whiney howl.

"Sorry, sorry, boy. You're a good boy."

With his accelerator almost flat on the floorboard, he raced onto the long stretch of highway to Vane's. His speedometer hit eighty-five, but he didn't care. At this speed, with no traffic and no cops stopping him, he could make it to Vane's in fifteen minutes.

He got his phone plugged in and glanced down at it. The battery indicator was green now. Using his thumb, he turned his phone back on and called Vane.

His high beams flared yellow against the black silhouettes of the trees.

This isn't anything like the day Meg died. It was night now, dark and dry, not a gray, rainy day. He wasn't standing on his porch, calling Meg, and watching a pair of cops make their way to him. Willing her to answer, while they marched on with the slow steps of mourners bearing a casket. *Mr. Moore?*

His call connected.

"Hi. This is Vane Riley. I'm not—"

Jesus.

He gripped the phone in his fist and hit his brakes, squealing onto the road to Vane's.

Now what? Call 9-1-1?

He gritted his teeth, the wheel slippery under his sweaty palm. Why couldn't he make a decision? *Just fucking call!* Somebody. Anybody. *Vane.* Doug needed to hear him. He couldn't leave Vane alone. What if... No, he wasn't going to die. Doug was almost there. He'd beat out an ambulance anyway. He'd save him the way he couldn't—

No, no. Don't think that. Flooring the accelerator, he called again.

"Hey."

The breath left his lungs in a blast. He hauled it back in again. "You scared the shit out of me."

"I dropped my phone. It rolled downstairs. It's okay though."

Okay, that was better. Full sentences. Doug liked full sentences.

"So you're downstairs?"

"Yeah."

"Where's Trout?"

"Um... I don't know."

Vane grunted.

"Are you getting up?" Doug asked. "You don't have to get up."

"I lost my cat."

Doug followed the last curve before reaching Vane's house. Hoyt slid closer. "Good boy," he whispered.

"We were going to bed," said Vane.

"You didn't let him out?"

"No."

Lights winked in the trees now.

"Okay. I'm here." He swung onto Vane's driveway. "Be in in a second."

His tires slid on the gravel, and he flung an arm sideways, holding Hoyt back against the seat. The pickup rocked to a stop. He jumped out and Hoyt followed him.

Vane appeared in the window, crossing through the living room. He was cupping the back of his head, a grimace twisting his face.

After the lock turned, Doug eased the door open and gave Vane time to step back. He got a smile and heaved a sigh.

"Hey." He cupped the hand Vane already had on his head and put his other one on Vane's waist.

"I have a lump," Vane murmured.

"Are you bleeding?"

"A little."

Doug tugged on his hand. "C'mon. Let's sit, so I can take a look. You sound better."

"I'm awake now."

Hoyt inched up to the couch where Vane sat under the hanging lamp and leaned against Vane's knee. Vane petted him with his eyes half closed and his head bending his neck. Blood matted his hair.

Doug pulled the strands apart, and Vane hissed.

"My whole scalp hurts."

The blow, or whatever it had been, hadn't split the skin. It looked more like an abrasion with a solid lump under it. It was also on the back of his head where he would have hit it on the floor if he had slipped and fallen backwards. But right now it didn't matter how it had happened.

"You're going to the hospital."

"No."

But he moaned it, so it sounded more like a complaint than a refusal. Doug sat down beside him. "What happened?"

Vane winced and rested his forehead on his palms. "Luis."

"Luis? Luis came over here and hit you?"

"Or Fisher. I dunno. I didn't see anybody, but Trout did. I found him. He's under the desk in the kitchen."

"Good." Doug stroked Vane's back. He was dressed, even to his socks, but his jeans weren't buttoned, and his shirt was wrinkled. "Now lie down. I'm going to go look around. I don't think Trout's going to be much help."

"Sorry," Vane mumbled. "I was going to bed and somebody hit me."

Doug nudged him until he settled against the arm of the couch. "Be right back."

"Okay."

With the light spilling out the living room window, the house looked warm and cozy. Still, strange things happened in the world, so Doug hunted for anything out of place. Nothing was. But he'd found no sign that anybody had iced the porch either.

Doug worried about Vane's insistence that Luis—or his ex—was out to get him. He refused to back down. But, in a lot of ways, Vane was pretty high-strung. Maybe that came from being an actor, but Doug was a work-a-day guy. He didn't get Vane's emotional life anymore than he could fathom why Vane was so happy with hiring Penny and Darelle. Darelle was a chatterbox, who bent everybody's ear. Penny sashayed her way through her shift every time Doug was there. Getting ready for her Broadway debut, he guessed. Personally, Doug thought Penny was a bit off, but the customers liked her.

Hoyt trotted into the kitchen with him. Then both Hoyt and the magically reappearing Trout followed him out. The doors were locked. All the windows shut and locked.

When he went down the hallway, Vane called after him. "Not my dad's room."

Doug bit back a sigh. "I won't."

After he checked the closet and half bath, he went upstairs.

The fresh scent of refinished floors assailed him. The walls were a clean eggshell. Nobody was in Vane's room, not even in the closet, and nothing led Doug to suspect anybody had gotten in. He checked the other rooms but stopped on his way downstairs to stare at the entrance to the attic. It wasn't likely anybody had been hiding in the attic, but...

"Don't."

His heart skipped for a moment.

Vane stood at the end of the hall, giving him a squinty-eyed look. "It's empty."

"I don't mind checking."

"No, I..."

Hoyt nuzzled Vane's hand.

A bewildered look came into Vane's eyes, but he looked down and rubbed the dog between the ears. "I have bad memories."

"Did you get stuck up there?"

He shook his head, winced, and lifted his hand to the back of his skull.

Doug approached, wrapped an arm around him and steered him back toward the stairs. "C'mon. I didn't call 9-1-1, but you are definitely going to the ER."

"I don't need to."

"You don't know that."

Vane didn't speak again until they reached the bottom of the stairs. "That's how my mom died."

Doug froze for a step. "I thought... Rose said she fell off a ladder."

After he gave Vane a little nudge, they moved on. The

sound of Vane swallowing was loud. "Yeah. That one. The attic one."

In the kitchen, after Vane stepped into his shoes, Doug lifted his jacket off a hook by the door and helped him into it.

"Thanks," Vane murmured.

"Wait," Doug said. Vane hesitated. "Not you. Hoyt."

"Oh."

"Were you here when it happened?"

"Yeah. I was the only one."

"I didn't know that."

"I'd made my dad's birthday present at school that day, and my mom put it in the attic to hide it. The ladder broke. A hinge or something."

They stopped at the side of Doug's pickup and Doug opened Vane's door. "I had no idea you saw that."

"She didn't die then. I was scared, but she sat up and kind of laughed. She died a little later."

Cold crept over Doug's body, and it wasn't the air. Vane's face was bleached under the interior light. Doug squeezed his thigh. "We need to make sure you're okay."

He went around to the driver's side and got in. Vane rested his head sideways, avoiding the lump.

He turned to Doug, and a small smile creased his face. "I'm such a screwup."

"No, you're not. You've had some bad luck in your life though, that's for sure."

"I went outside to play. Rose found her."

Doug backed onto the road, shifted into drive, and sped off. "How old were you?"

"Six. After she got up, she said I should go outside and sat down to watch TV. She said she was going to rest before dinner. I didn't help her," he added after a moment.

A musing tone floated into his voice, as though he only now thought of the possibility he could have. *Poor kid.* Doug doubted he could have done anything. Even his mom hadn't realized the danger she'd been in.

"You couldn't know."

"That's what Rose always says."

His tone had a dead sound. And Doug knew why. The one person Vane had needed to tell him he'd done nothing wrong was dead now too. "You should listen to her."

"I try."

He sighed, silent after that, and a few minutes later his breath was slow and regular.

Doug let him sleep until they reached the hospital parking lot. Vane was shivering by the time they got inside. Doug sat him down in the mostly empty ER and approached the intake window.

They took Vane in right away. Doug watched him go.

After the doors swung shut, he ran his hands through his hair and sat down in Vane's vacated chair. It held none of the warmth from his body because he hadn't been in it long enough. The news was on the TV. Doug stared, but the announcers spoke in jabberwocky.

After a while, he stood and wandered to a vending machine. In the hall that attached the ER to the rest of the hospital, a machine the size of a go-cart made its way past the doorway. It reminded him of a street cleaner.

He got a Coke and drank half of it before a nurse appeared.

"Are you Mr. Moore?" She waved him over. "You can sit with him. We'll be sending him home as long as you can stay with him. He said you could?"

"Of course. No problem."

She led him through the swinging doors and pulled back the curtains on a room midway down the hall. Vane reclined on the bed, tilting his head sideways with a smile. Doug didn't know what possessed him in a public place, but he crossed the floor and pressed his lips to Vane's forehead. Vane shivered, and Doug drew back.

"Are you cold?"

"I have an icepack under my head."

He cupped Vane's face, stroking his cheek with his thumb. Soft skin roughened into whiskers. He smiled too. "Well, that's pretty damn high tech. I'd never've thought of it myself."

Vane giggled. "Don't make me laugh."

Doug bent down and kissed him on the mouth this time, and Vane quieted. His breath blew warm against Doug's face, and shoes squeaked and padded in the corridor behind them.

Maybe people looked in. Maybe people cared about Doug kissing Vane. But Doug didn't. Not now. He'd never hidden his sexuality, but he'd never talked about it either. He'd told himself it was a complication he didn't need, and being with Meg had made it moot for most people. But he'd been hiding, and hiding now was the same as lying, even though it scared him to sink his heart into Vane.

Would he stay?

But the thought of losing Vane revived the panic for Meg that had dug into Doug's belly and chest on the day she'd died. He'd told himself she had good reasons not to return his calls, but the whole time he'd known something was wrong. She wasn't just taking a long bubble bath or catching a movie. She wasn't waiting for him, ready with the curvy smile he'd always loved, his beautiful pixie, light as air.

He closed his eyes for a moment, and Vane's fingers tightened on the back of his neck.

"Are you okay?"

He straightened, swallowing his emotions. "Yeah. I'm fine. I didn't hit my head."

"I didn't hit my head, either."

Doug bit back a sigh. "If you're sure somebody hit you, we need to report it."

"You aren't sure?"

"I didn't see anything, but I'll check everything again. What about the attic? Are you sure nobody could've gotten in there?"

Vane groaned. "No. I would've heard that. I... I..."

"What?"

"I... I don't know. I was pretty sure... Shoot, I can't remember now."

"Okay. Just relax. We'll report it tomorrow just to be safe, and I'll call a friend of mine who puts in alarm systems. But seriously, Vane. It wasn't Luis. Accusing him isn't a good idea."

"He's hiding something."

Vane's voice held no doubt. Doug locked eyes with him. No lie either. No hysteria. Vane believed it. But if it wasn't Luis... If it was anybody—who?

"Is this something your ex would do?"

Something flickered in Vane's eyes. "I don't know. He replaced me. Help me sit up."

He cupped Vane's elbow and took his other hand. "Did they give you something for the pain?"

A voice came from behind him.

"Acetaminophen for pain and an anti-nausea pill. No aspirin or ibuprofen, okay?" The nurse was looking at Vane.

He nodded, and she turned to Doug. "It's a mild concussion, but he should take it easy for the next couple of days. No driving for at least twenty-four hours. Keep alert for any changes—increased headache, irritability, confusion—that sort of thing. But we don't expect any."

She turned back to Vane. "I just need you to sign your discharge papers, and you can go."

A few minutes later, Doug was holding the door of the pickup open, and Vane was climbing in.

At home, Doug got him into bed, returned downstairs, and let Hoyt into the back yard.

No lights lit the sky and no moon glowed. The only sound was the rustle of Hoyt through the weeds and the breeze through the trees.

Doug stepped off the porch and walked to the corner of the house.

Nothing but trees looked back. Vane's nearest neighbors lived in a stone monstrosity three stories high.

They had a five-car garage, a pool house, and in-law quarters. The surrounding acreage was theirs, and they seemed to have no inclination to sell any of it. Vane was isolated here, but five minutes away, over the hills, was civilization.

Was he safe? Was anybody really after him?

Who? A crazy fan?

Doug snorted. He loved—*liked*—Vane, but few people knew he'd ever acted in anything. *Ranging Wild* was ten years ago. Time had marched right on past pretty Vane.

So who? His ex?

Definitely not Luis. Doug knew that. He trusted Rose, and Rose liked Luis.

The tinkle of Hoyt's tags grew louder, and Doug turned around and headed back.

"C'mon, boy."

Upstairs, he stopped in Vane's doorway and gazed at him with a fluttery heat inside. It melted him like candle wax and stuttered through his heart like a guttering flame. Vane was sound asleep on his side, his hands folded underneath his cheek. Doug placed the tea he'd made on the nightstand, removed his boots, and stretched onto his side beside him.

He doubted Vane felt it, but Doug brushed his whiskery chin with the back of a finger.

"Clumsy oaf," he murmured.

But Vane was sound asleep and didn't stir, which was just as well because the words didn't ring true this time anyway.

27

THE FACE IN THE MIRROR

THE FLOOR OUTSIDE Vane's bedroom creaked. He pried an eye open as a rectangular shadow slowly widened. The door seemed to be swinging in on its own.

"The house is falling down," he muttered.

Doug chuckled and tugged him closer. He wriggled back into the cocoon of warmth and settled his head on Doug's outstretched arm. Toenails clicked on the floor, and Hoyt huffed at them.

"Go," said Doug.

The golden huffed again but swung around and trotted away.

"You too," murmured Vane.

Doug nuzzled the back of his neck. "You want me out of here?"

"Uh-huh." He pushed his ass back and rubbed against Doug's crotch through the bed sheets.

"Doesn't seem like it."

"You have a business to run. You can't watch me forever."

"Oh, but I can," Doug murmured.

The scrape of his whiskers lit the side of Vane's neck with shivery sparks. "You can come back."

"With my trusty golden retriever?"

"Trout wouldn't have it any other way."

"No dancing of jigs while I'm gone?" Doug asked.

Vane twisted his head. Doug's face loomed over him, his eyes so close, looking like a forest floor of golds and browns and greens. A smile pulled at Vane's lips. "I'd just fall. It's been three days anyway. I'm fine."

"Fine is relative."

"Funny."

Doug released him, and he rolled flat. "What will you do while I'm gone?"

"Just relax. Watch TV."

"Turn it off if your eyes start to bother you."

"Yes, nurse."

Doug stood, already dressed. "Two hours. I'll bring home dinner."

"Okay."

Home.

The sound of the word floated inside Vane's head. He hadn't had a home in years. Now he had the house and Eileen's and Doug and Trout.

A shiver tickled his spine, but Doug gave no sign he noticed.

Vane followed him downstairs. He waited in the doorway until Doug and Hoyt had gone, hesitating before he stepped onto the porch. He had only pajama bottoms on, but didn't want his neighbors thinking he was turning into a dude version of a cat lady. Though he only had one cat.

Quiet settled as the sound of Doug's pickup drifted off.

Wandering slowly, Vane circled the house, ruffling the bushes under the windows. Nothing looked disturbed. There were no broken branches, just tiny buds nestled in the crooks of leaves and stems. *Hydrangeas.* White and delicate like lace. He thought lace was in the name of the variety but had forgotten.

When he reached the backyard, he swept his gaze from the low hillock the well sat on to the line of trees on the other side. Nothing unusual stood out. Then a voice shouted, "Hey!"

He jumped, and a second later, the kid on the bike blazed by him. He shouted back. "I'm gonna report you!"

The kid laughed.

Isaiah.

He was a juvenile delinquent. It bugged the bejeezus out of Vane that Doug talked to the little reprobate while he was working here. The kid kept plowing across Vane's property like he owned it.

"I think we ought to make a path for him," Doug had said one day. "Line it with a split-rail fence and make it look like a country road."

For a moment, Vane hadn't been sure they were on the

same planet. He'd pointed across the yard to the strip of pavement out front. "That's a road."

Doug had just shaken his head. "Tough guy."

Vane didn't know why the kid bothered him so much. Maybe it was because he'd always been too timid to do something like ride across somebody's yard as if he had the right to. He'd always followed the rules, as though... his dad would like him for it?

He watched Isaiah disappear over the top of the hill. Now his eyes smarted in the sun, so he turned to go inside. The breeze was cool, but it would be nice to sit out here in a few weeks. Images of tables and lanterns appeared to him. He hesitated, but then the images faded, and he reentered the house through the back door.

Trout streaked by.

"Better enjoy your free time. Hoyt's not gone for long."

He made himself a cup of soup and took it into the living room. But he was weirdly restless despite not having done anything for three days.

He turned on the TV only to turn it off again and eat in a silence he broke within seconds by talking to Trout.

"I used to love being alone."

Trout stared at him from his perch on the stairs.

"I don't really mind it now. It's just—" He prodded at his head. The throb woke under his fingers, but the minute he took them away it stopped. "I'm scared."

He got up and petted Trout through the railing. The cat smiled as Vane stroked his nose with a thumb. The rhythmic motion eased him too.

"My mom died from hitting her head."

She'd probably had no idea that was possible. He tried to remember all the words they'd shared that day, but they had long ago slipped away. It had been a normal day with no sign that he should hoard every memory. But at six, he couldn't have remembered everything anyway.

"I could've died too, I guess."

Trout kept smiling. Could haves and should haves just weren't that important to a cat.

After a while, Vane pulled his hand back and turned toward the couch. Then he stopped again when his stare went down the hallway to the closed master bedroom.

He loosened a fist he barely noticed he was making.

The next thing he knew he stood in the hall, resting his fingers on the doorknob. Turning the knob slowly, he waited for the click of the latch, pushed the door open, and looked inside. Nothing bad happened. He wasn't sure what he expected. From where he stood most of the room was in view. It was tidy, and he guessed that Rose had straightened and cleaned it. As far as he could tell nothing had changed. He might as well have never gone away.

You aren't a star, and nobody in LA wants you back anyway.

The only sound came from the heater vents. The carpet muffled everything else, so the brush of something against his leg was silent. He startled, but it was only Trout. The cat leaped onto the bed, and Vane froze, but no cyclone of dust spun in the air. Maybe a gossamer twinkle by the window, but that was all. The light drifted in calm and shady.

He stepped into the room.

Trout yawned at him.

The carpet was a low, cream-colored pile, and he thought the walls had been cream too—the memory was faint. White or cream, but they were so old the paint had faded to a whisper over the sheetrock. In the shady light, they had a gray cast. Vane let his eyes drift. He took in the bed and the crucifix over the headboard and his mother's writing desk and the dresser and the mirror and—

The cans. The three cans he'd decorated for his father's birthday.

His heart clenched, and a flare of pain sucked his breath away. Why were they here? They should be in the attic where his mother had put them.

"It must have been Rose," he said, gazing at Trout lying belly up now. Would Vane's father have brought the cans down and displayed them on his dresser knowing what they'd caused? It wouldn't have taken much insight to put two and two together—the cans in the attic with the day Vane's mother fell.

It made more sense that Rose wanted Vane to believe his father'd found them and brought them down.

"That's it," Vane murmured.

He buried his fingers in the ice-cream-sundae-colored fur and got in two strokes before Trout jumped up and ran off. Vane didn't blame him. The room was cold despite the heater. Funny how it was colder inside than out this time of year.

Trying to distract yourself? Thinking about nonsense?
Maybe.

A car zoomed by on the road and a bird cheeped in the tree outside the window.

Normal sounds and nonsense.

He clenched his hands into fists, strode to the dresser, and stared at the cans. He had painted them red, white, and blue at school and decorated them with silver sparkles at home with his mom. Each one had a round tag tied to it with a piece of string. Two tags had the letter D written in red felt-tip. The other had an A.

D.A.D. Vane's birthday present to his father.

A birthday present his father never got because he was busy burying his wife.

Vane picked one of the cans up, surprised by the tinkle of coins inside. He set it down and picked up the next one. That one contained receipts. The last one, paper money. That meant—

"It wasn't Rose."

Vane's emotions bounced between happiness and wonder at the thought it was his dad who'd found them. But how could he have used them every day but not have thought to let Vane know? It might have stopped the crazy questions in his head.

What if I hadn't made them? What if I hadn't added the sparkles, and Mom had gone up to the attic earlier? Would she have gotten back down before the ladder broke?

Maybe she'd still be alive. Had his dad thought that too?

"*Mow.*"

Trout was back, fat butt planted in the doorway.

"I'll let you out in a minute."

He got a baleful stare before Trout stalked off again.

His head swam for a moment as if it were about to float away. He stepped back toward the bed. Before he sat though, he noticed the photograph stuck into the corner of the mirror's frame. He tugged it loose and sank down onto the mattress.

The photo was old and turning yellow. Vane didn't know where it had been taken. The house in it wasn't this one. He smiled at his mom's image. His dad was in the picture too, but he'd probably kept it because of her. Her hair had been dark like Vane's, but he'd clearly taken after his dad. Same cleft in the chin, same nose, same cheekbones.

Why had he never noticed that before?

Maybe he hadn't wanted to.

Could Vane have gotten his dad's personality too? The guy looking up at him looked like the kind of guy who'd yell at a kid on a bike. But he'd also been the kind of guy who'd feed a cat like Trout, because somebody had been feeding him. And he had to have known Isaiah was riding across the yard, so maybe he'd let him.

Vane squinted into the stern expression. So glum, so... disappointed. And he'd looked like this even before Vane's mom had died. None of what Vane was seeing now matched his memories. He'd always thought his father hadn't wanted him anymore, and he'd been desperate to fix his father's life and be somebody his dad would've been proud of. But... this picture.

His smiling mother squinted at the camera. His father looked impatient and annoyed at having to stop and pose.

Vane got up and tucked the photo back in the frame. The face in the mirror was pretty but not happy. He scowled and became his father.

Geez, the guy had always been like that.

Nothing that Vane had told himself—nothing he'd based his life on—was true. He'd built everything on the belief that he'd ruined his father's life by being the reason his mother died. He'd wanted nothing more than to make his father love him again and find the dad he'd made those cans for.

Except that guy had never been real. The one in the photo was real. The one who had cast gray on a sunny day. Yet, his mom had found something likeable in him and so had Rose and Isaiah and even Vane's egotistical jerk of a cook.

When the sound of tires on gravel cracked in the silence, he let go of a sigh he hadn't known he'd been holding. A tremulous panic took its place.

Who are you?

Vane. An actor.

A low creak broke the quiet in the house, and the sound lanced his head with pain. He was going to be a famous actor. His dad would be proud of him. The two things entangled like his memories of his playing self and his dying mother. *It wasn't my fault.*

He rubbed his face and heard the kitchen door open. A moment later, Doug shouted, "Hey, we're back!"

That sound—the thump of a grocery bag on the counter, a dog's tags, the buzz of a TV—was what Vane thought a home should sound like. It was noisy and chaotic, and his heart stuttered with a mix of grief and happiness he couldn't make sense of. He wanted to be happy, but he was afraid to be too. He wanted to forgive himself, but what if he still had to pay?

You will stumble and fall...

28

PIES AND PORTENTS

VANE LEANED FORWARD and squinted through the slash of his wipers at the blurry highway.

Holy moly, it was coming down hard. The rain cut through brilliant sunbeams like streaks of silver. The clouds were a mix of plum and champagne, and shadows swept the sunlit hills.

On Round-About Way, where the rain fell softer under the canopy of oaks, the wet road followed the edge of Poppy Brush until it met the main thoroughfare again. Vane turned off at a sign that read Vista Oaks. As he passed a shopping center and a movie theater on the other side of the road, the rain eased but the sun faded.

He was supposed to stay on this road until he reached Meridian. Then from Meridian he'd turn on Lincoln.

He hadn't told Doug why he was coming over, only that he had something to show him. A part of him had thought Doug wouldn't want him at the house and would think of him as an intruder in Meg's space.

But Doug hadn't resisted, at all. In fact, he'd sounded happy about the visit.

Vane's surprise at that had shocked him into forgetting something he was supposed to do. He'd emailed Carol his script changes for the Founder's Day skit in case that had been it, though he didn't think that was what he'd forgotten. At the end of his email, he'd added, *I was thinking about putting on a talent night at Eileen's —Interested?*

YESSS!!!

He'd laughed until a troop of butterflies had taken flight in his stomach. *"I bet you fail at that too,"* the voice in his head had whispered. *"You'll be a laughingstock."*

"Shut up," he'd muttered back.

Now, as he turned onto Meridian, his butterflies stirred again. Two blocks down, he found Ladybug Circle, which was a cute cul-de-sac with bungalows on wedge-shaped lots. All the houses had earth-colored facades and stone columns framing the steps. Doug's house was a woodsy green with a lush yard of hydrangeas, butterfly bushes, and hostas.

The rain pitter-pattered down on him when Vane got out of his car. He opened the back and removed a two-tiered pie carrier.

Doug met him at the door, shoulder resting against the frame, arms crossed in front of him. He was barefoot and wore jeans and a thin sweatshirt with the sleeves cut off. His lower arms were browner than his upper arms and his biceps bunched from the way he had them folded. A small smile played on his lips.

Vane released a giddy breath. "Hey."

"Hi there." Doug motioned with his chin to Vane's pie carrier. "Is that your surprise?"

"Yeah."

Doug straightened. "Come on in."

Glossy floors spread across a larger room. There were built-ins on either side of a fireplace with a large white mantle and a green-tiled facade.

"Wow," said Vane. "This is beautiful."

"Thanks."

It was sparsely furnished, but all the pieces looked plush and comfortable.

Doug gestured down a hallway. "Kitchen and family room are back here. You can set that down."

Vane followed him to the back of the house. "Thanks for letting me come over."

Doug chuckled but didn't say anything.

They entered another open space with windows overlooking another wooded yard, and a second fireplace, this one with clay-colored tile. The kitchen was modern but seemed to fit the style of the house anyway.

"Did you do all this yourself?"

Doug took the pie carrier away from him and set it on the counter. "Built the house? No. I refinished the floors, and we remodeled the kitchen. Meg decorated. All the colors, furniture. Those were her picks."

"Good taste."

Doug cupped Vane's face in his hands. "I had good

taste. Still do," he added before leaning in and pressing his lips to Vane's.

Vane relaxed into him, wrapping his arms around Doug's neck with a zip to his heart.

After a moment, Doug released him and stepped back. "I'm glad you made it."

"Hm. Me too."

"I made fresh coffee. Want a cup?"

"Yes, please."

Of course, he had to ruin the perfect moment by bobbling the ceramic mug Doug poured his coffee into. He didn't know what weird demons possessed his hands and made them jerk like a puppet's. The mug plummeted to the floor and broke, splashing coffee everywhere.

"Oh gosh. Shoot, shoot."

"Hey, hey..."

Was Doug laughing? Yes. He was laughing as he stepped around the puddle of coffee and cupped Vane's neck. Doug pulled him close and kissed his face.

"Gosh," Vane muttered.

"Don't worry."

"I broke your cup."

"Just the handle. I have others."

Vane gazed down at the mug. It was a mossy green with golden swirls and probably a favorite with his luck. Maybe it had been Meg's favorite. This was her house. Her design. Her decor. Her... husband.

"Was it special?"

Doug returned from the sink with paper towels and a rag. "It. Was. A. Cup."

"I'm a klutz."

A smile grew on Doug's face. "You're a disaster. I like it."

Vane snorted. He didn't. It had made his life a horror at Fisher's, and it wasn't that Fisher had said anything or gotten mad, because he hadn't needed to. His expression had been enough to make Vane want to crawl into a hole.

He collected the two pieces of mug while Doug mopped up the coffee.

"Go pour yourself another cup."

He nodded and found another mug, this one red with blue streaks. This time he wrapped his hands around it, holding it tight as he took a sip.

"Sit."

He complied, sliding onto a stool by his pie case.

Doug opened the back door, and Hoyt barged in, did a double take at the sight of Vane, and bounded over.

Vane let go of the cup and grabbed Hoyt's head, rocking him back and forth. "Happy boy."

"Yep," said Doug. He came around the counter, took a sip of his own coffee, and nodded at the pie case. "Am I getting any of that?"

"Do you want it?"

"Do I?"

"Do you like sugar?"

Doug raised his eyebrows, smiling over his cup. He took another swallow and said, "That depends on the package."

"Round... Gooey."

"Gooey. Um. I dunno."

Vane unlatched the pie case. "Creamy."

"Creamy, I like."

"It's good for you too."

Doug eased closer. His body heat wrapped around Vane like warm arms. The smell of coffee and Doug filled his head.

"Show me," Doug murmured.

Vane stared at him. So close. The green in Doug's hazel eyes was the color of moss today. Green swirls in pools of gold like the mug Vane had broken. He shivered. Doug's hand stroked his arm and cupped his neck.

"Are you going to give me some?"

Vane frowned. "Give you some?"

"The pie, babe."

"Oh... Oh yeah. Look." He pulled off the lid. The pie was covered in creamy swirls and peaks. "It's carrot." Doug's eyebrows rose. "I don't call it that though. I'm calling it Eileen's Sunshine Pie."

"Carrot?"

"Yeah." Vane set the lid down and sank back on the stool. "Like a carrot cake."

"Well, I love carrot cake."

"Cool. Let's try it."

Doug went around him and opened another cupboard. "You haven't tried it either?"

"No."

Doug shook his head, opened a drawer, and retrieved two forks and a knife. "I don't know how somebody can make something out of nothing."

"You're building a house."

Doug smiled, but sadness flashed through his eyes. *Thinking of Meg.* "I have a blueprint."

"Me too."

Doug flipped the knife over, handing the handle to Vane. "Cut it."

"Okay. Here goes."

He stuck the top of the knife in the center and drew the blade toward the edge of the pie tin. Good. It wasn't solid like a cake.

"What's the top made out of?"

"Cream cheese and whipped cream. I pureed the carrots like pumpkin."

When Vane slid the first slice onto a plate, it looked like a bright orange summer sun.

"Damn," Doug murmured. He passed a fork to Vane. "Share with me."

"You first."

He watched as Doug cut into the slice with the side of his fork and slid a bite of the pie into his mouth. His gaze stayed on Vane's for the first few seconds. Then his eyes rolled up and closed. A moan escaped his lips. Vane watched him swallow.

"Yeah," said Doug, opening his eyes. "I love carrot cake."

"Pie. Eileen's Sunshine Pie."

"Take a bite."

Doug smiled at him, eyes at half-mast, as he followed the direction of Vane's fork. His lips parted when Vane opened his mouth and muttered, "Oh my gosh," a moment later. Cream cheese, sugar, and spice coated his tongue. He swallowed and moaned. "Oh yeah, that's good."

Doug laughed. "You sound shocked."

"Well, geez, it's a carrot cake pie. How weird is that?"

"It's your unique selling proposition."

"My what?"

"The thing that makes you different. Besides being the clumsy, sexy, nervous bastard that you are."

Vane didn't move as Doug leaned closer and closer. Their lips met, and the tip of Doug's tongue, sweet as sugar, tickled its way in. Vane opened. Cinnamon and cloves swept in with hints of coffee. He closed his eyes as Doug cupped the back of his neck and ravished his mouth. He gave him kiss after kiss until Vane's dick threatened to burst his zipper, and he yanked back with a gasp.

"Wow."

Doug rubbed Vane's lower lip. "I like wow."

"Hm... Me too."

Nails clicked as Hoyt danced.

Doug chuckled. "I don't think so, buddy." He stabbed at the pie until he got another forkful and brought it to Vane's mouth. "Eat it."

Vane took the bite, smiling over it. The piece melted like pumpkin pie, but the whipped topping lingered, sticking to the roof of his mouth. The aroma of sugar and tangy cheese filled his head, and the spices tickled his throat. He moaned and sank into the kiss Doug planted on his lips, thrumming under the flutter of Doug's tongue against his palate.

What if he never came up for air? Could he survive on Doug's?

He wanted to try, but finally Doug pulled back and gasped, "Damn. You taste so fucking good."

Vane straightened dizzily, dragging in a breath. "Eat some more."

Doug ignored the pie and devoured Vane's mouth, and Vane did nothing to stop him. He relaxed against the arm Doug curled around his back, though for a split second, he thought of Meg. Had Doug been like this with her? Ravenous? But then, teeth nipped his lip, and a warm palm cupped his crotch, and he forgot everything but the pleasure.

When Doug surfaced for air, Vane gasped—"I guess you like my pie,"—and Doug laughed and leaned in again. Closer. Almost—

"*Woof!*"

With a groan, Doug dropped his head and stepped back. "You just came in."

Hoyt spun. "*Woof!*"

"Fine. Just a sec?"

Vane nodded. "Beats a puddle on the floor."

"Ha. Yeah."

Doug turned and Hoyt scrambled to the door.

Vane followed as far as the window. Smaller panels of glass framed the inside of the sill on the top and sides. The small panes were etched along the edges, and the trim was white like the walls. The floors were a glossy, reddish wood. The room was beautiful. The whole house was. Not like Vane's that seemed to be falling apart even as Doug repaired it. Drafty. Too cold in some places and too warm in others.

Fisher would have had a coronary living in Vane's house.

Vane remembered the feeling of... no feeling in Fisher. The guy was as modulated as his temperature-controlled climate.

As Vane stood there watching, Hoyt took off after a squirrel, and Doug strode barefoot onto the damp grass. "Hey! Quit that."

The rain had stopped, but the light had gone too. Under a gray sky, the shadows outside crept into one. Trees and bushes rimmed the yard, and the air was fresh and damp by the open door. He took a deep breath and turned back into the room. Doug's voice came from behind him.

"Want a fire?"

He turned again. Hoyt trotted through the door and plunked himself down on a giant pillow by the couch. "Yeah. Can we?"

"Sure."

Vane wasn't sure why he never had a fire in his own fireplace, except it had always seemed like too much work.

"I didn't ask," Doug said. "Are you staying?"

"I don't have any plans." *Right?* That little niggle hit him again. *What the heck was he forgetting?*

"Good. We can order a pizza or something." Doug pointed at the cabinet by the TV and took a log off the hearth. "Pick a movie."

"Don't you have Netflix?"

"Yeah. That's an option."

When Vane opened a drawer below the TV, he grinned and said, "I like these better anyway." Doug glanced over. "Your not-suitable-for-work collection," he added.

"Oh." Doug chuckled. "Yeah, not so much." He lit the crumpled newspaper wedged under the logs.

"Why don't you watch online?"

"I don't like porn on my computer. Definitely not on my phone. I know. I'm weird like that." He wrapped his arms around Vane from behind, chin on his shoulder. "See anything you like?"

"Um... Het? No." Doug breathed onto his skin before biting his neck, and Vane pulled in a shaky breath. "But... Um... Yeah. This I like," he murmured, shuddering at a nibble beneath his ear. "We can... do this."

"Do what?" Doug's lips ghosted back down to his shoulder. "Watch it?"

"Act... act it out."

Now Doug drew away. "Act it?" He didn't sound against it. "These things are usually pretty vanilla."

Vane showed him the cover on the DVD he'd picked up. One guy was practically standing on his head, another looking like he was drilling for oil in the first guy's ass.

Doug laughed. "Won't you pass out?"

"You think that's me on the bottom?"

"Yeah, babe. I think that's you on the bottom."

Well... *yeah.*

Vane leaned against Doug's chest until they were nose to nose and wrapped his arms around him. "We act it out.

It'll be fun. I'm getting a beer and wine license and putting on a talent night once a week. Thursday nights maybe. I want to build some outdoor seating. A garden area. Skits and songs. With my special Eileen's Sunshine Pie."

Doug tipped his head back. At first, his face was expressionless. Then his eyes twinkled, and his smile grew. "I love how your mind works." *Love.* "There's no rhyme or reason to it."

Vane shrugged. "Makes sense to me."

"Put the DVD in. Show me what panties you have on today."

"Manties."

"Show me," Doug whispered.

Vane tucked the DVD under his arm, kicked off his shoes, and shucked his jeans. His dick brushed against soft cotton, pushing against the pouch that surrounded it. Doug grinned and Vane's cheeks flamed.

"Are those new?" Doug asked.

"Yeah." He huffed. "Not real comfortable." The pouch was too tight, the seams pressing into his skin.

"Yeah, but... damn."

Vane slipped his fingers under one of the red lace ties that crisscrossed the front of the gray briefs. He flicked it in Doug's direction. "Want me to take them off?"

Doug shook his head. "My job."

Liking the sound of that, Vane inserted the DVD into the player and hit the power button on the remote.

"So how are we doing this?" Doug asked.

"Well, it'll work better if you're naked."

Doug whipped his sweatshirt off, and Vane asked, "Do you want the sound on?"

"Hell yeah. That's the best part. Low though. I want to hear you over it."

Imagining himself moaning and groaning like a porn star woke Vane's inner wanton. He cupped his dick and squeezed it, pushing into his palm. "I think you have a bit of nasty in you." *Too.*

Doug kicked his jeans halfway across the room, took Vane's waist in his hands, and stared down at Vane's crotch. "Rub it."

Vane giggled. "You see? You like to watch."

"I like to watch you. I like the way your chest and neck get all red. I like the way you bite your lip. Like that." He tugged it from between Vane's teeth. "I like that you like it. Me watching you."

Vane nodded. Doug's glassy eyes drew a moan from his throat. He followed the tug of Doug's hands and dropped onto the couch with him. Tags jangled as Hoyt hopped up.

"Stay," Doug said.

"I'm not going anywhere," Vane murmured. "We have to watch the video." He pointed the remote, fast-forwarded, and hit play.

A guy on his knees popped onto the screen, his mouth full of another guy's dick.

"Yeah," said Doug. "I got this."

He hooked his fingertips in Vane's waistband and lifted. Vane groaned. The air on his hot skin sent shivers over him. Doug scooted down and blew on the tip of Vane's dick.

"Oh gosh," Vane whispered. "I'll watch for us."

Doug chuckled. "You do that."

But the swipe of his tongue made Vane drop his head onto the back of the couch and arch. "Yes!"

He lifted his hips, and Doug pulled his panties down mid-thigh. Another warm swipe of tongue drew a sigh from him. He raised his arms over his head and stretched, forcing his gaze to the TV. The throat bulged on the guy on his knees, and his face had gone red. The other guy pulled out a spit-slick cock. Vane hissed and thrust higher as the warmth of Doug's mouth enveloped him.

"That... Yeah." *Oh yeah.*

His memory told him this felt better than it had ever been with anybody else. His caution was lost, and when he smashed his elbow into the wall, he didn't care. He just rolled forward and curled his fingers in Doug's hair while the scene on the TV blurred. Forget what the porn stars were doing. He was his own porn star, presenting his crotch for Doug's pleasure.

He felt a thousand eyes on him.

The bop of his dick against the back of Doug's hot, tight throat lit a fire in his balls and belly.

He fought to open his legs wider for the touch of the air on his skin, but something wasn't working.

Doug popped off. "Wait."

Vane slumped back, gazing down the length of his body. His panties bound his legs. Something about that constriction sent a million tiny fingers dancing across his skin.

Doug pulled the fabric down but held onto Vane's ankles. "Keep these on."

"Yeah?"

"Yeah."

He let his knees loll to the side and curled his arms over his head again. "Do what you want to me."

Doug grazed his nails from Vane's nipples to the creases at the top of his thighs. Vane arched again. His tendons stretched while a combustive pressure built between his legs. His dick strained, a string of precum quivering above his belly. Doug swiped a finger through it, pulling it free, and carrying it to Vane's lips.

He opened his mouth and tasted himself.

"Yeah," Doug whispered. "Like that. You're so damn dirty."

He moaned and laved Doug's finger. Images of being tied bare to a tree with his own underwear bombarded him. He wanted people watching as Doug jerked him off, and he spurted steaming cum into the air. He rolled his hips, straining for a touch on his dick.

Doug pulled his finger out of Vane's mouth. "Want something?"

Vane nodded. "Suck me."

With his gaze trailing Vane's body, Doug worked his jaw side to side as though mulling this over. "I dunno. I don't want to spoil my dinner. Or my dessert."

A loud grunt came from the TV, and Doug turned to it. Vane followed his gaze. One of the guys was upside down now, his weight on his shoulders, the other guy's face buried in his ass.

Vane pointed the remote at the screen. "Do that."

Doug got on his knees. "I can do better. Pause it." He hooked a hand under Vane's knee and tugged his leg away from the back of the couch. "Flip over but keep your panties on."

"Manties."

Doug stood, and Vane crawled onto his elbows and knees.

"Face down."

The press of Doug's hand on the back of his head made Vane melt again. He wobbled, weak and woozy with a bizarre pleasure that swept through him as soothing as a tub full of warm water. He laid his face against the rough fabric of the couch, ass in the air. He didn't know he was rocking until the cushion sank beneath him, and Doug's warm hand on his hip held him still.

"So pretty."

"No..."

Well, yes, he was, so he didn't know why he'd said that. Maybe because Fisher had wanted him to be pretty, but not clumsy or anxious or hopeful or—

"Oh gosh."

A sticky substance coated Vane's ass between his cheeks. He flung a look behind him and caught his breath. With a wink and a smile, Doug licked the substance from his fingers.

A raspy wheeze left Vane's throat, followed by a giggle. "Is that pie?"

"Yep."

"Oh, my gosh."

Doug smoothed his palm up Vane's spine again, pushing his face back into the cushions. Vane spread his knees, balancing one on the edge of the couch.

"Oh, babe. You are so beautiful. You have no idea."

"I have pie on my ass."

Doug flicked a cheek with the tip of his tongue, and a shiver fluttered its way to the top of Vane's head. All the hair on his body stood on end, and his cock jerked at every swipe of Doug's tongue. It was torture. His balls ached from it.

"Touch me," he moaned, and teeth sank into his cheek. "That's... biting."

Doug dug his thumbs high into Vane's inner thighs, and Vane bucked at a sensation that confused him. His cock jumped too, but it might have been from pain. The feeling hit him like a fist in the belly, and he arched into it, sticking his ass straight onto Doug's hot, ravenous tongue.

Oh gaaawd...

Doug hummed. The sensation of that tongue and the humming rolled through Vane's body. He bent his head on the cushion and peered between his legs at Doug's chest and chin. Kisses danced over his cheeks and upper thighs, and the tongue flicks drove more shivers through him. The throb in his belly deepened into an ache. Moans and gasps fell from his lips as erotic as any porn stars. The flutter of air against his bare skin raced through him like every midnight fantasy.

He knew when the pie was gone. His spit slick skin contracted, sizzling under Doug's whiskery rubs as Doug probed his hole.

"I'm gonna come," Vane moaned.

Not even touching himself. Just by bouncing his hot dick in the air.

Doug grabbed Vane's cock and squeezed him tight. "Nope. Not yet."

"You're killing me."

A chuckle followed his whine. Doug let him go and rocked his jeaned crotch against Vane's ass. "I think I went a little off script."

Vane twisted his head to look back at the TV. "You think?"

"You want that?"

He gawked at the upside down guy on the screen. "Well, if I'm staying in character."

"A consummate professional."

"That's me," he agreed, pushing himself onto shaky arms.

Doug stood and said, "Back in a sec." He pointed at Hoyt. "Stay."

Hoyt gazed at Vane, worry in his frown.

"S'okay, boy. We're having fun."

Hoyt snuffled and sank onto his pillow. Sitting back on his heels, Vane let his other foot slip to the floor while his gaze drifted from the TV to the window behind it. The lamplight cast a glare against the dark glass and shadows moved across the panes.

The trees?

A creepy-crawly feeling of self-consciousness slithered through him. He covered his crotch with his arms.

"Now you're shy."

Well... People watching him for real didn't have quite that allure as fantasy people watching him. But dang, that fantasy got him going.

He uncovered his crotch. His dick was still hard and rosy tipped.

Doug grinned at him, dropped a condom and tube of lube on the couch, and peeled his jeans and briefs off in one motion.

His cock bobbed, and Vane's unease fled as he leaned over, eyes on Doug's, and Doug nodded. Vane ran his tongue up the hot column of flesh, laughing as Doug pushed into him. He took the tip in his mouth and flicked the slit.

Doug hissed and squeezed his shoulders. "Not too much. I'm gonna blow."

Vane pulled back. "Only in me."

Doug nodded. "You like that?"

"Your dick in my ass? Oh yeah."

He was a hardwired bottom, that was just what he liked, but with Doug it was...

Happiness.

Thoughts he didn't want to think about right now swirled under the currents of his desire. They whispered about emotions he was terrified of opening himself up to. What if Doug got tired of him the way Fisher had or couldn't get over Meg? What if Vane's talent night bombed and he lost the diner he'd begun to care about? He had a track record of screwing things up, after all. Maybe it was better to keep things light and fun like the scene on the TV.

Vane hit the button on the remote. Grunts filled the room as he rolled onto his ass and leaned over the edge of the couch.

"You know this is fucking awkward as hell," said Doug.

"I know, but I've always wanted to try this position." Without the possibility of catapulting himself out Fisher's two-story-high window. Certainly no romance was involved, just play and fun and...

Gosh, he was as nervous as if it were his first time. Wriggling in a way that turned Doug's eyes dark, he rested on his elbows and pointed his ass toward the back of the couch.

Doug's smile was a whisper on his lips. "Ready?"

"Yeah. Blood's already starting to rush to my head."

"I don't think that's where it's supposed to be."

"Hurry up. I might pass out."

Doug stepped onto the couch between Vane's legs, cupped him under the knees and eased him onto his shoulders. Now the TV was upside down, and Vane had to twist his head to view the action on the screen. Geez. The top was banging the bottom into the floor. Grunts exploded like shouts. Was the guy getting hurt? How much did they get paid for that?

"Look at me, babe."

Vane rolled his head back as Doug stroked his dick and pulled a shiver out of him. The snick of the cap on the lube got his heart pounding. Doug dribbled it onto his hole and rubbed it in with his thumb, and Vane clenched at the pleasure. "Oh yeah," he whispered.

A moment of tension filled him when Doug leaned

away, but then he heard the snap of a condom and Doug returned. "Hold still."

Vane blinked at the peculiar order. "Please don't add 'you won't feel a thing' to that."

Doug laughed. "Jesus, Vane."

"What?"

Luckily, he did feel it. The luscious burn of Doug pushing into his hole and blowing every thought he had into the stratosphere. His eyes rolled, and he let out a belly-deep moan.

Doug leaned over him and flattened his palms on the rug. "Fuck," he murmured.

"Yeah," Vane gasped, opening his eyes again. He rested his heels on Doug's back and rocked. His belly pressed into his chest, and the back of his shoulders scraped the rough fibers beneath him.

Hoyt scrambled off his pillow and whined at the back door.

"Like hell," Doug grumbled.

Vane chuckled and cupped Doug's face. "Are you going to move?"

Doug didn't say anything. He vibrated. The tremors ran up his arms and shook his shoulders. The pinned strength was scary. His face reddened, Vane's too, probably. "Hold onto me," Doug said.

Confused, Vane nodded anyway, hooked his heels at the top of Doug's ass and wrapped his arms around the back of his neck. Doug dropped a foot to the floor and worked his arms around Vane's body. Then he straightened, carrying Vane with him.

Vane gasped and held on. *Holy moly.*

Now they were upright, face to face, the tip of Doug's cock still in Vane's ass. Vane sank down on it, basking in the glow of pleasure on Doug's face. His eyes were soft pools of woodsy shadow. When Vane was fully seated, Doug lowered him onto his back on the couch and smiled. "Like this."

"Like this," Vane agreed, though this was the thing he was afraid of. Something had opened inside him between the brutal grunts on the TV and now the noise faded to only a distant hum. Hoyt's tags. Doug's breath. His own blood pounding in his veins.

Sweat, slippery and hot, collected between them.

Doug cupped his head, bending him double, the slide of his dick in Vane's ass burning hotter and hotter. Vane reared until their lips met and their breaths mingled. The smooth in and out didn't vary, the burn deepening, the pressure building until Vane gasped, "I can't... I can't..." Formless thoughts swirled in his head. He wasn't sure what he was saying. "Doug!"

"I'm here."

Vane rocked, trying to break Doug's rhythm. The next thrust hit his sweet spot, and his eyes rolled. Sparks flashed in the dark of his head.

Now Doug's thrusts came fast and slow. He rocked in deep, and the stab shot all the way to Vane's heart.

Vane groaned and pulled Doug down to him again. "Kiss me."

Hoyt barked.

Then Doug's lips touched his, a flutter as soft as his

tongue had been on Vane's rim. Doug's pants sawed at the air, the pounding of his heart knocking its way into Vane's chest.

"Faster... faster..."

Doug nodded. Sweat beaded the sides of his nose. Vane gasped, his tongue longing for a taste, reaching with a mind of its own. But Doug's lips met his instead, his hot breath baking Vane's brain until his thoughts burned away. He bucked, his dick sliding through his fingers, pressure building... building...

Doug panted. "This... this..."

Yes. This. Love making. Ferocious. Wild. Like nobody had ever done to him. Vane's fist flew. "I'm... I'm gonna come."

"Do it."

Fire raced up his spine in a burst of sparks and shot out of his dick. The release shattered his senses. He rolled his head back, tugging on his cock. With a shudder, he milked the last dribbles while Doug collapsed onto his elbow on the edge of the cushion.

Thoughts in a tumble, Vane let go of his dick and wrapped his arms around Doug's shoulders. "Don't fall."

Doug rocked his head against Vane's. "I won't."

Vane wanted to float away, but the couch wasn't comfortable, and Doug's weight rocked him as he sat up. "Okay?"

Vane forced a smile. "That didn't go according to plan."

Doug smiled too. "Not exactly. I need to get rid of this," he added, pulling off the condom.

"Can I clean up?"

How weirdly formal. Like they'd never had sex before.

"Sure. Go back down the hall. First door on the right."

He rolled off the couch, body screaming at him, grabbed his clothes, and headed for the bathroom. It was a pretty half bath with flowers etched into the mirror.

Don't look in there.

He washed, got dressed, and splashed water on his face. Two white hand towels with peach-colored roses along the hem hung from a rack beside the sink. He pulled one off and buried his face in it.

The smell of flowers enveloped him, light and old fashioned, like his mother's hydrangeas.

He lowered his hands and met his gaze in the mirror.

Stupid. I said don't look.

All the sex flush had faded into shock white. He leaned closer to the glass. Was love a visible thing? Did it live in the eyes? Had it ever been in Fisher's? His own eyes were so dang pale. As translucent as water and underlain with fear. He was lousy at living up to expectations.

Love.

Say it.

"Love," he whispered. "I think I love you."

Don't say it.

He hung the towel back on the rack and rubbed his thumb over the embossed roses. *Meg's?*

The minute he hit the light switch, it cut the fan overhead, and the sound of pounding on the front door reached him.

He stepped into the hall, and Doug headed toward him.

A voice came from outside.

"Hey, are you going to let me in? It's raining out here."

Dorcas.

Doug glanced at Vane, eyebrows rising in a curve as he strode by. He yanked open the door, and Dorcas stormed in, shot a look between them, and slammed her hands on her hips. "No wonder you stood me up."

She was staring at Vane. His mouth fell open. "Stood you up?"

"I waited for almost an hour. You both have texts from me, by the way."

"Oh gosh." Vane clapped his hands to his head. "The reading."

"I should make you pay for it." She glared at Doug, who was leaning against the door, laughing at them. "It's not funny."

"I'm sorry," said Vane.

She pouted at him, but then she pursed her lips and shrugged. "It's okay." Her gaze turned baleful, though, as she shifted it back to Doug. "I guess I understand."

"Don't look at me," said Doug. "I didn't invite him over."

"Hey."

"Well, I was worried," said Dorcas. "That's why I'm here. Scary things have happened."

Doug raised his eyes to the ceiling. "Don't encourage him."

She rested her hands on Vane's shoulders and kissed his cheek. "Well, I believe you."

"Thank you."

"I have to go. I have a date."

"Oo la la," murmured Doug.

"I'm ignoring you. You, " she said, turning back to Vane and hitching up the strap of her shoulder bag. "Tomorrow. One o'clock. Take a long lunch if you have to, but don't miss it this time."

He nodded. "I promise."

"Good." She waved at Doug. "You. Out of my way."

He opened the door for her. "Why are you mad at me?"

"Answer my texts. I could have been lying dead on the floor."

"Then you wouldn't have been texting me."

"You know what I mean." She stepped onto the porch, stopped, and turned back. "Where is Hoyt?"

A frown crossed Doug's face, and he glanced at Vane. "Inside, right?"

"I didn't let him out."

"Are you sure?" asked Dorcas.

"Yeah," said Doug. "I told him to stay. Hoyt!"

Tags clattered as Hoyt skidded around the corner and raced toward them. Doug raised a palm. "Stop."

The golden dropped to his belly and slid on the glossy floor. Keeping his eye on Doug and Dorcas, Vane bent down and gave Hoyt's side a couple of hollow-sounding thumps.

Doug was frowning. "Why did you ask?"

"Your side gate's open," Dorcas said. "On the garage side. I saw it when I drove up."

"Are you sure?"

She nodded and blew a kiss at Vane. "I'm looking out for you, sweetie, so don't forget. One o'clock."

"I'll remember."

"I need to check the gate," said Doug.

He padded out on bare feet and disappeared around the side of the house with Dorcas. The sound of their voices floated back while Vane gazed into Hoyt's upraised eyes. "Glad you didn't get out, boy."

Glad somebody's looking out for us.

He hoped blowing off his reading for sex wasn't going to come back and haunt him.

"Don't panic," he murmured.

Hoyt chuffed.

29

DORCAS READS FOR VANE

THE PEANUTS SAILED out of Dorcas's hand and clattered onto her cobblestone patio. At the sight of a green garden hose curled under the spigot, Vane shivered, though the day was warm. Doug still didn't believe somebody might have turned on Vane's hose and frozen his porch. Or broken into his house and hit him on the head.

Not somebody.

Luis.

Or... *Fisher.*

Dorcas brushed off her hands and turned back. The minute she stepped inside, a blue jay shot down with a raucous squawk. It hopped on the water-stained cobblestones, grabbed a peanut, and flapped off again.

"You must be popular in the bird world."

She laughed and slid the door shut. "I enjoy it. I feed the hummingbirds too. Come on back."

He followed her into a hall with one door at the end

and one midway that opened onto the shop. Vane glimpsed display cases, clothes racks, and bookshelves. Candles and glass bowls piled with colorful stones covered the countertops, and strings of crystals hung from the windows.

"I close at lunch for readings usually. Nobody will bother us."

The air was dark and spicy with incense. At the end of the hall, they entered another room that was probably supposed to have been a den or a study. It was a plain square with a small window covered by a dark green bush. The play of shadows from the leaves reminded Vane of Doug's coffee mug. *Meg's mug.*

A square table sat in the center of the space, and floor to ceiling bookshelves covered two of the walls. The titles revealed books on tarot, reiki, and divination. Half a dozen crystal balls, glass bowls, and pillar candles stood among the books. More candles sat on the table.

"Do you use these?" He touched one of the crystal balls with his fingers. The surface was warm.

"Yes. Sometimes," Dorcas said. She gestured to the table. "Sit."

He pulled a chair out. "How did Meg die?"

Dorcas shot him a look from where she stood at a dresser situated underneath the window. Her lips parted, but she turned away without answering and opened a drawer. "Didn't Doug tell you?"

He almost shrugged but stopped himself, surprised by the dismissive gesture. He wanted to know how Meg had died, but when he thought about it, maybe he didn't want to know about *her*. He knew she still had a hold on Doug, and maybe he was afraid she'd never let go, but did he really want her to? Did he want Doug and Poppy Brush to be his life?

"I know it was an accident, but I didn't ask much. I didn't really know how."

She set a box down and sat across from him. "Well, it's a hard thing to talk about, isn't it? To bring up the one who came before you?" She gave him a small smile.

"I don't know." Despite her place in Doug's heart, he wasn't sure being Meg's replacement drove his question. He didn't think he was that shallow, but he was fumbling through the memories Doug kept to himself. "I don't want to hurt him."

"Everything about Meg hurts him, honey, not just talking about her. The fact he's stuck with you means something though. It's been over two years now." Her voice softened. "I was waiting for him to pick up his life again. I guess he was waiting for you."

Vane didn't comment on that. He was hardly the screwup people waited for. "How'd it happen?"

Dorcas lifted the lid of the box and stared into it for a moment.

"Carbon monoxide poisoning from a furnace. This was at her office," she added. "I still don't understand. The building was old, but her landlord maintained everything. There was no reason to think anything was wrong. Things break, I guess. Doug was out of town. He said he had a bad feeling when she didn't return his calls. He left a message for me to check on her, but I was working that day and didn't get it on time. I don't know why he was so sure something was wrong. They were that close though."

"Geez," Vane said. "That's really awful."

"Yeah," Dorcas murmured. "I don't always believe it."

Goose bumps tickled his skin at the thought of being here one minute—one second—and being gone the next. He ran a hand through his hair, fingers lingering on the back of his head.

Dorcas gazed at him. "Things had just gotten—"

Her voice trailed off, and he waited. She removed a rectangular-shaped item wrapped in a silky red cloth and a match from the box.

After lighting the candles on the table, she said, "I'm going to tell you something. You can't tell Doug. I just want you to know the way he might think about Meg's death."

Dread filled him. What the heck was she about to tell him?

"What?"

"The police asked this. They wanted to know... Well, they considered that it wasn't an accident."

The goose bumps on Vane's skin turned into icicles. "Are you saying somebody killed her?" In a way that looked like an accident? Like—

Falling on ice?

His vision narrowed but focused again on Dorcas gaping at him.

"Of course not," she said. "I mean... They weren't sure why she didn't get out. Was the detector not working, or did she turn it off? There didn't appear to be anything wrong with it."

She took a deep breath and continued. "I know Meg and Doug fought over his job. The amount of work he was putting in, but that's the way of it when you work for yourself and you're starting out. Meg had her own business too, but it was a franchise, so it really wasn't the same thing. Anyway, what I'm saying is, they had gone through a rough patch. I don't believe Meg would kill herself. Ever. But I think Doug thinks I do because she stayed with me after one of their arguments. She was pregnant and didn't want to be alone."

"Would she—?"

Dorcas shook her head. "Somebody else from her office came in to work a few hours too, I guess. She told the police that Meg was just sitting in a chair by the door with her coat and purse in her lap. She wasn't even sure anything was wrong at first. But there wasn't a note, and she didn't leave a message with anybody, so the police chalked it up to a horrible accident."

"Dang," Vane murmured.

"Plus, it would be seriously far-fetched to think she took advantage of a malfunction like that. It's not something you plan. I researched this too and found out some people don't have symptoms. And the leak was bad, not just a buildup, which is usually what happens. So anyway, the police thought she'd started feeling sick and got her things ready to go and..." Dorcas swallowed. "Didn't make it."

"Oh my gosh. So Doug?... Doug believes she didn't mean to, doesn't he?"

"I hope so, but I'm not sure. I've tried to get him to talk

about it without coming right out and asking him to. I don't know how to bring it up either. I'm sure she never meant to die, but Doug doesn't want to talk about it. You know him. He's focused, sets his sights on a project, and goes for it. In the meantime, he doesn't notice a lot. Meg wasn't happy for a while. Maybe he didn't see it at first, but I know he was trying to change, and I believe—really believe—it was a tragic accident."

"I hope so," Vane murmured.

Dorcas smiled, and the candlelight in the gloomy room cast shadows on her face. "You're good for him."

"I think I might be a little high maintenance."

She laughed. "You're just right, honey, and it's time for him. Some things work out. When I was a kid, my sister, Violet, was sick, and my parents spent every waking moment trying to make her life better." She paused and chewed her lip for a moment. "I still feel awful about this."

"What?" Vane asked.

"Well, she was so sick, but she really wasn't a nice person, and I don't think being sick had anything to do with it. There was something not quite right about her, but my parents didn't see that. They couldn't do anything but watch her get sicker and sicker. She was never capable of living without a lot of care, and my folks gave her everything they could. They were heartbroken when she finally died, of course. But now they're living in Florida, young enough to enjoy the rest of their lives."

"Well, that part's good."

She nodded. "Everything happens for a reason. Now. Are you ready?"

"Uh... Yeah."

He didn't know what he thought was going to happen, but now he had butterflies in his stomach, and he hadn't come in that way. Somehow, all the kitsch in the shop and the lush green garden in back faded into menacing shadow. He wasn't sure he wanted to know what Dorcas's tarot cards would tell him. He kind of wanted to go across the street and buy a too-sweet, too-frothy coffee and browse a normal bookstore.

But here he was... trying to discover if he was paranoid and the biggest klutz in the world, or if somebody was truly trying to hurt him.

Was Luis that determined to get rid of him?

Or was it Fisher wanting his pictures back? Vane never had gotten around to sending those off. Jesus, why not? Was he crazy? Holding on in case—

"Vane?"

He blinked. "What?"

"You drifted off on me."

"Sorry. Just tired."

Her lips twisted in a half smile. "Maybe you shouldn't stay up so late."

His laugh sounded a bit like a titter. "Probably not."

"Okay. This is what we're going to do. I'm going to shuffle the deck and give it to you. You shuffle it and give it back to me. I'm going to spread the deck out on the table and you are going to pick seven cards, one at a time. You give me each card after you pick it. What do you need to know, honey?"

"I want to know if somebody's after me."

She made a face, scrunching her lips on one side, before smoothing her expression again. "I won't be able to be exact. We can guess based on the signs. See what forces are at work in your life right now and things you need to know about where you are going or might be going. Lessons you need to learn, or damaging patterns and old hurts you need to release before you can move on. Tarot shows you what your spirit guides want you to know to help you."

"Can't you just look in a crystal ball?"

Her expression froze for a moment, a stiff smile breaking it. "No. Well, yes. That's... stronger. But still in symbols. You can ask Spirit to help you see what you need to know. Or if you're following the right path with Eileen's. Or we could do a love reading."

"What I need to know? Like if somebody's after me?"

"The cards could portend interference or a powerful person working in your life. You might get a strong idea from that. You can ask just that—what do I need to know about my life right now."

"Okay."

"Take a deep breath and relax."

He nodded. Dorcas unwrapped the rectangle-shaped bundle she'd removed from the box earlier. The cards were innocuous, not the satanic images he was half-expecting. Of course, it was hard to judge with the cards face down. Still... He swallowed when Dorcas rapped the deck with a knuckle three times. "Just to clear any lingering energies," she said.

Great. Energies. Why couldn't he get lazy spirits?

He nodded and took the deck from her. "How many times do I shuffle?"

"As many times as you think you need to. Don't force it. Relax and do what feels right."

The cards were stiff and not that easy to manipulate. He thought he should shuffle more than three times, but he wasn't sure. Was a voice going to tell him, *"Stop. That's enough."*

Heat crept into his face. *Get a grip. This isn't real.* But what if it was? Like a fortune cookie. *Don't panic.* Now the butterflies in his stomach buzzed like hornets. He imagined Doug rolling his eyes at him, but Vane's inner early warning system bellowed—*Get out! Run!* But run from what? The truth?

Was he that afraid of everything he'd made of his life and all the things that might come back to haunt him now? *Duh.*

He shuffled five times and offered Dorcas the cards back. She set them on the table and fanned them in a smooth, perfect crescent.

"You could be a poker dealer."

She grinned. "Nope. Not in the cards."

He groaned. "Gosh, Dorcas."

"What? I thought it was cute." She pouted at him before she dipped her chin toward the table. "Okay. Pick your cards."

He let his fingers hover. Dorcas said nothing. He wasn't sure if anything drew him to the card he chose, but he picked one and handed it to her. Then another. She set them down until they formed a U-shape and only flipped them right side up when he was done.

Her eyes flickered as she studied the layout, and flame shadows danced across the face of the cards. *Satanic.* They looked satanic to him now. Rough, childlike scrawls in mostly yellows and blues and blacks. He shivered. But then Dorcas smiled and a surge of hope rolled through him.

"I love this spread," said Dorcas. "It's called the horseshoe. It's not as famous as the Celtic Cross, and it doesn't touch on as many elements. What I like is the broad view you get—past, present, and future, your hopes and dreams, and the world around you right now." She tapped a card at the top of the spread. "This is your recent past."

"It's effing Death."

It said Death right on the freaking card. A guy in black riding on a white horse with panic-stricken people falling on the ground. *Death.*

"Or transformation," said Dorcas. "Also, in your past."

"My dad?"

"Maybe. Notice the sun peeking out in the background? This isn't a negative card, really. It suggests an end, the loss of someone or something important to you. It might mean you have old patterns or wounds that don't benefit you any longer and you need to let them go. The sun in the background suggests hope ahead, so don't be afraid. The Chariot here—"

She tapped the card below Death. "This is your present. And the Ten of Wands at the bottom here is you in the world you're living in now. That means all the people you know and interact with and all the things that you're doing. Your house. Eileen's.

"The Chariot is a mostly positive card. It's a major arcana card, like Death and the Sun, which we'll get to, and represents spiritual lessons. The Charioteer is a pedal-to-the-metal kind of guy. Look at how straight and tall he is. He's fearless. But the black and white sphinxes are opposites, the light and dark of ourselves. The Chariot is ready for the journey, but we have to reconcile our two sides before we move ahead. So, this is a sign for you to look into yourself, and stick to your guns about your true purpose."

"Diner owner," he said dryly.

"That's a legitimate occupation." She leaned in closer. "Coming from a fellow business owner."

"Sorry. I'm nervous."

"Breathe."

"Breathing," he murmured.

"You are overwhelmed."

He forced his eyes not to roll. "Well, yeah."

"No, silly. The Ten of Wands. This is you, right now. Where you are in your life and the world. You are being crushed under the weight of everything you feel about your life right now."

Duh again.

Dorcas ran her finger over the image of a guy on the card and continued.

"See how he's bent under the weight of all the wands he's carrying? Well, you don't have to be him. You don't have to carry the weight all by yourself. You've been through a lot. You've lost your dad and put your career on hold to come home and save the family business. And maybe you resent that. Or don't want to do it. It might be holding you back. It's definitely a lot of weight, but you have friends and family who love you. Take help wherever you find it. And if you don't want to bear this weight, don't feel any shame about letting it go."

Something had pulled him back home to Poppy Brush though. He hadn't dropped everything and run here because he'd wanted to. He'd wanted to be Marvelous Marcel. Instead he'd become the hapless guy with ten wooden staffs on his back. Well, Vane didn't have to be him if he didn't want to be. He could always sell everything and go somewhere else if he had any idea where it was he wanted to go.

He swallowed and lifted his gaze to meet Dorcas's.

"What comes next?"

She smiled at him. "Next is the Knight of Wands."

"Is this like the *Game of Thrones*?"

"Stop."

"Okay."

"Anyway," she said. "This is you charging pell-mell after your goals. The Knight of Wands isn't going to let anybody stop him. He doesn't care what's in front of him. He's ready and eager to meet it. You will be moving forward, but be careful. The Nine of Wands is your environment and suggests that you are wary of the people around you. This card matches your worry, Vane. You feel threatened, and the Nine of Wands reflects that. You can tell from his expression that he expects an attack. He's holding on tight to his wand, and he's going to fight off whoever comes after him."

Cold dripped from the inside of Vane's head into his chest with every one of Dorcas's words. "Somebody is after me," he whispered.

"I don't know. The warrior on this card is strong and brave and willing to fight to defend his position. It is a card of defense and strength. He's hurt but not beaten. Can you see something you are willing to defend? Something you've been hurt fighting for, but you aren't going to back down?"

Marcel. My career.

"Or," she added. "You are defending something valuable inside of you. Some part of your heart and soul you don't want to let go of. All of these cards relate to you and your situation. Your dad's death. Your desire to save Eileen's. The renovation of your house. The burdens of your new—maybe temporary—life here. It starts with the Death card. What have you lost? What are you letting go of?"

His head was spinning. Trying to make sense of this wasn't going to work. He laughed. "I don't know about all this."

Somehow in the course of ten minutes, he'd gone from thinking this was a joke to believing it. The shadows in the room blurred the walls until it was only him and Dorcas and the colorful cards. Two bright white and yellow cards remaining. Cheerful cards.

"Does it get better?"

She smiled and tapped the second to last card.

"Your hopes and fears. This is the Page of Swords. Young and brave. He's ready to deal with any enemy, but he's not all geared up for it. He's also smart, but I don't think he's a person in your reading. He's younger than you, so I don't think he's you either. His presence tells me that everything you've been working for is going to pay off. Just keep your eyes open and be ready to take advantage of opportunities. Notice he's alert and a little wary. Pay attention to the people around you and listen to everything. But..."

She grinned now. "Your future is the Sun. You are going to find your happiness, honey. You've worked for it, and it's going to be yours. Eileen's or Hollywood. Sometimes this can mean being reunited with somebody or being more creative in your life. Not that what you're doing now isn't creative. I know you're trying to be, so have faith. Everything's going to be worth it. These are really wonderful cards in the grand scheme of things."

He snorted. The idea of being dragged over the coals to his happy ending had little appeal. Plus, she hadn't told him who was after him. "I wasn't making all that stuff up."

She drew her brows together in a frown. "What stuff?"

"I didn't freeze my own porch or hit myself over the head."

"You didn't call the cops either."

No, he didn't because... Doug told him not to? Well, not exactly. Doug had reported it the next day and had a friend of his install a top of the line alarm system. One Vane kept forgetting to arm. "I guess I'm crazy."

Dorcas was quiet for a moment as she fanned out the

cards again, blew across the tops and gathered them back into a deck. "I believe you. I want you to think about the cards though. We don't always see what's right in front of us. The truth is in plain sight, but we're busy looking behind or ahead of us. Whatever is happening to you is right here."

So, not Fisher? That meant Luis. Or Doug. Or... Dorcas.

"Why didn't you and Doug ever get together?"

She laughed. "Oh, my God. I was so in love with him when we were kids. It just didn't happen and now... Well, yuck. Doug's like my brother."

"You believe in all this?" He waved his arm, taking in the room.

She wrapped the cards in the silky red cloth. "I guess so. I was... Well, I told you, didn't I? I won a reading and got into it after that. Personally, I think I was always... attuned. I sense and see things. Maggie, the woman who taught me, used a crystal ball or a mirror. Scrying, it's called. It's very popular. People do it all the time. When you look in a mirror and stare at yourself, trying to figure something out, that's basically scrying. But it can be very deep too."

She pulled the candle she'd lit earlier closer and gazed at the flame. "You can even read fire. I can anyway. It's different from tarot. You see actual things, but usually they're symbols, so you still have to interpret them. I saw my sister's death, but I didn't know it right away."

"Oh, geez, that's awful."

"I had a vision of water and giant waves and imagined I was drowning. But it was her, drowning in her own fluids."

He reached around the candle, and she grabbed his hand and squeezed it. "I'm okay," she said. "Don't worry." She pushed the candle away. "But I don't often scry anymore. That was a bit much for me. I think there are some places people shouldn't go." She stared into his eyes, and a shiver ran through him. "We can do it though. If you..."

He shook his head. "I'm a disaster."

"You are not. Who told you that?"

"Doug."

He grimaced a smile, and she huffed.

"Ignore him. You just upset his plotted out little world. He likes to organize everything and make sure it's in its place. You aren't a disaster. Meg used to lock her keys in the car all the time. It drove Doug nuts. 'Why doesn't she put the damn things in her purse? Why does she even have a purse?'"

She rose and returned the box with the cards to the dresser drawer.

"Just remember, the sun is your future. That's where you're going."

Back to sunny LA?

To Fisher?

He wasn't Riley Vane anymore. The image of him in LA had all the substance of a paper cutout now. A flimsy facsimile he'd clipped from a magazine. It wasn't real to him anymore, and that scared him. He'd given up and wasn't anything like the Nine of Wands guy, who dug his heels in and faced everybody off. Vane waited tables in a diner.

He was clumsy and disastrous.

Like heck. I'm going to be the cook, and Luis can just get over it.

Dorcas followed him into the shop. He flipped her *Back at 2 pm* sign over and bent into her hug. "Well, that was interesting. Thank you, I guess."

She slapped his shoulder and pushed him away. "Go on. You don't have to believe. You and Doug can laugh at me all you want."

"I'm not laughing at you."

She hooted. "Maybe you aren't. You wait though. Doug'll see the truth one day. The doubters always do. See you later, honey."

She shut the door on him, and it flashed the sun back into his eyes, blinding him for a moment.

30

FLOWERS

V ANE DUCKED WHEN he saw the weed Doug had just pulled out of the ground behind Vane's house hurtling toward him. He slapped it away. "Knock it off."

"Get a shovel."

"So I can hit you over the head with it?"

Doug set the shrub he was carrying down by the two other shrubs already there and flashed a grin at him. "Outdoorsy type, are you?"

"Ha ha. I never said I was."

They had two shovels lying on the ground. Doug fetched one and started to dig.

A bump on the leg drew Vane's attention to Hoyt, who huffed at him over the tennis ball in his mouth. "I'm not playing," he said.

"*Huff.*"

Hoyt dropped the ball, and Vane picked it up. Its fuzz was patchy and somewhat leprous looking to Vane. He gazed down on the golden, who wriggled and switched his tail through the weeds.

"Want this?"

Hoyt whined.

"Don't be mean," Doug grunted as he jammed his shovel into the ground.

Vane tossed the ball down the incline, and something brown and cream shot out of the weeds and dashed toward the trees. He grimaced. "Sorry, Trout."

"What part of mean didn't you understand?"

"Ha ha."

A few seconds later, Hoyt raced back, tags jingling, and dropped his soggy ball. *Eww.*

"Don't use the dog to get out of digging."

"I didn't bring him."

The sun blazed, but luckily, they were standing in the shade.

"C'mon," said Doug. "These are gonna look fantastic next spring."

Ribes, Doug had called them. The picture on the tabs showed a plant with hot pink flowers dangling like grapes.

Vane swatted at a buzzing thing coming near him and staggered at another bop from Hoyt. After he righted himself, he fetched the other shovel and stuck it into... cement. For gosh sake's, the ground actually pinged at him.

"Sounds like you hit a rock there," murmured Doug. A laugh bubbled under his voice.

Vane stomped on the shovel until the tip sank. Then he leaned back on the handle, and the blade scraped up a paper-thin layer of dirt. Gusting a breath, he rolled his eyes toward Doug and said, "I got bad dirt."

Doug laughed. "Wanna switch?"

"Yeah."

Doug tipped his head at the shrubs. "Why don't you bring one over?"

Hoyt padded alongside him and circled the plants. Vane grabbed the pot nearest him and brought it to Doug, who turned it upside down and whacked it with his palm.

"I don't know why you want an outdoor space at Eileen's," Doug said. "You hate the outdoors."

That thing was buzzing around Vane's head again. A zigzagging, bright orange flash. He flung his arms at it and spun in a circle. Hoyt skittered backwards.

"I don't hate the outdoors."

Doug guffawed. "You could've fooled me."

"I like gardens."

"Yeah?"

"Just not... this... effing wasp."

"That's a carpenter bee. A male."

That stopped him. Vane dropped his arms. "How do you know it's a male?"

"It's orange. Hold onto the pot, will you?"

After Doug set the shrub on the ground, Vane pressed down on the pot's rim. The root ball released with a sucking sound, and he inhaled the fragrance of damp soil. "I wouldn't mind a garden back here."

"If you want to sell, it'll help. If not—well, then it's yours."

"With a lawn?"

"No. With something crazy and wild. Like you."

Vane snorted. "Not very."

The shrub sat in its hole now, and Doug held onto the top of it and turned his gaze on Vane. "That's kind of how I see you."

"Oh."

He might have said more, but the bee chased him in a circle to Doug's other side.

With a smirk, Doug handed him his shovel, and Vane took it and poked the dirt with its tip. It slid in. He stomped on the blade. It slid down even farther, so he wiggled it and pushed the handle toward the ground. A shovel full of soil broke free. He tossed it aside in a clump and stuck the shovel back into place, stomping on it again.

After a few minutes, the hole sank a good two feet before the ground became sticky again. But at least Vane had made some headway this time. When he stopped and swiped at his forehead, his gaze locked on Doug's.

The other two shrubs had been planted, and Doug was leaning on his shovel, grinning at him. "You're cute when you're all hot and bothered."

"Just plain hot."

The bee was back, after his sweat probably, the vicious little vampire.

Vane swung again and smacked it. *Oh shoot.* The evil thing roared back in a buzzing arc, and Vane staggered sideways, losing his balance. His eyes flew wide, and Doug leaped and nabbed his shirt, yanking him out of his backwards tumble. He landed against Doug's chest with an *oomph.*

"Careful. You almost fell in the well."

He hadn't been thinking of the well, even though he'd been working by it for half the day, but now he looked back at it. The sides were waist high, and the bleached-out lid covered the top. "I'd have to jump in it, Doug."

"Stop abusing the wildlife."

"Me? I'm not the one dive-bombing it."

"It's a bug."

Doug's chest threatened to combust against his own. "It's hot," Vane murmured.

"You are."

"Yeah?"

Doug didn't let him go, gazing into Vane's eyes with a look he couldn't decipher. His excitement had a flavor of fear to it. Doug started the butterfly gymnastics in Vane's gut with only a look. He wanted to lean in and sink into him while his nerves warned him that Doug might push him away.

I'm too crazy. Crazier than any garden.

I'm a guy.

But he wasn't being fair, though in the back of his mind, he half-expected Doug to tire of him. Maybe Vane was just a lark, a test run before Doug went back to a woman. After all, Vane couldn't keep Fisher, and Fisher loved guys.

His voice cracked. "Has Dorcas ever read for you?"

A frown creased Doug's forehead. He stepped back. "No. Why? You said nothing happened at yours."

"Nothing did."

Liar.

"A lot of effort for no return."

Vane shrugged. "It was fun. Like getting your horoscope read."

"I don't believe in that either."

"Is that why you haven't let her do a reading?"

Doug's hesitation was brief but there. "Yeah. I don't see the point."

"Well, I didn't get any advice from on high, so I'm stuck making my own decisions it looks like. I want a garden." He brushed the leaves on the nearest shrub. "They look nice."

"You'll love these in spring."

Will I? Would he still be here? "Will you help with it?"

"Sure." Doug stepped back and picked up both shovels. "I'm working with a client with an incredible garden. Exactly the kind of thing I like. There's one section that would look great here. The owners are going to be out of town next week, so I can show you around. Why don't you bring some sandwiches and meet me there after work? Maybe Tuesday."

Vane frowned, pursing his lips. "Sandwiches? You want to have a picnic at somebody else's house?"

Doug laughed. "No, goofball. We'll go to my place after."

"Oh. Okay. We can do that. You know what I want though." Vane slid between the two shovels Doug was holding and wrapped his arms around him. He almost groaned at the feel of Doug's heat baking into him again. "I want a secret grotto where we can have sex outside and nobody can see us. It has to have a water fountain too."

"No," Doug murmured. His voice fell and hummed in Vane's ear like the bee. Vane shivered and drew in closer. "I see a pond with water lilies. At night, the moon will shine down and your face will look back at you."

Vane's laugh squeezed out of too-tight lungs. "Wow. A poet."

"Only for you," Doug said and leaned in to kiss him with warm, soft lips.

31

LETTING GO

DOUG SET HIS glass of beer down. "What is it?"
"Agate."

Dorcas lowered the stone and its chain to the glass table, picked up her lunch, and took a bite. How she managed to find her hotdog under the mounds of condiments she'd dumped on it was a mystery to Doug.

Messy damn concoction.

While Dorcas hummed in pleasure, Doug gathered the necklace on his palm. The stone was smooth and glossy, a light color somewhere between sand and peach.

"Why don't you give it to him?"

She licked her fingers and picked up her beer. "I don't want to wait, and you'll see him first. I ordered it a week ago. I have tourmaline at the shop, but—" She frowned and shook her head. "It didn't feel right. Tourmaline is a very powerful stone too though."

"What's the agate supposed to do?"

She wrinkled her nose at him. "Not supposed to. It wards off negativity and evil spirits."

Doug looked straight ahead, though every part of him wanted to roll his eyes to the back of his head. He was never sure how much of the new age spiel Dorcas actually believed. She'd smirked over it often enough, but Dorcas had a weird and flighty sense of humor. Maybe she was smirking about other things. Meg had insisted her readings were spot on though.

But evil spirits?

"You know he's Catholic, right?"

"So am I."

He blinked because he'd forgotten that. "Okay." Shifting sideways, he slipped the necklace into his pocket.

"This afternoon," she said.

He cut off a bite of his chili dog and nodded. "This afternoon." After chewing a few times, he swallowed and added, "He can use it to ward off Luis."

Dorcas snorted, half-choking on her beer while Doug bit into his chili dog and chewed through his grin.

"You're bad," she said after a moment. "I can't believe he's relegated himself to baking his pies at three in the morning just to avoid Luis. They work together."

Doug shrugged. "I think it's more to get it done before the place opens, and for the peace and quiet. Those pies are important to him. Luis pisses him off."

"That was sweet of you."

"What?"

"Getting him the order."

"Well, he won." Doug was proud of him. Out of sixty-four entries in the pie cooking contest on Founder's Day, Vane had come in sixth place. When a business friend had wanted an unusual dessert to serve at a luncheon, Doug had brought up Vane's win, and the guy had ordered fifteen pies.

"I wish he'd been happier about winning."

Doug shrugged, but the truth was, he'd ached for Vane the whole time he'd posed with the other winners. His fake smile couldn't hide the fact his heart had been torn out.

"Sixth place," Vane had muttered when he'd returned to his little cheering section of Doug and Lucy and Ricky.

With a smile after frowning into space for a moment, Lucy had said, "You beat fifty-eight people, Uncle Vane. That's in the top ten percent."

Vane had forced another smile. "Wow. Really? You're good at math."

"You know Vane," Doug said now. "He isn't happy unless he's kicking himself across town a couple dozen times."

"You could be more sympathetic."

"Or I could be honest," he said with a wink.

Dorcas rolled her eyes and drank the last of her beer. "You are incorrigible, and I have to go."

Doug grabbed a napkin and wiped his mouth. "I'm ready too. I'll walk you back."

A few minutes later, he drove to a job across town where his guys were adding onto a closet-sized kitchen. Not having a place to cook was a hardship on the family

Doug wanted to make as brief as possible. From there, he headed to a client meeting that ran longer than usual. By the time he arrived at the house with the gardens he'd told Vane about, his guys were gone, and Vane was waiting for him.

Doug turned off the engine but didn't get out. He sat still, watching Vane. The picture he made leaning against his car was almost artsy looking to Doug.

Vane squinted in Doug's direction, but with the sun in his eyes, he couldn't see into the pickup.

Watching him was a pleasure Doug wasn't about to give up. For a moment he stayed where he was and feasted on Vane's form.

After the first few seconds, Vane hooked his hair behind his ears. It had been long when they'd met and now fell past his shoulders. He had his long, denim-clad legs crossed at the ankles and wore a black, sleeveless shirt. The sleeveless part was unusual to Doug, but it fit Vane.

He looked relaxed as he leaned against his car, but Doug guessed he wasn't. Doug not stepping out of his pickup was probably inching Vane's nerves to freak-out status right now.

He opened his door, and Vane pushed away from his car, smiled, and swiped his palms on his legs.

"This house looks like the one you're building."

"Mine's smaller," said Doug.

"More comfortable."

Doug didn't comment again. He took Vane's face in his hands and pulled him in for a kiss. Vane made a sound in his throat that rolled into Doug's body. He deepened the kiss, basking in the heat of Vane's skin against his fingers. Closing his eyes, he breathed in a scent that was warm like sheets on a clothesline. Vane's mouth was soft and sweet, and Doug sucked on his lower lip before letting him go and smiling into his glassy eyes.

"Wow," Vane murmured. "What was that for?"

He still cupped Vane's face, stroking his thumbs across his flushed cheeks. "Everything you are."

"You aren't breaking up with me, are you?"

Doug laughed and pushed him away. "You unromantic brat."

"I can be romantic."

He stepped under the arm Doug raised, and they walked down the side of the house with their arms around each other.

"You can show me how romantic later," Doug said.

"I have to go in early though. My pies."

"I remember. Did you look around?"

"No, I was waiting for you."

"The thing I like about this garden is that it doesn't look like one. The owner put a water fountain on the patio but a pond in the yard, so it looks natural."

Vane leaned into him and breathed hot air onto his neck, making him shiver. "Like the one by our secret grotto?"

Doug strangled on a chuckle. "Oh, that one."

"Yeah." Vane's lips brushed his neck. "That one."

"I might add a pedestal. You can stand naked on it."

"I'll probably fall off."

Doug laughed. "Well, there is that, isn't there?"

When they came to the back corner of the house, they stopped and stared at the tumble of plants in front of them. Unlike Vane's yard, which was ringed in hills, the property here stretched in a flat field to the edge of the woods. The open space was half an acre in size and lush with grasses, flowery bushes, and trees.

"What do you think?"

"I'd lose Trout."

"Until you opened a can of food. Let's take a look. The landscape's divided into sections, but you can't really tell. The way it's planted makes it look like it's all blended together."

"This must have cost a fortune."

"I imagine. We can't recreate it, but we can take ideas."

Vane took his hand. "Show me what you like."

"All of it." He laughed, but a bizarre tension gripped him. He didn't know where it had come from, but it followed on a flash of the bushes they'd planted at Vane's. A feeling that the yard belonged to both of them. He didn't know why that made him uneasy or why the sight of Vane's smile as he looked back at him sent a stab of pain to his heart.

Because Vane's not permanent. He's a flibbertigibbet destined to fall off the pedestal you build him.

Except that Doug had never put him on a pedestal.

Which was good, because a second later Vane tripped over the edge of a walkway half hidden by a carpet of thyme. Still clasping his hand, Doug held onto him.

"Geez," Vane muttered.

"A hot mess."

"I know." Vane pulled loose. "So what do you like?"

You.

"Over here," he said.

He led them to a wall of white oleander and Cecile Brunner.

"What's this?" Vane asked. "A rose?"

He ran his fingers under one of the pink blooms.

"Yes. It's one of the ones I think would look great in your yard. The oleander too."

"It's huge. I can block off that Isaiah kid."

"You know," said Doug. "I never would've pegged you for that grumpy old man in the neighborhood all the kids hate."

"I'm not old."

"You're grumpy as hell."

"Whatever. This is pretty though."

"Come through here."

A couple yards down the wall of bushes an archway appeared. Doug stepped through it, and Vane followed.

Doug thought this area was somewhat forgotten by the family, but it's what he loved best. The pond here was the smallest one and unadorned—a still pool at the bottom of a shallow hollow. Wildflowers bloomed in patches surrounded by wooly rose bushes, lavender, and rosemary. A small weeping willow swayed on the other side of the pond and birds sang inside the foliage. "Like it?"

Vane stood still, and Doug wasn't sure of his reaction. Vane's hair stirred against his cheek, and he brushed it back. Stubble shadowed his jaw. He was beautiful, and standing still, only strong and sure. But when he turned, Doug fell into eyes as pale as a pool of water. He saw sky and a tumble of murky clouds under the surface. A storm that rose and swelled as he stared.

"Would you help?" Vane asked. "I can't do anything like this."

Doug grinned. "You planted the ribe."

"I was in danger the whole time."

Now Doug laughed. "A disaster."

"Yep. That's me. I think this is pretty though. I like it. I wouldn't have to do much upkeep."

"Weed whack."

"Where will my pedestal go?"

"We'll find a special place."

"Okay. I like that big rose. This reminds me of your place."

"A little. We hired a landscaper, but Meg designed it all."

"And decorated?"

"And decorated."

"But she was...?"

"An accountant."

Vane's eyes searched his, and Doug's heart skipped a beat.

"Dorcas told me about her."

"You can ask me anything, Vane."

He shook his head. "I don't need to ask you anything. I'm just confused. I... I don't know what I'm doing. We should go."

"Hey."

But Vane kept on walking. Doug followed, eyes on Vane's long legs, waiting for him to fling himself across the yard. How anybody was that clumsy, he didn't know. It went far beyond anything Meg had been. But they both had a kind of grace that wove inside him like a peaceful song or a quiet twilight. Something that stilled the busyness in his soul. Watching them in their nonclumsy moments was an exercise in calm.

His blood, his heart, his breath beat in harmony with the long swing of Vane's legs.

Before rounding the corner of the house, Vane stopped and turned. His bottom lip was red. He must have been chewing on it.

"I wrote a screenplay," he said. "Fisher has it. I brought the wrong thumb drive with me when I left. I'm not sure I can get it back, so I'm writing the screenplay again as a novel. I might be only half way in, but I already like it. I probably like it more than acting. It's just... acting was my first love, and I didn't give it up because I wanted to. I... I don't want to just let it go."

Doug's lungs shrank, and he steeled himself when Vane's eyes hung on his. He was probably supposed to argue with Vane and talk him out of his silly dream.

It's never going to work out. How much of your life are you going to give away?

But a part of Doug urged him to just let Vane go. Why had he let himself get in this deep? If they had never met, would Doug's life be easier? Would he have reconciled himself to never loving anybody as much as he'd loved Meg?

The question tore him apart because answering it felt like losing her all over again. He'd loved her more than anything, but... *I love you too, sweet boy.* How could he be grateful for a love he'd only found because he'd lost Meg? He couldn't be, so letting Vane go should be easy.

He took a breath. "Vane, the only reason I know you is because I don't have Meg anymore."

He held Vane's stare. It was Vane who broke it, turning slightly in the direction of their vehicles. He ran his hands through his hair. "I don't know what to say to that."

"You'd leave me for a part, Vane."

But Vane shook his head, though he shook it too hard, and his voice wobbled from the force. "I didn't say that. I wouldn't."

Doug approached him again. "This was supposed to be fun, you know."

Vane snorted. "I don't know what's wrong with me."

"What did Dorcas tell you?"

Half of Vane's mouth twisted in a wry smile. "Am I gonna get her in trouble?"

"I know Dorcas is opinionated, and I know what she thinks."

"About Meg?"

Doug nodded. The dread that it was true Meg had known the furnace was broken and had just let it go was a shadow deep down inside him. The kind of thing that could graze him with its shady edge and he'd not be quite sure what had touched him. But he knew who Meg had been and that she'd never willingly risk anyone's life, including her own. "It was an accident."

"Dorcas says it was too."

Doug sighed. "The cops brought up the possibility. That's their job, I guess. Meg was too... I don't know. Mystical? That's where the garden came from. She decorated the house and designed our yard. The decorator Meg was clean and simple. The gardener Meg was wild and overgrown and spiritual. She loved Dorcas's readings and believed in all of it. That was her gardener side. That's you too. Totally uncontrolled."

A smile crept onto Vane's face, and Doug went on. "The decorator side was her accountant side. Practical. Her gardener side was... free. And faithful. I know—deep inside—she would never make a choice that wasn't hers to make. We were having trouble because of me and my work, and she was lonely, but we talked it out. The cops... The fact that she must've turned the alarm off and was just sitting by the door. So damn close..."

The pain hit him like a wall, not even a tidal wave. The crushing weight of masonry.

"So close," he whispered. He sensed Vane closing the tiny space between them. But he was staring down at the shadowy weeds, darkening as the sun sank. "I'm sure she was confused from the fumes, and her purse was open, so I think she sat down to call for help." He let out a breath. "Five feet from the door. This is why I stay away from Dorcas and her crazy cards. I can't change anything." He raised his head. "Did this come up in your reading?"

"Before. We talked." Vane huffed. "Everything I'm

doing is wrong. I can't save the diner. I won't let you fix my house the way you want, and I won't be able to sell it now. I can live in it, but I won't have a job. I don't think my cat really likes me. Bugs hate me. I'm..." His voice fell, and Doug drew closer but didn't touch him. "A runner up," he murmured. "Sixth place."

"Will you quit? That was a win. You invented the pie. You coached your acting class into putting on a fantastic show for Founder's Day."

"Mr. Kam's acting class."

"You wrote their lines. You beat out fifty-eight people in a pie cooking contest."

Vane squinted, and Doug noticed the violet shadows under his eyes.

"I'm not first though."

Doug inhaled. "For fuck's sake, Vane. I can't explain this. I can't explain it to myself. I don't regret Meg. I don't regret you. I want her back. I want you. I know it doesn't make sense."

"Not really."

Doug lost himself in those eyes again, but they were deepening with clouds. Vane wasn't like Meg, at all. Her faith was something she drew out of the air. It trusted. Vane stumbled, inside and out. Worried. Fumed. Bit his nails down. Doug imagined a lifetime with him. Day after day of this. And what if he did stay with Vane? What if they lived together for thirty or forty years? He'd only been married to Meg for six. Would he still be the husband she'd loved when she drifted into the shadows of his memory?

"You worry too much," he said.

"I worry all the time," Vane answered.

He said it so matter-of-factly Doug had to laugh. "A hot mess."

"I guess so."

"C'mere."

But he was already there. He leaned in, and Doug wrapped his arms around him and held him close. Vane's chin rested on his shoulder, cheek against his face.

"I used to think you fit your name. That you were just an arrogant asshole from Hollywood. I was as wrong as I could get." He pressed a kiss to Vane's temple. "You are too. About your life. Just relax and give yourself a chance."

"Maybe my pie will become famous," Vane whispered.

"Did you hear a word I said?"

"All of it."

Doug sighed and gave him a nudge. "Come on. Let's go home."

LEMONGRASS AND BASIL PERFUMED VANE'S kisses. He'd made their dinner—Thai basil shrimp with jasmine rice—because he'd forgotten to stop for sandwiches. The little fucker could cook. *I oughta tell him.*

But Doug was too busy humming into Vane's mouth —*hmm.* He tasted of licorice and citrus and Sam Adam's, and Doug lost himself in the slippery textures of cheek and tooth.

Vane giggled every time Doug flicked at the roof of his mouth.

When he pulled away, Vane's tongue followed his, so

he met it again, trapped Vane's bottom lip in a kiss a moment later and got a sigh.

They were lying on the couch. Doug pushed himself lower, kissing Vane's jaw and throat. The thrumming pulse mesmerized him. He let it flutter against his lips and swore the vibration echoed in his balls.

"You feel so good," he murmured.

Vane held his head, fingers ruffling his hair while Doug went under his shirt until he found a nipple. The hard, warm nub rolled under his thumb, the drum of Vane's heartbeat tapping underneath. Doug pinched him, and Vane arched with a sigh.

"C'mon," Doug said. He kissed Vane's jaw again. "I want you in bed."

He took Vane's hand and pulled him to his feet. Vane followed without a word, and Doug was silent too. This was different, but he wasn't articulate enough to say why it was, and he didn't want to ruin it with words.

Hoyt jingled behind them.

Leaving the main light off, Doug switched on the lamp by the bed, throwing shadows on the walls. When he turned down the comforter, his sheets looked gray. For a moment he didn't want Vane lying there, afraid he'd disappear. It took him a moment to shake the feeling off.

By the time he turned around, Hoyt was sprawled on his bed in the corner, and Vane stood in the middle of the room with his shoes off and his hands at his sides.

Doug went to him and cupped the hard curves of his shoulders. So solid and warm and real. He stroked Vane's skin, imagining it was Doug himself who'd disappear into the sheets. He wondered who he'd be when he resurfaced. If he'd be somebody Meg had never known.

He gazed into Vane's eyes and brushed his hair back with his fingers.

Vane groaned with the low, achy sound of something breaking under a strain.

Doug drew him closer and kissed him. First was his forehead, his nose, and his lips, parted and soft and hot with his breath. Next was the cleft of his chin and the notch at the base of his throat where his pulse thumped.

He unbuttoned Vane's sleeveless shirt and slipped his fingers under the collar. Warm skin met his, goose bumps roughening his way. The shirt fell, sliding down Vane's arms. Doug put his thumbs over Vane's sternum and drew them down to his belly button. When he pushed in, Vane bent with an "ooph," and his lips curled.

"That's sensitive. Right to the balls."

With a widening grin, Doug lowered his hand and cupped Vane's junk through his jeans. He tightened his grip, forcing Vane onto his toes. A hiss escaped his teeth, followed by a "yessss."

"Any sexy underwear today?"

He moaned his answer. "You decide." Pouty moans. His eyes were half lidded, and Doug's dick strained against his zipper at the sight of the lust in there. He brought his lips to Vane's temple, brushing kisses down to the side of his mouth.

"Want me to fuck you?"

"Until I fall apart."

For a guy always on the edge of collapse, that was an odd thing to say. But Doug wondered if it wouldn't be a relief—to just give up and give in. Come apart and figure out what to make of all the pieces later.

He cupped Vane's face, and Vane pressed his lips into Doug's palm. "I won't let you go."

"No," Vane agreed.

He unfastened Vane's belt before letting Vane take over and push them down his legs. He stepped sideways to free his feet.

"Fuck," Doug murmured. He cupped himself and squeezed, dizzy from the drumming of his blood.

How this guy managed to come up with an endless supply of the world's sexiest underwear was a mystery to Doug. Today, he wore black lace with a pouch that barely contained him. The waistband was low across his pubic hair and black straps hugged his hips.

"Are those comfortable?"

"The pouch is cotton inside. Do you not like them?"

"I fucking love them. I think the designer should win a Nobel Prize."

Vane laughed, making his junk bounce in its tenuous support. "I don't think I remember that category."

"The Nobel Prize for Art. Turn around."

Doug caught his breath as two pale cheeks appeared. He pulled off his shirt and cupped the warm ass in front of him. The flesh was solid and round but gave under the pressure of his fingers.

He leaned over Vane's shoulder. "Make it bounce for me."

Vane giggled. "You like to watch."

"I love to watch. I can't get enough."

After shucking off his pants in a breathless rush, Doug sat on the end of the bed and shifted Vane closer. A push and pull later he had Vane where he wanted him and let him go. "Bounce."

Vane jumped on his toes. His ass jiggled. Not a loose jiggle but an undulating roll on landing, a ripple rising from the bottom to the top and down again.

"Yeah. Like that. Do it again."

He bounced a few more times, and Doug stroked up his legs and squeezed the warm globes of his ass again. The flesh puckered under his fingers. Sliding his thumbs up, he pressed on the small of Vane's back, and Vane spread his legs and bent.

Bliss. Fucking bliss.

Vane's balls hung low in the black lace. The straps crossed his thighs under the curve of his ass. All of it framed the deliciousness that was the crack in front of him.

Doug was obsessed with things like this. The down and dirty details. The loose, rosy flesh of a pussy. The curly, bristly hair between Vane's cheeks.

He drew his fingers down the cleft, and a quiver ran through Vane's legs. His hole was pink and grayish-lavender with a tiny dark dot in the center. Doug touched it, and it puckered.

"You are so fucking delicious. I don't need any pie with this."

Vane groaned long and loud.

Doug licked his finger and rubbed Vane's hole until Vane's entire body quivered. He was visible through the split in his legs, digging his fingers into the threads of the rug. Doug blew on the wet skin and watched the knot of flesh go in and out. He soaked his finger, gripped Vane's hip, and pushed inside him. The ring of muscle tightened and tugged. Doug wiggled his finger, rolling it until Vane's hole loosened and widened. He pulled out, and Vane whimpered.

"Wet my fingers," he said, sticking his hand through the vee of Vane's legs.

Vane bobbed halfway up. "Suck your fingers? Are you crazy? Those were inside me."

"What? I can eat your ass, but you can't?"

"Sicko."

"Okay, fine. My thumb."

While Vane sucked on one thumb, he sucked on the other one.

The smell of Vane's musk was making him dizzy. Soap and a little sweat and the sweetness of his ass.

Doug pulled his thumbs away and pressed them inside Vane's hole. He followed with his tongue, dancing the tip around the delicate flesh outside.

The sounds of gasps and the jingle of Hoyt's tags filled the room.

He ignored it all and slipped into the drumming echo of his own pounding blood. His dick ached, jerking fitfully in the air. He ran his tongue along Vane's taint, scraping the lacy edge of his panties. Circling back to his hole and down again. Tracing the edge of the straps across his thighs next.

Vane shook. "Shoot... shoot... shoot..." The word went on and on as though he didn't realize he was saying it out loud.

Diving back between his cheeks, Doug fucked Vane's hole with the tip of his tongue. He pulled back, spat on it, rubbed the spit in with his fingertip, and went back to licking and probing.

The word changed.

Now it was, "Doug... Doug... Doug..."

He sat up, head swimming.

Vane straightened too, yanked his panties off, and spun around. He threw himself into Doug's arms, sending them both crashing back onto the bed. Their foreheads clunked, and they both said, "Ow," at the same time and dissolved into laughter.

"You make me feel so good," Vane whispered.

"Kiss me."

Vane lowered his face and parted his lips to let Doug in. His hair fell over Doug's face. His mouth was warm, his lips sweet. Doug kissed and nipped and held his face. "That was your ass you were tasting, you know?"

"That's different. That's like sharing cum."

Silky hair slipped through Doug's fingers as he brushed it off Vane's cheek. "I'll keep that in mind."

Vane nuzzled his palm. "Have you always been kinky?"

Doug laughed. "That's not kinky."

"You like to watch."

"Not just watch," he said, and Vane smiled and bent down for another kiss.

Doug melted into the bed and the warmth rocking on top of him. The hot slide of Vane's dick against his sent sparks exploding inside him. He cupped Vane's face and broke the kiss, watching as Vane slipped off his body and twisted sideways.

He hooked one of Doug's legs with his own, reached into the bedside table, and grabbed a condom and lube.

Vane's cock curved toward his belly, its tip glistening with moisture. It was ruddy, but it never got very dark. The veins under the skin were delicate, not like the ropes that swelled in Doug's. Vane's balls were heavy though, and darker than his dick. Doug rocked them on his palm, and Vane rolled his eyes and pushed his hips out, but only for a moment.

In the next instant, he took Doug's wrist and pushed him away. "My turn."

"Your—"

Doug's breath left him. Vane licked a stripe from the top of his cock to the bottom. His tongue was scorching, and his hot breath steamed Doug's skin. He spread his legs and tensed under the palm dragging up his thigh.

Lifting his head, Doug watched the tip of his dick disappear into Vane's hot mouth. The sight of Vane's hollow cheeks mesmerized him. His pleasure rocketed through him, jolting his heart at the touch of Vane's hand against his balls, the feel of his fingers sliding back, stroking the skin of Doug's taint.

Doug dropped his head back, enjoying the fire burning in his groin.

"Stop," he murmured, knitting his fingers in Vane's hair.

But Vane didn't stop. He swallowed instead and the squeeze of Vane's throat on his dick sent shockwaves through Doug's body. His hips lurched in an upward jerk. Vane gagged and popped off.

"Jesus. Sorry," said Doug.

Vane laughed. "I'm not. You pounded my throat."

Doug rose onto his elbow, patting the bed to locate the condom. "How about I pound something else?"

"Aren't you clever?"

"I try."

Vane found the condom and tossed it to him. "My hole awaits."

Doug burst into laughter. "I can't believe you said that."

The sparkle of Vane's grin lit the room. Doug brought him down and kissed him, and for a moment after the kiss, held him there, forehead to forehead. Vane's hair tickled his palm, and heat built between them. Doug whispered, "You are a hoot, Vane Riley," and watched his eyes crinkle at the corners.

By the time, he got the condom on and slick, Vane was on his elbows and knees, ass in the air.

"On your back," Doug said.

But he didn't comply right away. First, he dropped his cheek to the sheets and smiled into Doug's eyes. His spine rippled like water under moonlight, a shadowy rivulet flowing out of a dark valley between soft white mounds.

Everything about this night struck Doug as strange and mysterious. He was floundering in waters that threatened to pull him under. But when Vane finally rolled onto his back, Doug crawled between his spread legs and rested his weight on his elbows anyway. Electricity sizzled inside him when his dick slid in the dip against Vane's hipbone. He rocked, keeping his gaze on the face below him.

Vane's smile slowly faded, and the silver of his eyes deepened to a dark gray. A faint line formed between his brows, his expression both pensive and hopeful.

As Doug stared down at him, he grew still, reluctant to stir, as though the whole purpose of his life hung on this moment. Vane's eyes, as gray as the sheets underneath him, swam with secrets far below the surface. But now, like mysteries only Doug had the clue to solve, they slipped past the veil that had hidden them for so long. The weight of the gift shook him.

"I love you," he whispered.

Vane's voice broke on a shaky gasp. "Love me."

Doug shifted his weight, aimed his cock at Vane's hole and inched it in. Vane sucked in his breath and winced.

"Okay?"

"Yeah."

Vane was touching him now, stroking his arms and shoulders, not looking away, not closing his eyes. He locked his gaze on Doug's, the frown between his brows growing deeper.

"I won't hurt you," Doug murmured.

Vane nodded, his pants blowing at the loose strands of his hair. His heat was intense, his ass working to pull Doug in deeper and deeper. He hooked his fingers into Doug's shoulders and lifted himself, touching his lips to Doug's. "I love you with everything."

Fuck.

Doug fell, spiraling into a gray light. "Oh, baby."

He bottomed out, enveloped in Vane's heat, wrapped in his arms, and he shivered at the graze of teeth on his neck.

"Good," Vane whispered.

This was a perfect moment. Doug rolled his hips, and Vane moaned and lay back until Doug locked gazes with him again, spellbound. The trust in his eyes rocked Doug to the core. Vane was at Doug's mercy, impaled by him, but it was Doug possessed by Vane, hopelessly in his thrall. He slowed his strokes, thrusting deep and swiveling his hips.

Vane gasped and tossed his head on the pillow. "Best," he moaned. "This is... the best."

Doug's heart swelled.

The power in him buzzed in his ears like an electric storm, swelling, stretching to the bursting point.

He slipped his arms under Vane's knees and rolled him double.

Vane gripped his cock. His breath puffed out of his half-open mouth. Their flesh slapped together, and Vane moaned, the sound a feather-touch down Doug's spine. "I'm going to come," Doug said.

Vane nodded and licked his lips. His hand flew, and cum spurted from his dick in short bursts. Doug froze, gripped and squeezed by Vane's ass. His climax shot down his spine in a bright burst, and he let loose with the sound of thunder in his ears.

"Doug," Vane whispered, face in his neck.

Doug had fallen onto his elbows, Vane's legs splayed underneath him, arms around his shoulders, holding himself against Doug's chest. A giggle, like one of Vane's, fell from Doug's lips. "Am I alive?"

"No," Vane murmured. "We're in heaven."

32

VANE'S NIGHTMARE

V ANE PULLED TO the back of the diner and got
out of his car.

Soft sounds gusted in the woods, but when he looked
over, all he saw was the blur of the garbage bins in the
corner. Doug had rented an extra one for construction
debris. He'd started working on the outdoor patio the day
after Vane mentioned wanting one. It would be a fair
weather venue, but Vane hoped people would like it
enough to visit regularly.

He unlocked his trunk and headed for the back door.
The light under the eaves was as shaky as the one that
struggled out of the humming fluorescents inside. The
narrow hallway gave him the creeps at night.

He opened the door and strode to the kitchen. The air
in here smelled of lemon-scented cleaner. He flipped on
the light and returned to his car. After removing his pie
cases and a grocery bag of supplies from his trunk, he
slammed the lid down.

The crash echoed, but underneath it something else tickled Vane's nerves.

He paused, probing the stillness for another sound. A leaf or scrap of paper skittered by, but that was all.

He took another step.

The dull light inside the hall drew him on, and he quickened his pace. When the sound came again, it was behind him, and his head swelled like a balloon about to burst.

Oh gosh. Oh gosh. Oh gosh.

He didn't try to turn. He lunged for the diner.

Light exploded but not the one in the hallway. A blow hit him on the back of the neck and drove him toward the door. His groceries and pie cases scattered as he crashed onto his hands and knees. A ringing panic jangled through him. Scrambling over the threshold, he slammed the door behind him and bolted for the office.

Shoot!

The door was locked, and he'd put his keys down in the kitchen.

For a second, he stood frozen, mind blank as he tried to decide if he had time to get them. Then a thump behind him jump-started his heart, and he plunged inside the refrigerator.

He yanked the door closed behind him and let his forehead fall against the cold metal. The rush of his blood filled his head with noise. He closed his eyes, took deep breaths and held on tight to the safety release.

Would it hold? It was supposed to let people out not keep them in.

He shuddered as he stared down at his white-knuckled fingers. He was cold too. What if—

The knob jerked in his hand. With a gasp, he pulled back on it and yelled, "You won't get away with this!"

Silence swelled behind the door. The knob jerked again. He held on. "I called the cops!"

Would his phone even work in here? Well, he wasn't letting go of the door to find out. *I bet Luis would know.*

He swallowed at a throb of pain in his head. Would he run out of air?

A loud crack came from the other side of the door, and he held his breath. Another crack and thrum followed a moment later. After that the condensers kicked in, and the vibrations rolled up his wrists. And then nothing.

The air seemed colder, but it was June, so he didn't even have a coat on, just his jeans, a T-shirt, and a pair of old sneakers. Would his toes fall off? Would he suffocate first? He rested his head against the door again, squeezing his eyes shut at the throb.

"Shoot," he whispered. "I knew this was going to happen. I knew I was gonna get stuck in here."

Everybody thought he was a nut job and now this.

Just be patient. They'll go away. You'll get out.

After repeating this to himself a couple times, he thought he might have dozed against the door. He wasn't sure how much time had gone by but found himself staring at the floor, and he wasn't sure how long he'd been doing that.

Tightening one of his hands around the knob, he patted at his pants pockets with the other. Of course. No phone. What did he do? Leave it at Doug's? Or in the kitchen with his keys? He didn't even know what time it was now. He was going to die here, and he wasn't even thirty-three yet. He had to get out. He couldn't stay in here.

The condensers had stopped again, and no sound came through the door.

They were gone. They had to be. It was too risky to wait around. Vane took a breath and pushed on the release, but nothing happened. He rattled the knob and pushed again.

It was stuck.

He was stuck.

Stuck in the refrigerator. He backed into the shelf behind him. He was going to die. His heart thundered in his chest, and he clapped his hand over it, and a hard lump bit into his palm. Dorcas's necklace. He pulled it out from under his T-shirt and held it to the light. Doug had given it to him before he'd left that morning.

"I almost forgot. This is from Dorcas. To keep you safe," he'd said with a laugh. *"Agate. I guess that's supposed to mean something."*

"You're a lousy friend laughing at her."

"I know. It's the cross I bear."

Vane rubbed the stone between his fingertips. The throb in his skull banged away behind his eyes now. The compressor thumped and rumbled, and he strained to catch other sounds underneath. Ominous sounds like scraping and chipping and match strikes.

But it was still, only disturbed by the panicky beat of his heart.

Within three steps he was back at the door. He laid his palm against the knob and pushed and wiggled it. *Shoot.* He'd never checked the gaskets. Hopefully, they leaked, but probably not. Checking things like that was something Luis would do. On-the-ball Luis.

He gazed at the light bulb stuck inside a cover that looked like a giant mason jar attached to the wall. Did lights eat air?

Was that something he should have learned in chemistry class? If he had his phone, he could look it up.

"Vane... Vane!"

The voice hammered through the wall—*Luis?*—sending fresh pulses of pain through his head. He flattened his palms against the door. Even if Luis wanted to kill him, would he do it now? It had to be light outside, or close to it.

"I'm in here!"

For a moment, silence fell again, and then a few footsteps thudded. They paused outside the door. His heart jumped.

"Are you in the fridge?"

"Yeah."

"Come out."

"I can't. The safety is stuck."

Luis didn't say anything. Vane strained to catch a word, but only muffled sounds came through. A moment later, he heard Luis again, closer now.

"What's going on?"

Vane bent his head back and frowned at the ceiling. "I told you. I'm stuck."

"The key's broke off in the lock."

He dropped his head and stared at the door. "Call Doug."

"We need the cops. We got robbed. They threw your pie stuff all over the parking lot."

The footsteps receded.

"Call Doug," he bellowed.

"I'm callin' the cops!"

Turning his back to the door, Vane closed his eyes and squeezed his fingers together. Shivers racked him. He cracked an eye and stared at the thermostat. Maybe Luis wouldn't call the cops. Maybe he'd let Vane freeze to death.

He swallowed and scrubbed his face. Who else but Luis would do this? Who else had known he'd be here? If Luis called the cops, it was because he'd lost this round and wanted to look innocent.

Until the next time.

"Try the knob again."

He jumped, startled by Luis's voice. "It's jammed," he pointed out.

"Wiggle it. Maybe I can get the key out with these pliers."

"Why?"

"Whadda you mean why?"

"Why do you want me gone?"

"Are you crazy?"

He didn't answer that. "What time is it?"

"Almost six. I can't get this key out. You just sit there, I guess. I need to get to work."

Just let me suffocate.

He didn't say anything, and neither did Luis.

Vane stared around the refrigerator. A vent appeared high in the wall, but it was screwed in place, and it only led to the compressor unit anyway. Another box without an exit.

He closed his fist around his necklace. The stone radiated warmth, as though an ember glowed inside it.

Funny that only Dorcas believed him. Or was willing to believe him.

He opened his fist and rolled the agate between his fingers. He wasn't sure if he believed in tarot or crystals or any kind of new age thing. He wasn't even sure of God. Well, maybe a little. He gazed at the stone. Light orange swirled in a sandy nugget the size of a pinto bean. It probably had no power, but maybe if he thought it did, and Dorcas thought it did...

"Vane!"

He spun. "Doug! Doug, I'm stuck in here!"

"Okay. I'm gonna get you out. Are you hurt?"

"No. I got away. That's why I'm in here."

"Okay. I'll be right back. I just need a few tools from my truck."

"Okay."

A few minutes later, something buzzed outside. The sound alternated between a high whine and a gravelly stutter. It didn't take long before the release knob wobbled on its stem and fell on the floor.

"Push," Doug said.

Vane leaned his shoulder into the door and shoved against it. It swung into the hall where Doug waited for him. Vane stepped into his arms and rested his head on Doug's shoulder.

"I'm not a hot mess," he murmured.

Doug squeezed him tight. "No, no. You're not."

"I don't think they took anything," Luis said from behind them. "Nothing's missing, and the office is still locked."

Vane lifted his head. "We weren't robbed."

Doug looked back. "What happened?"

"I got hit."

He'd wanted to say somebody hit him. But it wasn't somebody. It was Luis. He met Luis's gaze, and Luis frowned at him. "Cops'll be here in a few minutes. I gotta get back to work."

He stalked off, and Vane stared at him until he disappeared.

"Vane?"

"Luis hit me."

"Luis? What the—" Confusion flooded Doug's face only to fade into exasperation seconds later. "Vane. Talk to me."

Vane exhaled. "Somebody hit me on the back of the neck." Doug reached for him, and he said, "I'm okay. But it was Luis."

Doug rubbed his face with one hand, dropped it, and said, "Okay. Come sit. I'll find you some aspirin."

While Doug went into the bathroom, Vane continued

to the dining room and slid into a booth by a window. Gray light washed through the dull glass. A few minutes later, a cop car pulled into the parking lot. He started to slide off his seat, but stopped short when Doug appeared with a bottle of water under his arm, Vane's aspirin, and a mug of coffee. "Stay. I'll bring them to you."

Vane pulled his coffee over. "Will you tell them?"

"You know it wasn't Luis."

He fumbled for his necklace. Doug's mouth tightened for a moment before he sighed and said, "I believe you believe it, and I will tell them."

Vane wanted to speak, but nothing emerged. He watched Doug stroll across the dining room and vanish into the hallway. A moment later, Luis poked his head past the kitchen door, glanced from Doug to Vane, and followed Doug.

Vane took a swallow of coffee, set his mug down, and rubbed the back of his neck. It hurt, but he felt no lumps or broken skin.

The possibility that anybody would believe Vane was pretty low. Luis had worked for Vane's dad from the beginning. He was a fixture. But, to Vane, that was why he had a motive. Vane was an interloper.

In every scenario, Luis would want him gone. If Vane stayed, he was the spoiled son of the owner and not worthy of Eileen's and not somebody Luis would want to work for. If Vane or Rose sold the place, Luis stood to profit.

Getting rid of Vane was an all-around plus. Luis hadn't hit him hard enough to kill him. It had been the same with the break-in at his house. The blow hurt, and it had knocked him senseless, but it hadn't damaged him. Hard, but not deadly. Maybe all he wanted to do was scare Vane away, but it could escalate. Or Luis could make a mistake, like he had when he'd iced Vane's porch, and now... Well, Vane ratting him out was going to piss Luis off twice as much.

He took another swallow of coffee, and his stomach burned with it. *You should've shut up.* He was an idiot.

He closed his eyes until the shouts started in the hall.

"Like hell! ...Okay, okay... Call her... I was nowhere near here!"

Vane straightened, gripping his mug between his palms. A part of him wanted to join them, not sit here like a scared kid, but the scared kid won.

It wasn't long before one of the cops strode into the dining room. Her belt looked like it weighed a ton. Doug would look good in a belt like that. *Cop arrests stripper. Stripper seduces cop.* She stared out of a face that was freckled and spotted and creased from the sun, but she was smiling, and she looked nice.

Vane smiled back and tried to relax, though he wasn't sure why, because it really wasn't his day.

The sound of Penny's, "Oh my God!" pierced his brain.

In the beginning, Vane had been jealous of the way Penny went about her life. She was bold and fearless and a chatterbox with the customers. Vane was pretty sure she was acting most of the time though. Nobody could be that cheerful and positive every second of the day. And maybe that had been Vane's problem. He just wasn't a very good actor.

Watching Penny on stage for the Founder's Day skit had mesmerized him. He doubted he'd ever been so free with a part. Who'd he been kidding all this time?

He'd wanted to be good so he could make people like him and had never experienced a time he'd gotten so lost he didn't know he was acting. Though sometimes... sometimes he slipped seamlessly into a scene he was writing. Sometimes he really was his crazy, jewelry-store-robbing cook.

Gasping with a full-on belly laugh, Penny disappeared into the kitchen. *Seriously? What was so effing funny?*

After a quick glance over her shoulder, the cop looked back at Vane. "Mr. Riley? I'm Officer Laws."

She didn't say anything else after the introduction, waiting for his reaction, he guessed. He wanted not to smile, but he failed. That name was certainly an ice-breaker. When he grinned, she gave him a smile with a wry twist to it. "Now that we've got that out of the way, I have a few questions for you."

"Okay."

He gestured at the booth opposite him, and she slid in and opened a notebook.

"You indicated to Mr. Moore that Mr. Flores assaulted you, is that correct?"

He nodded. "That's right."

She wrote something in her notebook that was a lot longer than *That's right.*

"Why don't you tell me what happened but without names for now."

"Okay."

She looked down and jotted notes as he spoke. Nothing in her face gave him any clue to her thoughts. She never blinked, not even when he told her about the other attacks or that he'd filed a report about the break-in. By the time he reached the end of his story, his head hurt again, and he wanted another cup of coffee. He was about to go get it when Doug and the other cop appeared.

Officer Laws raised a finger and said, "Excuse me for one moment."

"Sure."

She stood, and Doug slid into her place and pulled Vane's hand into his. He smiled, and it was the kind of smile you gave somebody who'd just won sixth place in a pie-baking contest.

"They don't believe me, do they?" he muttered.

"He has an alibi, babe."

"What alibi?"

"He was with his wife."

Vane rolled his eyes. "That's not an alibi."

"She's pregnant. He has no reason to lie. He doesn't want to lose his job."

Vane shook his head and looked away. His gaze landed on Luis, who stood in the hallway swinging his hands as he talked. Something rushed through Vane at the sight. Anger or maybe grief. Something that pinned Luis as an enemy no matter what Luis said. Letting his arms flop down now, Luis leaned back against the wall as though he owned the effin' place. Vane jumped up, startling Penny, who froze with the coffee pot in her hand.

"I thought you might want a refill."

"In a minute."

He barreled down the hall, eye on Luis, who straightened as Vane charged up, pointing a finger at him. "I know you want to get rid of me."

"So what?"

"So how far will you go?"

"Is this like an actor thing? Making a big drama of me not liking you? I don't have to. I just work here. I want this place to be the place your dad wanted."

The two cops stood in the outer doorway. Officer Laws stepped closer. "Mr. Flores has provided us with his whereabouts earlier this morning. We've corroborated that he wasn't near here at the time of your assault."

"Maybe it was one of your friends," said Vane.

The next thing he knew he had Luis's finger in his face, and Doug's hands on his shoulders. "You know what?" said Luis. "I'm gonna file a complaint on you."

"Mr. Flores, you're going to have to take a step back, please."

Luis showed his palms and moved to the other side of the hall. "All of this." He swung an arm again, gesturing toward the dining room. "You don't deserve it. I was here. I was the one your dad talked to. Not you, Mr. I'm-Gonna-Be-a-Famous-Movie-Star. Working in a diner? That was too low for you."

"So why am I here?"

Luis didn't approach but stretched his neck as he leaned closer. "Cuz. You. Failed."

Shoot, that hurt.

The squeeze of Doug's hands halted the lunge that had rolled through Vane's body without his noticing it.

"Knock it off," Doug said. "You don't have to make this personal."

The other cop waved a finger at them. "Are we gonna be okay here?"

Luis snorted. "This ain't new. Just a normal day."

Officer Laws stepped forward. "We have all we need, Mr. Riley. According to Mr. Flores, nothing was stolen, so we assume you interrupted a robbery in progress. I advise you to continue to report any suspicious occurrences like the earlier ones. You have my card. Please use it."

"Okay. I will."

In other words, have a great day, and this was your fault.

As soon as the cops returned to their car, Luis turned his glare from Vane to Doug. "I'm not the one making this personal."

"You might actually show some concern," said Doug. "The bottom line is somebody broke in here and attacked Vane. He was lucky to get away. I'm on your side, Luis. I always have been, but you have to cut him some slack right now."

"Well, convince him," said Luis. "I wouldn't hurt his dad's kid. Ethan was my friend. A friend I needed. I was lucky I had an alibi. I have strikes against me. Your dad knew an' didn't care, but I don't trust you. You can fire me,

I guess. I can't do anything about that, but I didn't want to give you a reason."

Vane frowned. Fog floated in his head. "You yell at me. That's a reason."

"I don't yell at you. You've been out to get me from the start. I know the only thing saving me has been Rose. You needed me, but the minute you found out..."

"Found out what?"

Luis took a breath, his chest swelling. "I told the cops. I can't hide it. I have a record."

"Record?"

"I'm an ex-con. Your dad gave me a chance. I remember it clear as day. Your dad took my application and put it in a file cabinet right in front of me. 'It stays here,' he said, and we never talked about it after that. I was a real person to him. That chance was a whole new life for me. I wish I'd had a dad like that."

A switch went off in Vane's head, a light snapping on. "Is that why you were sneaking around the office?"

"I wasn't sneaking around. That was between me an' your dad. You didn't need to see it. You were the one so fucking paranoid you locked up the office."

"Those are confidential papers. I was taking precautions."

"Put them back in the file cabinets. You can leave the door open, you know? So I can use the computer instead of my phone."

"How was I supposed to know?"

"You don't need to. Your dad knew. Your dad trusted me."

"My dad is dead."

His voice bounced off the walls. He was leaning back against Doug, held there by Doug's hands on his shoulders.

But Luis didn't yell back. He straightened and said, "I know that every day," before stalking off to the kitchen.

"Shoot," Vane whispered.

"It's okay," said Doug.

"No, it's not."

The many reasons it wasn't swam before his eyes. He was confused, and his head was pounding again. His father was a stranger. Another guy's father. Vane hadn't been enough. Hadn't been what he'd wanted. And now... Well, whoever wanted to hurt him was still on the loose, waiting for another chance. Because if it wasn't Luis, who—

A face popped into his head, bronzed and gold.

Fisher.

33

TEMPTATION

L UIS DROPPED TWO plates on the pass-through. "Order up."

Vane scowled at him, grabbed the plates, turned, and bobbled them like a drunk juggler.

Fisher!

His breath wedged in his throat like something he'd swallowed and couldn't get all the way down. Fisher gave him a tentative smile and sank onto a stool at the counter. A clammy sweat broke out on Vane's skin. Was Fisher here to finish the job?

Well, of course, he wouldn't do anything in public. Vane was safe for now. Should he call the cops though? And tell them what? Jesus, maybe he was insane. That's probably what they thought. He had no evidence of anything. He couldn't go around accusing people. He had to be sure, so he swallowed his stuck breath, forced himself across the room, and set down the plates.

Dave had the ketchup bottle ready, lifting the top of his

French dip to smother the roast beef with its contents. Dang, that was weird.

"So, when's the show here gonna start?" asked Ollie.

Vane cleared his throat. "Two weeks." *Hopefully.* "We'll be closed the last two days in August to paint and spruce the place up. You're coming to opening night, aren't you?"

Because he wasn't sure anybody else was and didn't want the kids performing to an empty house just because he was a loser.

"You bet," said Dave. He took a bite of ketchup-dripping sandwich while Ollie asked, "What's it going to be about? Not sure I get it."

"It's a revue. So songs, dances, some skits. Our first is going to be called Rosie the Riveter and Troupe. Stuff about workers and unions for Labor Day."

Dave nodded. "I like that idea."

"Regularly, we'll do a mix of things. Let people sign up. Poetry readings even."

"Can any people sign up?" asked Ollie.

"Yeah. Do you want to?"

"Well." Color as red as Dave's ketchup was rising into Ollie's cheeks. "I do write a little poetry."

Dave paused with his glass of Coke halfway to his mouth. "I didn't know that."

"It's a hobby."

"Share it. It'll be fun," said Vane.

"Maybe. We'll see."

"Well, okay. You enjoy."

Vane turned away, though he didn't want to have to face Fisher again. The whole time standing there, he'd felt the stab of Fisher's stare into his back. But what he got when he completed his turn was a view of an empty counter.

Shoot. Where was he?

Pulse yammering in his ears, Vane rushed across the diner and drew up at the entrance. Well, he wasn't gone. His car sat beside Dave's rusty white pickup.

"Is it always this slow?"

Holy—

Vane spun around. "No." *Yes.*

Fisher sat on the stool again. "I like it. The place has an appealing Americana feel."

Vane pressed his lips together. No way was he thanking Fisher for the compliment, but he wasn't about to make a scene either. Not in front of his customers anyway. So he went around the counter, poured Fisher a cup of coffee, and sloshed half of it onto the floor.

Well, of course, he did.

For Pete's sake.

After setting the cup down, he snatched a handful of napkins from a holder, mopped up the liquid, and asked, "Are you ordering?"

"Um... Sure."

Vane snagged a menu out of the nearest condiment stand and passed it to him. "I'm making new menus," he added, wishing he could kick himself the minute the words spilled out.

Idiot. Why don't you tell him about the water stains in

the bathroom and the threadbare carpets you have to replace?

Fisher was used to Ribbets. Eileen's was the kind of place he avoided. Feeling queasy, Vane turned away and gasped in horror as his wad of soggy napkin flew out of his hand and shot through the cutout into the kitchen. He froze, waiting... Luis's head popped up. He locked a glare on Vane, and Vane spun back to Fisher.

"The pepper steak is good," he said.

"Can we talk?"

"About what?"

"Outside?"

Outside? Did he want to talk about the new patio? How did he even know it was new? Then it sank in. Outdoors. He wanted to talk outdoors. Vane licked his lips. What a dolt. Fisher just brought out the worst in him. All his confidence crumbled. "I'm working."

"Just give me a few minutes. Right out front."

In plain sight is what Fisher meant, so he knew what Vane was thinking. Vane's face flushed, and he gritted his teeth. The last eight and a half months swept away like nothing. After all he'd gone through, he was back to the Vane afraid to spill crumbs on Fisher's perfect white rugs again.

His nerves jumped as Fisher stood and tipped his head to the door as though nothing was the matter. "Come on."

And like an idiot, Vane followed him.

When they got outside, Fisher slipped on his sunglasses and smiled. Vane squinted.

"I've been wanting to talk to you since our last

conversation. After you never returned my calls, I realized I had no choice but to come up here. But you're worth it."

Vane's forehead crinkled. "I don't have your thumb drive with me."

"That's okay. I don't have yours either."

"What do you want?"

Fisher took a breath, making a show of holding it in before he let his chest deflate in a gust of air. "Two... three reasons."

Vane shifted. The sun beat down on him, but Fisher looked cool. His body threw a shadow that Vane wanted to step into. "I'm working, Fisher."

Fisher grinned. "Taking a break when you want is one of the perks of being an owner. You look amazing, by the way."

"I look like a wreck."

The smile drifted off of Fisher's face. "I'm really sorry. I shouldn't have grabbed you like that."

"Grabbed me?"

"That was a bad time for me."

"Really?"

"I'm trying to apologize."

Vane gaped at him. Fisher sounded contrite, but he'd sounded that way before, and Vane had no other suspects to blame the attacks on now. He still liked Luis for it, but Fisher fit, too, and Vane had something of Fisher's. *He* was Fisher's.

He stared at the drawn-down mouth, slightly crimped at the ends. Fisher tipped his head, waiting, eyes invisible.

"Will you take your glasses off?"

"Um... Yeah."

Fisher slipped them into the pocket of his bone-colored linen slacks. His shirt was silk. Had to be. New grass green. A shade brighter than his eyes.

Why wasn't Fisher a movie star? He'd make the perfect celebrity.

But Fisher wasn't an actor, and he looked sad and thinner than Vane remembered. "I guess I just don't believe you'd come all this way to apologize."

"Yet, here I am."

"You want something."

"A couple things. I want to talk about us for one."

"There is no us. You have Stan."

"I told you that wasn't anything. I made a mistake. I was lonely."

"Lonely how, Fisher? I lived with you. You cheated on me."

The bunch in the jaw came from the Fisher Vane remembered, and he retreated a step.

"Oh, for fuck's sake, Vane, I'm not going to do anything. You aren't the victim here. I had meaningless sex with somebody who looked like you. What did you expect of me? I loved you, and I was losing you *to* you. How long did you expect me to live with the hollowed-out guy I came home to every day? I needed somebody who hadn't given the fuck up."

Vane took another step back and hit the wall of the diner. Even though he had nowhere else to go, every cell in his body screamed at him to bolt. "That's a lie."

"Really? How many parts did you not even try for?

Sure, you could get some boring-ass commercial nobody would remember in a year. That was no problem. But something good, something good for you—"

"Marcel," he whispered.

Fisher didn't whisper. His voice rose. "And what happened with that?"

"You hit me."

Fisher waved his hand. "You left. You weren't filming yet. You could have stayed. You would have been fine in a week or so."

"You. Hit. Me."

Fisher grabbed his head, pressing in at the temples before running his hands through his hair. "I broke, Vane. I'd had enough. I watched you just... almost disappear. You let all your dreams go."

"I effing tried, Fisher. All the time. I could taste it. I had it."

"You weren't even close to having it. For God's sakes, who cares that you had one part a decade ago? Everybody else in that show went on to do other things, and do you know why you didn't? Because you didn't get what you wanted out of it. Daddy didn't come running to throw his arms around you. It didn't work. It was never going to work, and being here now won't change things either, so you better think about that."

"You don't know me."

"I do. I know acting meant nothing to you anymore. You just pretended because you felt like a failure. The thing you'd wanted was lost to you."

"I didn't know you were so smart, Fisher. All this psychobabble is amazing. You should bottle it."

Vane was cold as his words died in the air. With the sun blazing down and the sweat on his skin, he was cold to the point of freezing. He didn't move as Fisher stripped all his defenses away like swaths of his skin. But Fisher's theory wasn't as neat and tidy as he'd made it out to be. Vane had wanted that darn part. He'd wanted to make it.

As though Vane hadn't spoken, Fisher said, "I showed your screenplay to a friend of mine, and she took it to a producer—"

Vane pushed himself off the wall. "Holy moly, Fisher! You want to steal that too." This he'd fight for.

"I didn't steal it. You left it with me. I'm trying to give you some good news. With some rewrites the producer is willing to take a second look."

"What producer? What producers do you know?"

"My friend knows him. You can act in it too. I know the Vern character is you."

"Why are you doing this?"

Fisher stepped closer. The air thickened with the smell of his cologne, and Vane wasn't sure his lungs worked anymore. Within a breath of touching him, Fisher rested his arms on either side of Vane's shoulders. "I can't let you not take this chance."

Vane slammed his palm against Fisher's chest. "Get back!"

Fisher staggered, grabbed Vane's shirt in his fists, and yanked him away from the building. Vane ducked, arms over his head, but before Fisher could do anything, the door beside them burst open.

"Hey!"

Fisher released him, smoothed his shirt, and stepped back. Luis met Vane's eyes and tipped his head to the interior. "A little help?"

"Sure." Luis stared at Fisher before he ducked back inside. "I have to go," said Vane.

"Wait." Fisher laughed. "You always got me going."

"No. I didn't. We barely spoke to each other. The hottest we got was when you hit me."

"Stop saying that. I never hit you. And anyway, I didn't come all this way to argue. I thought you'd want to hear the good news. I wanted to give you this chance because I love you, Vane. I love you, and I want you back, but I want you to grab onto your dreams too. I'm here for you, but no matter what happens with us, I want you to be happy. Don't let this chance go by. Think about it." Fisher took a step back. "I want you to come home."

Vane's mouth opened. In his head a bellow formed—"*I am home!*"—but his voice stuck in his throat. He spun, yanked open the door, and rushed inside.

34

CALLING IT QUITS

A WARM BREEZE stirred the grit in the diner's parking lot and kicked it under Doug's pickup. Two other trucks and four cars were parked nearby. One of the trucks was Luis's, and one of the cars was Vane's, which left four vehicles for customers. Good. Vane's pie was a hit at the farmer's market. He wasn't going to survive on twenty pies a week, but it was getting Eileen's name out there and that counted.

Breathing in burger- and onion-scented air, Doug pulled a cardboard box from the back of the truck. He carried it to the patio area and set it down on a floor of gray slate the same gray blue as the rest of the diner.

When he turned round to fetch his ladder where it leaned against the wall, he caught sight of Vane through the patio doors, carrying an armful of plates across the room. His hair was in a short ponytail, one stray lock across his cheek.

Sometimes Doug's lust for him was little more than a

flicker, a pent fire smoldering close to his heart. Vane had turned out not to be who Doug had thought he was. People were always a mystery though. The moments of their lives were as fragile as wind-buffeted clouds. He thought of Meg in her old office building, hunched inside her big winter coat.

Had she known how close the door was and that she couldn't make it? The thought she might have died afraid killed him.

I'm so sorry, Meg.

After Vane headed out of sight around the counter, Doug returned his attention to the patio. He set the ladder in the center of the space and retrieved one of the packages of outdoor lights he'd brought with him. The white, slightly gaudy crackle glass was right up Vane's alley. Doug climbed the ladder with the lights and a staple gun and got to work.

A half hour later, he glanced down when the French doors opened, and a flicker of worry woke his nerves. It might have come out of nowhere, but it didn't. It emerged with Vane and his strained smile.

Doug smiled back anyway. "Hey, babe."

"Hey."

Even from a distance he could see the frown lines around Vane's eyes. He turned back to the lights, finished with the staples, and climbed down the ladder.

Vane stood by the doors with his fingers stuffed in his back pockets. "It's almost done," he commented.

"Yep. Just the fountain after this. I'll set it up this week."

"Still have to paint the rest of the place," said Vane, moving away from the doorway now. He wandered to the edge of the patio and faced the highway.

"What's up, babe?"

He turned back. "Nothing. I was just thinking."

"About what?"

"All this work, it's—"

"All you. You've been sticking this out hard. Don't give up yet."

Vane smiled. "Darkest before the dawn?"

"Yeah, that."

Doug bent down, grabbed another set of lights, and opened the box.

"We had a pretty good day."

"I saw."

"Fisher came in."

Doug continued pulling the lights from the box almost by reflex. For a moment, he stared dumbly at them, as though he wasn't sure what to do with them, but his brain was a jumble of activity. He knew where this was going. He'd dated often enough before Meg that he knew he was about to be dumped. What bothered him was that Vane was bothered. But that was typical Vane. Working himself into a huff over the issues he had with other people and stumbling right past the things he was doing to himself.

Doug gritted his teeth, trying to swallow the bile rising up. He was his own worst enemy. When had Vane ever been someone anybody could count on? Doug had warned himself over and over to steer clear and had still fallen for the guy. It wouldn't even be Vane's fault. It wasn't like

Doug hadn't seen the signs. Even now, from what little Vane was doing, Doug knew exactly where this was going even if he didn't know why.

Slowly, giving himself time to collect himself, he pushed the lights back into the box. "What did he want?"

Vane tugged his hands out of his pockets, crossed his arms over his chest, and scratched his shoulder. "The usual. Everything's my fault."

"He came all this way to tell you that?"

Vane frowned. "I guess so. I mean, I think he came to see me, not just passing through or anything."

"Just to tell you everything was your fault?"

Vane dropped his arm. "I was thinking if it wasn't Luis after me... I guess it wasn't Fisher either. I... I thought I'd never get my screenplay back. I kind of gave up. So... you know. I was rewriting it."

"I know. I'm proud of you."

Vane's eyes locked on his. "You shouldn't be. It probably sucks."

Doug really didn't want to play this game. He didn't want to build Vane up only to get smacked down himself. But he played anyway, hoping it didn't finish with him getting hurt in the end.

"Come on, will you? Give yourself a chance."

Vane laughed and looked away. "I don't know if I'll finish it now."

"Why wouldn't you?"

"Fisher wants it. A friend of his showed it to a producer who might buy it. I... I might have a part in it too. A part in a movie."

The last part sounded like a plea, and Doug knew he should understand. He should be bigger than the jealousy and fury washing through him, but he wanted to win, and he wasn't going to. "He's doing this out of the kindness of his heart?"

Vane didn't ask what he meant. "No."

"He wants you back."

"That won't happen."

"What will?"

"I don't know. Maybe nothing."

"You'll let this opportunity go?"

"I don't want to." His voice fell as soundless as the heavy air. He was staring hard into Doug's eyes again.

"I guess... Congratulations."

"You won't stop me?"

The stillness didn't leave Vane's face, and a sudden panic ran along Doug's nerves. Could he fix this? Was that what Vane was waiting for?

But how? Doug didn't have a clue, and maybe it didn't even need fixing. Fisher was offering Vane a chance at his dream. Doug's not thinking it was going to make him happy wasn't a reason for Vane not to take the chance. Wouldn't Doug take it? A chance to... *Have Meg back?*

Wasn't that what it always came down to for him? He couldn't forget Meg or let her go, so maybe this wasn't Vane's fault. Maybe Doug wasn't ready either. Meg had taught him that he couldn't always have it all. He'd lost her to a dream that was fucking cold without somebody to hold onto.

"I want you to be happy. I just don't think I can wait for you."

Vane removed his other hand from his pocket. "You don't have to. I can do both. I mean, if it works out and I get other parts, I can come back in between."

"And run Eileen's?"

"I'll sell it. To Luis."

"Vane, I—" Doug ran a hand through his hair. "You won't come back. You might try. You won't though."

The sound of Vane's voice was almost too soft to hear. "Are you breaking up with me?"

"I'm not."

"I just want my chance."

"I get it, Vane."

And he did now, but his focus was on the empty hollow in his gut. It echoed, as empty as his house without Meg in it. He gritted his teeth and a band of muscle squeezed his temples.

Vane was yanking his ponytail loose, running a hand through his hair. He tugged it free and swung his arm at the space they stood in. "This. I don't know how it's going to work. I was being positive. I didn't want to disappoint you."

"Me? I was helping you, Vane. Was I just spinning my wheels? Aren't we trying to make it work?"

"It's not much of a sure thing, that's all."

"That's an excuse. Some things work out and some things don't. If you don't think this is worth the risk, don't spend your time or energy on it. Or mine."

"Well, thanks for the pep talk."

"What do you expect?"

Vane flinched and backed away. "Nothing," he said.

Doug shook his head and gazed down on the lights. He had two more strips to fasten, but not now. "I'll finish these later."

Vane said nothing. He didn't try to stop Doug from packing the box and leaving. *Well, hell. You didn't try to stop him either.* But the thought of trying and failing was like a knife in his chest. He couldn't take losing somebody again. Walking away was easy. It didn't matter that the rocks under his feet burned like glowing coals. He sped up and didn't look back.

35

DORCAS GETS SERIOUS

VANE GROANED WHEN Dorcas's name appeared on his phone the next day, but he wasn't surprised. He didn't answer it though. He put his phone back in his pocket, grabbed the plates Luis slid to him, and carried them to his customers.

Later, after the diner had emptied, he took a Coke to the patio and called her back.

"Oh, my God, Vane. You almost got killed, and you didn't tell me?"

He winced. He forgot he hadn't told her about the last attack. He sat on the new stage in the sun, put his phone on speaker, and said, "I thought you were calling about Doug."

"I'm calling about you. I never thought I'd hear myself say this, but maybe leaving isn't such a bad idea."

"What if they follow me?"

"Well, who is it?" Dorcas asked.

"I don't know. Maybe I'm crazy. Maybe it was a

robbery. That's what Doug thinks. Anyway, it was two weeks ago."

"And don't think I'm going to forgive you for not telling me right away. What do you think? I think it's too coincidental to be a robbery." Her voice dropped. "Maybe it's your ex."

"I doubt it. What for?"

"To get back at you. You took your love away. The things people do for love are scary."

"I took my love away? Is that a song?"

"How lovely you can joke."

"Beats crying," he said.

"True. What are the police doing?"

"Investigating a break-in, I guess, but I didn't have any property loss or damage, so..."

"What about you? You were damaged."

"To them, it was random."

"Does Rose know?"

"No. And don't you tell her. I told Doug not to either. I don't want to worry her with as far away as she is. Plus, she's got the kids and a new job, you know?"

"Are you going back to Hollywood? Maybe you should. Unless... Unless it's a crazy fan."

He snorted his Coke and coughed laughter before gasping out, "I don't think so."

"Well, are you?"

He rubbed his burning nose and took another sip of his Coke. The sun was a blanket on the back of his shoulders.

"Vane?"

"I lived for acting."

"Funny you should say live. Things work out for a reason, usually."

"You think I should go?"

"I'm worried about you. LA's not that far away, so I think it can work for a while, as long as you come back and stay with Doug on the weekends, of course. You can't just walk out of my life either."

Vane bent his head and felt his necklace shift under his shirt. "Thank you for the agate. Maybe it helped."

Dorcas blew out a breath. "Good, and I'm glad, but I think we need more."

"More what?"

"I want to do another reading."

Vane frowned. "I don't understand. How's that more? You do readings all the time."

"I don't mean tarot. I want to try something more powerful. You know I believe you, right?"

"I know. I'm not sure I believe me anymore though. I sound crazy."

"So did Joan of Arc."

"Didn't she burn at the stake?"

"I didn't say you were Joan of Arc. Stop making light of this."

"You're scaring me." He said it lightly, but the truth was his stomach was starting to flutter. "I don't know if I'm up for it. I think I just want to go home and watch TV."

"I'm worried about you though. Doug too. Something or somebody is trying to split you up."

"Me."

"Or other forces."

"That's creepy," he muttered.

"Come to the shop tonight. I don't think waiting is a good idea. I want to try something."

"Am I going to like it?"

"I won't. But I'm doing it for you and Doug. Tonight, Vane."

Maybe he would have blown it off for himself. He'd had a reading and didn't think it had done much good. Didn't he get the Sun? Well, his life was a piece of garbage right now. But... Doug. Could he walk away from something about Doug?

"Okay. Couple hours."

She disconnected, and Vane drank the rest of his Coke. When Darelle arrived an hour later, he went home and opened a can of food for Trout. Then he sat on the back porch and gazed into the yard that wasn't a garden.

Trout came and sat beside him.

"Think you can be a city cat?" he asked.

Trout glared at him.

"I guess not."

Holy moly, why couldn't his life be simple? But maybe it was, and he was just too dumb to appreciate it, or clinging to a fantasy he was too dumb to let go of.

When he thought about it, the dreams he'd had no longer drove him. They hadn't gone anywhere, but the farther he got away from them, the less he cared. He spent days now without a single thought of LA or Fisher or the condo. But when Fisher came back...

Vane was an idiot. He was just like the guy frowning beside his still-living wife in the photo in the master bedroom. Everything his dad had cherished in life had been right there beside him, and he'd scowled as though he'd had a million better things to do than get his picture taken with his wife.

"You were so alike," Rose had said.

Well, he didn't want to be like the guy in that picture. He wanted to be like the one Luis had liked. The one who probably didn't yell at kids on their bikes.

"I'm a slow learner, Trout. That's why I was born on Thursday. Thursday's child has far to go."

"Ow."

He sighed. "Yeah."

He wasn't sure what he'd just agreed to, but Trout smiled. He wasn't sure if he needed Dorcas and her reading now either, but when the light faded, he stood and drove into town.

The cobblestones behind her shop were damp again, and a faint coolness softened the air. He stepped through the open glass door. No lights were on, though the sun had dipped low.

"Dorcas?"

"Back here, hon."

The main part of the shop was muggy, as if it had been closed all day. The last of the light struggled through the blinds on the windows. For an eerie moment, the shop felt still and not quite real, as though Vane had only imagined the people here before.

In the hallway, another light glimmered. He turned through the doorway, and his gaze fell on a massive candle set in a bowl of water.

Dorcas turned from the dresser that held her tarot cards. "Come sit."

"This is weird, Dorcas."

She squeezed his fingers and smiled. "That's not what you mean."

It wasn't. He meant 'this is some scary crap,' but he didn't say it. He sat. Dorcas returned to the dresser and picked up a glass. "I have wine. Would you like some?"

"No, thanks."

"I don't usually drink before a reading, but I haven't done this in a long time." She laughed, and his skin tingled. "This is the real stuff we're going to do. At least for me."

"What's tarot?"

She made a humming sound. "Hm... More like insight. Guidance."

After a swallow of her wine, she pulled her chair out. She wore a long, loose dress in a black knit. *A shift?* That sounded right. He glanced around, taking in details that didn't matter. An upside-down book. Candles and crystals. She bobbled her wine as she leaned down to set it on the table. *Like me.*

"So what are we doing?" he asked.

"Scrying. Usually, you do it for yourself. Anybody can, like tarot. It's a very old practice. As simple as gazing into a mirror or reading tea leaves." She sat down. "I get... strong impressions. Close feelings. It's like looking into a crystal ball."

"You have a crystal ball."

She smiled. "I know. I have several. I like fire." She

opened a box of long matches and lit the candles on the table.

"What's that smell?" he asked.

She took a breath. "Oh, that's white sage. Incense." She blew out the match. "Maggie, my teacher, was big on scrying. She used mirrors. I see things in fire. Visions, I guess."

Her eyes didn't twinkle. She didn't wink at him.

The tingle on his skin crept to his spine, and the hairs on the back of his neck stirred. "Visions?"

She sighed. The flicker of candlelight made shadows under her eyes. "Sometimes, I'd look at my sister and see another face slide over hers. A mask but almost invisible. And it was... horrible. I didn't know what I was seeing, but sometimes... you just know something isn't right about somebody."

"Like Luis."

"But it wasn't Luis."

"Well, it was somebody."

"I got those vibes from my sister. My sick sister. I felt wicked." A quirky smile twitched on her lips. "Until she burned our house down. My parents thought it was an accident. By then, she had almost no control over her body."

"Did she want to die," he whispered.

Dorcas was silent for a moment. "She wanted us to die."

"Jesus, Dorcas. I don't know what to say."

"I haven't even told Doug this. I don't really know why I'm telling you. What we're about to do is... so powerful. I was the only one who thought the fire was deliberate. I trust my instincts."

"Mine suck," he murmured.

"No, they don't. You just aren't listening to them. But..." She tossed her hair back and straightened her dress on her shoulders. "We're going to fix that."

"How?"

She grinned, again the happy Dorcas he was used to. "Together. I want you to hold my hands. I'm going to gaze into the candlelight. I want you to just sit with me and be open with your thoughts and your heart. No fear, no worry, no doubt. Only positive energy. Only love. And don't give me that look."

"I can't shake the feeling I should be wearing a bullet proof vest, and you tell me to throw flowers in the air."

She leaned against the table. "We are the only two people who believe that you *might* be the object of a crazed fan."

"I don't think that, and whadda you mean might? Now you don't believe me either?"

"I believe you. I think something's going on. That's why I'm doing this. I wouldn't do this for just anyone."

That ripple of nerves itched his spine again.

"I don't want you to do something you're afraid of, Dorcas." He didn't. Everything had gotten complicated the minute Fisher had shown up. All Vane's resolve to not be like his father had flown out the window. He'd done exactly what Fisher had accused him of, trying to get his father's love. He didn't want to hurt Dorcas too. "You don't have to. I... I'm not going anywhere."

The candle flickered. Just a flicker. *That wasn't a flare... Right?* But in Vane's imagination it had jumped and brightened from orange to gold. He tore his gaze from the wobbling flame and stared at Dorcas.

She cocked her head with a frown. "Well, I can't forget about Doug either. I can't get rid of the feeling something's wrong for him, too, and maybe I can't read *for* him, but I can see him through you. I know I sound a little looney. I kind of base my business on that, to be honest. But it's for real too."

He swallowed the bitter fumes in his throat that made him look for the incense tickling his nose. But the wisps of smoke from the sage was sweet and light and not like the sourness rising inside him. He didn't want anyone doing anything. He didn't want strange or looney. He wanted Trout. He wanted to kick back on the couch with Doug. He wanted to go to lunch with Dorcas and work on the skits with the kids. He was such an idiot.

He shook his head. "I'm just saying you don't have to. I'm staying with Doug."

The candlelight filled her eyes with shadow, the rest of her face luminous. "I know that."

"I... we had a fight. About my ex. About me going back to LA."

"I knew something had happened. Are you talking about staying for good?"

"No. I'd split my time."

"Well, I never thought I'd say this, but I think it might be a good idea for now. For. Your. Safety. You two would never make it in the long run with you in LA for good though. I know Doug."

He sighed, and the candle flickered again. "I do too. I don't want to lose him."

She flashed another grin and waved her fingers at the air above her head. "I have my angels with me. Let's do this."

With a nod, he held her hands on either side of the candle in the bowl of water. Dorcas reached out and squeezed his wrists.

"Just relax and gaze into the flame."

He wanted to close his eyes.

Instead, he took a deep breath, let it go, and stared into the candlelight. The table was wide enough that he wasn't close to it. The flame flickered orange and yellow and black. It was pretty, but he drifted.

His back itched.

Then his nose.

The room grew warm.

He imagined a clock ticking, though he couldn't see one. It was probably dark outside now. Maybe he'd do some window-shopping and enjoy the warm summer evening. Or call Doug and confess he was a total idiot who didn't deserve good things in life. *Yeah. Doug. That's—*

Dorcas jerked, a sudden snap of her spine before she clamped down on his wrists. "That isn't you," she whispered. Cold fingertips skittered along his spine. He pulled back, but Dorcas held on tight. "You don't look right."

"Me?"

"Shush," she whispered.

The shadow of the flame moved over her face. Her gaze rose to his, and she released him, taking the warmth of her fingers away. The air froze his wrists.

He drew his hands back and stuffed them into his armpits while a shaky laugh rose in his throat. "That was it?"

"I... thought I saw you."

A strange expression crossed her face. He imagined it mimicked his, which made no sense to him, because Dorcas had no reason to be scared.

A fluttery smile curved her lips. "You looked... crazy. Like maybe you were acting in a part."

But the last few words sounded like a question. He shrugged and shook his head at the same time. "I don't know. Maybe the skits?"

"No. This was... too real. I don't think staying here is a good idea."

"I do. I'm always running. I'm gonna stay this time."

She gripped the edge of the table, and her knuckles turned white. Her nails were red. He hadn't noticed that before, and he fixated on it now, as the color seemed to deepen into the reddest of fires.

"This isn't a game."

He looked up and shivered again, and now it annoyed him. "Well, it isn't real. I'm sick of everybody trying to make me go. I live here. Doug is here."

Dorcas's face was empty in a weird and unfamiliar way. No smile or twinkle. No glimmer of light heartedness.

He stared into a blank oval and imagined a mirror filled with shadows.

As the seconds passed, a weird, ominous dread crawled over his skin, and he swallowed in a dry throat.

Snippets of memories flashed through his head.

Meg's death. Her suicide? Her accident? Hadn't Doug asked Dorcas to check on her? But Dorcas hadn't answered her phone.

And what about the day Vane had slipped on the sidewalk on his way to meet her? Had that given her an idea? Was it...

Dorcas?

But no. No, it couldn't be. He was crazy. *Crazy.*

He jumped to his feet. "I have to go."

"Vane—"

He bolted from the room, his blood drumming in his ears. He barely got a yard away before Dorcas clamped down on his arm. He wrenched free and spun around to confront her.

She drew back, white-faced, no candlelight bringing her to life now. "Go home," she said. "All the way home. You aren't safe here. Doug isn't safe."

He took a step back and spaced each word leaving his lips. "This is just a game."

But Dorcas shook her head, a slow back and forth. "No, Vane. This is real."

He bolted and rushed through the muggy shop, flung open the door, and stumbled out into the warm summer night.

36

DOUG MAKES A DECISION

D OUG RUSHED IN and out of the shower that morning and almost slipped across the bathroom floor on the wet tiles.

Of course, he thought of Vane.

Ignoring the pain in his heart, he swiped off the mirror and picked up his razor. A sheet of foggy glass faced him. He frowned and swiped it off again. A few minutes later, he stood against the counter with a bowl of cereal cupped in his hand.

Hoyt wiggled at his feet.

"I don't think so," Doug murmured.

He took another bite of his breakfast and gazed down into Hoyt's desperate eyes. Hoyt got to his feet, danced a jig, and plunked his ass down again.

Doug shook his head. "Nice show but no—"

A sudden crash against the window almost drove his heart into his throat. Hoyt scrambled, barking for the back door. After grappling with his bowl for a few seconds, Doug set it down and strode across the room.

"Jesus, was that a bird?"

Hoyt threw his head back and howled. Who knew his golden had a wolf in him? Doug bent to thump Hoyt's ribs before he stepped outside.

At first he didn't see anything. Then the blue jay that hit the window darted into a bush, and a whisper of wings pulled his gaze across the yard. He gaped, a chill stirring the hair on the back of his neck as an owl lifted off his fence and glided out of sight with one slow swoop of its wings.

An owl in daylight? Was that normal?

He dropped his gaze to the bush, but nothing moved inside it, so he stepped back inside and shut and locked the door.

"I hope none of this is an omen," he muttered.

Hoyt whined and shifted his weight from foot to foot.

"You can't come," he said. "It's too hot." Hoyt's whines grew louder at the last two words. "Too. Hot," he repeated. Not now, of course, but later.

Hoyt whined again, but Doug ignored him, dumped the rest of his cereal down the sink, and headed out.

He was halfway to his truck when his phone vibrated. By the time he pulled it from its clip, he'd missed the call, but he paused, waiting for a message that never popped up. The screen stayed blank. *No missed call banner either?* Frowning again, he tossed the phone and his portfolio on the seat beside him and started the engine.

What if it had been Vane?

He reversed onto the street and headed for the highway.

Well, what would Doug say to him anyway? *Don't go. Stay. Your dream won't keep you warm at night?*

Dorcas would want him to call. *Swallow your pride,* she'd say. But it wasn't his pride that held him back. He wasn't proud at all. He was afraid of taking a chance with his heart and losing it anyway. Losing Vane, even when a little voice whispered, *"He's already gone."*

So he didn't call. He spent the morning with a client and bought his lunch from a hotdog stand at the hardware store. The next time his phone rang, he swiped the green button and got a blast of static. It resolved into a fuzzy garble that lasted a few seconds before it cut off completely.

He frowned, dropped the phone on the seat beside him, and headed out of the parking lot.

The static reminded him of the day Meg had died. He had driven home knowing something was wrong but telling himself he had no reason to worry.

Now he tried to wipe the memory out of his mind. This was a different day. He had one more appointment before he could go home.

Two hours later, he pulled back onto the freeway. By now, a layer of thin, wispy clouds darkened the sun.

A while later his phone buzzed again, but this time the name of Dorcas's shop came up, so he pressed the speaker button. "Have you been calling me?"

"Duh, Doug."

"Well, all I've been getting is static."

"That's weird. It rang on my side."

"What's going on?"

Her exhale whistled like the static. His skin crawled at the sound. "Vane hasn't answered my calls either."

"Sounds like a problem with your phone."

"I upset him."

He groaned. "About us?"

"Yes. No. In a way. I gave him a reading, and I saw... something."

"Okay."

"I was using a candle, and the flame kept jumping up, and all of a sudden I saw it. A vision of Vane. It flashed for just an instant, but I know what I saw. Doug, he was bloody and crazy and... and holding a knife."

"Well, fuck." Doug gripped the steering wheel and pushed back into his seat. The stiffness eased in his muscles. "Let's think about this logically. You saw a knife. He works in a diner."

"It wasn't a career reading, Doug. It was about the attacks."

"Attacks? Accidents and one robbery."

"Who would rob Eileen's?"

Well, there was that. "I have no idea."

Dorcas sighed. "The whole thing scared me. I want to do another reading. Something isn't right about this."

"I think that would just confuse things. I get that you believe it. Meg believed it, but sometimes, Dorcas, it makes sense to step back and look at a situation from the outside. I love him. You know that. I want his happiness, and the only way for him to get that is to be sure about what he wants. I wish I had known to do that with Meg."

"I miss her too."

"I know."

"Vane is in danger. I tried to get him to go back to LA for a while."

"That's over the line, Dorcas."

"I can't let it go. I saw it, Doug. My vision."

He squeezed the steering wheel, shoulders tense again. "Just give me some time with him."

"I'm right about this."

"I know you think you are."

"I love you both."

He flexed his fingers. "We love you too. You know that."

"Keep me posted?"

"I will."

He cut off the call and a blast of static sent shock waves through him. He dropped his phone on the seat and turned off at the next exit. On the street below, he pulled to a stop and looked around. Nothing about the scene was different from any other day. The sun flooded the valley. The sky was blue. A butterfly bobbed by the windshield. He needed to let Hoyt out.

But when he turned, he headed for Vane's.

37

TIRED OF WAITING

V ANE'S HEART JUMPED the minute the buzz
reached his ear. He spun and flailed at the air, and
the bee zipped away.

"Motherfugging..."

He sucked in a breath. Jerkoff bugs. Maybe he was
possessed. Maybe that's what Dorcas was getting at. Soon a
swarm of flies would swoop down on him. *You have an evil
spirit. Selfish. Coldhearted and—*

He gave another swipe at the air and stared at Trout.
"Really?"

The cat's back rose in a half moon, and his ears lay flat.

"I was swatting a bee."

A ripple ran over Trout's spine—*getting rid of the bad
spirits?*—and ended in a flick of his tail. After that, he gave
Vane a withering look of disdain, lowered his spine, and
strolled off into the weeds.

"Weirdo," Vane muttered.

He stood in a circle of bare earth now. That probably

meant something too. It looked like a freaking pentagram in a cheesy seventies horror flick.

Sweat stung his forehead. He swiped it off and marched down the hillside. Screw it. Doug was just gonna weed whack the place anyway. If Vane still had Doug. A sharp pain twisted inside him at the thought of what he might have lost because he was an idiot.

In the kitchen, he splashed some water on his face, dried off with a paper towel and got a beer out of the fridge.

Why hadn't he called Doug?

He should.

But he was scared. He stared at the refinished cabinets and the wood floor and the yellow walls. The space was wide open now. Pendant lights hung from the ceiling where the old cupboard had been attached. Now light from all the windows spread across the surfaces.

The laundry room door was open, and Doug's tools and equipment hugged the walls. Everything was done except for the master bedroom. He wanted Doug to help him with it. White walls and dark wood, that's what he'd get.

He took another swallow of his beer and looked outside. Trout sat in the center of the bare spot Vane had made. As he watched, the cat shot a stare at the corner of the house. A clomp floated on the breeze. It sounded far away, but he didn't think it was. He thought it had come from out front. A car, though, not Doug's truck.

Dorcas?

He took his beer into the other room and peered

through the living room window. A bright purple Kia sat on the driveway behind his car. Penny? He went to the door. By the time he opened it, she was coming toward him, half running, a panicked look on her face. He stepped a bare foot onto the porch, and she full-on ran the last few paces, lurching to a stop in front of him.

"Vane. Oh, my God. You were right. Luis is out to kill you."

"What?"

Now that it was somebody else saying it, it did sound kind of ridiculous.

"I c-c-couldn't believe it, but I heard him talking to his wife. I was on the patio, and he didn't see me."

The scenery outside rotated, and Vane reached back to hold onto the door frame. That made no sense. Not anymore. And why was Penny pushing him inside? She stared at him with glittery eyes. Her long hair had loosened from her braid and fell around her face in tangles. A thought he'd had when he first met her came back to him. *She looks like me.*

"We need to get inside."

He stumbled on the edge of the rug. "Why?"

"To hide."

"I'm calling the cops this time."

He turned, and the door slammed behind him. A moment later, he stumbled. Something had hit him in the back. He wasn't sure what it was. A part of him continued on toward the kitchen. Another part of him panicked, and his vision went dark. The beer in his stomach curdled, and he landed on his knees and spat a mouthful of fluid on the floor.

Gosh, this... hurts.

Pain dug into his back. He twisted and sat on his ass. "Shoot, Penny."

She held a knife and the knife was dark.

No sense. It made no effing sense.

She smiled. "This was fun, chasing you around and making you scared. I have to stop now though. Classes start next month, and I want to be settled before that."

He scuttled backwards. He wanted to let go of his beer, but his fingers held on.

"You're bleeding," she said.

"You stabbed me."

As he scooted backwards, he dragged his hand through something wet. Blood. But it wasn't as much as he thought it should be. What did that mean? That he was bleeding internally, or that he wasn't badly hurt? Terror pushed his pain away while his survival instinct was doing a number on his terror.

Calm wrapped around him.

Everything rang loud and clear in his ears.

"I don't get it. I gave you a job."

"You have no respect for jobs."

Thoughts dropped out of his head with a clunk. Dull-looking thoughts that made no sense. "What?"

"You killed my brother over a job."

"No, I didn't. I swear to God. I was a waiter. I didn't kill anybody."

He was past the halfway mark to the kitchen but had

no idea why he wanted to get there. Penny crept after him, step after step, like a cat with all the time in the world to kill the poor little mouse. *Shoot!*

"You were up for the part Cory wanted, but they didn't want him. They wanted you or Stan Zolenski. Hollywood kills all the good people. Nobody cares about anybody else in that place. Nobody cared about Cory. You didn't. He was so excited, but you took it away."

"Marcel?" he whispered.

She nodded. "Marvelous Marcel."

Now it was clear. Sickening clear. Cory Conway. In a flash, he remembered the last name. The guy who'd killed himself.

"But I didn't get it."

"You walked away," she said. "You spat on the thing that killed him like it was garbage. Like he was."

"No. I didn't. I swear, I didn't. I had no control."

He scuttled back another foot. She leaped and slashed her knife across his thigh. It caught him in a graze, slicing through his jeans and burning his leg. He hurled his beer at her. She ducked, and the bottle thudded onto the floor.

Smiling now, she came at him again.

"We were all alone. They broke us up after our parents died. Sometimes we couldn't talk for months, but we stuck together afterwards. You don't know the things Cory went through with the family that had him. I do. I supported him so he could go on auditions. I wanted him to be happy. He deserved it. Cory... Cory had nothing but pain, so it was fun to scare you and hurt you. You didn't honor the part like Stan. You took something Cory died for and threw it away."

She lunged at him again, and Vane scrambled into the kitchen and slammed the door. She kicked it open. Her face was a twisted mess. Her eyes glittered like metal, her words grating like the scrape of gravel on gravel.

"You threw his life away!"

He shook his head, and she bared her teeth.

How the heck had this happened?

As though answering his question, she said, "I followed you here, and I watched you. What a slut letting somebody fuck you up against a tree."

Oh, geez. His chest heaved, and his fingers slid against something cool and smooth.

"Cory deserved respect. And. You. Are. Going. To. Pay."

He hurled Trout's food bowl at her and rolled. Something crashed behind him. He got his feet under him and bolted out the back door.

If there really was a God, Vane was going to have to thank him for that fight-or-flight instinct. It was an effing stroke of genius. He got halfway up the slope they'd planted the bushes on before his lungs emptied of air. He couldn't make his chest pull in a new breath. He stopped and swayed. He didn't know where he was going anyway. Where was he going?

Oh.

The houses. Help.

His chest stuttered back into action. He breathed and took a few more steps. The back door crashed open.

"Mother fucker! You're going to die!"

Geez, geez...

He plunged through the weeds, fell, and groped for something to hold onto. Metal. His fingers closed on it. A padlock.

He threw a glance behind him.

Penny was a yard from the bottom of the hill, her face garish with streaks of blood.

He grabbed the lock, flattened his feet against the well, and yanked. The plate the padlock was attached to pulled loose and threw him backwards. A bolt of pain shot through him. He rolled sideways and spat out another mouthful of beer and bile. Then he threw the padlock at her and knocked her back down the slope.

Now on his knees, he pulled the cover off the well, rolled over the edge, and dropped.

The slam of his feet on the ground and the pain in his back dug in with red-hot claws. He screamed.

Another scream rained down.

"I'll get you!"

My little pretty.

Too much Hollywood.

His sweaty forehead dragged down the side of the well. From his knees, he sank to his hip and sat there, panting. A second later, something hit him in the head. A rock. *Shoot.* He curled his arms over his head. She beaned him a few more times. Luckily, he didn't have many rocks in the yard.

"You wait." He looked up. She stared down at him. "I'll burn you out."

Cold stole over him with creepy-crawly fingertips, squeezing ice into his blood. "You can't."

"I can."

"There's water down here. It'll go out."

"Gasoline won't."

"I don't have any gas."

"I have it in my car."

"How will you get it out?"

"I'll figure a way." She yanked her head back.

Oh gosh.

The minute his feet had hit the ground, the numbness had worn off. The pain was like new knives now, wrenching and twisting. He climbed to his feet with a whimper and groped at the walls. The surface wasn't smooth. And now that he was at the bottom of it, he realized the well was shallower than he'd thought it was, so maybe he could pull himself up.

He dug his fingers in and rose to his toes. The pain clawed at him. Biting off another scream, he slumped back against the wall.

"Hey, mister."

The whisper made a raspy echo as it floated down. Vane looked up. A shadow hung over the edge of the well. "Who are you?"

"Isaiah."

"Go. Get out of here."

"She can't see me. She's out front anyhow. Shit."

Isaiah disappeared. Vane's heart thumped in his chest. The bright, hard clarity of a moment before was ringing in his head again. He stared into the circle of fading daylight.

"Okay," whispered Isaiah. "I'm gonna get you outta there."

"It's too dangerous."

"Naw. She went back inside. Your friend's outside. The nice one."

"Doug?"

"Guess so."

"Call the cops!"

"I— Oh fuck."

"What?"

"I think your house is on fire."

"What? Wait! Isaiah!"

But the kid was gone. A cold sweat broke out on Vane's face. He spread his legs and flattened his palms against the well on either side of him. A few minutes later, Isaiah was back, and something was sliding down into the dark. A garden hose.

"What about the cops?"

"I called. I told them your house is on fire. I think it is anyway, but I didn't get up close. Climb up."

"I can't, and you can't pull me."

"I bet I can."

Vane laughed, burst into tears, and grabbed the hose. "Okay." His voice was shaky and thick.

"Just walk up the wall like Spiderman."

His breath hitched. "Okay. Like Spiderman."

He put his foot against the wall and climbed.

38

SURPRISE!

A PURPLE KIA was parked behind Vane's car. Penny's?

Doug pulled in behind it, shut off the engine, and got out. Vane's front door was open, and a tingle in the back of Doug's neck made him pause and stare at the house.

"*Mow.*"

He looked away, scouring the yard for Trout, but nothing moved. "Hey, buddy. Where are you?"

"Oh."

He turned back toward the house. Penny stood in the front door with a basket in her hand. Her hair was tangled, her face shiny and red, and a streak of—*Was that blood?*—smeared her cheek.

She smiled. "Hi, Doug." Then she turned and went back inside.

He followed her, but the living room was empty by the time he crossed the threshold. He stood there staring while the tingle at the back of his neck spread like a cold breeze over his body. He remained still, the drumming of his heart thumping in his ears. But his nose burned. Smoke? *A fire?*

Where?

"Vane?"

He moved now, heading for the kitchen. A snap sound quickened his steps. *There.* Orange flickered, dancing against the kitchen door. A cacophony of noise from a crash behind him spun him back toward the stairs. He didn't quite make the turn. A blow to the base of his head hurled him to the floor, and Penny's voice swirled down through a tumbling fog.

"I lost my damn knife."

39

VANE DIGS DEEP

O H SHOOT. NO... *no.* Vane couldn't do this. "C'mon. Keep moving. You can do it. Just a couple feet. I'll grab you. That girl is crazy. I saw her in there—somebody anyway—like the place isn't on fire. I can see it now. You better hurry."

Where was Doug?

"Climb."

It hurts! I wanna lie down.

Go play.

Go play?

Why would he play? He needed to get to Doug.

"You got it. You're almost up."

He wrapped the hose around one hand, put his foot against the wall and pushed. The pain was like ropes of barbwire wrapped around him. He screamed and drew his other foot up. The sound of an explosion rocked through him like shock waves. He squeezed his eyes shut and dug in. Air touched his face, and an arm got underneath him. He scraped the rim of the wall and rolled over the top and down the hill, coming to rest with Isaiah panting beside him.

The kid stood and tugged at him. "You can't stay here."

Vane's eyes flew open. He stared at the pale sky as he lay in shade, cool and floaty. *This is nice.*

Then Isaiah's face appeared above him. "You need to get up. I don't know where your friend went."

A crackling sound drew his attention. He looked across the yard. Flames consumed the back door. Another window exploded, and Isaiah jumped.

Your friend. "Doug!"

Vane staggered up, swinging his arms for balance until Isaiah grabbed on and held him up. Together they crossed the yard and headed down the side of the house. Sirens blared over the roaring in Vane's ears.

Too far away. Where was Trout? *Doug?*

On the driveway, Isaiah let him go and fell against Vane's car. Vane bolted for the house, pain thudding through him. He hit the porch railing and dragged himself up the steps.

"Wait!"

Inside, smoke puffed out of the kitchen and flames already crawled along the ceiling. Penny stood smiling at him. She didn't have a knife anymore. She had a... *rolling pin?*

His rolling pin.

She stood over Doug, straddling his legs.

"I lost my knife," she said, swinging the rolling pin like a baton. "This works."

Vane roared, "Don't!" and rushed her.

His body felt weightless. A high-pitched whine filled his ears and obliterated his pain. Penny swelled in front of him, filling up his sight. She swung the rolling pin over her head and slashed down with it. Vane plowed into her, the collision like a semi knocking him flat. Penny flew, hit a dining room chair, and went down with it. Fire and smoke billowed out the door in a hot blast, and flames licked the plaster over her head.

Vane scrambled back, scooped Doug under the arms, and dug his heels into the floor. Gouts of smoke filled the room. His eyes stung and he coughed.

Penny loomed above him. "Die!"

She'd lost her rolling pin. Vane wasn't sure how she was going to make him die without it, but he didn't feel like sticking around to find out either. Heels still braced on the floor, he stiffened his legs and scooted them back a few inches. Doug lolled. *Shoot.*

With a hacking laugh, Penny swung her fist, and Doug caught it. Vane gasped in surprise, drawing in a lungful of smoke. As he spat it back out, Penny spun sideways, and Doug twisted her arm. The crack it made was louder than the roar of the fire.

Penny screamed and fell.

Still holding onto Doug, Vane kicked at the floor. He couldn't breathe anymore. Smoke gusted above him. He was floating in it. Floating outside where he gazed through the leaves of the tree Doug had made love to him under. *Love, you witch.*

"Vane!"

Doug was calling to him. He wanted to answer, but the dark swept over him again.

40

THE GRAND REVEAL

THE DAWN BROKE with a thin blue edge above the tree line. Eileen's was closed, the road out front empty and quiet.

"It's going to be light soon," said Vane.

"Want me to wait for the blaze of day?" Doug asked.

Vane grinned. "We'd get arrested."

"Probably."

Vane sprawled on the stage by the patio, one bare foot braced against Doug's shoulder. A few tiny pinpoint stars still winked above him. Other than that, the only light came from a single strand of crackle lights. A wisp of a glow that flowed around Doug's form and hid his face. But his eyes gleamed, so Vane stared into the gleam and smiled. "I never thought I'd be here."

Doug stroked Vane's legs, brushing his thighs with his fingertips. "Honestly," Doug said. "I never thought you would either."

"Remember the night we hooked up?"

"You were scared of somebody seeing us."

Vane rolled his hips. "Things change."

With a dip of a shoulder that let the light shine through from behind, Doug slipped his fingers around Vane's cock. "And sometimes they don't," Doug murmured.

Vane thrust, half closing his eyes.

After a few strokes, Doug let go and cupped Vane's knees, spreading them apart. Vane let his legs fall wide and opened his arms. The scrape of Doug's clothes against Vane's skin as Doug sank over him sizzled like sparks. "You aren't naked," Vane murmured.

"The important parts are. You are." He brushed Vane's lips with his. "The important part."

"With you."

Now a single star fluttered in the sky. It had a tenaciousness Vane admired. *Shine on, no matter what.* He kept his eye on it and gasped as Doug's cock slid against his. The fire on his skin felt as cold as blue flame. He sank under Doug's weight, and the ache in his back gave a sullen pulse. He ignored it and arched his neck, pushing his throat against Doug's lips.

"That feels good."

Doug hummed against his skin.

He bucked, looking for friction, and grazed his dick against Doug's, his tip brushing Doug's T-shirt. Red, white, and blue sparks burst in his eyes like fireworks on the Fourth of July. He hissed through his teeth. "Shoot," he whispered.

"Wait a sec."

Doug slid out of his arms and stood again. His features

in the growing dawn formed like a lost city taking shape under the surface of a misty lake. Rising onto his elbows, Vane twisted a look behind him, but the road was still empty. The clatter of a belt drew his attention back to Doug, whose pants had fallen to his shins.

A smile tugged at Vane's lips. "That's a good look on you."

Doug laughed. "Like lace on you."

"Fishnet?" Vane murmured.

"Oh, babe. Yessss."

Doug broke open a packet of lube, and Vane spread his legs again. They were going bare now, and every time Doug pushed into him, Vane sank into the promise of it. Nothing stood between them. It was new, nothing he'd ever done with Fisher.

Luckily.

He'd told Fisher to go screw himself the day before, but he hadn't shared that with Doug yet. He wasn't going anywhere. Doug was rebuilding Vane's house—"The same as it was," he'd promised, but Vane knew there'd be white walls and dark floors.

And he wanted that. He wanted the promise of permanence and family he inhaled in the smells of paint and varnish and wood. He wanted Trout and Hoyt.

He stroked Doug in an overhanded grip and groaned at the slide of Doug's finger over his gland.

"Nice sound," Doug whispered.

Vane had dreamed about this in the hospital.

At first only nightmares had visited him—skeletal demons and blackened trees. Then Dorcas brought him a bag of crystals, and the nightmares floated away. Only one stayed. He dreamed he saw a window exploding and Penny walking with a smile into his burning house. That one had had the weight of concrete, and he clung to it, though Doug said she'd tried to get out and had gotten lost in the smoke. She hadn't killed herself.

But Vane had seen her, strolling to a triumphant death with a smile on her lips. Having her use his house like that should have upset him and made him want to burn the rest of it to the ground, but it didn't.

It was his house. His home.

He groaned again as his ass stretched around Doug's cock.

"Yeah... That."

Doug grunted and settled on his elbows with a gasp. He moved his hips, dragging out, pushing back in.

"Good?"

Vane whipped his dick and bit his lip, grunting, "Yeah." This was his real dream. His everything. His desire was his home. His passion was the story growing in his imagination. His obsession was... Doug. "Yeah... yeah."

He dug his fingers into one of Doug's shoulders while he pummeled his dick with his other hand. Doug's mouth was open, eyes rolled up. Embers glowed in Vane's heart and belly, and the friction of the cock inside him spread fire into his balls.

"Oh..." Vane panted. "I'm... close."

Sweat trickled down Doug's face, gossamer pearls in the dawn. The warm splat on Vane's chest set fire racing down in his spine. He sprayed on his belly and froze in a curve of pleasure, the smell of his cum strong in the cool air. With a groan, Doug thrust in deep, pushing against Vane's ass, and sinking into his core.

The wash of bliss that rolled through him stole Vane's breath. He melted into the wood surface beneath him.

His dick twitched at the touch of Doug's belly hair against it. He smiled at the whisper of butterfly kisses on his face.

Then Doug sighed and pulled out, and a thumb took the place of his cock. He played with Vane's hole. Then he bent down and kissed the tip of his dick.

Vane moaned. "Don't go."

But Doug slid back and stood. "Want Luis to walk in on us?"

"Maybe."

Doug chuckled. "I have to go if I want to come back and help."

Vane pushed himself up and slid off the stage, scouting the area for his clothes.

"Here." Doug tossed him a Towelette.

Vane grinned. "You're so romantic."

"This isn't romantic."

Doug finished tucking in his shirt as he approached and pulled Vane close. His chest pressed Vane's and his breath was warm as summer.

Vane sank into him, drank his kiss, and crushed him in his arms. The moment stretched out long and sweet.

Then Doug pulled back and touched their foreheads together. "Everything I feel for you is romantic," he murmured.

Well, geez, that sure was.

"You hear that?" Doug whispered.

"What?"

"Tires."

"Oh shoot."

Vane got his clothes on while Doug took another Towelette over to the stage and wiped it off.

"Okay," said Vane.

He hooked his fingers in Doug's, and they headed inside. The light in the kitchen spilled into the hallway. Doug lifted a hand as they passed. "Hey, Luis."

"Morning, Doug."

In the parking lot, Vane took a breath of the cool air. It came off the hills carrying the scents of the trees. Tomorrow was the diner's reopening. Today was the paint party that was the last thing Vane planned to do to renovate the diner. The last thing he could afford for now.

Doug turned and wrapped his arms around him. "I'll be back at noon."

"I hope this works."

"Time to relax, babe. You've put your all into it."

Vane tipped his head back and met Doug's gaze. "That's what scares me."

Doug smiled and ran a hand down Vane's back. His fingers brushed over his scar. It was deliberate, though Doug never mentioned why he did it. Vane thought it was a way for Doug to convince himself the attack had happened. The scar was evidence that people could get through the bad times. Maybe Doug had lost Meg, but he hadn't lost his love for her. He'd almost lost Vane, but here Vane was with the scar to prove it.

"Enjoy yourself today," Doug said. "It's a party."

"A party that smells like paint."

Doug laughed and got into his truck.

"See you, babe."

Vane waited until Doug pulled onto the highway before he turned and went back inside. The smell of bacon lured him to the kitchen. "Can I have a piece?"

Luis scowled at him and gestured with his spatula to the plate on the warmer. "You want."

He took a piece and ate half of it. "Thanks for coming in to cook for us. You didn't have to."

For a moment, Luis was quiet as he scraped a pile of onions to the back of the griddle. Then he said, "I don't mind. I want Eileen's to make it. And your dad—" He paused and Vane waited. "I think he felt bad about pushing you away. My dad was like that too. I could never do good enough for him, an' your dad accepting me was special. Losing him hurt. Maybe I took that out on you. Your dad woulda been proud."

Vane wasn't sure his voice worked. He swallowed the taste of bacon, and all he could manage was, "Thanks."

Luis nodded and scooped a handful of raw onions from a tub of water by the stove. He tossed them onto the hot surface and waved his spatula through the steam.

Vane turned away. Light filled the dining room. He couldn't be sure his dad would be proud of him because Vane hadn't known his dad. Luis had. But this work on Eileen's was all for him, and it was the last gesture Vane could make. He'd have to live with that because the rest of his life was his now.

His and Doug's and Trout's and Hoyt's.

THE SUN BLAZED DOWN ON THE PARKING LOT AND it was crowded with cars.

Vane opened the front door and braced it with a water bottle, hoping for a cross breeze to blow away the smell of paint. Doug had opened the patio doors and now he plugged in the fan he'd found in the office and set it on one of the tables.

"I like blue an' all," said Carol, looking at the patch of wall she'd just painted, "but this is gray blue."

"I know," said Vane. "I like it."

She sighed and wagged her head at him. "So dull."

Darelle grinned at them from her perch on the step stool beside Carol. Her boyfriend, Malcolm, stood on a ladder, cutting in the gray paint around the light fixtures. "Better than builder beige," he said without a glance at any of them.

"Iced tea, anybody!"

Rose held up two pitchers.

"Me," said Isaiah, darting underneath the ladder. "It's like a hundred degrees in here."

"Ninety-nine," said Vane.

Isaiah snorted. "You should be painting my house. We have air."

"I should be charging you a toll."

"You are determined to be that old grump nobody in the neighborhood likes, aren't you?" said Rose.

"Whatever."

"Grump," Doug murmured against his cheek, giving him a quick peck before he headed to the patio with his glass of tea.

Vane scowled. He liked the gray-blue paint. The ceiling was in the process of turning light gray, as soft as a cloud. He watched Malcolm move the ladder and climb back up.

It wasn't until he inhaled something like burned sugar that he remembered his pies. *Oh shoot.* He rushed into the kitchen and stopped dead in his tracks. His pies sat on the shelf over the stove.

"You took them out?"

Luis glowered at him. "You wanted 'em burned, you shoulda told me."

"Oh my God!"

Dorcas.

Vane returned to the dining room and gaped at the couple in the open doorway. Mr. Kam? With Dorcas? They stood arm in arm, both gazing at the color going on the walls. Mr. Kam carried a shopping bag in the crook of his elbow.

Vane cleared his throat. "Hey, guys."

Dorcas shot him a grin, released Mr. Kam, and opened her arms. "Happy Reopening Day, honey. I'm sorry we're late. I had an emergency reading."

Vane hugged her and stepped back. "Emergency reading?"

She nodded. "That's my story."

Heat flooded his cheeks. "Geez, Dorcas."

She laughed and swung her arm at the room. "I like it. It's beautiful... in a very conservative kind of way."

He sighed. "I like blue."

"Gray blue!" Carol shouted from across the room.

Dorcas patted his shoulder. "Blue is the color of faith and heaven."

"Really?"

"Yep. Oh. I almost forgot." She turned and took the shopping bag Mr. Kam held out to her. "I got you a present. A diner-warmer."

Vane snorted. "I don't think there is such a thing."

"It'll be our tradition."

Mr. Kam sauntered off, and Dorcas set the bag on a stool and removed a box wrapped in orange paper. Up close, gold threads became visible. "Wow. That's bright paper."

"Orange is for happiness and success."

"Really?" he said again.

She leaned in and kissed his cheek. "Much happiness," she whispered. "It's for you and Doug. Now point me to the brushes."

He got her started, ducked under Malcolm on the ladder, and took his box to the patio. The sweet fragrance of cold water on hot stones greeted him. There were damp patches on the pavers where Doug was assembling Vane's water fountain. He glanced up as Vane approached, got to his feet, and deposited his screwdriver in his toolbox.

"What's that?"

"A present. From Dorcas. For both of us. It's heavy."

Doug bent down to plug in the fountain. Vane watched as water bubbled in the center of a flower, splashing down into the blue bowl. The flower was bright yellow with a bumblebee on one of its petals. Vane frowned at the bee for probably the tenth time since Doug had hauled the fountain out of the truck.

"You have a sick sense of humor," he said.

Doug shrugged. "The blue matches the decor. I didn't even notice the bee."

"I bet."

"Open that before you drop it."

"Ha ha."

Doug chuckled, and Vane stepped into the sun and sat on the edge of the stage. He unwrapped a black box and waited for Doug to sit beside him before he lifted the lid. They both laughed.

"A crystal ball," said Vane. After he twisted to set it on the stage behind him, he added, "Bah humbug."

Doug leaned back on his palms. "Bah humbug, my ass. You believe it."

"I don't know," Vane murmured. "I have a picture in my head of my future, but I could be wrong."

Doug was quiet for a moment, his expression tipping toward wary. Then he said, "What do you see?"

"You tell me. Confirm my vision."

"I don't believe in that."

"Tell me my future."

Doug sighed and looked at the sky. "Okay. What do you want to know?"

"Will Trout stop trying to kill Hoyt?"

Doug grinned. "Eventually."

"Will I keep Eileen's afloat?"

"Time will tell."

"Wow, you have a talent for this."

"I know. Keep going."

"Will I get my house back?"

"Just the way you want it."

"My cupboards burned up. Penny died in there."

Doug sat up and brushed off his hands. "Your mom died there too, babe." He gestured behind them to the crystal ball. "I don't know about things like that. But I know Meg is with me every day, and I know your mom—and your dad—are with you. And I promise. Your cupboards will look just the way they did. Everything will look the same."

"I might want some white walls and dark wood this time."

A smile grew on Doug's face. "Well... that's a good look. It's your house though."

"I'm getting used to company."

Doug's stare held onto him for a moment. Then he gazed in the direction of the road and the trees on the other side and said, "I'm selling my house in the meadow. I'm not going to finish it." He glanced back. "I'll finish yours. You don't have to worry about any of it. Worry about Eileen's, but personally, I think you're going to be okay here. That doesn't mean you have to stay though. You can sell it or keep it, whatever you want. Go back to Hollywood and—"

"Doug."

"Take that part. Live your dream."

"I am."

"You want to act."

"I want to write my book. I can do that anywhere, anytime. I want you."

"You have me."

Vane got lost in Doug's smile and the way it crinkled the corners of his eyes. Some lines stayed whether he smiled or not, signposts for every smile he'd ever given. Slowly, Vane leaned in and kissed him, closing his eyes, so he could steal every bit of sensation from the kiss.

He melted at the warm slide of Doug's fingers along his neck, holding him close until Vane finally pulled away. "I like this life."

Doug's eyes flickered, searching Vane's face. "I won't go anywhere," Doug said. "You can take your chance, and I'll be here waiting for you."

"Tell me my future."

Doug opened his mouth, but all that emerged was a puff of air. Then he pulled another breath in and said, "You live happily ever after."

"With you."

Doug nodded, a smile on his lips.

"You build my house," said Vane.

"And a secret grotto."

"Yesss," Vane whispered.

"And I buy stock in a sexy underwear company."

"Yesss."

Doug's smile crinkled his eyes again. "Tell me my future, Vane."

"You live happily ever—"

"Hey, you guys!"

They glanced at Dorcas leaning through the French doors. "A little help."

"Yeah, yeah," Vane grumped.

He stood, and Doug smacked him on the ass. He wiggled it for a few steps before he stopped and glanced back. "You live happily ever after with me."

Doug's smile slowly widened. "Deal."

A few hours later, they folded the drop cloths and sat back down to admire the place. The fresh paint looked good, as serene as heaven if heaven was muggy, sunny, and smelled like acetone. But this was okay. Vane was happy. His dad would be happy.

"Looks fabulous," Rose said.

He turned as she set another pitcher of tea on the counter. Coming up behind her was Luis, carrying trays of sliders and stuffed mushrooms. Everybody flocked to the food and filled their plates and glasses. Dorcas and Mr. Kam took the table beside the booth Doug and Vane sat in. Vane ate a mushroom. *Too much bacon. Needs something spicy. I could make this hecka better.*

After they ate for a while, Dorcas licked her fingers and said, "You opened your present, didn't you?"

"Oh yeah."

"Show everybody."

Vane stood and returned to the patio. A breeze stirred, blowing cool air off the water in the fountain. He grabbed the crystal ball out of the growing shade and hurried back, skirting the paint cans and...

Tripping over something.

Or maybe over nothing.

But he stumbled, and the ball soared into the air. Mouths fell open and rounded eyes followed its trajectory.

Oh shoot.

Vane crashed into a table. The ball fell out of its arc and...

Doug caught it. Gasps filled the room, followed by laughter and shouts.

"Whoa!"

"Look at that!"

Mr. Kam stood and clapped. Dorcas threw her arms into the air and clapped with him. "Bravo!"

Rose just laughed and shook her head, but Doug winked and mouthed, "I love you."

And for the first time since the day his mother died, Vane had no fear of falling. He took a bow and laughed at the applause. *Blind, chinless actor arrives on red carpet with the love of his life and lives happily ever after.* Somehow, through all the strange twists and turns of fate, his fortunes had come true. And it didn't matter if he stumbled now, because Doug would catch him.

ABOUT THE AUTHOR

Kayleigh Sky is an m/m romance writer of complex stories of love and redemption that always end in happily ever after. Love matters, and everyone counts.

Peace.

facebook.com/kayleighsky

twitter.com/skyboundlove

instagram.com/kayleigh.sky.writer

Other books by Kayleigh Sky

Backbone

A universal vaccine eradicates all known viruses from the human population, but in the wake of this miracle, a deadly new virus suddenly surfaces. As the death toll rises, people riot in panic and civilization collapses. Brey Jamieson, a convicted felon, is suddenly set loose in this violent new world. Desperate to reunite with his family, he sets out on a journey across the country but is captured by a brutal man who plans to sell him into slavery. Hank Kresnak is a cop in the new world. It is his job to preserve the law. But when he sees Brey, his belief in everything he has built his new life on begins to crumble. Memories of a dark and terrible time reawaken. He was the cop who arrested Brey, and with one look into Brey's eyes, he knew his life would never be the same. He was a married man with two daughters, but he couldn't forget a man he barely even knew. Now his wife and daughters are gone, and he must struggle to save the man of his dreams from a nightmare fate.

Pretty Human

Seeking absolution for his past in a fiery death, a young space force pilot crashes his ship on a desert planet.

When Ellis Ligoria, King of Xol, witnesses a space ship hurtling to the planet's surface, he rushes to the scene of the crash and joins the search party for survivors. As night descends, a strange compulsion leads him to the site of an underground city. Here he rescues a badly injured Jem. During his recovery, it is discovered that Jem is part Xolan. Not only that, but he's a genetically submissive variation called a Xolani. Ellis has no desire to care for a Xolani but cannot resist his desire for Jem. Taking him under his protection, he brings him home to his family.

Desperately wanting this new life, Jem claims to be a solitary Vagabond, a loner without family or home. A man nobody wants or is looking for. Safe for the first time in his memory, Jem has hopes for a happy future. He is falling in love with Ellis and adores his new family. All he wants is to live a quiet life as Ellis' consort, but as his secrets sink him deeper and deeper into a prison of lies, he knows that he can't hide his true identity forever. Marrying Ellis is a dream come true, but he'll never escape the brutal man he is running from.

Soon called upon to make the ultimate sacrifice, Jem must battle to stop a powerful monster bent on revenge.

Doll Baby

Todd Rifkin has sworn off love forever—until he loses his heart to a badly scarred rent boy and stumbles into a deadly game of cat and mouse with a brutal stalker out for revenge.

Struggling to make enough money to buy a friend's bar and grill to fulfill a promise, Todd Rifkin vows to let nothing stand in his way. Nothing, that is, until a friend's call for help. Bailing his friend out of trouble might cost Todd his dream. Now he is scrambling to make up the loss and reluctantly takes on the job of errand boy for his boss' spoiled ex-lover.

Bliss Busby has no memory of the attack that scarred his face. Scared and reclusive, he has no interest in Todd's intrusion into his life. No interest, that is, until somebody starts scattering cinnamon hearts at his door. Now Todd is the only one standing between Bliss and a mysterious stalker.

Years ago, Todd lost the love of his life in a violent twist of fate. After a night with a knife-wielding maniac, Bliss lost everything. Thrown together by circumstance, Todd and Bliss must unite to battle a hidden force from the past. As Bliss struggles to remember the attack that wrecked his life, and Todd struggles to save him from an attacker that is closer than either of them realizes, their reluctant friendship becomes a passionate love that just might have the power to heal their wounded hearts.

If they live.

Trinkets

On the run with a stolen teddy bear and a couple hundred dollars in cash, Alex's life takes a strange turn when he crashes his car in a freak accident. Stranded in the desert with no water, he is rescued by a crow that leads him to the home of Lars and Lars' five-year-old niece, Holly.

Lars is a man with secrets, and he'd just as soon Alex was on his way, but delays in the repair of Alex's car compel him to offer Alex a place to stay in exchange for babysitting services. Alex accepts the offer and soon falls head over heels for Holly and the mysterious Crow.

Over the course of several weeks, Alex finds himself embracing a life he'd only dreamed of. A life of warmth and comfort—and a passion that almost makes him forget the past he's running from. *Almost.*

As Lars and Alex fall in love, secrets about Lars and Holly, and a dark danger pursuing Alex, threaten to destroy their newfound family.

Alex was rescued once by the quirky crow he now lives with. Will Crow be able to save the treasure trove of a family he's collected in Alex and Lars and Holly one more time?

Angel Dork, *a short story*

Christmas is fast approaching, and eighteen-year-old Oliver is on his own for the first time. After aging out of foster care, he knows he's lucky to have found a welcome in the couple who own the diner where he works. Of course, his life would be easier if a pack of bullies wasn't out to get him, and if one of them wasn't so gorgeous. It's a terrible idea to crush on a guy like Liam.

At the ripe old age of twenty, Liam wears his cynicism like a second skin. He doesn't trust anyone, and definitely shouldn't care about weird little Oliver. But in Liam's world of bullies, disapproving parents, and lonely Christmases, Oliver is somehow a beacon of light.

When Liam and Oliver are forced to work together on a class project over winter break, they'll have to find common ground. And with the help of a kind-hearted couple, a down-on-her-luck kitten named Lola, a mysterious Santa Claus figure, and a snowstorm, Oliver and Liam might learn the true meaning of the season, too.

Jesus Kid

Thirty years ago, an asteroid struck the Earth. Now killer plants hunt the last surviving humans.

Ori Scott is a young junkie running from his mother's prophecy that he'd one day save the world from the killer plants. Her preaching made him a laughingstock and now he hides in his drugs. But he can't hide the change in his veins. They are turning green, and the prophecy is dragging him into a dark struggle between invisible forces. Set up on bogus drug charges, Ori is taken to a secret facility where he becomes a test subject in experiments to discover an antidote to the alien plant's sting.

Jack Doll is a cop with a vendetta against the plants that killed his best friend. All he has in the world now is his old friend's lover, Rive. Together they form an unbreakable bond—or so he thought. Jack has never liked Rive's friend, Ori, but he believes in Ori's innocence and doesn't understand Rive's strange indifference to Ori's conviction. Struggling with his suspicions, Jack can't help digging into a mystery that draws him closer to Ori than ever before—and closer to somebody who has secrets to hide.

Alone and scared, Ori is grateful for Jack Doll's friendship, and his longtime crush soon blossoms into love. But Ori has no plans to accept his fate. He wants to escape, and he doesn't care if he takes the cure with him.

Made in the USA
Columbia, SC
14 March 2019